SONG

IN THE

SILENCE

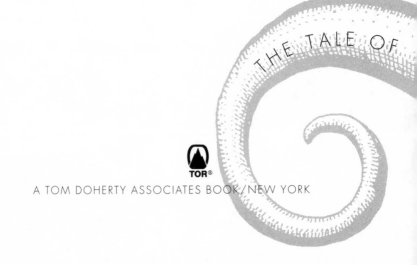

THE TALE OF

A TOM DOHERTY ASSOCIATES BOOK/NEW YORK

SONG

IN THE

SILENCE

LANEN KAELAR

ELIZABETH KERNER

SONG IN THE SILENCE: THE TALE OF LANEN KAELAR

Copyright © 1997 by Elizabeth Kerner

This book is printed on acid-free paper.

A Tor Book
Published by Tom Doherty Associates, Inc.
175 Fifth Avenue
New York, NY 10010

Tor Books on the World Wide Web:
http://www.tor.com

Tor® is a registered trademark of Tom Doherty Associates, Inc.

Design by Lynn Newmark

Map by Ellisa H. Mitchell

Library of Congress Cataloging-in-Publication Data

Kerner, Elizabeth.
    Song in the silence :   the tale of Lanen Kaelar   /   Elizabeth
Kerner.—1st ed.
        p.   cm.
    "A Tom Doherty Associates book."
    ISBN 0-312-85780-2 (hardcover   :   alk. paper)
    I. Title
PR6061.E74S65   1997
823'.914—dc20   96-29345
                                                                CIP

First Edition: February 1997

Printed in the United States of America

0 9 8 7 6 5 4 3 2 1

To the glory of God

and to

Alan Bridger

heart's-friend and support
and survivor of many years of rewriting

Deborah Turner Harris

treasured friend, longstanding and patient mentor,
terrific writer and top-notch kicker-in-the-pants
(bare is the back without a brother)

and

Margaret Lynn Harshbarger

dragon-souled friend, moral support,
ace plotter and desperately needed teacher
of the realities of being an artist

I dedicate this work.

CONTENTS

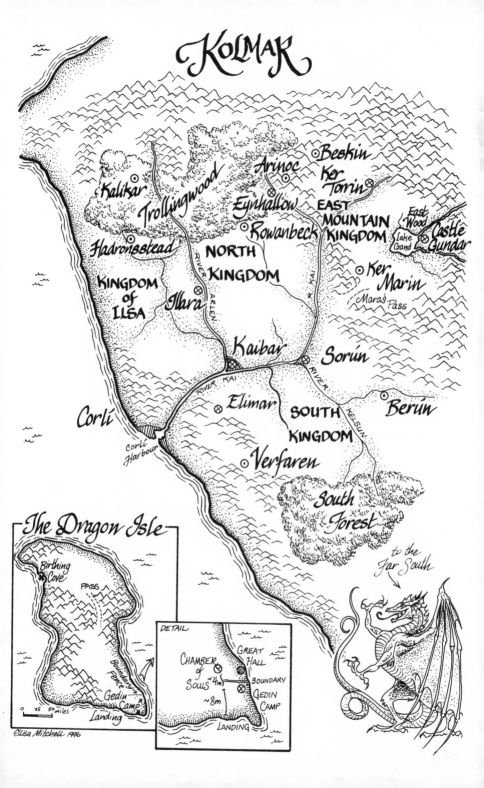

PROLOGUE

AS LEGEND HAS IT

The powers of order and chaos are in all things, and in the life of all races there comes a time when they must learn there is a Choice to be made. When Kolmar was young there were four *shakrim,* four peoples, who lived there: the Trelli, the Rakshi, the Kantri and the Gedri. They all possessed the powers of speech and reason by the time the Powers were revealed to them.

This is what the Four Peoples made of that Choice.

The Kantri were first. It seemed to their Elders that although chaos is the beginning and end of creation, it is order which decrees this. Thus they decided to serve order, indeed to become the representatives of order in the world. For this, they were granted long lives and a way to remember all that had gone before.

The Trelli chose not to choose. They did not wish to be governed by such Powers. They had only the merest beginnings of speech, but managed to convey their denial of both chaos and order. In that decision was the seed of their ending, for to deny the great Powers is to deny existence.

The Rakshi were already of two kinds, the Rakshasa and the smaller and less powerful Rikti. Both unhesitatingly chose to embrace chaos. In this they balanced the Kantri; but chaos cannot exist in a world of order without the two destroying that world between them. The Kantri were eldest, so the Rakshi for their choice were gifted with length of life to rival the Kantri, and a world within the world for their own, with which they were never content.

The youngest race, the Gedri, discovered after great turmoil that they could not reach a single decision, but unlike the Trelli they did make a choice. They desired Choice itself, giving each soul the chance to decide which to serve in its own time. Thus they had the ability to reach out to either Power and bend it to their own wishes; and although both the Kantri and the Rakshi were creatures of greater power, it was the Gedri who inherited the world.

> A prose rendering of the opening
> verses of the Tale of Beginnings,
> as transcribed by Irian ta-Varien.

INHERITANCE

DREAMS IN THE DARK

And the Dragons' song, so wild and strong,
fell from the sky like rain
upon my soul; which, watered well
bloomed with a joy no words can tell
where once was a dusty plain.

My name is Lanen Kaelar, and I am older than I care to remember.

I have heard the bards call me Queen Lanen in their tales, and that I fear is the least of their excesses. I cannot stop the songs they sing or the stories they tell, but at least I can write with my own hand a record of those times, in the slim hope that anyone might be interested in the truth.

Now I put my hand to it, I would I knew how the trick is turned. Where should I begin? Wherever they start the tale seems the only possible place, no matter how much has gone before. I suppose the only sensible beginning would be at Hadron's farm.

I was born at Hadronsstead, a horse farm in the northwest of the Kingdom of Ilsa, which was the farthest west of the Four Kingdoms of Kolmar. The stead and the village nearby were a few hours' ride from the Méar Hills to the north, and two weeks to the south and east lay Illara, the King's seat. Farther south yet the fertile plains of Ilsa began, a land full of farmers and crops and little else, and west over field and mountain lay the Great Sea.

Ilsa does not encourage women to go beyond the narrow boundaries of home, but from my earliest memories that was all I ever wanted to do. As a child I lived for those times when I managed to escape for a few hours, taking my little mare north to the Méar Hills,

walking among the great trees that marked the southern edge of the
Trollingwood, the vast forest that covers all the north of Kolmar. But
always I was fetched back to the farm, and a closer watch kept on
me.

Hadron was a good man, I do not say otherwise—he simply did
not care for me. My mother had left him soon after I was born, and
for some reason I decided that his close hold on me was because he
feared I would do the same. When I came of age the summer I
turned twelve, I asked to go with him to Illara, to the Great Fair in
the autumn. By then I was grown nearly to my full height, and since
I was clearly no longer a child—I stood nearly as tall as Hadron even
then—I thought I was due some of the privileges of being of age.
Instead, Hadron brought my older cousin Walther, his sister's son,
to live with us. When autumn came, Hadron calmly announced that
he and Jamie would go to the Great Fair, and that Walther would
look after me until they returned. Hadron never understood why I
yelled and fought with him over that decision; to him it was obvious
that I needed a keeper, and Walther was enough older than I to make
sure Hadron's words were obeyed. Needless to say, I hated Walther
from that moment.

I wasn't overfond of Hadron, either, but then I never had been.
He always kept his distance while I was a small child, and when I
grew so tall so young he seemed appalled. From the moment I came
of age he despised me, though I never knew why. I could do nothing right in his eyes. Sometimes I gave in to despair, knowing I was
an evil creature who had no heart, since my mother had left me and
my father did not love me. The worst of it to me, the true darkness
in my heart that frightened me most and that I whispered to no one,
was that I did not love him either.

But there was one bright light in my world, one beacon of hope
and love and caring in all the desert of indifference I saw around me.
Jamie.

For me, any words of Hadronsstead must begin and end with
him. He was there from my earliest memory, Hadron's steward and
his right hand on the farm. Jamie managed the crops and the other
livestock while Hadron ignored his child and made a name for himself as a breeder of horses. But to me, Jamie was ever love and kindness.

When as a child I needed comfort, it was always his small, dark, wiry figure I looked for, not the cold tree-height of Hadron. It was Jamie who made sure I was always looked after when Hadron forgot, Jamie who was a quiet friend when I so desperately needed one, Jamie who later taught me to see my strength and man-height as an advantage instead of a curse. When at fourteen I began to walk stooped over, trying to lessen my (I thought unnatural) height, which I feared made Hadron hate me, Jamie it was who took me aside and told me kindly that I reminded Hadron of my mother, it was nothing I had done, and he persuaded me to stand tall. Against Hadron's wishes Jamie taught me to read and write, and when I begged him he also taught me in secret how to fight without weapons, and how to use a sword and a bow. He was always there, never complained through all my needing him that I can remember, had a soft word for me even when my temper lashed him instead of its true target. He loved me as a daughter, as Hadron could not, and in return was given all the love I could not lavish on a heedless father.

I can hear the young girls wondering why I did not think of marriage. The true answer is that I did, sometimes, late at night as I lay in my too-short bed and dreamed. But there is a good reason I did not escape by marriage. I have seen some of the paintings the young ones have done of me in my youth, and they do make me laugh! I am now and always have been no more than plain. Hadron told me so all my young life, and I learned to believe him. Men were the same then as now; the young ones want a beauty, the old ones want a young one, and after being trapped so long on the farm I had the heart of an old woman and no beauty to speak of. The best that can be said is that I was tall as a man, strong as a woman well can be, brown as a nut from years of farm work in the sun and rain, and had a temper I only occasionally managed to keep in check.

Most nights, to be truthful, I thought more of love than of marriage, and more of going away than of love.

That is the real deep truth of me, now and as a girl. I longed to see the world, to go to those places that rang on the edge of stories like sweet distant bells. Even the sight of the Méar Hills to the north pierced my heart every time I saw them. Autumn was the worst, when they put on their patchwork winter coats and beckoned like so many red-and-gold giants. Lying on my bed in the dark I wandered through those trees a thousand times, laughing—sometimes aloud— as I watched the sun through the stained-glass leaves, breathing in their spicy scent and soaking in their colour until I could hold no more.

But my real desires lay beyond the Méar Hills. All of Kolmar was mine in the dark, covered with a quilt, weary from the day's needs but with mine still unfulfilled. In thought I roamed east and north, through the dark and threatening Trollingwood to the fastness of Eynhallow at the edge of the mountains, or into the mountains themselves, into the mines where jewels sparkled from the walls in the light of a lantern held high. Sometimes, though not often, I would venture south to the green kingdom of the silkweavers of Elimar—the north always called to my heart with the stronger voice.

But those times I most resented what I was forced to do, when despite the duty I owed him I would have cursed my father for making me stay, when even Jamie could not console me and the bleakness of my future came near to breaking me—then I would let loose the deep dream of my heart.

In it I stood at the bow of one of the great Merchant ships, sailing for the Dragon Isle at the turn of the year. The sea was rough, for the Storms that lay between Kolmar and the fabled land of the Dragons might abate but they never ceased. The ship swayed and groaned beneath my feet, spray blew keen and salt in my face but I laughed and welcomed it. For all I knew I would find naught on the island but lansip trees, and the long and dangerous trip there and back all for no more than my pay for harvesting the leaves more precious than silver. But perhaps—

Perhaps the Merchants' tales spoke true. It might be that I should be chosen to approach the Guardian of the trees, and perhaps as we spoke I would see him, and he would not be some giant of a warrior as everyone but the Merchants said.

I would feel no fear. I would step towards him and bow, greeting him in the name of my people, and he would come to me on four feet, his great wings folded, his fire held in check. In my dreams I spoke with the Dragon who guarded the trees.

Now, everyone knows that there are dragons, poor solitary creatures no bigger than a horse who live quietly in the Trollingwood away to the north. They pass their lives in deep forests or in rocky caverns, and almost always alone, and generally dragons and men do not trouble one another. Sometimes, though, a dragon will acquire a taste for forbidden food—a village's cattle, or sheep, or human flesh. Then great hunts are gathered from all the villages round and the creature is slain as quickly as possible, or at the least chased away. These little dragons have only faint similarities to the True Dragons of the ballads. They have fiery breath, though it is soon exhausted; they have armoured scales, but their size tells against them, and they seem no brighter than cattle. Unless they fly away—and they do not fly well—they may be killed without too great difficulty.

The Merchants, however, have the word of those who have been there, and they say that the Dragon Isle is the home of the True Dragons of legend. They are as big as a cottage with wings to match, teeth and claws as long as a man's forearm, and a huge jewel shining from each forehead. Of course the Harvesters who returned were asked about them; but the last ship to return from the journey to the Dragon Isle came home to Corlí more than a century ago, and there are none living who can swear that the True Dragons exist. It is said that within certain boundaries it is safe to visit that land, but some old tales whispered of those who dared to cross over seeking dragon gold and paid the price. If you believe the tales, not one of those venturous souls ever returned.

The bards, of course, have made songs of the True Dragons for hundreds of years. Usually the tale is of some brave fighter attacking one of them against terrible odds, defeating it but dying in the process. All very noble but more than a little absurd, if the Merchants recall truly their size and power. Still, there are some lovely lays about such things.

Every now and then, however, you come across a story with a different turn. The Song of the Winged Ones is a song of celebration, written as though the singer were standing on the Dragon Isle watching the dragons flying in the sun. The words are full of wonder at the beauty of the creatures; and there is a curious pause in the middle of one of the stanzas near the end, where the singer waits a full four measures in silence for those who listen to hear the music of distant dragon wings. It seldom fails to bring echoes of something beyond the silence, and is almost never performed because many bards fear it.

I love it.

I heard it first when I was seven. The snows were bad that year, and a bard travelling south from Aris (some four days' journey north of us) on his way to Kaibar for midwinter got stuck at Hadronsstead for the festival. He was well treated, given new clothes in honour of the season, and in return he performed for the household for the three nights of the celebration. The last piece he sang on the last night was the Song of the Winged Ones, and I fell in love. I was just warm and sleepy enough to listen with my eyes closed, and when the pause came I heard music still, wilder and deeper than the bard's but far softer. I never forgot the sound. It spoke to something deep within me and I resolved to hear it again if ever I could. When I mentioned it to the singer later he paled slightly, told me that people often imagined that they heard things in the pause, and swore to himself (when he thought I had gone) never to sing the wretched thing again.

I spent the next seventeen years waiting to hear that sound, and dreamed of meeting a True Dragon, a Dragon out of the ballads, huge, wild and fierce, yet possessed of the powers of speech and reason. And he would not kill me for daring to speak to him. He would respond in courtesy, we would learn of each other and exchange tales of our lives, and together the two of us would change all of Kolmar. Humans would have someone new to talk to, a new way of seeing life and truth, and it would happen because I had dared to do what few had even dreamed about.

And they would grant me the name I had chosen in the old speech, those who came after and knew what I had done. They would call me Kaelar, Lanen Kaelar, the Far-Traveller, the Long Wanderer.

And there the sweet dream would end, and I would cry myself to sleep.

My world changed in my twenty-fourth year. Hadron, rest his soul, finally had enough of raising horses and a daughter with no prospects. He died at midsummer, and Jamie and I laid him in the ground high on the hill overlooking the north fields.

After Hadron's death his lands and goods came to me, which shocked me to the bone. I had always thought Jamie or Walther would be his heir, but in death Hadron was more gracious than ever he had been in life. I was amazed by the extent of his lands, many of which I had never seen, and by the wealth he had gained. I knew well enough how to run the place—I had been Jamie's right hand for years—but the sheer size of it all took me by surprise. I still thought of Jamie as my master, and he still taught and helped me in those first months, but to my chagrin I found that I was blessed as well with a valuable steward in my cousin Walther.

Walther had for many years now made his peace with me, though I could never forgive him for siding with Hadron in keeping me caged. It did not help that even as a child I found him dull and a little slow. All his thoughts were of the farm; his one-fond wish had ever been to become as good a breeder and trainer of horses as his uncle. He had not known what his place would be when Hadron died, but since working for me did not seem to concern him I never mentioned it.

Hadron's death came just as he was starting to prepare for the Great Fair, and with him gone there was more to do than hands to do it. There were a good dozen of the horses old enough, broken in and ready to be sold this year. Hadron and Jamie had always gone to Illara, but Hadron's part now fell to me as the heir. If I had been a little less tired I would have been delighted at the prospect of finally seeing the King's Seat of Ilsa. As it was, grief and weariness outweighed all else. I did not pretend to mourn Hadron greatly, but I felt his loss, and grieved quietly to myself that I had cared so little for my own father. In great part, though, I must admit that I felt a weary weight lifted from my shoulders.

I could see no further than that until the night before we left, when my eyes began to open.

The horses had just been brought into the barn for the night. We would have to rise early to begin the journey—the fair was in a fortnight's time and we would travel most of that, Jamie and I and the three farmhands who were coming to help with the horses. Still, the night before leaving had always been exciting even when I was not going on the journey; a time of ending and beginning, full of promise and change. Jamie had already gone to his bed and the other hands to their lodging. Walther and I had just finished the last chores, and I was trudging across the paving stones of the courtyard when he laid a hand on my arm and stopped me in the torchlight, saying he had something to ask me.

"What is it?" I asked, wondering why we had to stop walking. I was filthy and exhausted and wanted a bath and my bed in the worst way.

"Lanen, I—it's been six weeks since Hadron died. There's been no man around here but me to look after you, and . . ."

He had to wait while I laughed. "You've a curious sense of things, Walther. None but Jamie has 'looked after me' for twenty years. Why should someone start because Hadron died? Besides, I've yet to meet a man who wanted the honour, and none I wished to give it to." I moved on towards the house.

"What about me?" said Walther loudly.

That stopped me.

"What about you?" I asked as kindly as I could, turning back to face him. All women have a sense that warns them of such things. I was shocked—he was all but betrothed to Alisonde from the village—but I could smell it coming and was desperately trying to think of how to get out of it without being too mean. I didn't like him, but some things demand mercy.

"Marry me, Lanen," he said quietly, moving close to me. He smelt of the stables even stronger than I did. "I'll not pretend there's more between us than there is, and I—I'll not demand a husband's rights, but you need a man to look after—to run the place for you. You know everything I do, but you haven't the touch."

That was true enough. I never was interested in horses the way he was, certainly, save perhaps when a mare was in labour. Still, even in my anger I nearly smiled to myself. Poor Walther always thought he was so subtle.

"Walther, this is so sudden," I said, unable to keep an edge from my voice. "What would Alisonde say? She deserves better of you than this."

He looked down. "She will understand."

If it had been morning, broad daylight, I might have held my peace and simply refused him; in the flickering torchlight at the end of a long day I let my armour slip. "Aye," I sneered. "She loves you well enough to take a mistress' place, as long as you never behave as true husband to your wife. What a charming life you offer me, Walther! Marriage without love or the comfort of your body, where you bring no more than my father's knowledge of horses as a bride-price." I knew the progress of my own anger by now, and tried to stop before my temper got the best of me.

He sounded only vaguely guilty at being found out. "Lanen, you don't understand—"

"Save your breath to fan the fire," I snapped. "You meant nothing else. You spent too much time with Hadron, you're beginning to sound like him." I stopped my words there, but I couldn't stop my memories. Years, too many years of Hadron's neglect, too many times being told I was too plain, or too tall, or too manlike, or simply not good enough to be my father's daughter, piled on top of me like so much stone, and just when I was beginning to learn my worth and value my solitude, Walther, Walther of all people, insults me like this. I stood and fumed, I could feel my eyes dancing with fury in the torchlight. "Why can't you just marry her and stay here?" I snarled, my last valiant attempt to speak reasonably.

He was long silent; when he finally spoke his words had to fight their way past a knot of anger in his throat as great as the one in mine. "And live my life as your paid servant? No thank you, cousin," he growled. "I haven't the money to go elsewhere and start fresh. I thought I could be your man, since you don't seem to need one like a real woman, and I could have the place and Alisonde, too."

That did it. I gave no warning, just drew back and hit him. I am only a little under six feet tall and strong with it, and Jamie's lessons were not wasted. Walther measured his length on the paving stones and I stood over him, battling my need to hit him again. "How *dare* you tell me what I need or do not?" I spat, barely resisting the urge to kick him. Repeatedly. "I am more a real woman than ever you could know, you cowardly lout. If you covet this stead then say so, but I do not take insults well. Shall I tell Alisonde what your marriage proposals are worth?" He still did not speak, but now at least had the grace to look ashamed. In a breath, my anger turned to disgust.

"Ah, get to the Hells, Walther, all seven of them, and take Alisonde with you," I said, and was about to add a comment on his manhood when I froze where I stood. Like the sun bursting into a dark cellar, where all had been darkness there was blinding light. If I could have spared the effort I would have laughed with delight, but too many other things were crowding in on me.

Dear Walther. Time wears down the sharp edges of youth and memory. I have spoken to him since and thanked him. He it was who made me see that things had truly changed, that my life could be my own. I had kept my soul alive through dreams in the dark, even after Hadron's death, until Walther with his absurd proposal shattered the darkness.

"Come, cousin," I said, my anger gone in the instant. I gave him my hand and helped him up. "Let us think of this another way."

"What way?" he asked, suspiciously, rubbing his jaw and watching my hands.

"Why, you were partly right. I shall need someone to look after the stock, to choose the right bloodlines for Hadron's horses, to care for them, to train them to harness and saddle. Surely you and Jamie are best suited."

"But what of you?"

I laughed. "I shall be gone, Walther. If you see me once in the year it will be more than I expect. But I do not renounce my inheritance; I am still Hadron's heir, still the possessor of his house and lands and all his goods. But I shall need funds." I stared hard at him. "This is what I propose, Walther. When the hands are paid and the year's accounts settled, any profits will be divided three ways, one share each to you, me and Jamie. I shall simply ask Jamie to keep my shares for me until I return to claim them. That way we are all three equals, you need not work for me and you will soon have enough to marry Alisonde. Now, does that suit? Or do I send you back to your father as you stand?"

He could not speak, so he nodded. "Very well," I continued. "I shall want a portion of the available moneys to see me on my way, and I shall take with me a third of the profits from the fair. Is it a bargain?"

He didn't move, so in the country fashion I spat in my palm and held out my open hand to him. He did the same and took mine in a daze. Well he might—in payment for an empty proposal meant to manipulate a weakling, he had received a decking and a secure future. I'd have been dazed, too.

I was awake all night preparing a contract for us three to sign, though I had to read it to Walther in the morning and help him make his mark. I had carefully put my few belongings into an old pack with my clothing and wrapped a good portion of silver in a pair of saddlebags. Jamie and I left before dawn with the hands and the horses.

I was happier than I could remember being.

LESSONS

𝒱 The way was long from my father's farm.

Illara, where the great fair was held, lay a long way east and a little south of Hadronsstead; we would be travelling the best part of a fortnight. Thankfully, old King Tershet of Ilsa was not yet in his dotage—there were not as many Patrols around as there might have been, but there were a few still out on the highways to keep order.

At the end of the first day's travel I had been awake for two full days. We found a clear dry place by the edge of a wood on a little hill; with the last of my strength I helped tend the horses, inhaled Jamie's stew and slept like a dead thing.

The next morning was a mixed blessing. I woke gently, lying on my back, to the lightening sky above me and the sweet sounds of waking birds all around. There was a smell on the dawn wind that spoke of winter's coming, and an elusive scent of late wild roses caught at my heart. The sun was nearly up, a bright clear glow in the east behind the trees. I rolled over and stood up, surprised at how stiff I was. I had ridden all day since I was a child, and worked long hard days, but I had never slept on the hard ground in the chill of early autumn afterwards. It made me swiftly and deeply aware of the distance I had travelled already, which was nothing that could be measured in leagues.

Jamie was already up and making the fire. He grinned at me. "Groan away, lass, you've the right, but don't expect any sympathy from me. You're the one always said you wanted to see the world! There's a stream down there," he added, pointing down the hill. "It's good and fresh. The lads have taken the horses down for a drink, but I could use more water myself. Just you take those buckets upstream a ways and fetch me some, and I'll have breakfast ready when you've done."

I might have protested at being ordered about if I had been awake, but Jamie knew me far too well. By the time I was awake enough to object, I was at the stream.

I had a black moment there. Stiff as I was, it had somehow not occurred to me before. Only as I knelt at the side of the water did I understand in my chilly bones that I would not see a hot bath for weeks. I suspect it was just as well I had something else to do before I saw Jamie again. My mind was delighted beyond words at being gone from Hadronsstead, but so far my body was not entirely convinced.

When I returned to the fire, though, I had a little surprise for Jamie. I had planned it for ages; indeed, when I was a child I dressed in that fashion most of the time. I had made the clothes in secret soon after Hadron died, and now I was looking forward to a little gentle revenge. When I returned to the fire Jamie looked up and stared. I was dressed as he was, in woolen leggings and good stout boots and a long-sleeved wool tunic that, belted, came some inches below my knee. No skirts, no shoes that smacked of delicacy, no fine linen showing (though I kept my good shirt on beneath the wool), and my hair bundled up under a shapeless hat.

He said nothing at first, but he had the strangest look in his eyes, as though he saw a memory rather than me. Finally he said, "Good idea. Better to ride in, at any rate, and other travellers will have to look twice to know you're a woman."

That was the idea, of course; but somehow it hurt to hear that from Jamie. Still, I was comfortable and sensibly dressed for riding, and I had seldom asked more of clothing.

We had the luck of the weather when we started out; it held fine for the first few days. I delighted in waking every morning to find myself farther and farther from the places I knew. I gazed about me every moment, cherishing the changes of the land as it grew more and more unfamiliar, the smells and sounds of unknown places. The hills around and about Hadronsstead began to give way to great plains. Much of the land was farmed—we stayed with the horses in one or two barns on the way—but some was yet untamed. The wild grasses grew high, now brown with autumn and heavy with seed. Usually we all slept under the stars, Jamie, the lads and me, and as the night wind blew through the grass I heard the voice of Kolmar whispering a welcome. The ground was hard and I still woke sometimes with a stiff back, but I was so glad to find myself on my way at last that I tried not to complain.

To my surprise, it was hard not to. No matter that I had tried to imagine the hardships of a journey as well as the pleasures—I had simply never been for longer than a day without the comforts of a well-appointed farmhouse, and I missed them. I had never realised what it truly meant to have four walls about me and a roof over my head. There was safety and warmth and comfort there, cleanliness and good order. Here on the road there was much to wonder at and enjoy, and so I did—but in those first days I was perilously close to complaining.

I found, too, that by the end of the first week I was looking about with a different eye. I began to grow nervous, checking constantly over my shoulder for I could not tell what. Jamie noticed but he never said anything.

After two more days of this I was ready to scream. Were all my dreams to come to this, a useless woman afraid of her own shadow, longing for her safe farm and searching always for something unknown? I could bear it no longer. I pulled up alongside Jamie. We had not spoken much lately, and I knew it was because he was waiting for me. Blast him.

"Well, then?" I asked.

"Well what, lass?"

"You know what I mean. What in the Hells is this, Jamie? I keep looking for something and it's never there."

"Aye, so I've seen." He smiled gently. "Do you know what you're looking for?"

"No! And if I don't figure it out soon I shall go quite insane and start biting the horses. If you know what it is I wish you'd tell me!"

He rode on in silence for a minute or so, then said quietly, "I'm afraid it's the walls of Hadronsstead you're missing, my lass."

I swore. Jamie just grinned.

"But I've waited years to get away!"

"True enough, but you've never been above a day's ride from there your life long. What more natural than you should look for your home?" He stared off into the distance, frowning. "That's the other side of the wandering life, Lanen, that you'd never learn by dreaming about it. This bout will pass quickly enough, you're just fresh away from the place. But if you take to it the way you say you wish to, I'll tell you now there's more to come."

"What more?" I asked, curious. Jamie had always been resolutely silent about his life before he came to us, and I had always wondered. This sounded promising.

"Ah, Lanen!" He sighed deeply with old memories. "I wandered the world from the time I was seventeen, fifteen years ere I came to

Hadronsstead. It might be well enough to wander if you've a place and people to come back to, but I tell you now there's no desolation like wanting to go home and truly not knowing where it is."

I had never heard Jamie so bitter. His voice had grown rougher; if I hadn't known better I'd have thought him near tears.

"Is it really so terrible?" I asked quietly.

He looked over at me and smiled. "Not for you, lass. No, we all long to change to the other way if we get the chance—or think we do. I wouldn't leave Hadronsstead for the world now, but you've known nothing else. You go on a-wandering, my girl. There's a wondrous lot to see out there," he said, nodding east ahead of us. "Including that storm, which won't wait for us to find it."

I saw nothing but a thin dark line out on the plain.

"We'd best get moving, we'll need shelter."

"Jamie, it's a good hour away at least."

"Not out here it isn't. Now move!"

We found nothing better than a small wood to take cover in before it hit. I had never seen a storm move so fast. It was a typical autumn storm otherwise, a windy blast of drenching rain followed by a cold drizzle that was better and worse by turns, but never stopped completely.

After the downpour was over we moved on through the cold rain. Jamie knew of an inn we might stop at, but it meant a far longer day's ride than we had planned. It was miserable on the road, but anything was better than trying to camp in that muck. We rode for hours in the dark and were soaked through completely when we arrived, just before midnight. By then Jamie and I had ridden some way ahead of the hands and the horses, to make arrangements for men and beasts.

I had only ever been to the village inn near Hadronsstead, and that had been much earlier in the evening. I had expected that all inns would thus be well lit and cheery. This was the first time we had so much as travelled after sunset, and I thought it easily the most dismal place I had ever seen. All was dark save for a tired red gleam of firelight under the front door. Such of the cobbled yard as I could see by cloud-covered moonlight was thickly tufted with grass, the sign of a slovenly keeper. I told Jamie as much.

"Would you rather ride all night in this damn drizzle and catch your death, then?" he grumped at me. He hated rain. "Besides, we should rest the horses. It may look a bit threadbare but it's not such a bad place. Just quiet." He slid stiffly off his horse and tried the door. It was locked, only sense in these parts after midnight to my mind. But Jamie was in no mood to wait. He pounded on the door, raising loud, startling echoes in the courtyard. "Ho, innkeeper!" he yelled. "There's travellers and horses here, enough to make your fortune in stabling fees."

There was no response. Jamie tried again, knocking and shouting. "Ho, within there! Open the door, it's raining like all Seven Hells out here!"

The door was jerked open suddenly by a man who made me feel tiny. He was well taller than I and made three of me sideways. "Come in then and stop your damned shouting," he rumbled.

Jamie seemed as startled as I, though he recovered quickly. "Your pardon, Master, but we've been riding all day in this muck. We've seventeen horses to stable, the others are coming behind. Have you room for us all?"

"How many of you?" the giant asked, warily.

"Us two and three more with the horses, maybe a quarter hour behind."

"The stable's that way," grunted the giant, pointing to the run-down building across the courtyard. He disappeared back within doors, leaving us to make our own way.

We left our two horses standing in the yard and groped our way inside. The door was not latched.

Jamie dug out a candle stub from his pack and managed to light it with flint and tinder. Carrying it before him, he found an oil lamp hanging from the wall and lit it.

The stable was in a terrible state; the reek of ancient manure rose from the stalls, old straw lay rotting everywhere, rusted bits and broken tack lay abandoned in odd corners.

I was furious. I may not have the touch, but I grew up with horses. This was appalling.

"A bit threadbare? Jamie, have you lost your—?"

"*Quiet!*" he hissed. "Keep your voice down or we're lost. I've never seen that man before, the old owner's died or worse. Get out your dagger."

I drew steel for the first time in self-defense. I was frightened, excited and sick to my stomach.

"We must get away from here, Lanen. You stand behind the door and—"

"I wouldn't do that, Lanen," said a deep rumble from the door. "Unless you're tired of the old man here." The candlelight caught the dull gleam of rusting steel as the giant innkeeper entered, preceded by a long wicked-looking knife. I hoped that all the dark red on the blade was rust.

"Just you put that little pigsticker on the ground, lad," he said to me, keeping his eyes and his knife on Jamie. I hesitated, looking to Jamie.

"Do as he says, lad," Jamie said, putting a slight stress on the "lad." I obeyed, but in a kind of shock. Not at the ruffian. At Jamie. His voice was the voice of a stranger, cold and hard and merciless.

"Good," rumbled the giant. He had not noticed the change in Jamie's voice, or had dismissed it as fear. "Now, throw down your purses. Business has been slow," he laughed. "Time this place made me a profit. Seventeen horses should keep me through till spring."

Jamie started moving slowly away from the door—directly away from me—and the giant followed him. "No, I don't think so," said Jamie in that wintry voice.

The instant the giant's back was turned to me I retrieved my dagger, slipping a little as I fetched it. I might as well have shouted.

"Drop it, I said!" cried the giant, whirling towards me. I drew back my hand and threw.

The dagger bounced off his hardened leather jerkin.

"Damn it!" I yelled without thinking, my voice high-pitched with anger.

"You're no lad!" he grunted, an evil grin breaking on his face. "I've all the luck tonight, you'll make a tasty change aftaaaahh . . ."

He slumped to the ground, blood streaming from his mouth. Jamie stabbed him once more through the back, twisting the blade, making certain.

I ran out of the stable and was violently sick.

I tried not to hear when Jamie dragged the body behind the barn. Suddenly he was beside me. "Come on, we're leaving. Bring the horses round to the road. Now."

He handed me my dagger and went up to the door of the inn, sword in hand. I walked my mare Shadow and Jamie's Blaze out to the road, slowly, calming them as best I could in my state. At least the rain had stopped.

Jamie soon emerged, carrying a largish sack.

I wondered if there was still blood on his hands.

"Lanen," he said quietly. His voice was as it always used to be, low and kind, the voice I loved more than any other in all the world. "All's well, he was alone. I found some decent food and a little silver. It'll be handy when we come to the next town."

I couldn't speak, though I did try. Words seemed meaningless.

"Lanen, I had to," he said, pleading against my unspoken words. "I never wished his death, but he'd have killed us both when he was done with you."

I forced myself to speak, unclenching my teeth only by an effort of will. "Jamie, I've seen death before. Hells, I tried to kill him myself."

"And forgot everything I ever taught you," Jamie said, trying to make light of it. "Never throw away your weapon, Lanen, not in close quarters like that, it's . . ."

"That's what made me sick, Jamie," I said through my teeth. "Not his death. You." I looked at him, I could see his face now a little in cloud-spattered moonlight, confused, hurt. "Where did you learn to kill like that? I never asked when you taught me the sword behind Hadron's back. Where did you learn it? Where were— what—damn it, Jamie, who are you?"

"I haven't changed, Lanen. I am who I have always been," he said quietly.

"No. I heard your voice, it was cold and hard and—"

"Lanen!" he said, and his voice was tired in the darkness. "Not now. We must get moving." In the quiet night we could hear the hands and the horses coming along the road. "There's another town not three miles away with a clean inn and a groom who knows his business. The horses are all tired, we have to get them inside and settled. We'll stay there and take a rest day. We've enough time before the fair."

I didn't answer. He reached out to me. Without thinking I moved away, my head full of the vision of his hands covered in blood.

"As you will," he said, his voice a blend of disgust, hurt and weariness. "Mount up, we've three miles yet to go before we rest."

He told the lads only that there was no room for us here and we'd have to keep going. We did not speak on the road, though my mind never stilled. I kept trying to understand how the quick, merciless killer in the stable could be the loving friend of my childhood.

We reached the town and woke the innkeeper. Jamie's only words to me were that I might sleep late if I liked, we'd not set out until the day after the morrow. I fell exhausted into bed and dreamt horrors.

Come morning the girl came knocking to call me for breakfast. I sent her down with orders for a hot bath and breakfast brought up. She had to wake me again when the bath was ready.

I emerged about ten. Despite my weariness of heart it was wonderful to be clean, my new-washed hair in a loose braid down my back, my filthy tunic and leggings scrubbed. I carried them down to dry before the great fire in the public room. I'd have used the windowsill in my room had there been any chance of sun, but it was a cold, grey day, with the certain promise of dreary rain morning to night. Somehow that fit.

Jamie was waiting for me at a table near the fire. There were no others in the room save for an older couple in a corner, and they paid us no heed.

My terrible night visions were largely dispelled by the sight of him. He had found the wherewithal to bathe as well. He sat waiting, at first glance looking much as he always had, neat and clean and utterly himself.

Though he didn't usually start drinking this early.

When I had draped my wet clothes over a bench I joined him. Without speaking he pushed an empty tankard over to me and filled it from the jug on the table. I drained it in moments, refilled it and ordered another jug.

"How did you sleep?" he asked. His voice was rough.

"Terribly. You?"

"About that well," he said. Now I was closer I saw that he looked years older this morning, dark circles under his eyes, his face scored with lines I had never noticed, the silver in his hair more pronounced than before. He lowered his voice. "I haven't killed anything but chickens for longer than you've been alive, Lanen. I assure you I take no pleasure in it, if that's what you thought. But our lives were over if he had lived."

"I know. Truly, I do know that I owe you my life. But—"

"But?"

I was still having trouble speaking, and I stared at my drink. "Jamie—you terrified me. Your voice—I never imagined you could—damn, I don't know how to say this." I glanced over at him. There he sat, his eyes as kind as they had ever been, his face full of sadness but still the face of my dearest friend. I started to look down again when I realised I had to say this to his face. I owed him that.

I spoke barely above a whisper but I looked straight in his eyes. "Jamie, you knew exactly how to kill him. Swift and sure. He dropped in the midst of a word, he was dead before he knew he was in trouble. I was—sickened at seeing that in you. I always thought you the kindest man alive. I've seen you walk away from any number of fights, but you killed him like one born to the deed."

He sighed, only the slightest sound of regret. "Very well, Lanen. If you wish to know, I will tell you. Be warned, this concerns you as much as it does me." The shadow of a smile crossed his lips. "I've meant to tell you for a while now, though I had hoped for a time of my own choosing." He emptied his tankard and refilled it, drinking deep. "There is much to tell, but now you've asked you shall know all of it. At the very least it will help you to see past last night."

Then he began to talk.

"I was born in the North Kingdom in the village of Arinoc, near Eynhallow at the foot of the mountains, hard by the border with the East Mountain Kingdom. I spent most of my youth there, getting into fights like most young men and doing badly at learning my father's trade. My parents died when I was fifteen, old enough to do without them but young enough to miss them. I found myself working in my father's stead for a while, but I was the worst cobbler the world has ever seen." A corner of his mouth lifted. "A lot like you and horses. I could do it if I forced myself, but I never liked it.

"A few years later came a series of battles along the eastern border. Seems one of the richer and bolder nobles from the mountains wanted a bit more fertile land to farm, so he sent raiders. When that didn't work he sent soldiers, and our King started recruiting his own. I joined up. I was out of money, and I'd have done anything that took me away from the cobbler's trade.

"I learned fast, what little they took the time to teach us. We managed to keep the raiders off, and it was all over in a year and a half. But by then I was changed. When our captain asked us to follow him to fight another rebel in the western half of the Kingdom, I was the first in line. I was nineteen and immortal and I hadn't the brains of a cabbage."

Jamie paused to wet his throat. I sat consciously holding my mouth shut for fear I'd let flies in. I had pestered Jamie about his past for most of my youth and finally given up; it was as if you had spent years battering your head against a wall, finally turned away, and heard behind you the soft sound of it crumbling into dust.

"Well, that battle led to another, and another, and in a few years I found that I was a mercenary. A good one, mind. By then we had fought together for a long time. I'd been trained by the best and I enjoyed it. We went wherever the battle was—and there are always battles, these little lordlings are always after more land and none of the Four Kings are strong enough to stop them without help." He sighed. "They were the closest I had to friends, those men. We fought together eight years, sometimes on land for petty barons, twice on the sea—once with the corsairs and once against them. But I grew weary of seeing my comrades killed, one here, two there— and finally I was badly wounded myself." His eyes were a thousand miles away. "It was the first time I had faced my own death, and I didn't like the sight of it. The Captain realised it and decided to send me on a very particular mission to shake me out of it. We'd been paid to stop the Baron of Berún, in the southern half of the East Kingdom. He was a particularly vicious bugger, the kind that kills women for the fun of it."

And there it was again. Jamie's voice had gone hard and cold, unforgiving, strong as a mountain's root and distant as forever. I shivered in the warm tavern.

"If ever a man deserved death, he was the one. He had a bunch of louts fighting for him, the Captain said it was cruel to kill the poor bastards. He decided to send in a small force to kill the Baron as a way to end it. He chose me. We went in at midnight, me and two of my comrades to watch my back."

Jamie closed his eyes and fell silent. I knew sure as I breathed that he was reliving that night, step by step, thought by thought. He opened his eyes slowly and looked straight at me, and his eyes were the eyes of one who has lost forever some part of his soul. "I killed him, Lanen. It was so simple. I slit his throat as he slept. No noise, you see, with a cut throat." His voice was full of loathing, and I knew it wasn't for the Baron. "We slipped out the window and past the guards, and the battle was over. No sense working for a dead man. We'd won."

He drained his tankard, filled it and drank it half down again before he went on. "When word got out—a careful word here or there, you understand, nothing in the open—we began to be hired to do it again. And again. There's quite a call for paid killers, if they're good at what they do."

He looked at me again, almost as if seeing me for the first time. "If you are wondering, Lanen, then yes, I hated it. And myself," he said, and dark bitterness dragged at his voice. "But even in such a profession there can be pride. I never caused pain once I learned how to avoid it; I never killed women or children; and I did not take just any work once I could pick and choose. Some I refused if I knew the victim, or if I felt in that small core of soul I had left that the death was undeserved. I was not always right, and I could not always choose—but when I could, I tried to keep some part of myself intact." He closed his eyes briefly and went on. "I lost the friends I had made in the company. Eight years of living and working together, and overnight they saw me as a creature they could not bear to speak to— one who killed in secret.

"I lived at the whim of those who paid me for many years, now on my own, now with others of like profession, and as time went on I grew harder of heart and smaller of soul, until I could barely stand to face a glass long enough to shave. I gave up the work—just for a while, I thought—and lived on my earnings for as long as I could, travelling where I would, working my way slowly back to the only place I thought of as home.

"When I finally got to my village, the first person I saw was Will Tanner, who used to sell hides to my father. He was old and half-blind, and I walked towards him about to speak. Then I realised what I had to say, and I knew I could not bear to corrupt this place with my presence. I left before sunset and never went back.

"I found I had nowhere particular to go, and even if my village was closed to me the countryside was mine to explore. So I wandered as the whim took me, learning more about the Kingdom of the North than I had ever known when I lived there. It took longer than I thought to go through my money, but when I was just turned thirty, not long past Midsummer's Day, I found myself without a copper to my name in a small town called Beskin, in the Trollingwood west of Eynhallow." Jamie's face relaxed, and the ghost of a smile crossed his face. "There was a man there, a blacksmith named Heithrek, with a good wife and many children. The eldest was a daughter he loved more than life. She had the height of the women of the north like her mother, though her hair was more golden than most. She was very like you, indeed, save for her arms." Even as he spoke his voice grew softer and his smile more his own. "She was truly her father's daughter! He had taught her the art of the forge and it showed. She was easily the match of any man in that village for strength and skill, so she would have none of them. She was leaving her home to see the wide world. Ever she longed to see what lay beyond the horizon."

He glanced at me as if to ask had I heard the like before.

"Her father hired me for a year, as a guard, to look after his daughter Maran Vena. It was a welcome change."

Maran Vena. That was my mother's name. My mother, who left me to shift for myself as best I could at Hadron's cold hearth. Jamie had been bodyguard to my mother.

"Old Heithrek was lucky to find me. I'm from those mountains myself, as I said. A man from anywhere else would have been horrified. In the North Kingdom the women are equal with men, sometimes rulers in their own right, but in the other three Kingdoms most men think of women as things to be protected, not people with their own ways. The idea of a woman setting out thus on her own would be scandalous.

"The mother was resigned, and it seemed to me almost glad to get this wild girl off her hands. But the blacksmith knew his daughter, and she knew her own mind. He never even thought to fear for her safety from me. I was no fool, I knew well enough those arms could fend me off even without the steel she bore. But she must sleep sometime, and there are rogues enough in the world.

"So, as I was down to my last few coppers, I swore fealty for as long as I had been paid, and we were ready to leave.

"I tell you, Lanen, I hope never to see another such farewell in this world. Both she and her fire-blackened father wept bitter tears

as they embraced. As it happens it was a meet parting, but at the time
I thought them the world's own babes. He was dead within the year,
it was their last sight of each other. Somehow they both knew.

"We left at sunrise, headed east. She wanted to go explore the
mountains, fool girl," he said, with a quiet smile, "so we set off while
the good weather lasted. We tramped from foothill to high peak until
autumn caught up with us." Jamie grinned. It was amazing to watch
him, to see the pain that had so filled him leave as it had come. "I
never did find out why she wanted to go up there. I suspect she
thought if she got high enough she could see all of Kolmar spread
out below her."

I kept silence, for I had had the same thought. More than once.

"We must have wandered over most of Kolmar in those three
years. We joined a party going south to Elimar and travelled over the
plains for a month, just so she could see the silkweavers at their task.
We went north and walked the Trollingwood end to end—now *there*
is a tale and a half for a winter's eve—then down to Sorún for Midwinter Fest, then over to Corlí and up along the coast, then back
across the width of the Four Kingdoms to the East Mountains.

"And through all our adventures, and they were a good many, she
softened my hardened assassin's heart and broadened my shriveled
soul. I came to love her, Lanen, as I have loved none but you since."
He glanced shrewdly at me. "And you are well old enough now to
know she loved me as well. She would not marry me, though I asked
her many times, but we shared a bed for more than two years, and
I have never known such joy before or since."

A wild hope rose in my heart, piercing and unexpected. Perhaps
Hadron never loved me because I was not his daughter. Perhaps
Jamie, all this time it was Jamie—

It was as if he read my thoughts. "And it's sorry I am, lass, but
she was wise and never quickened from all our loving in those days.
It was best for her, I suppose, but I have regretted it all my life."

My newfound longing died a swift death.

"Yet after three years, I knew her not half so well as I thought.
We left the mountains to travel west again for the Great Fair at Illara in the autumn, and I swear we had no sooner arrived than she
fell into Marik's arms."

I stared at him. "Marik? Who's Marik?"

"Marik of Gundar," said Jamie, his voice deepening with anger.

"Son to Lord Gundar, a very minor noble in the East Mountain Kingdom. Marik's own father had thrown him out of the family, and Marik was just beginning to make his way as a merchant. I know only a little of what has become of him since, but I can tell you for nothing that he was as nasty a son of the Hells as ever escaped the sword."

"What happened?" I asked. I was like a child at the foot of a bard, spellbound, listening to the tale of my mother's life unfold like a ballad. I had forgot Jamie's killing of the ruffian for the moment, forgotten all but the weaving of my mother's past.

Jamie sighed. "It's not a tale I relish telling." He poured himself the last of the ale—a small matter indeed—and glanced mournfully into the depths of the jug.

Despite myself I laughed. "You old liar! This is your way of getting another round out of me."

He smiled. "True enough, it wouldn't go amiss. But I'll have to get a few rounds out of me to make room first." I couldn't help myself, I grinned as I called for the ale. I stood and stretched, checked my still-damp clothes before the fire and turned them over, and visited the necessary myself. When I returned Jamie was seated at the table again, and as I sat down he leaned forward on his elbows, gazing into my eyes, searching for I know not what. He must have found it, though, for without further words he poured a fresh tankard for us both and took up his tale.

iii

JAMIE'S TALE

🗡 "Marik. Well, he was a handsome youth, I suppose—when we first ran into him, he was in the center of a bevy of young beauties. Give him credit, the beggar, he saw your mother and the others dissolved like the dew."

"Was she beautiful, then?" I asked in a whisper. I had heard all my life, from Jamie and Hadron both, how much I looked like my mother, but that was always where it stopped. And to be so tall, man-height they called it, and strong with it—"look twice to see you're a woman," indeed! It cost me the world to ask, but I had to know why this handsome young man had been so drawn to the mother I was so like.

Jamie was silent for a moment, considering. "I honestly couldn't tell you, my girl," he said at last. "I don't remember her being a great beauty when first I saw her, but that never seemed to matter. She was—she looked—ah, there's no words for it. She was so *alive,* that was what you saw, and beside her the others were candles to the sun."

So, I thought. *Not beautiful, but attractive.*

There are worse fates.

"Tall as Maran was, he stood yet taller, though he never stood straight—but he was a scrawny thing, compared to her. Altogether he minded me of a red hawk, stooped in the shoulder, nose like a hooked beak and green eyes flecked with yellow. To this day I don't know what your mother saw in him. When I asked her she hadn't the words, though she seemed to think his voice the best of him. It just sounded high to me, soft and mannered like a man who never deals with men. But then I wouldn't know." Jamie stared into his tankard. "I never did understand it.

"The long and the short of it is, she left me for him that very day, with barely a word after three years." Jamie's voice grew softer, just for a moment. "I would have laid down my life to keep her from harm, and she ran to it fast as she could go." He looked up at me and a rueful smile touched his lips. "You'd think I'd have been furious, wouldn't you?"

"I would have been," I answered, a little sadly. "And I was just starting to like her."

He snorted. "I'd been at it longer. I had told myself all the while we travelled that there'd come a time when she'd leave, but I never believed it. And even as her name was linked with his by the marketplace gossips, I waited. I found odd jobs, nothing much, enough to keep me near her, for my heart misgave me, and I would not leave her to him so swiftly.

"It was two months before I saw her again to talk to, and it was the last thing I'd have imagined that made her turn to me again. I began to weary of waiting, and I had gone to the marketplace with some idea of buying provisions and leaving—though in truth I had no thought of doing such a thing—when someone grabbed me by the arm from behind.

"Well, you don't live long in my profession if you let that kind of thing happen. Without thinking I whirled and braced in a fighter's crouch, my dagger in my hand though I didn't remember drawing it, distance between us that I pulled from thin air.

"She laughed, part from surprise, part from something else, something I had not seen in her before.

" 'I never thought to see you here,' I told her, putting my blade away, the anger of two months washing through me. 'Lover boy leave you, or you him?'

" 'Neither,' she said, her eyes troubled. 'Take me somewhere private. We have to talk.'

"For a bent copper coin I'd have cursed her and left, I was that angry, but even as I turned to go I finally recognised what was new in her. It was fear." Jamie shook his head gently. "I had travelled the breadth of Kolmar with her for three years, Lanen. We'd fought off winter storms and treacherous cliffs and the occasional band of roughs and worse, and in all that time I had never seen fear in her. I swore to myself then that I would banish it if I could, and if that bastard Marik had somehow frightened my fearless Maran, I'd put the cap on my career and kill him. Cheerfully."

He took a drink. "Of course, it didn't work out that way. Usually doesn't."

He fell silent for a moment. The couple in the corner clattered about, having a meal served them. I waited, but Jamie seemed to have lost himself in his memories. "Jamie?"

"Eh? Oh." He picked up my tankard, felt the weight and set it down again. "You're not drinking," he said, looking at me with a slight frown. "Something wrong?"

"No," I said, lying. "Go on. Please."

"It's not pretty, my Lanen," he said sadly. "Make you a deal. You drink, I'll talk. You stop drinking, I stop talking. Done?"

"Done," I replied. I lifted my tankard and half-drained it, filled it back to the brim and made a point of sipping at regular intervals. The brew was starting to affect me, but I kept my mouthfuls small and listened with all my might.

"We found our privacy in a hidden nook in a crowded pub, much as you and I have. Seems she had found a secret passage in Marik's house—and being who she was, instantly went in. She heard voices, Marik and a stranger, a voice she didn't know. 'He was bargaining, Jamie,' she tells me. 'The stranger is a demon master called Berys. He said he was a Magister of the Fifth Circle, whatever that means.

He was angry at Marik and said he needed more gold. When Marik asked how he should gain it, Berys told him to send a ship to the Dragon Isle!' "

Jamie paused, glancing at me. "You've stopped drinking again, lass," he said, a wry smile ghosting past his lips. "And remember to breathe while you're about it." I nodded and took a deep breath. He went on.

"Maran told me that Marik tried to beg off that particular venture, because of the storms and because every last one for a century had disappeared without trace. Seems Berys didn't much care. 'He told Marik to call on him again in thirty or forty years,' she said. 'Berys started to go but Marik called him back. He said he needed power now, not in thirty years. So Berys said he would make a Farseer for Marik. Thank the Goddess Marik's gasp was louder than mine. I thought such things were only legend, and so did Marik, but Berys was serious, and the price is to be—oh, Jamie, it turns my stomach!' she said, covering her mouth. When she could speak again, she said, 'The price is his firstborn child. I thought for a second he was jesting, but he meant it.' She caught my eye and shook her head. 'And no, I've not quickened, he doesn't have a child. Not yet,' she said, shuddering.

" 'Then Marik asked if Berys intended next to go to his rivals and make Farseers for them, but Berys said there could only be one of the things in the world at any time, and that if he never had children there would be no price extracted. Marik asked what would happen if it were stolen from him. Berys would only say that if he were unlucky he might live.'

"Well, the long and short of it was that Marik agreed to the bargain and signed away the life of his firstborn child in blood. The ritual was set for that very night at moonrise." Jamie wrapped both his hands around his tankard and stared into its depths, and his voice dropped to a rough murmur. "We talked for a while about what to do. She had the start of a plan, and together we worked out the details. When all was set, I—I offered her my services." He swallowed hard. "As assassin. I asked her if she wanted me to kill them. I had not killed in more than three years, and the very thought made my gorge rise up to choke me, but if she needed me to . . ."

I sat frozen, my throat thick with dread. For me, no matter what came after, this was the center of all Jamie's telling. I could not breathe. I had to know. And below dread, below thought, deep in the center of my soul, I prayed faster and harder than ever I had before. *Blessed Lady, Mother Shia, please, please let it be that my mother did not ask Jamie to kill for her....*

A tiny corner of his mouth lifted, he glanced at me, and I breathed again.

"She took me by the shoulders and turned me to face her. 'Jameth of Arinoc,' she says, solemn as judgement, 'rather would I cut off my own arm. If you have forgotten, I haven't. I may be fool enough to take a dark soul like Marik as a lover, but while I live you are the man I care most about in the world.' "

I saw the tears slip down his cheeks, this man who was farmer and assassin and all but father to me, and I knew that he remembered those words as if she stood before him and spoke them fresh at the very moment, and that they were all he had of her to remember.

"I believed her, though I could see her own words shocked her. And me. 'I swear to you, Jamie,' she says, 'if either of us has to kill anyone it will be only to save our own skins.'

"We waited until just after moonrise; then she led me through the house to the secret passage. I was dressed in my old uniform, a kind of mottled black tunic of silk with no clean edges. I left her halfway down the passage, as we'd agreed, and crept on to the room at the end. There was a little light—only a few candles—but it was enough. I waited at the corner some few minutes, listening, until I guessed they were too interested in what they were doing to notice me. I peered round the wall just as the voice I assumed was Berys rose high and loud in a kind of incantation. Just as I looked round the light changed, from dim candlelight to a bright red glow, and I heard a hissing voice like nothing I'd ever imagined.

"There, above the small altar between Berys and Marik, a figure of nightmare hovered in the air above glowing red coals, and it was much the same colour. It didn't take much to guess that it must be one of the Rakshasa, a demon from the Seven Hells. I'd only ever come across the Rikti, the minor demons, on one of my jobs—it was a pleasure taking out that demon caller—but this was its older cousin, and a foul, fierce thing it was. The voice made my skin crawl.

"That was a bad moment, because even if the men couldn't see me the demon sure as all Hells could." He smiled grimly. "I had forgotten the nature of the things. They don't give away spit. It probably hoped I was there to kill them, which would leave it free to go. In any case, it never even hinted to them that I was there.

"I don't remember what they said—there was a lot of bickering, threats, and empty posturing on both sides. I remember Marik's voice swearing his firstborn child to Berys, though, and Berys saying it was time for the blood sacrifice. I didn't think much of it until I heard a small sound, startling in that place. Even in those days I knew the sound of a waking infant when I heard it.

"It took me a few seconds to understand that they were going to kill some poor, nameless child then and there and give its blood to the demon for the making of this Farseer.

"You must understand, Lanen, that all the while I was watching and listening, I was planning when and where to strike. All those years of killing left me with a good sound sense of survival and strategy." He frowned. "I wish I could say my first impulse was to rush in and try to save the child. I thought about it, but I knew that the best that could happen was that I would be killed myself and do Maran and the child no good. Maran and I had decided it would be best to take the Farseer once it was made, and I knew I had to keep to the plan." He lifted the tankard before him, which he had ignored for some while, and drank deep.

"I watched it all, Lanen," said Jamie, his voice deep with old sorrow. "Berys chanting, the child crying louder and louder, screaming in fear and pain, then suddenly, horribly silent. I moved no muscle, invisible in the shadows that hid me at the back of the room, but I swore revenge for that babe as it died.

"Then Berys told Marik that he would have to give of his own blood to seal the spell. The craven bastard yelled near as loud as the child had, and cursed Berys through his teeth when his arm was opened to let the blood. I began to slip my dagger from my boot. A poignard would have killed, but somehow, in the face of that evil, the thought of giving more death to that creature made me sick. My hands were stained enough as it was.

"There was a loud hiss as Berys poured the mingled blood of Marik and the babe over the hot coals, and the voice of the demon slithered through the air. 'It iss done, Masster. Behold that which you dessire.' There was a globe on the altar now, of what looked like smoky glass, about the size of a small melon.

" 'It is done, slave,' says Berys, calm as could be. 'Begone to the Fourth Circle of Hell that spawned you, but know that if this is not the true Farseer I will have claim to your miserable hide for a year and a day.'

" 'Ssso bee itt,' the thing hissed, and with a loud pop it disappeared. Then Marik grabs up the globe and says, 'Show me the head of the Merchant House of Hóvir.' I couldn't see exactly what was happening, but from his expression the thing worked well enough. With that kind of power Marik would quickly rise to lead the Merchant Houses. At least.

"I felt my jaw draw tight as my body set itself for an attack. All of Kolmar's trade ruled by demons? Not if I had word to say about it.

" 'Do you accept this Farseer and seal our pact?' asked Berys, calm as if he was asking about the weather. Marik should have seen it coming. Idiot.

" 'Yes. I will take this in exchange for the life of my first child, whensoever it might be born,' replied Marik, staring into the depths of the thing like a man in a daze.

"Then Berys laughed, and it was a terrible sound. 'It is done! Fool! Could you imagine the road to power so swift and simple? Ere ever you sought me, ere ever you were born or named, a prophet of our brotherhood knew this would come to pass. For his pact with the Lords of the Hells he was given visions of endings and beginnings, and for the four Kingdoms he prophesied:

" 'When the breach is healed at last—
when the two are joined in one—
when the lost ones from the past
live and move in light of sun,
Marik of Gundar's blood and bone
shall rule all four in one alone.'

" 'What is this gibberish?' snarled Marik. 'My blood and bone are within my body. You are the fool, Berys, it is simple enough to ensure that I never have issue. Then I shall rule Kolmar, I, Marik of Gundar!'

"Berys never moved, and his voice went cold and calm. 'No.

Your destiny is merely to bring into being the child who will rule all of Kolmar—and now the child is *mine!*'

"I had heard enough. I spoke low but loud, to shock them and alert Maran. *'Now.'*

"I threw myself at Berys, but I might have saved myself the trouble. Somehow I'd have thought a master of the Fifth Circle—there are only seven—would have safeguards against just this sort of thing, but the luck was with me. I can only guess he couldn't have summoned the Raksha with his guard about him. A few cuts that wouldn't kill him to get him into position, one deep wound to keep him down, and that was it.

"I turned just in time to see Maran deal with Marik. He had disarmed her, but she never was much for weapons." Jamie grinned then, all the way up to his eyes. "He'd grabbed her right arm to keep her off balance. Idiot. Spent all that time with her and never noticed she was left-handed. She hit him in the stomach like the hammer hitting the anvil. I heard ribs crack from where I stood. He'd doubled over, of course. Then she straightened him out. He dropped like a stone.

"She wrapped the Farseer in her cloak and we ran for the horses I'd left nearby. May I never again face such a wild ride in darkness. Our noses were pointed north and west and we followed them, caring only about putting as much distance as we could between us and them.

"We had been going for some half an hour when something made me turn in my saddle. There behind us I watched as two red smears of light streaked towards us in the darkness. They were at about the same level above the ground as we were, and they were gaining on us far too quickly.

"The horses saved us, I think. They caught wind of the things and bolted. I thought they were running before, but sheer terror is a wonderful spur. We fairly flew.

"And just as well, for despite our speed the things caught us up. I knew of nothing to do against such creatures, and I had no idea what would happen, but I learned soon enough. A red mist covered my sight, and every inch of my skin crawled as though a thousand ants swarmed over me. The itch swelled from a burning to a knifeprick to a deep stabbing pain. I never meant to, but I cried out, about the same time Maran screamed."

He stared deep into the fire. "I don't know how we managed to stay on our horses, but we did, and that's why I'm alive to tell of it. Who could know that so simple a thing as sheer distance would be our saving?

"It was sudden as blowing out a candle. The pain just stopped as we clung to our poor terrified mounts and sped away from Illara. We slowed and stared at each other in amazement, and together we reined in and looked behind.

"There behind us in the road were two red patches of light, dissolving like sugar in rain even as we watched. The horses, poor things, fell into an exhausted walk once the smell of the demons was gone. We got down to give them a rest, and because I at least wanted the feel of solid ground under my feet.

" 'Jamie, what happened?' says Maran. 'I thought we were done.'

" 'My first time, too,' I told her. 'Why don't you try the Farseer?'

"She pulled it out of its swaddling in her saddlebag and said, 'Show me Berys.' As I leaned over her shoulder I saw, despite the darkness, a clear vision of Berys looking near death, and of Marik behind him looking little better. They were being tended by a healer. From the way Berys was lying, I guessed he'd fainted.

" 'Is he breathing?' Maran said, almost to herself.

" 'For all of me he is,' I told her. 'Did you think I'd kill him? I admit I was tempted, but I'd had my fill of death in that place already.' And suddenly I was crying like an idiot. It had washed over me, that poor babe, dying alone and terrified that we might live. I still owe someone for that, you know," said Jamie thoughtfully. "I swore it to the child."

He stopped to down his ale. I sat unmoving, unwilling to break into his thoughts, wondering when he was going to get to the part that affected me. He kept silent, though, and I couldn't stand it. "What happened then?"

"What, am I a bard now?" he asked lightly. "If I am your hospitality is lacking. I'm starving," he said. "It must be two hours past noon."

I shook myself and looked out the window of the inn. He was right, noon was long gone. It was still raining, but the sky was beginning to lighten in the east with at least some hope of an end to the soaking. The couple in the corner table had finished eating and seemed to be in the midst of an animated discussion.

Jamie stood and stretched. "I should get out to the stables and check up on the lads," he said. "I'll get the innkeeper to bring them some of that stew that smells so good, if you'll arrange the same for us. I'll be back soon."

I ordered the stew and a large loaf of fresh bread. By the time it had come Jamie was back, bringing with him a whiff of the stables. It almost smelled homey.

We sat together, as we had always done, and broke bread together. I found myself blushing for the way I had treated him. Blast him, he always could see my thoughts clear as daylight.

"So you're over your horrors, are you?" he said with a wry smile. "About time, too, ye daft thing." He leaned across the little table and took my hand. "I never meant to shock you so, my girl, but it's time you learned there's more to most people than meets the eye."

"I know, Jamie. I just thought I knew you." I stared at him, trying to see in him all the Jamies I had met: oldest friend and truest companion, lover of the mother I had never known, killer for hire, to whom now I owed my life for dispatching—but twelve hours past—the ruffian who would have killed me.

He squeezed my hand. "You do know me, Lanen. Better than any save your mother." He let go my hand and grinned. "Better than you might wish to, I dare say. But at least such friendship means that after we eat I can finish the tale for you."

Jamie said it was good stew, but I hardly tasted it. The instant he was finished with his bowl I whisked it away, filled his tankard again and sat it squarely in front of him.

"Right. Talk," I demanded.

He laughed—louder than usual, I suspect the ale was finally affecting him, though his capacity was legendary—and settled back in his chair, gazing at me. It was a measuring glance, though I could not think what he was seeing.

"You know, you've been right all these years. You never did suit Hadronsstead, not from your first breath. We've not talked so much for years, my girl, save just after Hadron died, and I've missed it sore." His smile broadened. "And you have never ordered me to do anything your life long. It suits you." This for some reason struck him as amusing. "Just like your mother," he added, laughing rather too loudly.

I drummed my fingers on the table. This sent him off into another gale of laughter, and I couldn't help it—I never could hear Jamie laugh and not join in. When he finally stopped, wiping his eyes, he sat and grinned like a cat who's found the dairy. "As I live and breathe, Lanen, Maran did that very thing when she was annoyed. Where did you pick that up?"

"Nowhere. I mean, I've always done it," I said, surprised. All my life I had gone without any word of my mother, and of a sudden it seemed that she had some part in me after all. "Jamie, why in the name of sense have you never told me any of this before?"

He sobered a bit at that. "I gave my word, lass. I swore to Hadron that I would not speak to you of your mother as long as I lived under his roof."

"But why?"

"Ah, well, that's the rest of the story." His grin broke out again. "And so you've brought me round to it. You're too damn clever by half, you know. Still, I suppose needs must. I've avoided it long enough." He sipped at his ale.

"You see, Maran and I were lovers again on the road away from Illara." He shot a keen glance at me, keener than I'd have thought him capable of at the time. I kept my face carefully composed. Whatever it was, I needed to hear it.

"We arrived at Hadronsstead not a fortnight before Midwinter Fest. We had not been there a week before Maran realised she was pregnant. With you. Only," he said, all his gaiety gone in the instant, "she wasn't at all sure who the father was. Me or Marik."

Without looking at me, without speaking, he drew out a small metal flask from his tunic and passed it to me. I took a swig and let the strong spirits singe my throat. I was glad of the sensation. I think it kept me from doing something stupid like fainting.

I couldn't think straight. Jamie's daughter. Marik's daughter. Marik's firstborn, promised to demons and to Berys. Maran, who abandoned me, so careless with her body she didn't know who my father was. Maybe Jamie's daughter. . . .

All of these were loud and most of them were frightening, but louder yet and triumphant, a song of release that soared above the rest, was the glorious thought, *Whatever I may be, I am not Hadron's daughter! He never was my father. His anger at me was not at me. He despised me not because I was worthless but because I was another man's child. Even though I did not, could not love him, it is not because my heart is barren. Despite all Hadron ever said and I ever thought, I am not a cold, heartless child. Dear Goddess, what a relief!*

But there had to be more to the tale.

"Jamie, why did Hadron take her in? Did he not know?"

Jamie sighed. "Ah, Lanen. Well I know you never saw the softer side of Hadron's loving, but you must believe me. From the moment he met her he was smitten. No matter that she was no beauty, no matter that she had no fortune, no matter even to his strict Ilsan soul that she had travelled with me for over three years. Her manner was free and her heart was light, she was a strange grey-eyed Northern woman who stood in truth head and shoulders above her sisters hereabouts. In a week she had swept him off his sensible feet, he who had never loved another his life long, with her laughter and her brave soul. Before the month was out he asked her to marry him. They were wed a month past midwinter, hardly three weeks after they met."

He paused, and I had to ask about what he had not said. "You tell me he loved her, very well, I believe you—but Jamie, what of what she said to you? What was it—while I live I shall love you best, something like that." His face, clouded before, darkened yet more. "Jamie, I can't believe it. How could she love him?" When he said nothing, I asked, "Did she love him?"

He closed his eyes, old pain sharp-etched for an instant in his face. "I don't know. She never told me."

When he looked up I had to look away. The silence between us danced with shadows, new to me and terrible, but to Jamie they were old ghosts. He knew them well enough; and though they made him sad, they held no longer raw grief, only old sorrow. He spoke again sooner than I would have dreamed he could.

"She wed him, at any rate, and you were born at the autumn solstice." His voice grew softer. "I'd never seen Maran so happy. She had a smile for you that no one else in the world ever saw." I glanced at him and saw that sorrow had left him, and now in his eyes and his voice lived softer memories of her. "I asked her once if she could see in you anything of me or of Marik, but she laughed and told me that she saw only herself in little." He glanced at me out of the corner of his eye. "Or maybe not so little."

"Thanks."

He snorted. "Wretched women, tall as houses the pair of you, and mean with it."

"You think I'm mean now, just you stop talking and see what it gets you."

"You're a glutton for punishment, aren't you? I'd have thought this lot was enough for one day," he said, finishing his ale. "Speaking of which, how about some more to drink?"

"Of course," I replied, and called the girl over. "A pot of chélan, with honey, and two mugs."

"Chélan? What for?" he asked.

"What do you think? You always told me that after a long drinking session it helped clear the head. We've been at this since mid-morning and it's near dusk already." My point was reinforced by our host, who came round with candles for the tables to banish the gathering shadows. More folk were coming into the tavern, their day's work done, to quench their thirst.

One corner of Jamie's mouth twisted up and he looked at me from under his brows. "And are you feeling the effects of all this ale, you who never drink more than two pints?"

It hadn't occurred to me. I was astounded to find that I was perfectly sober. Jamie laughed at my expression and clapped me on the shoulder. "You have just learned one of the great rules of drinking, my girl. When you are deeply concerned, when your heart is troubled by deep grief or sorrow, drink makes no difference no matter how much you take. But I will say, chélan sounds good."

"Fine, it's coming, now would you get on with it?" I said.

He sighed. "Lanen, must we finish this now?"

"Jamie, I've waited twenty-three years to hear all of this. I think now is as good a time as any."

"Very well." He sighed. "You see, Lanen, the men of Ilsa have odd ideas about women. They are very possessive, and Lady rest his soul, as dense as Hadron was even he could count. The old wives in the village simply leered at him, assuming that he and Maran had been lovers from the day they met, but he well knew they had not. She had denied him until they were wed, as would any good, quiet Ilsan maid. He thought his life long that you were my daughter, but when Maran left, he made me swear never to speak of her, and for the sake of his good name I must always refer to you as his child."

"Jamie, why did you stay? You knew the truth, such as it was. Why did you cleave to Maran when she had denied you not once but twice?"

He turned his quiet countenance to me and smiled gently. "I stayed because I loved her, Lanen. And because as long as there was even a slim chance that you were mine, I would stay at your side to protect you."

"And Maran?" I asked, my voice tinged with the bitterness I could not hide. "I have asked you all my life why she left, and you never answered. Tell me now."

"She left because she had to," answered Jamie, sitting back in his chair with his mug of chélan hugged to his chest. "Not for herself, though she was miserable with Hadron. She unbound him when she left, did you know that? Their joining was dissolved in the eyes of the Lady. I have since come to believe that she wed him because she needed somewhere safe for you to grow up, and knew she could not provide it." He was staring into the depths of his mug, for all the world like a village wiccan preparing to read the future in chélan stains. "When you were six months old, she looked in the Farseer. Berys and Marik had recovered, more's the pity, and were preparing to hunt for her. Seems we were lucky in one thing—from what she could gather, the Farseer itself protected her from their sight. But she was convinced in her bones that they would find her, and she didn't want them to find you." He looked up at me. "Just in case."

I had finally heard all that my heart could bear. I felt dizzy and had to brace myself on the table.

"She left right then, dissolving her ties with Hadron but leaving you in the only place she could think of where you would be safe. I begged her to let me come with her, bringing you, but she refused to take either of us into danger. She seemed to believe that somehow Hadronsstead would keep you safe. I was angry with her for years, hurt and miserable, but for whatever reason you are still alive. I have not heard from her since that day. And that is the end of it.

"And so, my lass," he said to me quietly, "that is why I have never spoken. I had to keep my word to Hadron, and since his death I have been waiting for the right time. That is who you are, to the limit of my knowledge, and that is the Jamie you saw last night. I feared I could not call on him, he has been so long silent, but when I saw you threatened I welcomed him and his skills." He coughed, then drank his mug dry. I was not surprised. I had not heard as much speech from Jamie in all the years I had known him.

Then he said quietly, one corner of his mouth lifted, "You know, that big bastard is still wondering how he happened to die last night. He never felt a thing."

And all was right between us. I found myself answering Jamie's grin, proud now of the skill that had saved our lives. How could I be angry at him who had been father to me when there was no other—who might be my father in very truth? And if death had been his trade he had changed it for another and better, and for my mother's sake. There had always been great love between Jamie and me; now it was closer and stronger than ever, and included my lost mother as well. I felt years older and shamed at my harsh child's judgement of him.

"Jamie, I—"

"Now, then, my little Lanen. All's well." He smiled, the smile he kept for me alone. "I'm the better for having told you. I should have done it ages ago."

"I haven't been anyone's little Lanen for ten years," I said, returning his smile. I had been well taller than Jamie since I was twelve.

"Ah, my girl, now there you're wrong. *My* little Lanen you'll always be." He took my hand for a moment across the table. "And now, my little one, it is your turn."

"For what?" I asked, genuinely confused. "You've known me forever, what could I possibly tell you?"

"I can't imagine," he said lightly. "You woke me the day we left to sign a contract it wasn't light enough to read, you're carrying silver enough for two months, and all this journey long you've said not a word about it. What could I possibly be wondering about?"

I grinned at him. "I can't imagine. Now I'm concerned about that little bay mare, she seems to be limping on the near fore—"

He leaned over and swiped at the top of my head. "Terrible child," he said affectionately. "Your turn. I'm dry as the Southern Desert. Enough of chélan, I want ale. Ale!" he yelled, and the girl scurried over with a jug. "Now," he said, "talk to me while I drink, my girl. Since you turned five I've known you would give your right arm to leave Hadronsstead—why now, so long after Hadron's death? Why did you not leave at once? What has brought you to it at last?"

I told him of Walther's absurd proposal in as few words as I could, but even so we were laughing heartily by the time I was done. "Ah, young Walther, he's not so bad a fellow, just a bit slow in everything bar horses."

"I wish the horses joy of him. I swear, Jamie, if you had seen his face—well, I hope he and Alisonde are happy and have the decency to keep out of your way."

"I won't mind them. I shall see her and think of you well away with a calm heart. But I must know for my own peace where it is you are going."

"I'm not sure myself. Away, mostly. There is a lot of Kolmar to see."

He narrowed his eyes. "Don't try that with me, Lanen Maransdatter, I know you too well. Come tell me, where are you going and what do you seek? You and I are all the family we have left now, unless it be Maran's mother or her brothers and sisters. I will follow behind you the rest of your days rather than let you go with no idea of where you are bound, or why."

Maran's mother, or her brothers and sisters. My grandmother, my aunts and uncles. I swore rapidly to myself in the silence of my soul that I would go one day to the village of Beskin and find that family I had never seen.

I liked the sound of "Maransdatter."

But for now—I took a deep breath and told Jamie the deep desire of my heart, speaking it aloud for the first time.

"I seek the Dragons, Jamie. True Dragons, on the Dragon Isle itself. I have dreamt of them since I was a child, since I heard that bard sing the Song of the Winged Ones, and I have longed for them beyond all reason. I heard them in the silence that night, you know, heard their wings and a melody beyond hearing; and I have heard them in my dreams all these years since."

"And what makes you think there will be a ship sailing, when so many have been lost? And what makes you think that you will survive where so many have died?" he asked solemnly. He shook his head, sadness in his eyes, but smiling at me as he always did when he knew I would have my will no matter what. "And what will you do when you find them, Lanen Kaelar?" he asked in a low voice.

"What? What did you call me?" I asked, shocked. How should he know that name I had chosen for myself?

He smiled, speaking very softly. "That was the true name your mother gave you. Lanen Kaelar, Lanen the Wanderer. I often wonder if she had the Clear-sight to go with the Farseer. It would explain a lot. I would swear she knew you would go adventuring as she did. Certainly she knew you would be a dauntless soul, you had no fear even as a tiny child. But come, answer me. What will you do when you find these Dragons that call to you so?"

"Talk with them, Jamie. Talk with them, learn the thoughts of those great minds that live a thousand years and more. Surely that is not impossible." I let him see my excitement, strong now with knowledge of my past, creating my future as I spoke. I had never dared say these things aloud, and the very sound of the words fired my heart. "I cannot believe that we two races should never meet. Why then can we both speak and reason? If there were but two people in all the world, would they not seek each other out? For companionship if naught else. I will find them, Jamie. Somehow, I will find them, and I will speak with them if I must risk my life to do so."

He was silent. I found I feared his disapproval as I had never feared anything else.

"I am not mad, Jamie, unless I have been mad my life long."

"I do not fear for your mind, my girl." He gazed into my eyes, the love of long years clear and strong. "But I wish with all my soul you did not have to risk your life on anything. Still, you are your mother's daughter. If you have this dream before your eyes, I know well that no power in the world may stop it." He smiled. "Just remember that Walther is not all that remains in Hadronsstead. I will be there still, waiting to hear the tales of your adventures."

He yawned, stretched and stood. "But for now I'm off to bed. We'll have a long day of it tomorrow. We're still three days away from Illara."

It was still early evening, but I too was exhausted. I wanted to say something to Jamie, but I had no words. What could I have said? I embraced him, bussed him on the cheek and bade him sleep well. I glanced at the couple in the corner, who had long ago stopped talking and now lay with their heads on their table, snoring gently. I smiled and went to my bed. I slept like a rock.

We set off early the next morning. The rain was still dropping showers on us as it passed, but at least we managed to dry out a little in between. By late afternoon the sky had cleared for good, and by the time we stopped—we rode only until sundown—the ground was mercifully dry. We camped at the border between a wheat field and a small wood.

The next morning I woke to a clear, crisp autumn dawn. Around me the kingdom of Ilsa gleamed, cold, rainwashed and wondrous with the dance of red and yellow leaves left on the tree boughs and the soft murmur of the late, deep golden wheat swaying in the wind. I stood still and let the land fill my senses, birdsong and leaf-whisper, sharp scent of fire and spicy smell of dying leaves, touch of wind on my face and taste of autumn on my tongue.

I shall never forget that morning. I woke for the first time with knowledge of my mother, with a sense of my own past and my own self; and with the knowledge that Jamie, friend and more than father, who had always been for me the love of family, bore within him the life and soul of a paid killer. I also knew what it had cost him and that both sides together made the truth of him. It was frightening, this new clarity of vision: but I felt free at last to know darkness as the other side of light, and that both were needed for sight.

And with that thought—it was almost as though I felt it in truth—the shackles of my old imprisoned self fell away at last. No more did I long for a warm bed behind safe walls. My heart drank in the beauty and wonder and danger of the world, and I saw for the first time that life was not something to survive, but something—the only thing—to be savoured in all its diversity. Light and dark together, mingled in all things, giving depth and substance where either alone was a pale shadow. I felt from that moment I might begin to find all things new.

I never lived in Ilsa again, but I never forgot that journey, the first of my long life of wandering. Forever after, the kingdom of Ilsa was to me the colours of autumn bright as sun after rain, and the sound of wind in the grass.

THE GREAT FAIR AT ILLARA

𝒱 "That's the one, the White Horse Inn," said Jamie. "Hadron always liked it. And keep to your plan! Believe me, during the fair the hostellers in Illara see single women as a losing proposition. He'll give you the worst hole in the place if he thinks you're alone. I'll get the lads and the horses settled at the fairground and arrange a cot for myself out there."

"Are you sure you won't stay here with me?"

He grinned. "And miss out on all the inside dealing at the grounds? Not even for you."

"Good luck to you then, because it's been forever since I've bathed and I'd kill for hot water. I'll meet you here for supper."

I watched Jamie and the lads ride off with the horses, who despite constant attention looked as much the worse for wear as I suspected I did. It was evil of me to leave the men with all that work, but we all knew the horses would be the better for my being gone. I was thrilled at being in Illara at last, and the last thing the poor creatures needed in this strange place was the smell of my excitement.

I turned towards the inn. Losing proposition, eh? Just in case, I had changed my filthy leggings for the only skirt I had brought. After I found Shadow a place in the stables I went around front. Now for it.

I took a deep breath for courage and went in. Coming in from brilliant sunshine in the late afternoon was like walking into a cave.

I don't like caves.

"Yes, milady? Come in, come in, what might I be doin' for your ladyship?"

Well, he sounded a little greasy, but not so bad as I had feared. I had never been "milady'd" before.

By now my eyes were becoming used to the gloom. The innkeeper was some way shorter than I, but made up for it sideways. (Surely there is somewhere a place where innkeepers are made; they seem all cut from the same cloth.)

"I need a room for the night and an evening meal for two," I said quietly.

"Certainly, milady." His smile made me long for clean water.

"Though I fear I'm near full up for the fair. I've only the one room left and it's the finest I have. I couldn't take less than a silver piece for it."

A silver was worth twelve coppers, or the hire of a man for six days. It was robbery.

I fought the impulse to accept it simply because I could afford it this once. "A silver for the week? That's fair," I said innocently.

The man laughed. Ugh. "Oh, no, milady. A silver for the night."

"A silver for two nights, with breakfast and supper for two thrown in," I said. "Or if that doesn't suit, I am certain there are other inns in the town."

It was twice what he could expect to get for any room he might have and he knew it. "Very well, milady. As you say." He oiled in front of me, leading the way. "It's lovely, truly it is, well lit and airy and plenty of room for you both. And it has a balcony as overlooks the river, you couldn't ask for better."

I could not suppress my smile entirely. "I'm sure it'll be fine. Send up a bath as well, please, with enough hot water for two."

"Yes, milady. And supper will be ready when you come down for it. My cook's a good hand with a stew, and the bread's fresh this morning, you'll be well pleased. Now if you'll follow me, it's just up this way."

He led me up a narrow stair and round a corner. "There you are, big and light like I told you," he said, opening the door for me. "You'll have come for the fair, I don't doubt. Have you travelled far?"

"Yes," I said, looking round. The room was indeed light and airy, the ceiling allowed me to stand upright, and the bed, thank the Lady, looked long enough so that for once my feet wouldn't hang over the edge if I stretched out.

"I suppose your man will be getting the horses stabled?" said the innkeeper. It was mere pleasantry.

Right.

"I took my horse to your stables before I came in. Your groom seems able enough."

The innkeeper frowned. "Then where—your pardon, milady, but where is your husband?"

"I don't have one," I replied. When he started to protest I cut him off. "I never said I did. You saddled me with him when I came in." I was far too pleased with myself as I watched the innkeeper's jaw drop. "I have been travelling for two solid weeks, to answer your question, and I will need enough hot water for two baths, one for me and one for my clothing. I have arranged to meet a friend here for supper, and now he can join me for breakfast as well. You are very kind."

He opened his mouth to object, so I kept talking. "And no, I won't move out of this room for some closet under the eaves. I like it here and my silver is as good as anyone else's. Now send up my bathwater and a bottle of your best wine. I'll be down later."

Before he could speak (or think) I had shoved him out the door and latched it.

I waited until I heard him go cursing down the stair before I laughed. Two days before, when we stayed in a village inn, I had been polite and found myself in a room I couldn't stand up in because the landlord discovered I travelled alone. This was a vast improvement. It was clean and well warmed by the sun, and there was indeed a tiny balcony with enough room for the little chair that sat by the bed. If I could make my peace with the innkeeper I thought I might stay here while I decided what to do with my new freedom.

Just then my bath arrived, a big caulked wooden tub with six large buckets of steaming water. I filled the tub with three of them and followed them in, lowering my aching body into the hot water with a deep sigh of relief. I lay back, legs hooked over the edge of the tub, letting the heat soak through to my poor mistreated bones and breathing in the steam like rarest perfume. That was the worst of travelling, I thought as I lay back—you so rarely got a chance to bathe. Smelling like a horse is fine for a while, but I hadn't bathed in hot water for nearly a week. I was *sick* of horse.

By the time I was clean and dry and the worst of the muck washed out of my clothing, the sun had set. I dressed in the spare linen shirt and clean leggings that I had been hoarding and realised with some surprise that much of my feeling of pleasure and well-being came from the simple fact of being clean again at last.

I took up the bottle of wine and the rough cup that had arrived with my bath and settled into the tiny chair I had moved onto the balcony. Spread there before me lay Illara at the edge of night. The light of the new-risen moon covered the city like a potter's blue-white glaze, broken only by the shimmer of silver where new-risen moonlight caught the river Arlen as it flowed on its way to join the Kai. And in nearly every window there was a light, like a skyful of stars come to rest. I smiled, filled with a quiet delight. I had dreamed of this for so long, dreamed of what it would be like to be in a city. I had never imagined there would be so many lights.

The first stars gleamed at me as I stretched out in my chair; long legs, long body, broad back and strong arms. Jamie had always told me that I looked well enough, but the glass told me clearly I was not beautiful. Still, if I truly was like Maran—*so alive, that was what you saw, the others were as candles to the sun*—yes, I could live with that. I was proud of my hair at least. Loosed now from its braid it lay draped about me to dry. It was the colour of late autumn wheat, thick and full, and when it was clean it fell to my waist like a waterfall of dark gold. And I had my mother's northern eyes, grey like the northern skies.

It was growing cold, I knew I should go inside, but the colours of the clear night were so lovely. I had not known such peace for a long time. I sat back and let myself be filled with moonrise over Illara. It was my first night in a city, and I was making a memory. By noon tomorrow I would have my third-share of the profits and be free to stay here or go where I chose.

The thought still seemed a little unreal. The heavy purse at my side, the carefully packed saddlebags with their hidden silver, made me into another person. No longer the sharp, neglected mistress of Hadronsstead, old before my time, a poor tired farmwife with no husband. I would miss Jamie—now more than ever—but from the moment he left, I would be my own woman, and I had all of Kolmar to discover in truth rather than in dreams.

I sipped my wine. Such a pleasure to be clean and dry, with the prospect of a real bed to sleep in again! I could stay here another few days, enjoy the fair, then off to—where? I wasn't sure I had decided yet. With all of Kolmar before me, the choices seemed endless.

I grinned then as I realised what I was doing. "I wouldn't have thought it of you, my girl," I said aloud. "Waiting still? Seeing all the rest of Kolmar while you wait for your dream yet a little longer? Idiot." I stood, leaning over the railing of the balcony, my heart beating faster, still speaking aloud to myself. "No more. I will wait no longer. If I am truly to be Lanen Kaelar then I must go where my heart leads. It is but the turn of the season. If by some miracle there is a sailing this year for the Dragon Isle the ships won't be setting out for some weeks yet. I can get to Corlí soon enough. Surely by the time they sail."

My gut tightened at the idea. There really was no reason to wait any longer. I could leave the moment the fair was over—indeed, as soon as the horses were sold—and get to Corlí in time to find out if any Merchant was daring or desperate enough to send a ship to brave the passage of the Storms. Corlí, whence the bold or the foolish were wont to board ships bound for the Dragon Isle, once in every ten years when the Storms abated enough to allow passage.

I knew perfectly well that this was the one year in ten, but we had heard no rumours of such a venture being mounted. Still, better chance of finding out here in Illara than wandering through the Ilsan countryside!

I started to laugh, for sheer gladness and for the delicious fear that stirred my blood. I could not be still, I had to do something— so I started to dance. Nothing graceful, believe me. I broke into a kind of leaping dance, of the sort done by the people of the Méar Hills before they went to war; a traveller at Hadronsstead once had taught it to me to pay for his supper. It involved sharp movements and leaping into the air and loud beating of the feet on the floor, and it was just what I needed. I started to sing the song that went with it when I heard (barely) a loud knocking at the door.

"What is it?" I yelled, striding towards the door.

A high, frightened voice answered, "The Master says will I please tell the lady to shut up, and that supper is ready in the common"— here I threw open the door—"room downstairs," finished the little maid with a gulp. She was a tiny thing, and from the look on her face the Master hadn't told her quite how large I was. Poor child.

I smiled at her. "Thank you, lass," I said kindly. "I'll be down soon. And dear, the next time your master sends you to tell a guest to shut up, try to soften the blow a bit. Telling someone that another guest needs sleep is good, or that there are rules about only singing in the common room. It makes it seem less rude."

"Y-y-yes, milady," said the girl. She curtseyed hurriedly, turned and rushed down the stair as if her life depended on it.

I laughed as I closed the door and began to put myself back to-

gether. Poor thing, she looked terrified. I caught sight of myself in
the glass and laughed harder. My drying hair was flung in all directions, my eyes gleamed still with my excitement—I looked positively
wild. I forced a comb through my hair again, braided it, and belted
my shirt about my waist. The wine had been lovely but the thought
of food made my mouth water. Jamie and I hadn't taken a noon meal
in our hurry to get to Illara, and breakfast was a dim memory of old
hard bread and older cheese.

I was halfway down the stair before I remembered. I returned
to my room and slipped the slim, sheathed blade into the top of my
boot. I knew Jamie would look for it.

I hurried downstairs towards the smell of stew and ale.

When I reached the common room, Jamie was waiting for me at a
table on the far side of the fire. "Is this place to your liking, my girl?"
he asked as he signalled to the innkeeper.

"It's lovely, Jamie. Are you sure you won't change your mind? I
hate to think of you sharing a barn with the horses when I'm lying
in such luxury."

Jamie grinned, the creases in his face deepening. I smiled with
him, when of a sudden I had a sense of ending upon me; it was unexpected and unwanted, as I felt for the first time a new aspect of
what I was doing. I stared at Jamie with the eyes of memory, trea-
suring this moment. Hadronsstead I had left with joy, Illara held no
regrets—but it would be hard, hard to leave Jamie behind. He was
the last of my old life, and the best; even before our journey he had
been the dearest soul alive to me. Now . . . I shook myself to hear
what he was saying.

"—and if I'm not there, I'll have no measure of what the other
stock are going for."

"Ah, well. I'm sure you know best," I said quietly.

He drew breath and I knew he was going to ask what was trou-
bling me; I could not bear that, not just then. I forced myself to smile
and mean it. "Oh, and it worked beautifully. The innkeeper never
knew what hit him, he was out the door almost before he had time
to object. I've the best room in the house, it's—oh, hello," I said
pleasantly, as the man himself arrived with two tankards of ale and
a jug.

"The girl will bring yer supper, let her know if you need aught else," he grumped, and left.

I leaned towards Jamie. "Do you know, I don't think he likes me."

Jamie grinned.

Our supper arrived moments later, and the same girl brought it as had fetched me. I smiled at her. "I'm not half so frightening sitting down, am I, lass?"

She smiled back, and with the confidence of her age replied, "No, missus, that you're not. And I hope ye won't mind, but I much prefer ye down and quiet to up and singing."

I had to hit Jamie to get him to stop laughing.

As we ate we spoke of selling the horses, Jamie told me some of the tricks of the fair, where best to take the horses to be seen by the wealthiest buyers, what time to catch the people there, how to drive a hard bargain. "Best leave that to me, for the first few anyway."

"Jamie, I may not have travelled much, but I've been bargaining in the village since I was eight!"

"Illara is no village. There are traders here could sell infant's clothes to a crone. For the first two, at least, watch me. Then we'll split up and do the best we can. Deal?" he asked, holding out his hand.

I lifted my palm to my face, county fashion, to spit in it, but he caught my wrist. "The first rule of barter in Illara is not to spit in your hand. The townsfolk think it a terrible insult."

"Do they still shake hands?" I asked.

"Aye, but just as they are. Deal?"

"Deal," I replied, extending my hand. I noticed that Jamie shook it twice instead of once. Another wrinkle. Another difference to learn, another culture to be part of. Excitement shivered through me again. How wondrous, to be in Illara at last, with Corlí before me and all my life beyond.

As if he read my mind, Jamie asked, "Will you be leaving soon after the fair?"

"I think so," I replied, confused by the wildly differing emotions coursing through me. My dreams lay bright before me in the glow of a fireplace I had never known, but the firelight gleamed as well on the face of the one person I loved. This was our last night together, who had never been sundered longer than the month of the fair. And he of all men would know just how I felt. "I'm going to do it, Jamie.

I'm going to the Dragon Isle, if it can be done. I'll seek word of a ship down by the river tomorrow, see if the rivermen know of anyone daring the journey this year. In any case I will be setting off for Corlí as soon as I can. Do you know how long the journey is? I never thought to ask."

He looked at me, measuring again, and said quietly, "It's the best part of two months to Corlí if you set out overland. The roads weren't good the last time I took them, and I don't expect in these days the old King has done aught about them. I've heard no rumour of strife between the lesser nobles on our travels, which bodes well; they aren't generally inclined to start anything loud and unpleasant with winter coming on. Still, the best and safest roads run by the rivers. If you go that way and ride easy, it's three weeks to Kaibar where the rivers meet and a little more again to Corlí after."

Nearly two months! "Is there no faster way, Jamie? The year's getting old. If they're going at all I might have four or five weeks at best before they leave. Surely it's not so far—"

"Trust me. And if it rains it will seem twice that, and it will rain." He shook his head, a wry smile on his face. "It must be inherited, your mother had no more sense than to set out just before winter either. But there is another way." He was silent for a moment. "You could go by riverboat in half the time. You'd have to leave your mare, though."

"Leave Shadow?" I asked, but knew the answer as soon as I said it.

"Or sell her," replied Jamie. "If you're going to take the ship you'd have to sell her in Corlí anyway, or find a boarding stable for her until you get back."

I hadn't thought that far ahead. That worried me.

But I couldn't sell Shadow. She was a last link with my past, and somehow I couldn't bear to part with her.

"Jamie—will you take her back with you? She can carry your pack, and"—Jamie was smiling—"oh, very well. I can't bear to think of her here in Illara when she belongs at home. I'll come and get her when I get back and I'll tell you all about my adventures. Deal?" I put out my hand.

Jamie took it; I shook twice and let go.

He laughed. "You'll do fine, my girl. Keep your wits this sharp and none can stand against you." He drained his tankard and stood up, yawning. "I'm off. We've an early start tomorrow. Mind you come well before dawn to help us groom the horses for the sale." I nodded. He leaned over and kissed my brow. "Good night to you then, Lanen Kaelar."

I grinned up at him. "Good night, you old bandit."

"Less of the old," he said, miming a blow to my head. I ducked obediently under it as he went out the door.

I sat quietly and finished my drink, staring into the fire. I never heard a thing until a voice behind me said, "Good even, lady. I see your companion has left, as has mine. I hate to drink alone. Might I join you?"

That voice.

It was the most thrilling sound in the world. That voice belonged to the man of my dreams—of any woman's dreams—light and in the middle range, so musical it might have been singing the words, but with a slight drawl that spoke promise of long slow nights of pleasure. I could not have ignored it to save my soul.

I turned in a daze. Before me stood a tall thin man with fair golden-red hair, eyes the green of spring grass and a nose like a fine hawk. He was fair enough to look at, but nothing could possibly match that voice.

"Of course," I answered, trying to keep my own voice steady. "Please—" I gestured to the chair across from mine.

He sat down beside me, his movements graceful as a cat. "I thank you, lady. Let me refresh your drink." He gestured to the innkeeper. "Are you here for the fair?" he asked, and smiled.

"Y-yes, yes, I've brought horses. To sell. Tomorrow." I stammered. I had been wrong. There *was* something that could match that voice, and it was his smile. It changed his nice-enough face to one of startling beauty and appeal. I was smitten like the greenest girl. I closed my eyes and tried to get my thoughts together. "My friend and I sell Hadron's horses tomorrow," I said, managing not to sound like a village idiot. But I couldn't keep my eyes closed, not with that face so close.

"Hadron's horses? Ah, my luck is still with me. I am seeking a mare for . . . light riding. Have you any suggestions?"

I gathered my thoughts this time before I spoke.

"There's a little chestnut with a lovely smooth pace. She's really a lady's mare, though, not strong enough for you."

He smiled again. "Ah, but she would be for a lady. Now," he said, leaning on his elbow, his face so close to mine we were almost touching. "What sort of a bargain might I strike with you?"

I nearly fainted. It was all I could do not to lean over—such a little way!—and kiss him then and there. His voice transformed all his words into purest seduction, no matter their real import. My heart was pounding. I forced myself to look away from those laughing grass-green eyes.

It was hard to deny him anything, even my own glance, but somehow that made it easier to think.

"I'm sorry, sir, but you will have to come to the fair like all the others. Though I will let you know which is the mare I'm thinking of." I turned back to him. He was sitting upright again in his chair, removed to a safe distance (thank the Lady!). Though if the opportunity arose again I didn't think I would have the strength to resist.

It struck me suddenly, despite the thrill of the encounter, that I was feeling and thinking things that had never occurred to me before—at least, not so swiftly. It frightened me. I stood, heart pounding.

"Your pardon, sir, but I have been awake since well before dawn and must rise earlier still in the morning. I hope to see you tomorrow at the fair."

"Then I shall bid you good night, lady, for I will certainly see you tomorrow," he said, his voice a gentle purr. He took my hand in his and kissed it.

I felt that kiss shoot along my nerves like raw lightning. I gasped with the power of it. He smiled that glorious smile at me, his eyes alight with good humour and laughter. It took all my strength to pull away and hurry up the stair; I felt his eyes follow me all the way.

For the first time since I left Hadronsstead, I did not dream of Dragons.

The horse grounds were busy when I arrived, an hour before dawn. I found Jamie and the lads already at work and, muttering a subdued "Good morning," took up a curry comb and got to it. By the time we finished the sun was well up and there were a good few folk about. Ours were not the only beasts for sale, of course, but once people heard these were Hadron's horses they crowded round, asking us all

questions, admiring the horses, watching as the hands took each one
for a walk and a little warm-up, showing them off to best advantage.
The horses gleamed in the morning light, and the grounds were
crowded with buyers and sellers. Jamie left me inside the ring and
clambered up on a tall stump near a grassy spot that he had picked
as a good place to gather buyers. He winked at me and began crying aloud, "Hadron's horses! Hadron's horses! Now or never, my
lords and ladies! Come and buy! Come and buy! Hadron's horses!"

I had to laugh. I had no idea anyone could shout that loud, let
alone Jamie. And it worked wonderfully. I decided I had missed more
than my childhood longing for travel by not being allowed on one of
these trips before; Hadron's was a name to conjure with here. There
was a large crowd around us in no time.

"The first to go will be this bay mare, my lords and ladies," said
Jamie, only a touch softer than before, to the crowd that had gathered. He gestured, and one of our lads started walking the mare
around the ring while Jamie described her and made the most of her
good points. He finished with "She's four years old, the best of
Hadron's breeding stock, with a sweet mouth and a cheery way about
her, and she'll run with a light load well into tomorrow. Now, what
am I bid for Hadron's bay mare?"

There was a chorus of voices, and in the end the mare went for
twice what I knew she was worth. The next was much the same, and
the crowd had grown even larger. "Change of plan, my girl," Jamie
said to me quietly. "We'll make our fortune today. I've never seen
folk more eager for Hadron's stock." His eyes twinkled. "Perhaps they
heard that Hadron has died, and there is no son to carry on his
work." I was appalled, and Jamie laughed. "I never said there was
no daughter or sister's son. It's all part of the game, my girl. Now I'll
do the next few, until my voice gives out, then you take over. Mind
you let them bid till they're tired and goad them on when they flag.
We'll do well today." In his chapman's voice he cried loudly, "Have
a good look and choose your favorite. Shame to take second best, my
lords and ladies! Hadron's stock, the finest in all of Ilsa, in all the Four
Kingdoms of Kolmar! Choose your favorite, my lords and ladies!"

I watched in awe as the next two went for the same kind of sum
the first two had. Amazed at Hadron's riches? Amazed now that he
was not more wealthy, the prices were incredible. When the fourth
went, Jamie called me to him. "I'm getting hoarse," he said, getting

a laugh from those closest. "Your go. Do me proud." He sat down and left me to it.

If the crowd had thinned, I couldn't tell the difference. I stood gathering my thoughts, looking out over the people who watched the handsome grey gelding in the ring, and after a short while I found myself scanning the intent faces for a particular one, hawk-nosed, fair-haired . . . *and that's enough of that, Lanen my girl,* I thought. I cleared my throat and stepped up onto the stump. "Very well, my lords and ladies," I cried, as loudly as I could. It was harder than I thought to make that much noise. "Next is this lovely grey gelding. Four years old, broken to harness and saddle, what am I bid?"

In deference to the change of auctioneer, someone shouted a ridiculously low figure and the others laughed.

Right.

"That'll get you his left foreleg, sir, what'll you bid for the rest of him?" The laugh was louder this time—the one who had spoken joined in—and the real bidding started.

After half an hour my voice was starting to go. Jamie and I took it in turns, until by the time we were down to the last it was my go, and Jamie's purse was full near to bursting. Most astonishing of all, it now held not only a river of silver, but several gold coins as well. Gold, the rarest and most precious of metals, and I had held one. It seemed unreal.

Jamie grinned at me. "I'm off to put this somewhere safe. You sell this last little lass and collect the fee, and I'll be back before you can count it."

The last to go was the little chestnut mare I had told the fair-haired man about. I had saved her for him. I scanned the remaining faces. Many had left, but when I glanced over them he was nowhere in sight. I gestured to the lad who was walking her sedately around the ring, and he brought her to a standstill. "This is the last, my lords and ladies," I said. I tried to speak loudly, but my voice was almost gone. I described her qualities as best I could, finishing with "She's three and a half years old, strong and willing, the prettiest lady's mare you'd wish to find. The lightest touch will send her where you want to go, and kindness is her best spur. Now, what am I bid?"

The bidding started high, as those who were left knew this was the last of Hadron's stock to be sold. It reached its limit soon enough, and I was about to announce the bargain struck when a light, melodious man's voice rang out, sending shivers down my back and naming a price full five silvers above the last call. It met with a stunned silence, and after repeating the sum three times, I called out, "Deal! Come forward, sir, if you please."

The crowd dissolved like morning mist, and there he stood. He was smiling that heart-pounding smile and holding out a purse. By the time I had counted out his silver—a ludicrous sum for the mare, good as she was—all the other buyers were gone. The lad brought her over and tied her to a post on the buyer's side of the ring, then left to enjoy himself.

I had been trying to think of something to say to this man after I was certain he'd paid the bidding price, counting slowly to let my fool heart slow down and my tongue unknot.

"You've quite a bargain even at this, my lord," I managed, giving the little mare a farewell pat and carefully not looking at him. "She's a good lass with a sweet temper—"

"You can stop now," he said cheerfully, "I've already paid for her." He reached out a long-fingered hand and took the reins from me. "I'm sure she'll be fine."

I couldn't avoid looking at him, so close. By daylight he seemed older—the sun found wrinkles the firelight had hidden—but the glamour about him was in no way changed or lessened. Indeed, it seemed that a touch of age sat well on his shoulders, adding an air of wisdom. His eyes perched above that sharp nose seemed only a moment away from laughter. I had to ask.

"Are you a bard, my lord?"

He did laugh then. It was like birdsong. "What a lovely thing to say! No, mistress, I'm no bard, just a Merchant with delusions of grandeur. I was told to find a good lady's riding steed, and I believe this mare of yours will suit perfectly."

I barely heard what he said, lost in the perilous music of that voice. "I'm glad you found what you sought. I—I never thanked you for the drink last night," I said. "And I fear I left rudely. I hope you will excuse me, I was so weary . . ."

"Rather I should ask your pardon, mistress—I know not what to call you. Might I ask your name?"

"I am Lanen Hadronsdatter," I said. It was my old name, but in my confusion I forgot the newer one I had taken. "And you?"

"Bors of Trissen," he said. "I am a lowly trader for a great merchant house in the East Mountain Kingdom. Surely, Lanen Hadrons-datter, the youth that abandoned us just now is not your only escort. Who accompanies you?"

"My father's steward, Jameth of Arinoc. He should be back at any moment."

"I would like to meet him," said Bors, sounding as if he truly meant it. He smiled at me again. "Have you ever been to Illara before, Lanen?"

"No," I said, and something made me add, "I've never been away from home before."

"Ah, so that is why you take everything in with those wide grey eyes of yours. It would be my pleasure to show you the fair," said Bors. I longed to say yes, but hunger and weariness had caught up with me; I would have accepted even then, but I caught sight of Jamie coming towards me and waved to him. Bors, watching, quickly collected up his little mare. "I'll be wandering round the fair this afternoon; perhaps we will meet then," he said softly. He made a simple walk round the fair sound wondrous desirable.

Jamie came up just then and asked if I was ready to eat. By the time I had turned round again Bors was gone.

Jamie and I walked in silence for a few minutes, heading back to the White Horse. Then I shot a sideways glance at Jamie and found him looking at me from the corner of his eye. We laughed, and that thrilling fear I had felt around Bors was gone.

"So, my girl. I hardly saw him. Why did he run off, and why did you blush when I looked at you?" asked Jamie with a grin.

"His name is Bors of Trissen. He's staying at the White Horse, and I seem to spend all my time around him blushing."

Jamie smiled still, but he looked puzzled. "That's not like you, Lanen. You, turning red around a man? I thought you were over that years ago."

"So did I," I said. "But did you hear his voice?"

"Barely. A bit high for a man, I thought."

"Oh, Jamie, how can you say that! It's the most beautiful voice in the world, I've never heard such music, even from the bard who stayed at Hadronsstead once."

Jamie said nothing to that, but changed the subject to the price we had gotten for the horses. It wasn't until we had eaten and polished off a mug of ale that he brought up the subject again.

"And so, Lanen, where did you meet this Bors of Trissen?"

"He joined me at the table last night after you left." I shivered with the memory. "I've never even imagined a man like that. Every time I see him my heart races and my face turns red. I've never blushed and stuttered around anyone! I swear, Jamie, I feel a complete idiot when he's about. Mind you, he is the most attractive man I've ever met, and that voice, that smile—"

"What?" Jamie seemed startled—or troubled.

"Don't you think he's handsome?"

He didn't reply to my question. "Lanen, would you say he had a glamour about him?"

"Absolutely."

Jamie's voice grew hard. "Now would you think about what you just said."

I did and got no further. "What do you mean?"

He muttered a few mild curses and looked up at me with a dark frown. "I wonder if I shouldn't tie you up and drag you back to Hadronsstead for a year while I teach you a few things." I returned his glance steadily. He sighed. "No one has ever told you about amulets, have they? No, I haven't and it's damn sure no one else would." He shifted in his seat to face me directly. "Lanen, you know of the minor demonlords, don't you? Sorcerers, demon callers?"

I nodded.

"Well, aside from meddling with more dangerous things, they often sell magical objects made with the aid of minor demons, to keep them in the materials they need for their damnable work. The most popular are amulets of Glamour. Their single object is to make the wearer irresistible to the opposite sex, and they work beautifully for that—but to those of the same sex the wearer is not changed at all." Jamie took my hand. "My girl, you know there is none would be more pleased than I to see you happy with a man. But this Bors, if that's his name—I only caught a glimpse of him, but from what I could tell he's no more handsome than I am, and he looks nearer my age than yours. Now tell me, if you can: did he seem to have a glow about him?"

"Yes, he did," I said. As I spoke I could see it, a faint outline of light around him. I didn't remember noticing it, but the memory was there.

And suddenly I was furious. Acting like an idiot child from the nearness of an attractive man was silly but no harm to any. Being *made* to do so was base deception and it made my blood boil.

Especially because I was deeply smitten with him. Damnit.

Jamie finished his drink and stood. "Right, then, my girl. Let's go."

He surprised me out of some of my anger. Usually when I was in this state he just let me stew. "Where?"

"Down to the river." I stared at him. "Or do you not want to learn when the boats set out for Corlí?" he asked.

My laugh surprised him. "I thought you were going to help me find Bors and pitch him in!"

Jamie smiled, a gleam in his eye. "That's an idea whose time has come, sure enough, but I don't think he's worth the effort."

I laughed again. "True enough. To the river it is!" We strode out of the inn and down the street, laughing as we went.

It didn't take us long to find the riverboats. We still heard no word of a sailing from Corlí, but several of the captains said word would never come so far north in any case, and we'd just have to go to Corlí herself to find out. When I asked about transport, I found that most of them moved goods rather than people, but Jamie and I did find one that was taking passengers all the way to the harbour ar Corlí. The owner and captain of the riverboat *Maid of Ilsa* was a young man named Joss. He agreed to take me, but where most were waiting until the fair was over some three days hence, he was leaving the next day at sunrise. He said it would take the best part of three weeks, which delighted me—it was less than half the time of overland travel. I paid him and promised to be at the pier well before dawn.

Before we left, Jamie took him aside and spoke with him. I strongly suspected that Joss was getting an earful of advice regarding my safety and well-being on this journey—at any rate, both he and Jamie seemed content when they parted.

As Jamie and I walked back to the fair, I was surprised that I was not filled with pleasure at the idea of setting out on my journey. Instead, sadness had claimed me; I left on the morrow, and from now the rest of my journey must happen without Jamie. I had thought all this time that being a wanderer on my own meant being alone, and the idea had seemed sweet. Now I saw with eyes grown older by two weeks of travelling with one I loved. It felt like years. I would miss him terribly.

As we drew nigh to the inn, Jamie said quietly, "Well, my girl, you're off at last." A smile touched his face. "At least you've the sense not to head into the mountains at this time of year. I've done that much good at least."

The sadness in his voice was hard to bear.

"Now mind yourself in Corlí, my girl. The docks are rough, and they're not above cutting a purse in the streets in broad daylight anywhere in the city, though they usually stop short of a throat before dark. Corlí is far larger than Illara, and that much more dangerous." He stopped, took my shoulders in his hands and stared into my eyes. "Are you still determined to do this alone, Lanen? Could I not come with you, as far as Corlí? I could tell the lads to take the silver back, they're trustworthy, I'm sure that riverman has another berth for the trip—"

I had dreaded this moment, but only truth would do between us. "Jamie, I've had this argument with myself ever since we left Hadronsstead." I blinked fast to keep the tears from my eyes. "You know I love you more than anyone alive. You're my only family. But I can't rely on you forever, any more than I could stay at Hadronsstead. If ever I am to live my own life, I must do this alone. I'm sorry."

He closed his eyes and let his arms fall away from my shoulders. "Aye, well. I thought I'd try." He looked up again, his expression echoing my own determination. "Lanen my girl, I hate long goodbyes. If I'm not to go with you I've no more business here, and to be honest I couldn't bear sitting around tonight waiting for you to leave. I'm off back to Hadronsstead tonight. I'll only need long enough to pack."

I stared at him. "But Jamie—"

"Now, don't you do it. You're right, it's best this way. You've the rest of the day to have a look at the fair, be sure you do, it's an amazing thing." The White Horse Inn was before us. "I'll not be five minutes packing, just you off and find the lads and tell them to get themselves ready. You get Shadow ready to go and I'll meet you in the tavern of the White Horse in a few minutes. Now be off with you!"

I left him in a daze. The lads I found all together at a stall selling ale in the horse fair grounds and told them they were leaving. I had expected to find them not best pleased, but they seemed not to feel too hard done by. I brought one of them with me to the White Horse to get Shadow, and left him to wait for the others while I talked with Jamie.

He was already in the tavern. We didn't take long to make our few arrangements. I decided that I had too much silver with me already, and sent my share of the profits back with Jamie. I stood by miserably while he had a farewell drink. He managed to chat lightly of the trip back, how it was always so much faster and easier than the trip out; of what he would have to tell Walther, of the new way things would be done now that he was Walther's partner rather than his foreman—"and more than partner, his overlord, as I have your voice as well as my own," he said with a wicked smile.

"Now, Jamie, don't rub his nose in it," I managed, trying to keep my voice light. "The poor soul is helpless enough as it is."

He grinned at me. "If I didn't know better I'd think you had a soft spot in your heart for him."

"Soft enough to flatten him," I replied. "But I didn't kick him when he was down. Perhaps you're right, I must like him better than I thought."

Jamie finished his drink. "There now, that'll keep me on the road until nightfall. Time I was off." I followed him out into the yard. All three of the lads were there, idly chatting and holding Shadow and Jamie's Blaze along with their own mounts. Jamie turned to me. "Now, then, my girl, I'll bid you farewell," he said. "Mind what I've taught you. Keep your wits about you, and try not to kill that Bors if he comes pestering you again."

I laughed, as he knew I would. "I promise I'll only wound him." I reached out to him and he gathered me in his arms and held me close. I was taken with a trembling. "Oh, Jamie," I whispered. He did not speak for a moment, only pulled me to his heart and embraced me with all his strength. "Lanen, daughter, go you safe and keep you safe, and come safe home to me," he whispered, his voice rising at the end as his throat tightened.

The smell of him, the feel of his arms around me, love and strength from my earliest childhood—I could not speak.

He loosed me from his embrace and mounted his horse. Holding out his hand to me, he drew me to his side and kissed me on my forehead like any father seeing a child off into the world. He held my eyes with his one long moment, then turned Blaze to the west gate out of Illara. He did not look back. The lads followed him, waving cheery goodbyes to me, and I soon lost sight of them among all the others on the road.

I dried my tears on my shirtsleeve. It was a strange feeling, being alone at last. My heart was full of his words and his look, but there seemed to be an empty space all around me where Jamie should be, had always been.

He called me daughter.

No matter that Maran never knew, no matter that we could never be sure—he was my father in every sense that mattered.

I wrapped my arms around myself. Despite the early-afternoon sun, there was a chill wind blowing in from the northeast. I took it as a sign from the Lady. I would let the winds blow me south and west, to Corlí; if chance and the Lady willed it, to the Dragon Isle, following the wind and my dreams—and when I wearied of wandering, at least now I would always know where home was.

And Jamie would be there.

He called me daughter.

I let the words sink deep in my heart. I could feel them like a cool drink on a summer's day, spreading through my body, quenching the hot dryness where I held images of a heedless Hadron. Sweet pain, that brought such a feeling.

I smiled. It had been a good parting after all, and the only one that mattered.

I turned back towards the inn, my heart and mind full of time past and time to come, and walked straight into Bors of Trissen.

We had to catch hold of each other to keep from falling. I was glad to find that my heart did not pound as it had before in his presence. Once I had my balance again I shook off his hands.

He was smiling, looking genuinely pleased. "Why, Lady Lanen, here you are! I've been looking for you. Won't you come fairing with me?"

I was on the point of swearing at him when I realised I could look at him without being dazzled. I wondered if that was the result of knowing about his amulet.

He laughed. "Dear lady, why so great a frown? I have no dark designs, I only want to show you the fair."

"Why so great a deception?" I growled. "I have no time for liars."

"What do you mean? How did I deceive you?" He looked all innocence.

"You know full well. My friend warned me, for the spell did not affect him."

"Oh, you mean the amulet," he said calmly. "Why, my lady, surely you knew—oh, your pardon! I never thought!" He went down on one knee to me, right there in the street, like a prince (or a player). He looked genuinely penitent. "Lady Lanen, I pray you will pardon this fool. I wore what I had purchased to find if it was what I had paid for. I should have realised you would not know of such things, I know they are rare outside of Corlí and Elimar. I beg your pardon most sincerely."

A crowd was beginning to gather. He looked such a fool kneeling there in the road, it was all I could do not to smile at him. An old woman called out, "Take him, lass, or leave him be, but don't leave him there in the dust!" It raised a general laugh. I reached down and drew him to his feet.

There was more laughter and the people dispersed. "You great idiot," I said, losing the battle and grinning at him. "A simple apology would have done."

"I am truly sorry, Lanen," he said humbly. "I am not wearing it now, you know." He grinned at me. "Though that night in the inn, I must admit I thought it was not working. I had hoped for a kiss at least."

"Be glad you didn't get one," I said. "If I had kissed you because of a spell and found out about it later, I might have—well, I should warn you, I have a vile temper."

Still he smiled. "I may not even hope?" he asked, teasing.

I batted at his arm to cover my confusion, not knowing whether to be flattered or insulted. He was still a handsome enough man when he smiled, and his voice at least was no deception. It still had all its power and music, undiminished by the absence of the amulet. With such a natural gift, I thought to myself, he could own the world if he so wished.

"Come then, you deceiver," I said, smiling. "Show this ignorant country girl the fair, and don't forget that you're the one who paid me three times what my mare was worth."

He laughed and took my arm. "And I shall buy you supper on the strength of it as atonement for my fault," he declared. And so we entered the fair.

We spent what was left of the afternoon going round the booths and tents. I had never seen so many things before in one place. It was like a swift glimpse of all the places I dreamt of seeing someday. There were silks in all colours and patterns from Elimar—and many things that claimed to be Elimar silk but weren't (Bors showed me the difference). There was jewelry from the East Mountains, heavy furs from the trappers of the Trollingwood, beautiful boxes and bowls made from the perfumed woods that grew in the North Kingdom, warm woolens from northern Ilsa. For supper Bors took me to a booth where they sold a spicy soup of fish and roots, a specialty of Corlí. It was delicious and I was ravenous. Bors laughed and bought me another bowl. Then in the gathering dusk our eyes were caught by a troop of jugglers passing by, tossing lighted torches in the air and catching them, crying the start of a performance. We followed them to a platform draped with cloth, where the jugglers disappeared and reemerged in costume. We found space on the ground and I watched their play, fascinated. Players never came as far as our village, and everything the bard had said about them was true. I tossed a silver coin in the hat they sent round just before the end and clapped delightedly for them when it was over. Then I looked around and realised that most of the Merchants were closing their booths.

Bors saw the look on my face. "Was there something you wanted to buy?" he asked. "They are none of them gone home yet, if we pound hard enough on the shutters they'll open—or we can come back in the morning."

"No, it isn't that I wanted anything—but it was such fun to look!" We both laughed. "I can't believe it," I said as we walked slowly back to the White Horse Inn. "So many beautiful things all in one place."

"That's why I became a Merchant," said Bors. He was trying to keep his voice light, but beneath it I heard a genuine passion. "I have always wanted to have beauty around me, to keep such things and make them mine so I could see them whenever I wished. I have to say, I wonder at you, Lady Lanen. I tell you true, I have never met such a woman. To look all day and buy nothing at all! I know perfectly well that you can afford anything you have looked at—I handed you enough of my silver this morning. Could it be that in all the fair you found nothing to please you?"

"I have no need of things, Bors," I replied softly. "I have spent my life surrounded by things and I leave them behind with a good will. I am going to see the world. Having more things means only a larger pack for my back. Since I sent my Shadow home," I added with a smile, "I must bear my own burdens."

He looked up at me, his expression unreadable, that glorious voice uncertain for the first time. "Are you a wizard, then?" he asked, his voice catching ever so slightly.

I burst out laughing. "Shadow is the name of my horse," I sputtered when I could speak. He had been truly frightened! Suddenly I cared nothing for the little deceptions he had practiced on me. Perhaps it was simply the custom of Merchants. I had spent the day talking with a man I had never known, who meant nothing to me and to whom I was only a country lass to be enjoyed as a novelty. I had never done anything of the sort before and I had had a wonderful time. The very distance between us was a comfort.

Do him justice, he laughed as heartily as I. The moon was not yet high, and I could not see his face when he said cheerily, "May you be the only woman in Kolmar who feels no need of my wares, lest my fortune wither! For I seek my fortune as a Merchant, Lanen, though I am but a young one as yet."

"Not so young anymore," I said lightly.

"Ah, sunlight is my enemy," he said, and I could tell he still smiled. "True, I am not so young as a man, though my wealth is such that as a Merchant I am barely out of my infancy. Though I think I have found a way to remedy that."

"To remedy age? Surely only lansip may do that," I said.

"I meant only to remedy my status as a Merchant—but you are right." He was silent for a moment, then said, "I am surprised you know of lansip."

"Even in the north we hear stories. It was lansip that used to send ships to the Dragon Isle, the leaves that preserve life, that restore lost years. But I have often wondered if the tales of their power are no more than legend."

"No, lady, the tales are true," he said, his glorious voice earnest and compelling. "So convinced am I of their truth that I have spent much of my fortune outfitting a ship. If you know so much, you must know that this is the year the Storms lose most of their force. My strongest ship leaves Corlí in little more than a month to voyage to that island, to bear home to me wealth beyond imagining and the means of life twice the span of mortal men."

I gasped and grabbed his arms. "Speak you truly, Bors? Your ship leaves for the Dragon Isle this year?"

"I have said so," he said, command almost smug in his voice.

I laughed. I laughed with delight so vast I was almost singing there in the dark street. I covered my mouth with my hands in disbelief, joy brilliant and sparkling all round me. I could barely see Bors, but I could feel his confused stare even in the dark. It made me laugh more.

"If you find me so ridiculous, I shall bid you goodnight," said Bors in a huff. Instantly I reached out to him.

"No, no, please, don't go, I'm not laughing at you, it's only that I can't believe it. Bors, I have dreamed of going to the Dragon Isle since I was a tiny child. Surely it is more than good fortune that brings us together here."

He took me by the arm and drew me into the light from the windows of the inn. There he studied my face intently, shook his head and said, "I don't see it. Why should you desire wealth or longer life, you who are your own mistress and withal so very young?"

"Not so very young," I said, faintly stung in my turn. "I turn twenty-four at the Autumn Balance-day not a fortnight hence. But I do not seek more life or wealth."

"What then could draw you to dare such a voyage? You must know that of the last ten ships gone out not one has returned," said Bors, wondering. "It is almost certain death to ride one of the Harvest ships. I risk my all for the hope of great gain. What do you seek that is worth your life?"

I let the one word speak the volumes I felt.

"Dragons."

It was his turn to burst out laughing, but his merriment was born not of delight but of ridicule. "Dragons? Why, away north the Trollingwood is full of them. They are small and harmless and stupid, cattle with wings. What could possibly make you risk death for—oh!" He stared at me. "And you laughed at me for seeking lansip. You are mad, you know that. True Dragons are an invention of the bards. And what could you possibly want with one if you found it?"

Thank the Lady I managed to remember that this man was my way onto the ship. I swallowed my pride and replied quietly, "That is my secret. But I must go, and I am delighted beyond words to know that you send a ship this year. Know you how I might join your Harvesters?" I wanted to fall to my knees and beg, offer to cook or clean the privy (if there was one) or wash the floors, anything to get on board. I managed to keep the pleading tone in my voice to a minimum.

"Of course, of course," he answered smoothly, the silk of his voice returned with all its force. "Perhaps we might travel to Corlí together? I have business to tend to, but I take to the river in three days' time. There would be time enough to find out more about Illara, and each other. Shall I come fetch you after you break fast? I would be pleased—"

Even his voice couldn't make the offer anything but ridiculous. I laughed aloud, breaking the mood he strove to create, and soon he could do naught but laugh with me. "Ah, Bors, you are tempting, but I cannot. I leave at dawn on the morrow, and I will be glad to deal with you as master of the ship you send once I get to Corlí, but you are too much the deceiver for my taste."

He sounded hurt. "Again you call me deceiver. How have I now deceived you? I told you I have left off my amulet. In what have I—"

"Don't worry, Bors. I don't know why you decided to be a player today, but it doesn't matter." I moved to the front of the inn and stood in the street before the open doorway. I smiled at him in the light that spilled out upon him, leaving me in shadow. "A lowly trader, indeed. How lowly a trader is it who can pay what you did for that mare? And you have sent your strongest ship to Corlí, have you? Your strongest of how many? You are master of your own Merchant House, that is clear, and your lady awaits you and my little mare at home. But I have enjoyed this day with you. You have been a true challenge. I have no idea what you might mean when you say anything, so I spend my time trying to hear what you do not say. With practice I might be good at it."

His voice smiled. "Ah, you have caught me, lady. After only a day you know more of me than do many. I may not tell you my true name here—I have many dealings with those in this city, some of whom have never seen me, and I have come expressly to discover if they are treating me honestly. I find I must again throw myself on your mercy—" He stopped, and I could almost hear the thought come to him. "And if it pleases you, let me proffer as recompense that which you have requested, as reward for your discretion. Meet me at the harbour in Corlí and I will see to it that you have a berth on my Harvest ship."

So simple. So easy. It couldn't be real.

But I wasn't going to argue. In fact, I could scarcely catch my breath. "It would please me greatly," I managed to whisper.

"Then I am well content," he said. "I shall see you in Corlí. Unless you will break fast with me in the morning ere you go?"

"I thank you again, but my boat leaves at dawn and I must be there well before," I replied. "Bors, I bless you from the bottom of my heart, but I am dropping with weariness. It has been a lovely day, but a long one, and I need some sleep at least. I wish you a good night, may your dealings prosper, and I will see you in Corlí."

He stared at me for a long moment, as if to fix my face in his mind. "I thank you, lady, for your good wishes and your good company," he said at last. "Goodnight, and farewell." He pulled me to him and kissed me softly. I met him with a good will. His lips were satin, smooth and soft but with more than a hint of the passion beneath. When I moved to put him off he stepped back and bowed and, smiling, his laughing eyes sharing their private joke with me, he turned and disappeared into the night.

I paid the innkeeper and told him I would need breakfast early, then went slowly up the little stair and into my room. The day had been long as years and I was exhausted. I felt I had done not badly for my first day loose in the world. I undressed in the dark and collapsed onto the bed, but I could not sleep immediately. It had been a pleasant kiss, perhaps more would have been even better. . . .

I turned over determinedly and crushed the pillow to me. "Go to sleep, Lanen you idiot," I thought. "You've to be at the dock before dawn. Then it's off to Corlí and ho for the Dragon Isle!" I smiled into my pillow and closed my eyes.

Not a bad day at all.

Marik

"By the price that was paid, by the power of blood, in the name of Malior, Lord of the Sixth Hell, I conjure a Messenger here to me. By this sigil ye are bound, by these wards restrained. I am your master. Come now and speak."

I poured the blood I had drawn from my arm over the hot coals on the altar, and in the rank steam there appeared a wizened figure no longer than my forearm. For a moment I was concerned. I hadn't asked Berys how I would know it was a Messenger—but then it opened its mouth. The mouth was half as large as the entire creature, filled with teeth like wicked thorns. When it spoke I started, for it was the voice of Berys himself.

"I trust you have good reason for waking me in the middle night," it—he—rumbled.

"Reason most excellent, Magister Berys. I have found her, the child of Maran Vena, here in Illara. She is the right age to be the child of my body, though I can see no trace of myself in her. For looks she might be the mother come again."

Berys's voice sounded much more awake this time. "What have you learned? Does the mother live, or does she herself have the Farseer?"

I laughed. "I had not long converse with her, Berys. There was no need. The young idiot seeks the True Dragons with all her heart, she is headed for Corlí on her own. She even thanked me for agreeing to take her on as a Harvester! Now I need not lose sight of her while I am gone, and when we return we will learn what we need to know, and this eternal pain of mine will end."

"Is she your child, Marik?"

"I have no idea, Berys, but I will find out once we are on the island."

"And if she is not?"

"It is well known, is it not, that Dragons are vicious killers? Simple enough, once we are there. In the meantime I begin to learn some of the joy of the cat with a mouse between its paws. There is no question that the mouse will die, but there is a certain contentment to be gained from playing with it."

"Indeed," replied Berys, his voice now calm, "but this could have waited for morning. Again I ask you, Marik, why am I wakened thus?"

"Reason enough. From the records I have found here, along with old seamen's tales and those I heard in Elimar, I cannot but begin to believe in the True Dragons. I am hoping that the legends of their gold are equally true. The difficulty will be to take what I need and get out alive, if the tales of this Boundary are correct, and if it is true that they can smell Raksha-trace on any who have dealt directly with the Rakshasa."

"Ah. This makes things more difficult." Berys was silent a moment. "It is well you woke me. I will need every hour to prepare all for you, if they must have the added virtue of removing all trace of Raksha-scent." Another moment's silence, then, "You must know that this will cost you dear."

"Let all be your best work, Magister," I answered him, laughing, "for when I return I shall pay you in lansip, a king's bounty that no king has seen in over a century."

"Very well. As we agreed, I will provide boots, cloak, amulet and the Ring of Seven Circles. Thus shall you be provided with silence and concealment enow for your task, and a chance of surviving battle should things go ill. As for dragonfire—there are ways. I could prepare an artifact, but there is a simpler method." The demon held silence for a moment, then Berys's voice said, "I shall send Caderan with you. He is well able to provide such protection, and he may serve you in other things as well."

"I thank you. Let him be sent to Corlí with the items you have spoken of. You must know, Magister," I said quietly, "that I show you great trust in this. I have no wish to end my days in a watery grave, in company with all the other fools who have attempted this journey. I have only the word of your 'prophet' that I will return alive from the Dragon Isle, with lansip for all my needs and to spare. Should that not come to pass, you should know that I have ensured that proper recompense will be made to you and yours. You understand me I trust."

"Indeed," replied Berys, sounding almost pleased. "But you need not doubt me. I will find many uses for a quarter of your journey's profits. Just remember, Marik. The child of Maran must not be harmed, lest she be your daughter. The bargain was for her whole. I know you would not let so minor a pleasure as she might prove rob you of the cessation of your pain."

"She will be whole, Magister," I replied smoothly. "You look to your side of the bargain, and I shall look to mine. I will speak with you again once we reach the Dragon Isle. Commend me to your masters."

Berys must have released the Rikti from his side, for with a noisome pop the creature that had spoken with his voice suddenly disappeared. I walked away from the darkened summoning chamber, going over and over my plans and preparations for this mad journey. My only crumb of comfort was that Maran's daughter would be on the ship with me, and was every bit as likely to die as I was.

It was small comfort, but better than none.

Caderan

"I am to go with him, Magister? But he is a lout, a bungler!"

"Then you are more foolish than I thought, Caderan. Do you not know who it is who has arranged for so many of our number to find useful work to do? No, Marik is no fool, though he is not nearly so wise as he believes." The Magister smiled. "For example, he does not know that by completing this first summoning, he has begun a record." The Magister showed me a thick volume bound in a strange, pale leather. The pages were blank except for the very first, which was half-filled with small, neat script. At the top of the page were written the words "By the price that was paid, by the power of blood, in the name of Malior, Lord of the Sixth Hell . . ." The very words he had spoken, the tenor of his thoughts between the words.

I turned the page and nearly dropped the book. An invisible hand wrote still. "I must remember to have that damned mare taken to Gundar. She'll make good breeding stock, at least. Now, where did I put that report from . . ."

The Magister snatched the book from me. "So you see, my apprentice. I will know all that he seeks to keep hidden from me, and I will know all that happens on this voyage as soon as he thinks it. The book will continue until he steps foot again on this shore. Go, attend him, and remember—I will never be far from you, either."

I bowed humbly, as befitting his status as a great demon master. "I will not forget, Magister. Remember me to our masters."

His laughter as I left was not reassuring.

RIVERS

Lanen

I was soon sick of water.

The first few days on the riverboat had been a novelty, living on the river Arlen, which is the border between Ilsa and the North Kingdom. I was disappointed to discover that the western marches of the North Kingdom looked so very like Ilsa, but as we moved south the land changed at last. It was greener, for one thing, and the air a little warmer, though each morning brought fresh promise of winter's approach. I had enjoyed seeing the land slip by, and the speed of the journey had been all that I could wish.

At first.

I soon learned, however, that the rivers in eastern Ilsa run through the flattest country imaginable, and after more than a week of it I was thoroughly bored. It began to rain on my birth-day, only a week out from Illara. Joss, the owner and captain of the *Maid of Ilsa,* set up a shelter of waxed cloth on the deck so we passengers need not spend all our time below in the dark—but whether we huddled under its slight shelter or sat cramped in the tiny space below, it made little difference. We were all wet and we were all miserable.

The next day there was some excitement, when we left the placid Arlen and joined the turbulent Kai; certainly Joss, silent before for the most part, seemed truly awake for the first time during the journey. He spoke with me and pointed out the many districts of Kaibar, the great trading town that had grown up on the north shore of the Kai and west of the Arlen. When we put in for a few hours to restock, I wandered about Kaibar, exploring, drinking in the new sights and smells like finest southern wine. Since I had brought only light clothing, knowing I would have to find winter garb somewhere along the way, I decided to look in Kaibar for a good heavy cloak.

After much contented rambling I found a tailor's near the waterfront. He heard my request, took one look at me and disappeared into the back room, emerging in moments with the loveliest cloak I had ever seen. It was dark green, double woven of beaten wool to keep off rain, and it had autumn leaves embroidered around the hood that spilled onto the shoulders. I was delighted. I do not usually care much about clothing, but this caught my fancy; it reminded me of the Méar Hills in autumn. It was even long enough. I am ashamed to admit I barely haggled at all, and walked out wearing it.

I returned to Joss's boat, warm at last and ridiculously pleased with myself. It was a pleasure I would need, for the next fortnight stretched endless before me. Now we were on the Kai's broad back we went faster, but after the first four days I felt we had been on it forever. The river could not flow quickly enough for me. I was growing restless—I had dreadful visions of missing Bors's ship and being left in Corlí with only my dreams. I finally approached Joss and asked if he knew when we should arrive, but his calm answer was "We'll get there when we get there and none the sooner for wanting it. Ten days, mistress, no less, no more."

Infuriating man.

But he did seem to prefer the Kai to the Arlen, or perhaps eastern Ilsa did not suit him. He started to talk to us a little more, not much and not long, but he let loose a few words here, a few sentences there. I found him kind and shy, willing to help but not to talk about it. He spoke with me more often than with the others—perhaps because I was the only woman, perhaps because I was alone and willing to be silent as often as I spoke. The others were a pair of youths, Perrin and Darin (I never wanted to remember their names, but I couldn't help it; I wondered what their parents had been thinking of), and three older comrades down from the northern hills with last year's furs—seems they had been trapping late the last spring and missed the season. They hoped to make a good enough sum from this early cold to return to the hills before the snows, and daily prayed to the Lady it would last until they came to Corlí.

I found I had to put off one of the old lads who fancied himself a ladies' man; but I made things clear and he backed off without much protest. A boot knife and a strong arm are good arguments, but man's height and a plain face are stronger yet.

The rain finally stopped a week out from Corlí and the weather set fair and cool. I spent most of my time now with Joss, helping here and there where I could, listening, talking when he welcomed it. I was at a loss with nothing to do, and I learned there was always enough to keep two busy on a boat. I enjoyed his quiet company, and he seemed to like mine better than solitude at any rate. We spoke of our lives, I told him of Hadronsstead and my journey so far, and I asked him where he was from and where he had been. I was delighted to discover that he had never been as far north as Hadronsstead. At last, someone who didn't know the lands I did! The days passed more quickly, and I was nearly surprised to wake one morning and realise we would reach Corlí on the morrow.

I found Joss at the tiller as always and brought him a mug of warm chélan. As had become our custom, I sat with him and drank my own. It wasn't very good and I muttered something about being tired of "poor man's lansip." Joss put down his cup and gazed at me.

"What is it that draws you so, Lanen?" he asked as we watched the banks slide by. "I've had passengers before who were anxious to get to Corlí, but seldom one like you." He smiled at me, a slow smile I had come to honour for its rarity. "He's a lucky man, whoever he is. There's not many can hold a woman's heart so."

I gazed on the passing fields, some golden yet, some stiff with stubble from the reaping, some already brown and ready to wait for spring. Joss's calm manner had entered my soul, and he had been a good companion. No reason not to answer.

"There's no man in my heart, goodman Joss. My dreams alone take me to Corlí. I seek passage on one of the great ships."

"And where will it bear you?" he asked, no whit disturbed. Indeed, he seemed almost cheerful. "The great ships travel all the seas in the world. Are you bound for the Desert Lands? The frozen north? No, you have not the look of a trapper. Surely not just a trip to the silkweavers of Elimar, you could get there as fast on one of your precious horses." I shook my head and returned his gaze steadily, smiling, wondering how to tell him of my destination.

To my surprise he turned away suddenly and cursed. "Another damned idiot!"

"What?" I was shocked.

"You're hiring on with the Harvest ship, aren't you?" he said harshly. I was amazed by the bitterness in his voice. "I heard rumour of one leaving this year. Bound for adventure, looking to make your fortune from gathering lansip leaves, maybe steal a little dragon gold on the side, if the creatures even exist? And you a grown woman! That makes three of you on this boat, and not one with the sense the Lady gave lettuce. You'll never get past the Storms." He growled his words, gripping the tiller. "And so pass a parcel of idiots, and the world well rid of the lot of you. If you don't mind, milady, I've work to do. There is room for you to wait at the bow rail."

I waited for him to thaw, sitting no more than a foot from him, but he steadfastly ignored me. Eventually I gave up. I pondered his words, his vehemence all that day. It was not until the sun began to go down that I dared approach him again. At twilight we had become used to taking a drop of ale together. The other passengers had gone to their bunks with the sun. I went to him as he stood at the rail that encompassed the forward part of the deck and held out a tankard.

"Come, goodman Joss—shame to part so," I said as gently as I could.

He looked at me, the twilight glow lighting his dark eyes. "Aye. So it would be," he said gruffly. He took the tankard and made room for me at the railing.

We were silent as the light faded from the sky, watching the twilight follow the sun. He was hanging the running lamps from their hooks when I asked quietly, "Who did you lose on a Harvest ship, Joss?"

"Never you mind," he growled. Silence fell again. There were no clouds—it would be a clear night, mercifully. The first stars twinkled as they rejoiced once more at overcoming the day.

"We'll come into Corlí at the second hour after dawn," he said as he stood in the gathering darkness. "You'll have plenty of time to get to your precious ship."

"Thank you, Joss," I said, looking not at him but at the water. "And I thank you as well for your company these last weeks. You have lightened my heart with your friendship, and I will not forget you."

I was not even certain he was still there when I heard him say softly, "Nor I you. Go with care, Lanen Maransdatter. The Storms are deadly and the Dragons are real, whatever anyone may say, and none who go to that cursed place come back unchanged if they come back at all. My grandfather told of his grandsire's wealth gained from harvesting lansip, and I lost my father and my brother both to those damned ships. Whether Storms or Dragons took them I know not nor care, but I hate that isle and curse every ship that sets out for it."

I heard the door of his tiny cabin in the stern shut quietly. Joss's bitterness stung my heart. I knew that note of helpless anger, I had sung it often enough myself—but there was nothing I could do save commit his anger to the Lady. Surely, as the laughing Girl of the Waters, she would know and move to ease the sorrow of the brother she bore on her back.

As for my own heart, it was full of his other words. *The Dragons are real, whatever anyone may say.* Those words had my soul singing so I could hardly breathe. *They are real!* I repeated to myself, over and over as the boat slid rapidly towards Corlí. *I am going to the Dragon Isle at last, and they are real!*

I fell asleep with Dragons dancing in my heart.

It started sprinkling just after dawn and kept raining on and off all morning. We came into Corlí in the middle of a shower. There was just enough wind and rain to make the little riverboat horribly uncomfortable for the last half hour. All the other passengers were huddled under the oiled cloth. The young ones were sick, the elders well on the way.

I am almost ashamed to admit that I recall feeling wonderful. I was out on the deck, at the bow railing, wrapped in my cloak and an oiled cloth, breathing in Corlí with the rain, riding the surge of the water like a galloping horse. For the last few days we had passed more and more villages along the riverbank, and for the last half hour there had been a solid rank of houses beside the water on either side. Now we were passing a crowd of small boats, and came shooting down on the current of the Kai into the true harbor of Corlí.

I took one look and gasped, turned away, overwhelmed.

Before me stretched a vast great plain of water.

I taunted myself into some semblance of courage and turned my face again to the sea to learn what lay before me.

Water. As far as the eye could see, water. There were what looked like tiny spurs of land to the left and to the right, but before me the water seemed to stretch into infinity. I fell back from the rail, shrinking into myself. I was terrified, I wanted to hide below the deck in the face of this immensity. It seemed alive, as if some great being dwelt beyond sight under those dark waters and breathed out its essence in words no one could understand.

I firmly believe that forcing myself to look again at the sea, just that small arm of the sea in Corlí Harbour, was the hardest thing I had done in my life up to that time. All the tales—true and false—

that have attached to my name since never mention the fact that my
first glimpse of the sea reduced me to a terrified, shivering wretch,
huddled against the rail of Joss's little riverboat for protection, turning my head away from the deep, the vast, infinite unknown.

We came to rest with a bump at a small pier, like twenty other small
piers around it. It was still raining.

Joss leaned down and shouted to the others below that we had
arrived. My five fellow travellers climbed out of the dark and into
the rain, and were not pleased about it. They grumbled as they assembled their bags, they grumbled as they left the little boat that had
been our home for three weeks. Joss managed a civil farewell to them
all.

I waited until the others had gone, taking my time to collect my
few belongings and pack them carefully. I dragged my pack up the
few rungs of the ladder, shouldered it with a grunt and went over to
Joss, who stood with his back to me.

I took a deep breath for courage, then went to him and put my
hand on his arm. I spoke quietly, the light rain making a small silence
around us as I spoke.

"Joss, I have wanted to leave my home and travel all my life and
never had the chance before now. I thank you for bringing me here,
even if you are right and I go to my doom. You cannot bear the burden for every soul that joins the Harvest."

He shook my hand off his arm but did not turn round.

"I am not your father or your brother, Joss. I do not seek wealth
from the lansip trees. I am going to talk with the Dragons, if I can,
and find out why they do not live with us, and see if I can change
their minds."

"You go on a fool's errand, Lanen," said Joss to the sea.

"Then my errand and I are well suited," I said with a laugh. "At
least wish me good fortune."

"You will make your own fortune, good or ill, whatever I may say."

I sighed. "Farewell then, Joss Riverman," I said sadly. "The Lady
bless thee."

"And may she lead thee to safe harbor in the end, Lanen Maransdatter," replied Joss. His face was still to the sea, his rain-soaked back
to me. "I will not curse the sailing of this ship, for it will bear thee

and thy dreams. Fare well, Lanen, and may the wind and waves be kind to thee."

I stepped onto the pier, surprised at the weight of my pack, surprised to find that the land seemed to rock as the water had. I laughed at myself, threw the long wet braid of my hair over my shoulder and set out for the center of the harbor.

I learned later that it is the custom of seafaring men never to watch a friend out of sight, as that would mean a long separation. Years after he told me that he had been on the verge of begging me to stay, for I was the first soul he had trusted in many years—but he knew I followed a dream and would not stay for a chance-met friend.

Lighthearted in my ignorance, I all but danced my way down the quayside as I sought out the Harvest ship.

vi

CORLÍ AND AWAY

C Corlí Harbour sits near the mouth of the great river Kai, where waters collect from every corner of Kolmar to mingle in a glorious rush and flow in a torrent into the bay. The warm swift southern current, brushing up the coast, then sweeps away the silt, leaving a natural harbour and meeting place for trade and shipping. The old saying "If you want to know anything, go to Corlí" comes from the Merchants and traders who fill the wharves year-round with the sights and smells of far away. (The rest of the saying is "If you want to know everything, go to Sorún." It refers to the Silent Service, based in Sorún but found everywhere in Kolmar—when they fail. It is said that enough silver will buy any information you might want, but that is another story.)

In Corlí you will find goods from all the kingdoms in their wondrous variety, like the fair at Illara in large; but that is not the only reason Corlí is renowned. It is from Corlí that the great Merchant ships set out west and north over the sea to the Dragon Isle. Lansip grows there wild, it is said there are endless forests of the stuff, but it will grow nowhere else. The seedlings and young trees brought back in the past always withered and died, the seeds failed to sprout.

If lansip were not so powerful, none would even consider the deadly journey. But even weak lansip tea is a sovereign remedy for

many ailments, from headache to heart's sorrow, and when it is concentrated into a liquor it has the power to give back lost years. They
tell the tale of a fabulously wealthy Merchant in his seventh decade
who bought a full Harvest, every leaf, and drank all the liquor that
was distilled from it. He passed through middle age and into youth,
until the day he drank the last of his lansip. He was found dead of
shock, with the look and the body of a youth in his early twenties.

When, rarely, the Harvesters find late fruit on the trees, it is
brought back with care, most valuable of all—for that fruit, eaten
without its bitter skin, can heal all wounds save death alone. The
Harvest journeys are said to have been the founding of several of the
Merchant Houses, and certainly kept the older ones wealthy.

However, despite the enticements of the Merchants—Harvesters
are paid the weight of the leaves they bring back in silver—Harvest
ships had always set out shorthanded. Few in those days feared the
True Dragons, for most considered them no more than legend, but
the Storms were real and known deadly, and in a hundred and thirty
years before we set out none had returned of all the ships that had
essayed the passage.

If I'd had any sense, I'd have been terrified.

I couldn't wait to go.

I know it sounds strange, but I hardly remember the first time I saw
Corlí itself. It is in my memory little more than a jumble of impres-
sions. I know it was wet, and that I was lost after I left Joss's boat. I
think I considered asking directions, but decided instead that I
wouldn't mind being lost for a while.

A few moments stand out from the mist. I remember leaving the
quay and wandering towards the harbour, getting wetter with each
step. There was an inn with a fire where I had soup, and the land-
lady gave me a cloth to dry myself. I waited there until the rain
stopped. The next thing I remember is being at the dock, seeing the
great ships for the first time and being amazed at the size of them.
To my eyes, used only to Joss's little riverboat, they looked huge, their
sails like furled wings gathered onto the yards.

Unfortunately, I remember very well what happened when I got
to the harbour. I went to the first dock I came to and asked where I
might find the Harvest ship. I drew any number of blank looks and

a few lewd remarks, so I walked on along the pier. I needn't have bothered to ask. Fifteen minutes' gawping walk from that first ship, I heard a crier. After selling the horses in Illara I knew enough to admire his lung power. Then I managed to understand what he was saying.

"Come aaall ye, come aaall ye! Sail for the Har-vest! Sail in three days' time for the Dragon Isle! Sil-ver for leaves! Sil-ver for leaves! Sil-ver for all the leaves you can carry! Come aaall ye, come aaall ye!"

I hesitated a moment before approaching him. I had meant to go up and mention Bors's name, but decided in the end I would rather not be indebted to him if I could help it. And I noted that for all the crier's enticements he was being given a wide berth by the passing sailors. Apparently lansip was not as real to them as death by drowning in the Storms.

The moment I came close enough for speech he dropped the foghorn of his voice to a more bearable level. "Come to sign on as Harvester?"

"That I am. What are the terms?"

"Same for everyone, unless ye've been to sea before."

"No, I haven't."

He grinned, and the sight wasn't for the fainthearted. He had more gaps than teeth. "I never asked," he said. "Ye've not the look." Then in a practiced singsong he recited, "Terms is silver, weight for weight, for all the lansip leaves ye gather. We provide passage, bags for the leaves and half your rations—and ye'll work for that half, let me tell you. You supply your own bedding, clothes—and get a waterproof or ye'll regret it—and the other half of your provisions. If ye disobey orders we'll not answer for your safety." For the first time his voice softened the merest touch as he added, "And ye must know that no Harvest ship has returned in a hundred and thirty years. There's rumour the Storms are weakening near to nothing this year, but all in all we've no better than one chance in two of coming back alive. Consider it well ere ye decide."

Ass that I was, I barely paused for breath. "I've decided. I'm coming."

He signed me on with no further argument. He gave me a list of the items I would need for the voyage and pointed me to a scribe nearby. With the infinite smugness of the slightly educated I thanked him and said I could read for myself. He nodded and said, "Then you'll have read that you signed on as assistant crew from this minute. Take the day to find your gear and be here at sunset, you'll sleep on the ship and take up your duties from eight bells at the change."

He might just as well have been a dog barking for all I understood him. "What change? Did you say eight bells? When is—"

"Midnight, ye useless thing. Now hop to it, get your gear into a sea chest and get on board before the sun's down. Move!" he yelled, his voice rising to its former level. He turned from me and began to cry again his enticements for Harvest workers.

I left a bit dazed—part from shock at what I'd done, part from the sheer volume—and turned towards the town. Thankfully most of what I needed I found in a series of shops near the harbour.

I'm afraid I spent a small fortune in Corlí. I know I was badly cheated in some places, but I really didn't care. I found a small, strong sea chest, some heavy tunics and stout leggings (they were not at all surprised by my clothing in Corlí, even in those days), and as recommended I purchased that curious and smelly garment sailors call a tarpaulin. It stank of tar and I wrapped it in my old blanket (though on the journey I wore it seven days out of seven and would not have traded it for its weight in solid silver). I got myself a new pair of good boots, some extra bedding, rations and a small luxury— dried dates and figs from the southern reaches of the South Kingdom, since even I had heard of the poor rations at sea. I packed away my old clothes, leaving my skirts and my fine new cloak at the bottom of the chest and everything else on top where I could reach it. I spent what little time remained to me wandering about Corlí Harbour, becoming accustomed to the smell of fish and salty air, watching the sea in fascination.

I reported as ordered at sunset. I carried my belongings on board in the fading light, jostled from behind by my fellow Harvesters, directed by the regular crew, who barely tolerated us. I stared all around me as I was led to my "berth" belowdecks—a tiny space in which to sling a too-short hammock and a smaller space in which to stow my gear—and told to sleep while I could. It was only just after sunset. I managed perhaps two hours' sleep before we were all roused by a loud voice calling something I couldn't understand, but which by the movements of my fellows obviously meant "Get out of bed and get to work."

It was eight bells at the change. Midnight. We all worked in the steamy hold, hard as ever I had worked on the farm, scrubbing the floors—they called it swabbing the decks—preparing the ship for I knew not what. Come dawn—about six bells in the dawn watch, or seven in the morning on land—I found out. We were all hurried back up to the main deck and put to work loading cattle and what I judged to be not near enough hay to feed them. What they were there for I could not even guess. For a brief while I worried that I had been fooled and that this was a trading ship, but soon there were more canvas sacks to be loaded into the hold than I had ever imagined existed. They were new and surprisingly good quality, and I eventually realised that they were waiting to be filled with lansip leaves.

My heart beat absurdly fast as I worked. The very touch of the rough canvas thrilled me. I was living my dream at last, and even the terror of the journey had no power over me.

For the next two days, with sleep snatched between watches, all I remember thinking was that if this was a dream I wouldn't mind waking. I'd had no idea. When we weren't working or sleeping, we were learning about the ship and its workings. I had never imagined such strange terms in my life, still less thought I would need to know them. The ship's Master had us practicing every waking moment until the movements began to feel familiar. Surprising how quickly such things come to seem normal.

My next clear memory is of the dark before dawn—five bells in the dawn watch, so late in the year—the day we were to sail. The sky was just beginning to lighten with the promise of morning. The smell of the sea, ever present in the town, was stronger yet at the dockside. The gulls cried their eternal longing, other birds fought with them for the foul bits of fish the incoming fishermen spilled on the dock. A light breeze blew from the water, blowing away the smell of the land altogether. It was clean and sharp with salt.

We had gained steadily in numbers since I came on board, but there were still a number of empty hammocks, so we all had plenty to do. There was a lot of cursing by the Master as we raw beginners fumbled with a rope (which I was beginning to think of as a line, but could never call a sheet without giggling) and despite all our practice nearly tripped each other up trying to follow orders. He was a hard taskmaster, but even I could guess that our lives would soon depend on knowing what he wanted done and doing it as swiftly as possible. Still, I managed to glimpse the gangplank being hauled on board and the last line cast off from shore. It all went very quickly. We were madly busy as we left our anchorage and I felt the ship begin to move. We were on our way.

I will never forget the feeling of hauling on a line to help set the sail, glancing towards the quay and watching the land draw away from me. With a moment's thought I stand even now on that deck. I can feel the gentle glow of the sunrise on my face as we set out. The air is salt and chill, with a hint of much colder to come.

I remember thinking, *This ship is as unlike Joss's riverboat as a full-blood stallion from a gelding pony; a different creature altogether. The river has its own kind of life, and all moving water a certain rhythm of its own, but a river flows only in one direction. For the first time I feel the sea rock the deck beneath my feet. It is a stronger feeling than I expected, and the sea wind is wilder, with more on it than salt. I remember my terror two days past at first seeing so much water, and shiver again with it even as I laugh at myself. I think even the bards cannot describe this feeling, this world so close to our world and yet so far. It is strange and wondrous to feel living water not dead rock beneath my feet, and the air cold and clean and other.*

Thanking the Lady for my farm-hardened hands, I finished helping to set the sails, unfurling the wings of the ship to catch the breeze. It was a wondrous feeling.

Just as well. It had to last a long time.

The space we had to live in was horribly cramped. I was easily the tallest person among the Harvesters, and I realised why after my first night on board. No tall person with sense would ever go near such a craft. I could hardly stand up in the morning—which was just as well, because there wasn't room for me to straighten there belowdecks. Once I could finally stand upright I found a free instant to ask the Master if there were a few feet of deck unused at night where I might sleep. That was where I first learned that, despite the empty berths (which by the time we left were packed with various odd items that would fit nowhere else, and securely stowed using the hammocks for netting), every inch of space was taken up by at least two things and I was lucky to have the space I had. There were so many people on the ship at that time that I never saw the half of them, especially if they were not among those of us who were working our passage.

I spent such free time as I could find with an older woman from

the East Mountains. Rella was a small woman, she came not as high
as my shoulder, but her strength was near the equal of mine. She was
sturdily built and managed most things well enough, but she could
not hide the crooked back that made many of the others shun her. I
barely saw it, for to me she was a window on a world I had not yet
discovered. Her accent was strange and she used words I had never
heard, and she was the first person I had met from the East Mountain Kingdom. I got her to talk about her home and every word was
gold to me, and she was grateful for the attention. She took to looking after me in her own gruff way. It felt good to have someone to
talk to, even someone as curious as Rella.

The first week of the voyage is mostly a blur, for which I am
thankful. The few clear memories I have are of badly cooked food,
horrible smells and some of the hardest work I have ever done in
my life. There was always too much to do, cleaning the ship constantly, tending the cattle we carried, drilling in the ways of the ship
until we could all but do them blindfolded. There was more to keeping a ship in order than I had imagined, but I was glad enough for
the exercise. The days were cold and growing colder and anything
that kept us moving I was grateful for.

The weather grew worse the farther west and north we sailed.

At the end of the first week even the greenest of us had gained
some semblance of sea legs, and the worse of the seasick had recovered. Others had taken to life at sea as if born to it. I leaned a little more to the second than the first, and thank the Lady I was not
seasick, but it took me ages to find my balance on this moving creature. At first I fought the movement and lost every time. Once I
started to think of it as a willful horse I seemed to manage a little
better, but as the weather worsened I had to spend more and more
time just staying upright. I caught a glimpse of the Captain as he
passed by one afternoon to take a reckoning on the mysterious in-
struments he used, and as if he had shouted I heard his thoughts
turning on the Storms.

That was when I began to be truly frightened.

That night things got worse. If before the ship had groaned in
the wind now it cried out like a wounded man, shuddering from top-
sails to keel when a contrary wind fought with what I had first imagined to be masts stout as trees, but now saw as tiny wooden sticks
that stood between us and a damp, mournful ending. A thin strip of

sail on each mast bore us flying westward over the rough seas. I learned later that the usual practice in rough weather was to strike all sails and wait out the storm—but here the Storm never ceased, and movement was our only safety. The waves battered at the hull of our fragile home, lifting and dropping us in a wild dance, rolling and pitching until the strongest of us felt queasy. There had been no cookfires for days, and the cold food within and cold water without were as depressing as the thick blanket of grey skies all around us.

The morning of the ninth day out, I at least was convinced that I would never see land again. I cursed myself roundly for being such a fool as ever to leave solid ground, and I swore that if I came out of this alive, I would never set foot on a ship over the deep sea again.

Well, I swore a lot of things back then. I meant it at the time.

That morning, though, I committed my soul to the Lady and prayed for a painless death. It felt as though every roll would be the one that sent us belly-up. The winds whipped through the rigging, plucking at the taut lines like harp strings playing an endless dirge. I was thankful for the regular duties that gave me something to think about rather than simply worrying about staying alive. Still, if I stayed working belowdecks too long, I felt I was in a cave. Better outside than in if we went over, I reasoned. Probably wrong, but I have always hated caves. Besides, the noise was louder down there, and I was terrified. My fellow passengers were no better off than I, and some were worse. The seamen were too busy to be frightened, but they none of them looked much better than we did.

Suddenly there came a shout from the bow. This was nothing new, it had been happening about once an hour for the last day and night. I never did find out exactly what it was they shouted, but the meaning was always the same—take hold of something solid and hope you can hold on. I reached for the rail and looked up.

And up.

A solid wall of water was poised to break on top of us and send us to the bottom.

I was too terrified even to scream. I closed my eyes, whispered, "Lady, protect us," wrapped both arms about the rail and hung on like grim death.

And the wave crashed down. There was a terrible splintering sound like a branch breaking from a vast tree. I was swept off my feet by the force of the water, flipped over the side still clinging to the rail, fluttering in the rushing water like a banner in the wind and fighting not to breathe in. I held on with all my might and blessed the pure strength of my arms and hands. As the water receded I struggled to pull myself back on deck, shaking in every limb, coughing out seawater.

The Captain said later that if our sliver of sail hadn't caught a wild gust just before the wall fell on us, we'd never have seen the sun again. We managed to shoot out from under the worst of the terrible weight of water, but still it stove in parts of the deck. The splintering I heard was the foremast, the one carrying that sail that saved us, breaking off halfway down its length.

And with that, the sea and the Storms had done their worst. The winds dropped almost immediately. The waves grew less and less, until in a quarter of an hour we found ourselves rocking in a swell no more than five or six feet high. If I hadn't seen it myself I would not have believed it.

I happened to look up and catch Rella's eye. She smiled, then she grinned, then she let loose with a laugh straight from her toes. I joined her, and in moments so did every one of the crew, laughing away our terror, laughing in disbelief that we had survived, laughing until we wept for wonder that we were still alive.

We learned soon enough that we had lost almost a third of the crew in the passage—all Harvesters save for one unlucky soul of a seaman—and though we mourned them, we found ourselves marvelling that so many had survived. I wondered how with a lesser crew we would ever live through the return passage, but when I spoke with the true seamen, they were certain sure of the lore, and swore that the trip east and home would be far easier than the trip out. I hoped in my soul they were right.

That night and the next day were spent furiously repairing where we could, making shift where we could not repair. A kind of spar was jury-rigged onto the stump of the foremast to bear what canvas it would, for now we were making best speed to the northwest. The surviving mast looked to me for all the world like a washing line, spreading vast bedclothes to the sun.

The rest of the journey, for all the work, was in the nature of a sigh of relief. When I had time to think about it, I was terribly proud that mere six-foot swells seemed tame to me now. The Captain passed the word one morning, about four days after we'd survived the Storms, that by his reckoning we would make landfall by evening. That brought a cheer—and I for one wondered what if anything could ever convince me to set foot on deck for the trip home. But the cheer was loud and heartfelt. I knew well that each of us had given up our souls as lost in the Storms, and to be not only alive but arrived at a place known to no living man—it set our blood racing.

That afternoon, just before sunset, the word was passed for all hands on deck. (We truly noted then for the first time how many of us had been lost; there was far more room for us all on deck now than there had been.) The Master congratulated us on still being alive—which brought another cheer, and not a little backslapping among us—said that land was nigh and it was time we heard from our new master what our duties would be on the Island of Dragons. He stepped away from the rail of the bridge and the Merchant took his place.

It was Bors. At least, it was Bors until he opened his mouth.

"I give you greeting all, brave Harvesters. We have done with the worst, thanks to our good Master and his gallant crew," he said, bowing slightly to the Master behind him. "Now in the name of the House of Gundar I welcome you to the place where all our fortunes will be made." He caught my eye, then, and a terrible smile crossed his face as he said proudly, "I am Marik of Gundar, and if you work till you drop for the seven days we shall remain here, you will return to Kolmar wealthy beyond your dreams."

Marik. My mother's mortal enemy. And Jamie had spent years telling me how much I looked just like her, damn, damn, damn. He must have known from the moment he saw me at the White Horse that I was Maran's daughter. Now there was no escape. I could not even hide in the crowd of Harvesters—I was a good head taller than the tallest of them. I tried out a curse that I had heard one of the seamen use during the Storms. It helped, but not much.

And whether he planned it or no, Marik had no more than announced his name and begun to speak of our duties when the lookout up aloft cried, "Land ho! Land off the port bow!"

We were there.

We did not come in full sight of the island for some while yet, and did not get near enough to it to land until twilight. It was decided that we would anchor off the coast for the night. No one mentioned a reason, but it occurred to me (and to others) that perhaps

Marik was delaying his meeting with the Dragons. I remembered that he did not believe they existed, and that he meant to prove the stories of the other Merchants false. Still, even if it was a matter of fighting other humans rather than negotiating with Dragons, better to wait until daylight. It would also be easier to deny the existence of such things in broad daylight than in darkness surrounded by an unknown land.

For the last time, as I slept fitfully that night, I dreamt in part of the Dragons that had haunted my sleep for so many years, gleaming in the sun, full of delight at our meeting, courtly and kind.

In the face of truth, dreams disappear like smoke on a windy day.

For alternating with that sunlit vision was one of darkness and blood, and Jamie's voice saying, "As nasty a son of the Hells as ever escaped the sword." Marik, who (Lady forbid it) might be my father—and if he was, who must want me to finish his bargain for him. My dreams tossed like our storm-racked ship between those images, and I woke sick with worry and wonder.

A small boat took Marik and his two guards to land at first light. They encountered neither Dragons nor warriors, either on the beach or as they explored farther into the trees that came almost down to the water's edge.

Once they decided it was safe enough, most of us were set to unloading the sacks and the cattle from the hold, along with tents, bedding and cookpots that could hold enough food for a village. The Master asked for volunteers to go ashore to unload the boats at that end—I tried to reason with myself that there was safety in numbers, I should stay on the ship, it was tempting fate to go ashore where there would only be me, a few Harvesters and Marik with his men.

I never did listen to reason.

THE
DRAGON ISLE

THE DRAGON ISLE

Lanen

If my memories of Corlí are as an autumn fog, my first step on the Dragon Isle is a crisp bright winter day, cold and sharp and clear as diamond.

The land seemed to rise up to meet me as I followed my comrades out of the boat and into the shallows. It may have been no more than the effect of land after twelve days at sea, but the impression remains. I walked out of the sea onto small black rocks, and thence onto the rough grass that grew nearly to the water's edge. The scent even of the grass under my boot was like nothing I had known—it smelled like spring in the morning of the world.

Crushed grass.

I will always remember.

As I stood on the shore my heart beat fast and high, and I felt as though there were iron bands about my chest like the faithful servant in the old tale, though mine were to keep my heart from breaking for joy, not sorrow. I worked hard to draw breath, there on the edge of my dream.

I took another step forward.

The island did not disappear under my foot or sink into the sea—or fade into the darkness of my room at Hadronsstead.

I walked on the Dragon Isle under the sun. My heart sang, and despite the danger I was in I laughed aloud for heart's ease. I beheld the world clearly, more clearly than ever before, and realised that I had walked in a fog all my life and not known it. The threat from Marik was real and could not be ignored, but joy took me for that time and would not be denied.

As I moved through the morning, working hard but taking every spare second to look around me, I met more and more that was new to me and I delighted in it all. This was the dream of the traveller made real and at its best, working and breathing in a new place. The sun shone, the air was cold and crisp and smelt of something I did not know; like cinnamon and nutmeg but wilder somehow and deeper. I soon learned that this was the smell of lansip in the autumn, as the dying leaves dried in the salt air.

Crushed grass.

I will always remember.

Kantri

I watched her as she walked and laughed in the sun. I longed to go to her. The others I had seen, more than a century past, knew only fear and greed. She was very different and I desired to know what made her the exception. I knew very well that only a certain few ever came to our isle, and for fewer reasons.

But she moved with a grace I had not seen in others of her race, and her joy was that of a youngling new-come to the world. Almost I could smell with her the air, almost myself laugh with delight at first knowledge of a new place, and for that alone I would have abandoned my post and gone to her. I knew she would not run. I hoped, I longed to discover that she was truly the one from my Weh dreams; and my wise heart knew her, even then.

Still habit kept me back, and obedience to the laws of our Kindred. I remained in hiding and waited.

Lanen

We had a fair walk north after we landed, through thick stands of lansip trees. A gentle breeze blew towards us from the north and the smell was glorious, spicy and invigorating. There seemed almost a holiday air among us all; I think it must have been the wonder of filling our lungs with that rare perfume not smelled in a hundred years. It was a marvelous sensation—at least, for those of us walking ahead of the cattle.

After about an hour we reached a small clearing, one of three. I was amazed to see that there were old cabins still standing, two of them, made of a dark red wood I had not seen before. As if they had known what to expect, Marik's men directed the Harvesters to the next clearing, which held no structures and was no more than a large open space among the trees. I could only guess they had old Merchant's tales to guide them. The place had an ancient feel to it, and lonely, as if it had been waiting faithfully for men to return and bring it once again to life.

The tents we carried were soon raised. There was room for four in each, but since we had lost so many in the passage I managed to get a tent for Rella and myself alone. We were all given our duties immediately, some to fetch water from a nearby spring, some to start a fire, some to see to the cattle. We noticed that most of the sailors who had helped carry supplies stayed on as well, and why not? There were fortunes literally on the trees here, no need to pass up such a chance of wealth.

I barely noticed what we were doing. I fancied I could smell Dragons on the air, feel their presence in the trees beyond, watching and waiting.

For me, of course.

Ah, Lady bless us. Was I ever truly that young?

Kantri

When I had tracked them to the Gedri camp and it grew clear that the one I watched so closely did not mean to call to me yet, I turned over the watch to Hadreshikrar. It was nearly time for the renewal of the treaty, if the Gedri remembered. More than a hundred years had passed. I knew from my studies that in their brief lives such a span encompassed three or four generations. Few of my people had even noticed.

Thus I was pleased to find at the appointed place and time a new Speaker. This one was tall for their kind, with hair of golden red—from the little I had seen I guessed he must be the leader of this Harvest. He waited but a moment before he called out, "Very well, it is noon and I am here. Show yourself, Dragon, I pray you; I have much to do." There was an insolence in his voice that surprised me. The Gedri are seldom so arrogant in the face of my people.

When the sun stood directly overhead I moved into the gap in the trees, where I might be seen, and answered him. "Greetingss, childt off the Gedri. Hwat bringethh thee ofer ssea to the landt of my people?" I make certain that my man-speech is archaic and a little rusty when the Harvesters renew the treaty.

The Speaker started violently when he heard my voice. "You're real," he said, his voice much lower and shaking now. "Forgive me— I was told—I thought you were legend." He stood in a cloud of fear.

"It hathh been many a yeear ssince thou hasst come for the hlanssif. Knowest thou sstill the termss off the treeaty?"

He managed to speak at last. "I—no, your pardon, Lord Dragon, I knew not even that there was a treaty," he said. I was struck by his voice. Despite his fear he sounded much like one of the Kindred— it was pleasing to hear a Gedri voice so musical.

"Thou art hhere for the hharvest nonethelesss?"

"Yes, Lord Dragon. But—what treaty—forgive me, lord, I didn't think you would be here."

"It iss ssimple, childt off the Gedri. The Boundary iss well sset to north and far away west, a ffence off woodt between thy people andt mine. Ssouth iss thy landing place, easst iss the ssea. Keep thysself and thy kindred on thine own sside the ffence, hwere the hlansif trees arre, andt for ourr part we sshall not cross the Boundary to interffere with thee. An thou or one of thy kindred dost cross oferr, thy livess are fforfeit and we sshall ssslay thee on ssight. Sshouldsst thou require to sspeak with uss, be heere at noon and thou sshalt be answsered. Thou hast until dawn off the sseventh day from thiss moment to gatherr hwat hlansif thou willt. On that day thou sshalt meet with me here to ssay farewell when the ssun riseth ofer the rim off the worldt. Ffail not off that meeting, ffor it iss the assurance that thou art departing. Shouldsst thou remain affterr, thy departure will be—assissted. Dost undersstand?"

"I—yes, yes, I think so. We stay on this side of the Boundary, we have six days to gather and I must meet with you before we leave at dawn on the seventh day. If we need to talk come at noon. Is that it?"

"Hyu lissten well, merchant. Hwat iss thy name?"

"I am Ma—Master Bors of Trissen, Lord Dragon. How should I call you?"

I smelt the lie and put a low growl in my voice. "Truth, Merchant. I assk only thy ussename, but I will have the true one."

"Marik. Marik of Gundar," he said swiftly. "And you are?"

I hissed my amusement. "I hight Hlorrd Drragon." He seemed disconcerted by my laughter. "Know that thou andt thy people arre watched alwayss," I told him. "Ssendt the cattle through the gate at ssunsset. Sshouldsst thou have needt to sspeeak with me, come to thiss place andt call for the Guardian. Barring ssuch a meeting, we sshall not sspeeak again until thou art ready to depart."

He bowed shakily in my general direction and left, far more swiftly than he had come.

That was the extent of the prescribed contact between our peoples, save a formal farewell when they left.

For me it was not enough.

There is among the Greater Kindred a longing which we call *ferrinshadik*. It may be, as some believe, a racial memory from aeons past, for it is felt to some extent by us all—but to some, as to me, it is a bitter pain to be borne. It is the deep longing to speak with another species; to converse with another Kind, to learn, to see the world through different eyes. It has been my burden all my life. I have learned all that is known of the Gedri among my people, thus trying to ease the pain, but it only grew worse.

How should I describe a deep longing of the heart for that which cannot be? There is a ban against our races meeting, for the dangers to both sides are too great. Since the coming of the Demonlord, there is too deep a temptation for my people to desire the death of the Gedri. That is why we first came to live on this island. The Great Ban has been in place for three thousand years, a long time even by my people's reckoning, and we could not see a way to end it without grave danger to both sides.

Some have tried to speak with trees to ease the *ferrinshadik*, but that slow ponderous speech takes a lifetime to learn, even one of our lifetimes; and it knows only wind, water, earth and fire, sap rising and leaves falling. The true *ferrinshadik* is for speech with a sentient being. The Trelli have all gone, as far as we know; we do not speak with our life-enemies the Rakshasa; there remain only the Gedrishakrim. Our old fear and loathing is hard to overcome, and most of the Kindred believe that it is foolishness to try—but the *ferrinshadik* is not to be denied, and I had it in greater measure than any I knew.

Hadreshikrar knew it as a scholar, but that is the lesser kind. My blood ran with it, my Weh sleep was plagued with dreams, and every year I waited for some sign that the time had come.

The one who laughed. My heart was full of her. I longed to speak with her, but I must not. I myself had helped establish the Harvest laws, and a king cannot act against his own decree. So I must wait and hope, and see if she also felt the longing.

She must come to me.

Lanen

After the tents were set up and we were more or less settled I had to fight my instinct to hide myself. It was not possible, of course. Marik knew I was here and there was no way to avoid him, so I decided, perversely, to seek him out. I asked Rella if she knew where I might find him.

"He's gone to talk with the Guardian, I hear," she said. "If he's uneaten yet he should be back soon enough." She seemed to have a hearty contempt for Marik, which made me feel a little better. At least it helped balance the fear.

But even as she spoke I saw Marik's long figure emerge from a gap in the trees. He seemed terribly excited as he strode along, and my good intentions vanished like smoke in a high wind. I ducked back in the tent and tried to keep hidden.

I might have saved myself the trouble. The Master called out to the company and told us all to assemble in a wide clearing just north of the one where we had set up camp. I realised that that was the direction Marik had come from.

I put up the hood of my old black cloak and wandered over to the gathering, despite all sense trying to walk hunched over and with bent knees. Marik stood nearby, but it was the ship's Master, he who had signed me on back in Corlí, who spoke to us.

"Here it begins," he said simply. "Lord Marik has spoken with the Guardian of the Trees and learned the terms of the treaty. That old fence along the trees—" He pointed behind him to an obvious line of trees with an overgrown but still visible path alongside it and a decaying fence before. "—is the Boundary. The fence runs for some miles to the west, and according to our records bends south to meet the coast. The sea is the Boundary east. We are allowed to collect any leaves we find on this side of the line, also any fruit, but there's no sense bringing back trees, they just die. It's leaves you're after. The more the better, we've sacks enough to strip bare every lansip tree on this island. Fruit still on the tree is to be brought in person by the finder back to Marik, who will occupy the larger cabin. The finder will be credited with the weight of the fruit in silver." Here his mask cracked slightly and the Master let loose his gap-toothed grin. "I hear the things weigh as much as a melon. Guard them with your lives."

That got an appreciative murmur.

His voice grew louder. (I was impressed despite myself; I knew how hard it was to make that kind of noise.) "But believe me when I tell you—you will not pass over that Boundary and live. I heard some of you on the way here saying the Dragons were something we Merchants had created to keep lansip to ourselves." He grinned again, briefly. "I wish we had, it's a wonderful idea. However, they beat us to it.

"No matter what you heard or didn't aboard ship, Lord Marik has now spoken with one of the beasts. The Dragons are real. They live here, this is their island, and you cross that Boundary on peril of instant death. All the records we have of the old voyages say that they will slay on sight anyone who tries to cross over, and the Guardian has said it again not five minutes past.

"Keep on this side, work like fury for the next seven days, and you should all be disgustingly rich when we get back to Corlí. Cross that border and you die, simple as that. Any questions?"

Silence.

"Leave your gear in your tents, get as many sacks as you want from the quartermaster after the midday meal. Dismissed."

The rest went their ways, leaving me staring still into the dark wood ahead. I could see no farther than a few feet through the thick branches, thinned though they were by autumn nakedness. I nearly spoke out then and there when the Master called to me.

It was not the time, I knew that perfectly well; yet I turned away reluctantly, staring over my shoulder until the clearing was out of sight.

VOICES BY MOONLIGHT

Lanen

By nightfall I reckoned I'd made back at least what I'd spent in Corlí before the voyage. I had a feeling for weight, and the leaves I'd carried even in half a day came to a decent amount in silver. Tonight and thereafter we'd have to go farther afield, but even I had already seen thicker groves farther off, and I wasn't paying much attention. True enough, I wouldn't object to the silver my efforts would bring me, but there were other things on my mind.

I still hoped that by the morrow I'd have found a Dragon to talk to. Marik had not sought me out nor sent for me—I began to hope that now he was here his mind was on lansip, not on me. But ever in my inner ear I heard a small voice whisper that this might be my father, and I long promised to demons.

The evening meal was warm and plentiful, and the moment it was over most of the others collected more sacks and went back to the trees. A few, with whom I remained, went into their tents, planning to start again as soon as they were rested. Most planned to rise after only a few hours. I was surprised to find that no watch was set on the camp and asked Rella about it as we were preparing for bed.

"And what would it be we'd watch for, eh?" she replied, bemused. "By all reports there's three creatures larger than a mouse on this island—us, the cattle we brought, and the Dragons. We're all either too tired to do any mischief or off gathering, the cattle are in the keeping of the Dragons now, and if a Dragon attacked nothing would save us anyway. Now go away and let me sleep, there's a girl."

I left her wrapped in blankets and went outside, up to the fire for warmth, waiting for the last stragglers to go to bed or back to the lansip harvest. My mind would not let me rest this night until I went to the Boundary and at least tried. I paced as I waited, and my thoughts seemed to travel round the same circle time and time again, like a yearling on a long lead. Partly I thought with solemn fear of Marik and whatever his purposes might be, but uppermost in my mind now were the Dragons themselves. Now I was here at last, at the end of my first journey and on the point of adventure, I was strung tight as a bowstring. Was Marik lying yet or were they real, now I was here at last? Had I wasted my life chasing dreams in the dark? And if they *were* real, why in all the world should one of them want to talk to me, rather than killing me where I stood for my insolence? And what, dear Goddess, what in the Seven Hells would I say? The fine flowery speeches I had made up in the silence of my chamber at Hadronsstead turned to dust, fell like dead leaves away from my mind, leaving not even their shadows behind.

Into that dusty darkness came a soft voice from the edge of the clearing.

"Lanen?"

I was close to the fire, I could not see past its light. But then, I didn't really need to. "Yes, Marik, it's me," I replied quietly. I looked up as he approached, and managed a slight smile. "Or would you rather I called you Bors? In any case I seem to be working for you now, so perhaps 'my lord' is more in keeping."

"I thought I saw you on board the ship, but I wasn't certain until yesterday," he lied cheerfully. "When the Master told me none had asked for a berth in the name of Bors of Trissen I was convinced you had decided not to come." He reached out suddenly and lifted my chin with his cupped hand. I put a tight rein on my temper; it would be far too dangerous to lose it now. "I had nearly convinced myself you were a dream. How wonderful. Now I am doubly blessed. I am certain you will be a hard worker, and"—he grinned—"mayhap I'll get back a portion of the ruinous price I gave you for that mare."

His smile was kind and his voice echoed it. But his slight stoop and his hawk nose seemed terribly reminiscent, in the flickering light, of the pitiless bird of prey Jamie had compared him to, and his eyes did not speak of kindness. Even in the firelight they were cold, with a peculiar quality, a flinty hardness I had seen only once before.

At least Jamie had been on my side.

In that moment I decided to play the innocent. What could it cost me I had not lost already?

"What keeps you wakeful this night, Lady Lanen?" asked Marik graciously. His hand was poised negligently on his sword hilt, as though there were no other sensible place to put one's hand. A coincidence, no more.

I looked down and swallowed, but could not banish my fear. My voice I knew would betray me, so I kept silence and hoped I might seem merely distracted.

He laughed softly. "I know the accommodations are not as spacious as those at the White Horse, but surely you don't mind a little rough living for the chance to make your fortune? Or do you still seek the True Dragons?" He smiled, chilling me. "You know I have spoken with one. They are real, as you believed and I did not. And I was the first to speak with one in more than a century." There was a portion of wonder in his voice, but underneath it lay a kind of petty smugness. He was pleased that he had spoken with the Dragons before I had, that he had taken that much of my dream from me.

I had no choice but to reply, and I feared he would hear it if I lied. "Yes, Marik. I still seek them, above even the riches of lansip, and I envy you the speech you have had with them." That at least was true enough. As for who he was, I prayed silently that the Lady would make my ignorance believable. At the least it was worth a try. "But I still don't understand about your name. Marik suits you better than Bors anyway, and what is the difference?"

He was surprised and more than a little suspicious. "Do you tell me you have never heard my name before?"

I smiled my most gracious smile, hoping it would at least be convincing by firelight. "Your pardon, Lord Marik of Gundar, but it is not an uncommon name in Ilsa. There were two Mariks in my village," I lied smoothly. How to get rid of him, how to protect myself—then I remembered something Jamie had taught me. *A lie is best served with an open countenance, a sincere voice, and buried deep in the midst of truth.* "Jamie once told me of a Marik, someone my mother knew, but he must be twenty years older than you."

"Your mother?" he said, slightly curious, no more. "Do you know, I thought you reminded me of someone. What is her name?"

"Her name was Maran Vena," I said, trying to hold my voice steady, frightened at being this close to truth.

"You amaze me. I did indeed know her, for surely there has never been more than one with that curious name. But you say was? Is she dead?" He tried to restrain himself, but even in firelight I could see his whole body tense, his voice give the merest suspicion of a waver as some strong emotion gripped him.

"I don't know. Probably. She left me when I was yet a babe in arms, I have no memory of her at all."

"Indeed. It sounds like the Maran I knew, if you will forgive me. She left me as well, after she stole a certain trifle from my home. Did she ever speak of it to you? Or"—and in one swift move he was at my side, not a handsbreadth away, and his voice was low and intense—"did she perhaps leave it with you for a birth-gift? It was a globe of smoky glass, no larger than might be held in two hands. A mere bauble, but I would fain have it back. Tell me, Lanen, do you have it?"

I turned to him, my eyes clear and truth in my voice. "I have never seen such a thing. If she took it, she must have it still, if she lives. I hope you find her—I owe her nothing—but I cannot help you. I have her looks, I am told, but apart from that nothing of her. I'm sorry."

He stepped back and bowed, and his eyes were a little more kind. "I thank you. But still I wonder," he said, "does not your father know where she might be found? Surely the life of a child is a bond not so easy to break—"

Help me, Lady, I prayed silently. "My father Hadron died at midsummer. If he knew where she was he took the knowledge with him."

"I see. Well, it cannot be helped, I suppose." He stared at me still, and I took advantage of the silence.

"My lord, it has been a long and wearying day, and I suspect I won't get much sleep for the next week, so if you will excuse me—?"

He hesitated a moment, then bowed gracefully, smiling, his dancing eyes on mine the whole time. "Of course. It is not as if you could leave me as you did in Ilsa. There will be time later to speak of such things—but for now, sleep well, and work hard for both of us. We shall speak again soon."

And he was gone, striding off to the cabins in the darkness.

I breathed again, but I knew my relief must be short-lived. He was right. There was nowhere I could go, and for some reason he seemed quite willing to wait. I felt like a mouse in the paws of a cat—I might provide him some entertainment, but in the end I was caught sure.

I went back to my tent, moving quietly so as not to disturb Rella, whose snores were reassuringly safe and homelike. I drew off my boots and lay on my blankets, my mind whirling. How if I was his daughter? From what Jamie had told me, Berys had made the deal to have control of an infant. I couldn't imagine what it would mean to be given to demons as a thinking adult, but I suspected that death would be preferable. I could think of no escape, no way out, when like a candle in darkness I saw all clear. I very nearly laughed.

The Dragons. Those whom I had sought all my life, they were my way out. If—no, I reminded myself grimly, when—Marik and his cronies tried to trap me, I would do my best to lose myself in the deep forest, but if that failed all I would need to do was cross the Boundary. I did not relish the idea, but death was not as frightening as being demon fodder. Unless, of course, my madness bore fruit before then. Unless I really did manage to speak with one of them.

And with that thought, I was whisked away from the intrigues of evil. I had meant to sleep for an hour or so, but I could no more sleep than I could fly. The Dragons were so near I could all but smell them. I could wait no longer. I rose quietly, slipped on my boots and from some sense of fitness I laid aside my old black cloak and wrapped myself in my fine new green one.

As I stepped outside I was thankful for the weight of my lovely cloak and the thick weave of it, for the night had turned cold. I pulled the hood over my head, for warmth and to cover my hair, lest it reflect moonlight and betray me. The moon was up and only a night before the full, but a thin layer of clouds obscured its light, scattering it blue around the clearing. The dying grass was soft under my feet; a noise like the sea surrounded me as I walked, listening to the light breeze as it swished the last lingering leaves against the sleeping branches overhead.

I kept to the shadows and moved as quietly as I could. It had occurred to me, belatedly, that I might not be the only one abroad; that thought saved me from crying out when I glimpsed a cloaked figure ahead of me. I was nearly at the Boundary when I saw it ahead of me, moving quietly through the tree shadows. I was about to call out when there was a break in the clouds, and the change in light made the figure whirl around.

It was one of the young men who had been on Joss's boat with me—Perrin or Darin, I couldn't remember which. I had seen them in passing on the journey over. Surely the idiot boy realised this was the very thing we had been warned against. Hadn't he listened to the Master? Or did he think . . .

Satisfied that he was alone, he turned north again, planted a foot on the top rail and disappeared into the dark woods on the far side of the Boundary fence.

Almost immediately I heard a huge hiss. It was oddly soft for the size of throat it came from, terrifying in that quiet darkness. It was followed by an immense sound just on the edge of hearing, as of air displaced by something very fast and very, very large. There was a single thin, sharp cry, then silence.

I stood trembling in the darkness and knew what had happened as if I had watched it. There was a guard at the Boundary—of course there was—and he had executed the man (*the thief,* I told myself) without an instant of hesitation.

It was horrible—a life snuffed out in the blink of an eye—but it was what they had said they would do.

I was not trembling with fear. I was trembling with the nearness of Dragons.

I walked slowly up to the Boundary.

"Hello?" I said softly to the night air.

Silence.

I realised they must think I was with the poor idiot they had just killed. Surely no one had approached them directly for anything but dragon gold, even in the days when these journeys were not so rare. How could I get them to listen to me? *Nothing for it,* I thought. *I'm going to have to call out.* I reached for breath, but hesitated—what could I possibly say? What words could make a difference, here at the edge of two worlds?

I stood uncertain in the deep night, knowing my words might bring my heart's desire or the end of all. My mind was whirling with the verses of bards' songs, finding only "Dragon," knowing in my bones it was wrong.

And suddenly I realised how I had thought of them ever since I heard the Song of the Winged Ones so many years ago, the song in the silence.

I drew in a breath and called softly, "My brother?"

There was a movement in the darkness between the trees.

I began to tremble in earnest now, my voice unsteady and my knees threatening to betray me, but it was too late for fear. "Oh please, my brother, please, come to me. I have waited for you so long—" and my throat closed against the words, as the memory of endless awakenings in my solitary bed at Hadronsstead rose up before me. I shook my head and banished those thoughts. That darkness was over; and the formal greeting I had crafted so carefully all those years before rose to my lips unashamed.

"I call to thee, my brothers of another kind; through the parting of ages I call to thee. I know not why our peoples live apart, but I summon thee through darkness to come to me, that together we may create a new light. I long for thee, through all my life I have sought thee, to learn thy ways and thy hearts, to tell thee of my own people and our dreams. Oh, my brothers of the Dragon kind, I summon thee by all I hold holy; by the Lady of the Moon, by Blessed Shia the mother of us all, I call thee brother and I long for thee."

I was come to the end of my fine words. I knew nothing else to say, and could only add in a desperate whisper, "Oh please, please—come to me."

A shaft of moonlight escaped its cloudy cage and glinted off something very large moving beyond the trees.

"Oh my brother," I breathed softly.

Kantri

I could resist no longer—or perhaps it is truer to say I did not wish to. I had felt her call, as though she were one of the Kindred, and when that voice in the dark called me brother I knew I must answer.

I left my hiding place, left the broken body of the thief. She was so different from the small-souled dead one, though of the same Kindred. There was so much we did not know of one another, so much to fear—but the faith and the longing in her voice shone like a beacon.

I moved slowly that I might not frighten her. I had long imagined how I would appear to one of them; they are so small and naked, and I with my silver hide was strange even among our own people. I felt my soulgem glow brightly in a shaft of moonlight and heard her gasp, but it was neither fear nor greed. I did not know what she was feeling, not perfectly, but it appeared to be a mixture of *ferrinshadik* and adoration. I had always been told that we could not feel the Gedri, but I had sensed her even before our meeting.

I found that without thinking I had assumed the Attitude of Protection of a Youngling, and my soul grew in that moment. I discovered it was possible for one of the Greater Kindred to care for one of the Gedrishakrim.

We stared at each other through the darkness, not speaking; but even the dim seeing was enough. I leant down a little to see her better. She did not cry out despite the fear I felt from her, though she did draw back a little.

She was a brave dreamer.

"There is no need to fear, little sister," I said quietly.

Her eyes grew wide with wonder, and her breath came short as if preparing to fly. "I'm not afraid," she said; then, "Well, not very afraid." For a long while we simply stared at each other, as though words would break the fragile spell and we would vanish disastrously from each other's sight.

Then she spoke again, very softly, almost to herself. "You are so different from what I dreamt. The songs don't even . . . you are terrifying."

She tried to go on but could not. Her mouth moved as if to speak, but awe still held her. She breathed as one tried with great exertion, but she stood in what looked like the Attitudes of Joy and Wonder and her eyes never moved from mine.

"You are the most beautiful creature I have ever seen," she said at last.

I bowed my head in thanks and moved closer still to see her better in the dim light, and to be seen. We were silent again, drinking in each other at close range. Her eyes gleamed in the moonlight, and I smelled saltwater.

"Is it the way of your people to drop seawater from their eyes?" I asked, keeping my voice as soft as I could.

She bared her teeth but I sensed neither fear nor threat. "No," she said. "It's—the seawater, it's called tears. We do it when we're very sad, or very happy."

I was fascinated. "So even do we with Fire, the same expression for great joy or great sorrow. We are not perhaps so different as is thought, little sister."

"We can speak and understand each other. Where is the great difference there?"

I hissed my amusement softly. "Little sister, I have taught myself your speech over many long years. If I spoke in my own tongue, the difference would be clear."

I stopped. She had started and drawn away when I laughed, and stood now uncertainly, ready to flee. "What frightens you?" I asked.

"Why did you do that?" she asked hesitantly.

"What did I do, little one?"

"You—you dropped your jaw and—hissed at me."

I just managed to stop my self from doing so again. "I did not mean it to distress you. It is a sign of friendship or mild pleasure. Did you not just now bare your teeth at me, when I spoke of seawater?"

She thought for a moment, then bared her teeth again, more broadly, and the flesh at the corners of her eyes crinkled. "It's called a smile. Do you mean the same thing when you drop your jaw and hiss?"

"I believe so, though I do not know the words you use."

She simply stared up at me, obviously standing in the Gedri way of Joy—she had changed from fear to gladness in the blink of an eye—and it struck me that we had changed the world as we knew it. For the first time in centuries, Kantri and Gedri had taught each other something.

My first reaction was great joy.

My second was the stirring of fear.

This, of course, was the reason why contact between the races was forbidden. The Gedrishakrim are always curious, and the Kantri seek to teach despite themselves. Without thinking we had exchanged knowledge, to our mutual delight; but old habit and long years of mistrust reminded me that, trivial as this exchange was, it was friendship between our peoples that had ultimately doomed the Lesser Kindred to live as beasts. For the first time the *ferrinshadik* dimmed and I began truly to understand the Great Ban.

"Little sister, forgive me, but I must ask you something of great importance," I said. "When you called to me, you spoke of dreams, of a life spent longing for my Kindred. You called me brother," I said quietly. "That is not a word used often or lightly among my Kindred."

"Or mine," she said. None of the awe was gone from her, but even these few moments spent in my company had made her bolder. "I called you that because that is how I thought of you," she said. "Even more now than before." Her voice wavered and she trembled, but not with fear. "Ever since I was a young girl I have wanted to speak with a—with your people."

Her words pleased me. She did not call us "Dragons"; deep in her heart she must know it was their word for us, not our own. I longed to tell her even then how we name ourselves, but I did not. Habit and old mistrust. The knowledge that this kind of meeting was forbidden sharpened suddenly into an urgent need. I had not known how strong the urge to teach was, how deeply she would affect me, how I would long to tell her of our Kindred and of myself—in truth, to teach her whatever she wanted to know. We had learned to our sorrow that the Gedri could use knowledge to evil ends. Our numbers were halved and the Lesser Kindred trapped in darkness because of misplaced trust between our peoples. I must learn why she had come.

"Why?" I asked her. "Why have you wanted to know us? What brought you here, so far from your lands and your Kindred? Speak truly, and tell me why you are here."

I asked her this aloud, and without thought repeated it in the Language of Truth. *"Why do you seek me/us out in the night? What brings you? Do you mean us harm, do you seek for gain? Why are you here?"*

To this day I do not know why first I used the Language of Truth with her. Every scholar of our Kindred had told me that the Gedri-shakrim were deaf to it.

To my great delight she proved them wrong.

Her thoughts were faint and not well ordered; they spilled out all together and sparkled with emotion like stars streaking across a dark night. It was much like speaking with a youngling—but it was the Language of Truth, undeniably.

"I come because I love you I want to know you, let us speak to-gether and grow to know one another. You are so beautiful/won-drous/not what I expected but real at last. I have dreamed of you so long, so long in the lonely darkness, it is glory and wonder to hear speech and reason from another creature A REAL DRAGON!" And below that, her underthought whispered, *"Is this real oh please let it be real if it is not let me never wake from the dream, oh my heart aches you are so beautiful!"*

She stood silent for a moment. "What did I—did you hear that?" she asked very quietly.

"Yes," I said, standing in the Attitude of Surprised Pleasure. "I did not know you had the Language of Truth, little sister!"

"I didn't either," she said.

"You have never done this before?"

She shook her head. "Never. I think it's—we call it Farspeech, but I've only ever heard of it in tales from the bards." She stared up at me. "I never thought it was real!"

"It is the Language of Truth," I told her. I had not lost all restraint, but how could such knowledge bring harm? "It is the true speech of mind to mind, and minds cannot hide a lie from one another. This Farspeech—you are certain you have never used it before?"

"No. I told you, I didn't even believe in it until now," she replied. She looked up and smiled. "I'm not sure I do yet." She seemed a little dazed. It was a common reaction among younglings, and I found myself wanting to cross the Boundary to comfort her, as though she were indeed one of the Kindred. I resisted with great effort. The least I could do would be to explain.

"With us it may only be used between two who consent," I told her gently. "It is very revealing, and younglings find it leaves them unsettled."

"Unsettled; yes, that at least. I wasn't expecting it at all." Her mouth drew up again, and I knew a small wash of pleasure as I realised that I was the only one of all the Kindred who could recognise the smile of the Gedrishakrim.

"You should warn a lady," she said.

I bowed to her. "I will."

And I realised only in the second after I had spoken that my words hung in the air like a winged promise. With those two words I had changed my life and hers. There would be another meeting, I would again use the Language of Truth with her. I knew not until I spoke that I meant to continue this frightening, forbidden, wondrous communion.

I stared at her, startled by my own words, and saw to my wonder that some postures are universal. She stood in Anticipation of Joy as best she could. It seemed we merely acknowledged a fate already decreed.

"There will be another time?" she asked. "May I come back tomorrow night?"

I waited, wondering, seeking a reason to deny her and not finding one. "Yes, little sister," I said at last, and the saying was a joy. "Come to me tomorrow at the same hour, alone as you are. We will speak again."

"Thank you, my brother," she said, and bent in the middle at me. It seemed to be a bow of some kind. *I must ask her about that sometime,* I thought, when she said in a different voice, "That man, the one who came just before me—did you kill him?"

"Yes," I replied.

"Why?"

"He had broken the treaty, our laws and yours. There was greed in him, and death in his heart for my Kindred. He reeked of the Rakshasa, he must have had dealings with them. He knew the price." I peered at her. "Does my killing of him frighten you?"

She paused, looking down, then answered, "No. It probably should, but no, it doesn't." She looked up at me again, and I longed to know what the glow in her eyes meant. "I trust you. I will obey your laws."

"That is well, little sister," I said. "You have nothing—" I caught myself. The temptation to trust was overpowering. I was amazed. I must have time, time to think about this strange impulse, ponder what it might mean. "Go now. We will speak again tomorrow, at the middle night."

"Must we part so soon?" she asked.

"Do not your Kindred require sleep?" I asked.

"Yes, but . . ."

"In our laws, and I suspect in yours, our two Kindreds are warned never to meet." I looked down on her and said kindly, "I think this first lawbreaking should not be overlong. There will be time enough, and we both have much to think on."

"That's true," she said. "You won't forget?"

I nodded. "We do not forget, little sister."

She smiled at that. "Then goodnight, large brother," she said. She bent in half again and turned to go, then turned back. She stood silent a moment, determined, hesitant.

"What is it, little one?" I asked.

And without hesitation she said, "I am called Lanen Maransdatter—but my true name is Lanen Kaelar."

And she waited.

The giving of a name is with us the greatest act of trust. Only father, mother and mate know the true name, or perhaps one true friend of the heart; but the name gives power to whoever calls it.

It would be stupid, it would be blind senseless, it would be madness to give her my name and thus power over me and my Kindred. How could I so break the ban and do so foolish a thing?

How could I not?

For trust calls out trust, and this powerless child of the Gedri had given me that which could cost her soul.

I moved to the very Boundary itself, stretching my neck so that our faces nearly touched.

"Lanen Kaelar, I am Khordeshkhistriakhor," I whispered, and closed my eyes.

"You honour me," she whispered back, and her heart in truespeech echoed her gratitude, her wonder. I shivered with the feel of her breath warm across my eyelid. "We will meet again, at midnight."

When I opened my eyes she was gone.

I returned to my hiding place, watching, thinking long on my folly and wondering where it would lead me, and was amazed to see the light rise about me hours later. For all my doubts I had never felt more alive.

I had never known the *ferrinshadik* to bring joy before.

Marik

I summoned Berys's Messenger the night we landed on the Dragon Isle, and no sooner had it appeared than it spoke with his voice.

"So. You have survived the Storms, and since you summon me the Dragons have not killed you. How goes the Harvest?"

"Greetings to you as well, Magister," I replied, speaking slowly to annoy him. "I am very well, I thank you. The Dragons remembered some treaty we had forgot, and all is arranged. Already the workers have made back the cost of the journey, and we have been here barely half a day. And you might be interested to hear that the child of Maran Vena is here as well. She knows nothing of the Farseer, but it is still possible that she is my child."

"Indeed?" asked Berys with a sneer. "I am not interested in your conjectures. We cannot be certain until we have made—tests. And for that we will need blood from her."

This was news. "Blood, say you? And how should I go about getting blood from her?"

"You have guards, do you not, and men paid to serve you? Take her captive and cut her. What could be simpler?"

I had been thinking the same thing, but since Berys suggested it I thought of an objection. "And if she is my child? Do not your Masters require her whole?"

"You need not remove an arm," he replied, disdain rich in his voice that came from the demon's throat. "It will take enough to fill a cup, no more. Doubtless one so clever, who has arrived whole at the Dragon Isle, will be able to discover some way to acquire that much." I would swear then that the small, distorted demon Messenger smiled with Berys's smile. "May the Harvest prosper, Marik. I look forward to my share of your profits."

The creature disappeared in a cloud of sulphur. I threw wide the shutters and left word for Caderan to attend me in the morning. There was much I needed to know if my search for dragon gold was to be rewarded with other than death.

ix

LESSONS

Kantri

I had gathered my thoughts and was preparing to return to my chambers when Hadreshikrar, my dearest friend among the Kindred, came upon me as I lay silent in the early dawn.

"Good morrow, Lord Akhor," he said cheerfully. "I am glad to find you here. I began to wonder if the Gedri had put you under some spell in the night!"

"It is not impossible," I replied. The idea had occurred to me more than once in the long darkness.

"Akhor, I spoke in jest!" said Shikrar.

"That is no surprise, my friend, you jest more than any three other of our Kindred." I did not want to tell him of my thoughts, though, not for a few minutes yet. "Still I live in hope that more of my people will catch this light malady of yours. Tell me, what makes you so winghearted this morning?"

"It is no great mystery. Such a wondrous time for my family! I bespoke my son Kédra this night past, and he tells me Mirazhe has left for the Birthing Cove. Their youngling will be born ere the moon is past the full! Is that not enough to lighten the darkest heart?"

"It is indeed," I replied, smiling at him as I rose. "And of course, any son or daughter of Kédra will be as great a blessing to the Kindred as his father has been."

I teased Shikrar and he knew it, but his pride in his son was too great to be affected by anything I might say. He had invested in Kédra all the love he had felt for Kédra's mother, his lost beloved Yrais. Kédra was, to his credit, a modest soul, and though he loved his father dearly he laughed at Shikrar's excessive praise. They got along well, Kédra was bright and well liked, and Shikrar never stopped talking about his wondrous child.

"And so it will, my friend, mock me though you might," he replied. "My Kédra has given me joy since his birth; I trust his youngling will do so as well. Mirazhe is a wonder, she all but glows with the littling. Idai stands birth sister to her." Shikrar gazed keenly at me, which I as keenly ignored. "And when shall Mirazhe return the favor, Akhor my friend?" he asked pointedly. "It is widely known that Idai leans to you, she has these many years, spurning all others. Can you not find it in you to return her regard?"

I sighed wearily. "Hadreshikrar, must we go through this again? As Eldest you should know better. Should I take Idai as mate out of pity? She would no more stand for it than I. I cannot count the numbers of those who have urged this joining upon me, nor the number of times you yourself have done so. Of your kindness, my friend, do not speak more of it. Idai is wise and worthy of all praise, but I do not love her."

"Ah, well, I shall keep my peace. But with our numbers so few, it pains me to see you still without a mate and Idai yet barren."

"That is her choice and mine!" I replied, stung by his bluntness. "You know I never said word, never asked any such devotion from her. If she chooses not to mate with another what word then should I give her to sway her? I will not bring a youngling forth where there is no love to sustain it, even if Idai were willing. And she would not be. Why should she settle for such a half-life when there are many who hold her in high regard and would take her as mate with hon-our? And it is no shame to choose a life of solitude."

"Forgive me, my friend," he said, as we walked a little away from the watch post. "I did not mean the words to gall. But the fire rises in me with the coming of a youngling, with my pride in my dear son—surely it is no wonder that I wish the same joy for you."

"Ah, Shikrar, you old meddler," I said. "You would have all of us mated before ever we left our mothers." Truth to tell, his words dis-turbed me more than I could allow him to know. So few younglings, so few of the Kantri even taking mates. I feared for my people, but I did not know what I could do. It was not a new problem, there have never been many of us; but our numbers were halved by the De-monlord, and despite the long years between we had not even begun to recover. Still, no need to speak of that with Shikrar while his heart was so light. "Not content with instructing the young ones, you would teach us all what we must do to keep old Hadreshikrar happy."

He laughed, as I knew he would. "That's better. You have been overgrim this morning, Akhor." He grinned at me. "Is it that old dis-ease of yours, eh? It does come round this time of year, especially when the Gedri are so close. Still, no one has ever died of the *fer-rinshadik.*" When I did not respond, he stopped and peered at me. "Do you know, I begin to wonder in truth if someone or something has not put a spell on you."

"As for the *ferrinshadik,* Shikrar, you are not immune yourself. Tell me if you can in the Language of Truth that you have no long-ing in your soul to speak with them, that deep in your heart of hearts there is no burning desire to learn of them, to have converse with another Kindred and see the world through new eyes."

He said nothing. I sensed no more from him than the amused tolerance of friendship, touched lightly by concern and by a grudg-ing admission of guilt. I went on, "But I do not recall the casting of a spell. Surely I would remember such a thing."

Instantly Shikrar's voice sang in my mind, worried, caring as only a soul's friend cares. *"Khordeshkhistriakhor, I ask as your namefast friend, what has happened to you? I spoke in jest, but truly you are not yourself this morning. Your thoughts are guarded against mine as they have not been in my memory. Does the Weh sleep come upon you again so soon? Or have the Gedri indeed cast binding spells upon you?"*

"Hadreshikrar, I warn you, much has happened this night," I replied cautiously, aloud. Then in the truespeech I added, *"I will gladly open my thoughts to you, but for friendship's sake do nothing, do not even move, unless you find the true touch of the Rakshasa."*

"I swear it, old friend."

I let down the barriers of conscious thought and let Shikrar see the events of the night before. In a moment he knew most of what had passed, and in that moment I threw my wings and my forearms about him and held him fast. I had not known him all these years without knowing what his first reaction would be.

"You swore to me!" I cried aloud as he struggled to throw me off, to take to the sky, to seek out this Gedri and destroy her. "Hold to your word!"

In his fury he struck at me as best he could while I held him, raking his claws across my chest plates. If he had had any leverage my blood would have drenched the grass. My wings had hampered him, but now they were vulnerable and I withdrew them; they were far too delicate to risk in a struggle. "You fool!" he cried, thrashing. "Would you damn us all? Shall we be cattle in the Trollingwood, shall we be *dragons* because you trusted some pawn of the Gedrishakrim?"

"Enough!" I cried. I felt my grip weakening. Shikrar was older and larger than I. I focussed instead on using all the power of truespeech to cry out to him mind to mind, where I could not be ignored. *"Hadreshikrar, listen to me! Did you find Raksha-trace?"* I shook him even as he battled to escape me, even as I felt my hold slipping. *"Tell me, your soul to the Four Winds, did you find any trace of the Rakshasa in me? Any trace at all?"*

He stopped struggling then, suddenly, bowing his head in defeat. *"No, Akhor. Your soul is as clean as the day you were birthed, you great fool,"* he replied. Then he spoke aloud, as if truespeech were too painful. "What madness possessed you? For since it is not the Rakshasa, it must be that you have in truth lost your mind."

I released my hold and stepped back, praying to the Winds that my tongue might be touched with the power of persuasion. If I could not explain this to Hadreshikrar, I could not explain it to any of the Kindred.

"Shikrar, do you remember my waking from my last three Weh sleeps?"

He stared at me, waiting.

"Hold your silence now if you will, but then it was you who spoke to me of my dreams. You reminded me then that it was the third time I had spoken of them, and how Weh dreams should be honoured as they are so rare. Do you remember my reply?"

"Is that it, then? Is that the basis for this madness, that you have dreamt a child of the Gedri calling to you? I tell you, Akhor, we have all had that fantasy—though the *ferrinshadik* has ever been a shadow over your shoulder." He stared straight into my eyes and said, "Do you tell me, Akhor, that she called you by your name?"

"No," I replied quietly. That had been a powerful element in the second Weh dream, that the Gedri had known my true, full name without being told. "She did not call me by name, my friend. But Shikrar, neither did she call me 'dragon,' either."

"What did she say? 'Hello you great idiot'?"

"She called me brother, Shikrar. Brother, as in the first dream. And she told me she had longed to know us for all of her short life."

"Did she also tell you that she had heard tales of dragon gold and might she please have some?"

I felt the fire grow in me, rising with my anger, but I fought it down. My own vehemence surprised me. "Have you so little respect for our fellow creatures that you will allow none of them to be greater than the worst?"

"Have you so far lost your reason that you forget what happened to the Lesser Kindred?" he growled. His anger was echoing mine and growing on it, flame fed by accusation. "Will you have us all live as soulless beasts? Shall we haunt the deep glades of the Trollingwood like the Lesser Kindred, slaughtered like cattle, with no soul and no reason? I am the Keeper of Souls, I have tried my life long to speak with the Lost, with the Lesser Kindred, to no avail. They were in the heart of their flower, Akhor!" he cried, as though the Demonlord's destruction were a blow struck moments before. "The youngest and best of us, struck down by that twisted child of the Gedri with no more thought than we give cattle." He could barely contain himself. He had begun to crouch, and I could see small tongues of flame in his speech even in the bright light of early morning. With his next breath he would challenge me, and I was in no mood for a fight.

"Shikrar, I charge you by our friendship, restrain your anger. Let us guide one another in the Discipline of Calm, but I charge you to follow that Discipline now as my namefast friend." I spoke quietly, with all the calm power I could muster. It did not move him at all that I could see.

I had hoped to avoid invoking my authority with so old a friend, but I could see no other choice. I bespoke him.

"If that will not reach thee, Hadretikantishikrar, I charge thee to honour my wishes by thy vow of fealty to the King."

The use of his full true name shocked him—as well it might—and it had the desired effect. He stared at me in hurt surprise. I gazed back at him, standing in the formal Attitude of Kingship, wings fully extended, and my soulgem gleamed in the early sun as I stood in my power.

He bowed to me formally, gathered himself and began the Discipline. I did the same. As we took ourselves through its measured paces I spoke.

"I would not have you judge this child of the Gedri without knowledge, Shikrar my friend. I know the fear you speak of, better now than ever before, I assure you. Even if my distrust had not been awakened by my own actions, your would have shocked me to awareness."

Shikrar finished the Discipline. When he opened his eyes the deep anger was gone; what was left more closely resembled regret.

"What would you, my Lord King?"

I had asked for it, but still it stung. Shikrar had been the friend of my heart for many a long year. I had hoped my reminder would shock him out of his anger, no more. Well, he would thaw in time.

"I would have you accompany me this evening, when I will meet again with the child of the Gedri," I replied. "I would ask you not to harm her unless she breaks one of our laws."

"Do you not break those same laws, Lord King, when you call out to this—this Gedrishakrim?"

"You bespoke me, Shikrar," I replied sternly. I would not let his formality wound me, nor allow myself to defer to our friendship. There was too much surrounding this meeting for that. "You well know that she called to me, not I to her, and that the law refers on their side simply to crossing the Boundary. As for my breaking of our laws—I ask you to let me carry that burden alone for now. We might find between us, you and I, that it is the law that is at fault."

Shikrar did not reply.

"I will meet you at the watch post on the Boundary shortly before the middle night," I told him, then in farewell said what we always said to the Guardian. The words came hard past my tongue.

"Watch well, lest we find a demon in our midst."

I did not need deep understanding to know that he was thinking it more than usually likely, and that mine would be the burden of having allowed it to come in. It was, after all, just possible that the little one—no, use her name, that Lanen Kaelar was a pawn in some greater game, not herself corrupt but allowing corruption to gain entry.

It was possible.

But the moment I left Shikrar I felt the deep joy of our meeting seeping through my anger and disappointment, and I could not believe that evil lurked near her.

It is unfortunate but true that the proof that there are rocks in the field is usually the fact that we have just hit them with the plough.

Lanen

I don't know how I managed to sleep at all that night. Every time I closed my eyes I would see that silver face so close to mine, the eyes vulnerable mere inches from me, hear that voice that sang in my mind, breathe in the wild, strange smell of him, and open my eyes to let out the tears of wonder.

I have discovered in the long years that I have been blessed above many others; for when I took the chance to follow my dream, I not only found what I sought in the deep shadow of trees beneath the moon—I was given the gift of not finding what I had hoped for. What I found surpassed my longing, my desire, my very imagination, beyond the power of my limping words to tell.

I was in a daze all the next day as I gathered lansip leaves with the rest, hardly speaking, not eating at all—but inside that daze I was gloriously alive. I heard every note of every bird's song, every rustle of wind in the lingering leaves high on the trees; I smelled the different woods thrown on the fires, the heady scent of lansip all around me, even the subtle hint of spice and healthy autumn rot below all.

I felt the smallest twigs crackle beneath my boots, and below that and around, the brown autumn grass bent and broke as I passed. The misty rain that came up in the early afternoon sparked cold on my cheeks. I opened my mouth like a child and sipped at the rain, and I could not remember a sweeter drink. The leaves as I gathered them in bundles were soft on my hands, harsh the raw canvas bags we stuffed them in, hempen rope rough against my palms as I tied the bags shut. I was like a child indeed, discovering the world for the first time, seeing all things new in this strange, frightening clarity, and in each moment and each sensation I came back to the wonder of the Dragon.

Kordeshkistriakor.

I had been afraid I would not be able to remember it, so long, so strange—yet as I came away from our meeting it rang in me like a wondrous bell.

I found, though, that the human mind can only bear a little exaltation. By midafternoon I was dropping on my feet, and I had to return to the tent and sleep while the others worked. Luckily I was not alone. It seems that the pattern among the Harvesters was to gather leaves until you were about to drop, then go back to camp, eat, sleep as little as possible, and back to it. I had heard people coming and going all night as I lay and tried to sleep, and all morning they came and went, no rhyme or reason. My comings and goings went unnoticed, for all were doing the same.

I did not rest long. I woke to a buzzing of voices and realised I had slept only an hour or so. It might have been five hours past midday. Marik had called us all to assemble by the cookfires. His lovely voice was grim. Around me the others murmured, wondering what was to do.

Marik stood by the fire, his men behind him, a horrible bloody bundle at his feet. "I was called by the Guardian this noontide," he said loudly. He need not have bothered, he had everyone's attention. "This poor dead fool decided I was a liar and crossed the Boundary last night. They returned his body this morning." He looked around at our closed faces. "I need your assistance with this, I fear. I would ask you to come and look at the body. I do not know this young idiot's face or name; perhaps one of you might be able to tell me."

I knew perfectly well who it was, but his brother was there long before me. I had not seen him in the darkness last night, the body was too far away; now I saw clearly, as could we all, the wreck of that young man. The huge gash in his body, the head at a sickening angle, and on the dead face a grimace of terror. It turned my stomach, I wrapped my arms about myself and was glad I had not eaten for many hours. I had seen death before, but this was horrible. I kept telling myself he was a thief, he was a thief—but it made no difference. He had been a young man with all his life before him to change his ways, to atone for any evil.

A general murmur arose, filled with outrage and anger. Marik was waiting for it.

"If you're thinking of revenge, you may as well give it up now," he said over the muttering of the crowd. "How should you revenge yourselves against creatures that can kill like that? I have seen them. They have claws the size of my arm and teeth to match, and they can fly. You fools, they are True Dragons! You could all stab at them with swords of the finest southern steel for a hundred years and they would never feel it. I tell you again; the Treaty protects us, the Boundary protects us, but if you cross it you will be as dead as—as—"

"Perrin," said his brother Darin brokenly, his face white with shock. "His name was Perrin."

Perrin, I thought. *Perrin. I will not forget.*

No one should die like that. Not even for being a thief.

Somehow I must say that to my large brother.

Marik

Caderan and I wandered back to my cabin together after the body was identified. "A useful lesson, at least," I said as we walked. "It should stop any more forays into the dragonlands. I can't afford to lose any more Harvesters."

"Indeed, my lord. It is certain that the Harvest cannot be extended? We are so shorthanded."

"If you want to go and ask the beasts and be killed for your pains, I do not," I snapped. He just looked at me. "Forgive me, Caderan," I said, "the pain is bad today. No, the Guardian told me six nights, leave at dawn on the seventh, and I intend to do just that. Now," I said as we entered the cabin, "we have gone over the artifacts that you and Magister Berys prepared—the boots that mask sound, a cloak of deep shadow to hide me in darkness, the amulet to cover scent, and all with no trace of the demons that made them. Now, what is this ring he sent?"

"The Ring of Seven Circles? It is a great work, Lord Marik," simpered Caderan. "There are none alive save Berys who have the power to make such things. This alone would be worth the tenth part of your harvest." He lowered his voice, as if he feared he might be overheard. "It is a weapon that will work against True Dragons. Each circle is more destructive than the last. With this, you may withstand one of the creatures easily—two, if you are prudent—but you must have it on your hand for the spell to work. Each circle has a release word—should you wish to fire off the first circle, you would point the ring at the Dragon, speak the word and twist the outer circle thus."

I took a close look. It seemed no more than an ugly piece of jewellery, but when I put it on I could feel the pulse of the fires that coursed through it. I quickly removed it. "Surely this is a last resort. My whole plan is to avoid a pitched battle, and if it works—what shall I do if I do not need it? What then of the price I have paid?"

"Magister Berys told me that he hoped you would not need it, for he could sell it at three times the price to any number of adventurers."

"Very well." Soberly I began to consider the possibility of having to fight Dragons. "There is one more thing to be done, though, and Berys said that you could do it. He said you would be able to weave a spell to protect me from dragonfire."

"Yes, he mentioned it to me. I have been gathering the materials I need, but a few things I still lack, and you must provide one of them."

"Somehow I am not surprised. What do you need, then? Lansip? More blood?"

"Something a Dragon has touched."

I was shocked for just a moment, then felt a broad smile cross my face as I realised what would serve. "Nothing could be easier. How large a thing?"

"Enough to fill my cupped hand. But if I may ask, lord, what—"

"I knew that death would be useful," I replied. So simple! "Certainly a Dragon touched young Perrin. He is yet unburied—if I ask his brother to allow me to arrange the burial, surely he will not grudge me a handful of flesh around the wound? Especially if he never knows."

Caderan bowed. "You are truly a worthy master. If I may enquire, what are your plans regarding the child of Maran Vena?"

"You know them," I said sharply.

"Forgive me. Your *immediate* plans."

"I shall wait." When he started to protest, I snapped at him, "I told you I am shorthanded. She is bringing in as much lansip as the others, it would be foolish to take her from that task before I must. Tomorrow night is soon enough, and I shall have had a full day's more work out of her. Tomorrow you will instruct me in the rite of summoning that particular Rikti that will tell us about her blood."

Caderan bowed. "In truth, my lord, I will be glad to, but know that we must call upon the Rakshasa for such information. It will not be cheap."

"It never is," I replied sharply. "Go now, and report to me tomorrow when you have finished your preparations."

He bowed and left. I sent one of my guards to make arrangements about the body with the surviving brother, then sat musing over a cup of lansip tea. It eased a little the pain that never left me, the price of the Farseer I had never used. *Oh, Lords of the Seven Hells*, I prayed, *let her be my daughter, that this agony might end!*

Tomorrow night I would bring her to be bled. We would know soon enough thereafter.

Lanen

Ever I waited for Marik to accost me again that evening. It was almost worse when he did not. All I could think, as I worked, was that he was waiting until I had done my share of Harvesting, that he might not lose by it. It seemed fairly petty, but I would not put pettiness beyond him.

I went out gathering with a group immediately after poor Darin took his brother's body away, just as the sun was starting to sink. I saw Rella and called to her, and we worked together for hours by lamplight, sorting lansip leaves from all others, making sure no twigs nor dirt went in with the leaves. We came back many hours later, stumbling and weary, and fed ourselves from the last of the late stew that had been kept warm over the fire. The full bags we all brought back from our forays were taken to the ship regularly, and by my rough reckoning there must by now have been hundreds of them.

I ate gratefully in the tent with Rella. She was complaining in a general way of how sore her back was, to which I added my hearty assent, when she glanced up and said, "And how goes your search, my girl? About given up after that specimen they brought in today, have you?" I had forgotten that I had spoken to her of my true reason for coming here. "They didn't talk much with him, I'd wager."

I hesitated. *Wrap it in truth, Lanen,* I reminded myself. "No, it didn't look much like talk. But I haven't given up. Marik said Perrin crossed the Boundary. I won't."

"Best not, girl. If you come back looking like that even I won't have to do with you."

"And you, Rella," I said, trying to make it seem natural. "What brought you here on this fool's errand? You never said."

"Not a fool's errand if it makes me filthy rich, is it?" she said with a grin. "I reckon it's the same as everyone else, bar you. Though I notice you don't hold back from gathering lansip, despite your words."

I laughed, though she worried me. I had made a particular effort to keep up with the others as best I could, so as not to stand out. "And why should I hold back my hand from riches when they are in my grasp?" I said, defiantly.

"And there's my answer to your question. Now either shut up or go away, dearie. I didn't sleep this afternoon like you did and I'm shattered."

I lay back on my bedroll, resting while I gave Rella time to go to sleep. This was the second of our six brief nights, and the pattern continued of Harvesters coming and going at all hours, for which I was desperately thankful. It was just before midnight and all was still in the camp when I rose as I had the night before, pulled on boots and cloak and went out into the night.

The moon was well up in the sky, full and bright, the night gloriously clear. I had not forgotten Perrin—or Marik—but for all my misgivings my heart was as light as a littling with nothing on her mind but wild flowers and a clear summer day; like a village maid new-struck with a lover and giddy with delight. I was living my dream at last, and even the shadow of death could not keep me from joy. I could barely keep my feet on the ground, barely keep myself from laughing out loud.

I sobered a little as I drew near the Boundary. I peered through the moon-washed trees but could not see him; I had opened my mouth to speak that name that lay gleaming on my heart, I had even said the first syllable, when a near-physical jolt struck me dumb.

All my lightness left me. I must not be stupid when I spoke with him.

I had been about to speak his true name aloud, betraying the trust he had given me without a thought. Thank the Lady I stopped in time.

Should I resort to "large brother"? Or use a part of the name? Or—

Ah.

I took a deep breath, concentrated, pictured in my mind's eye that silver face close as a whisper to me, and murmured a whisper back in my mind. *"My brother?"*

I could hear his pleasure as he replied. *"Well met, little sister."*

I knew where to look for him now, I could make out the fragments of his silhouette among the branches. As close as he had been to me last night, it had been terribly dark save for fitful gleams of moonlight through the clouds. This night, though, was beautifully clear and near as bright as day. The wind had slackened to a soft breeze, and the full moon looked down on our meeting place. He moved to meet me, and for the first time I saw him clearly in all his splendour.

His face was terrifying, all sharp and hard, like shaped steel armour. There was a spiny ridge that started at the top of his head and ran down the length of his back (as best I could see) to the tip of his tail. His wings, vast and leathery, were folded against his back; his fangs were huge even from a distance, and showed sharp and cruel even when his mouth was closed.

That was the frightening part.

The rest of him took my breath away.

He looked like the moon on moving water, the moon on the sea. His hide seemed to have a light of its own and it shimmered when he moved, glittering in the blue moonlight. As he came towards me his long sinuous body moved with a slow grace and the veiled promise of terrifying speed. His scales seemed to stop just under his jaw and at the top of his head, leaving his face one solid surface. It looked as though it had been hammered out of purest silver, and the darkness I had seen in his forehead last night showed itself a bright green gem like a vast, living emerald set in a silver lake. A great pair of curving horns swept gracefully up and back from his head, all in a piece with the rest of his face.

I could not speak.

"Little sister?" he said softly. "Does something trouble you?"

I found myself breathing hard, near overcome. I wanted to run away, wanted to fall to my knees and worship this creature, and knew that both were wrong. I closed my eyes.

And that deep sibilant voice, with a truer gift of music than Marik could ever hope for, whispered, "Little one, are you not well?"

With my eyes closed at least I could speak.

"I'm fine, my brother, I—forgive me, I've never truly seen you before. It was so dark last night . . ." I opened my eyes again. He wasn't quite so overwhelming this time. "You are so beautiful."

He dipped his head on his long neck, and the Language of Truth sang in my mind, rang in my heart, nearer than ever whisper might come.

You honour me, Lanen Kaelar.

I felt my heart fill like an empty cup, fill to overflowing, felt a wash like light sweep over me from top to toe until there was no room for darkness.

I had heard my true name spoken by one I loved, however disparate our races, and I would have died content at that moment. I would have missed other, more wondrous things, but I knew even then that there is no greater joy.

Kantri

"Well met, I say again, Lanen. Is that how you would be called?"

She smiled up at me, her eyes bright in the moonlight. "Yes, Lanen is what I'm called. How shall I name you?"

"I am known as Akhor." I returned her smile in the way of my people. (She did not flinch this time, though I learned later that the sight of my teeth was still frightening.) "And still you leak seawater. Do tears come so easily to you, Lanen?"

She laughed. "No, not usually. Only since I met you, and then only for joy."

I bowed. "May all your tears be for joy then, sister Lanen. And have you thought on our words last night?"

"I have thought of little else, Akor, all last night as I lay awake and all today," she said. I noticed she could not truly pronounce my name, but from her "Akor" was meet. "Can you tell me something? You said that our meeting was forbidden. I think I know what you meant, but if your people have laws I don't know about, please tell me." She paused, but I did not speak yet. "I don't want to cause trouble for you over our meeting. I didn't know if it was an actual law or—well, ever since I left my home I've talked to people about wanting to meet you—your people, I mean. And everyone I spoke to thought I was crazy. One accused me of wanting gold, one said you weren't real—and I think the only one who actually believed me spent most of his time wondering how he might get a trade advantage."

I had to laugh—I had heard variations on those arguments from my own people for hundreds of years. She did draw back at that. When I asked, she wrinkled her head at me and asked if I was amused or angry.

"I laughed. That is the word, is it not? Laugh?"

"Laughing means you find something funny. Is that what you meant?"

I hissed my amusement at her. "Yess, Lhanen. If you think, you do the same—I saw you, the day you arrived—but as you are not creatures of fire, there is no steam or flame to accompany the laughter."

"We're a damn sight smaller, too, and don't have near so many teeth," she answered in what seemed a wry tone of voice.

"To answer your question about the ban, littling, would require the telling of a long tale, and that must wait. Suffice it for now to say that my people have made it a law that we should not come too near friendship or trust with the Gedri, for in the past great evil befell my people and yours because of such trust." I bowed. "Indeed, I have broken that law to speak with you even so much."

"But why?" she asked, genuinely puzzled. "How could I possibly hurt you? Your lightest thought could destroy me." Then she shook me as she echoed what I had said to Shikrar. "Forgive me, my brother, I speak in ignorance, but could it be that your laws are too harsh in this?"

"You speak with my words!" I stumbled as I spoke, so many thoughts were trying to come out at once. "Where now are the insurmountable differences between us? It is true, I had to learn your language, but I understand your Attitudes without thought. I am not as certain of the changes that come over your face. I know they have meaning, and I suspect that they mesh with the Attitudes of your people; but taken all in all they are not so strange, and with a little time I will come to know them. We both laugh when we are amused, we shed flame—or tears—with great emotion, we watch out the night when there are great things to ponder . . . and we do not bear well under laws that are too strict. Surely, my soul to the Winds, there are no creatures in all the world so similar as we two, for all our differences."

And a deeper voice from behind me said quietly, "And it appears that the Gedri also are heedless in their encounters with other races."

Lanen

I must have jumped back ten feet. I landed in a fighter's crouch—bless Jamie!—for all the good it would do me here. They just stared at me, with what I hoped was curiosity. The newcomer had moved forward a little, and the moon was higher now. I could see them both very clearly indeed.

It didn't really help.

The first thing I noticed was the other was considerably larger than Akor. His great fangs gleamed as he spoke, the vast wings tucked against his body rippled in the moonlight. His hide was much darker than Akor's, but I could still see the gem in his forehead, above and between the eyes. Both gems caught the moonlight and sparkled, though I suspected that much of the sparkle came from within. (A fleeting thought struck me that if Marik ever saw those gems he would move mountains to get hold of them.) His horns, as he stood, framed the moon for a moment. It was frightening, but it was unutterably beautiful.

And to be truthful, I was fascinated. I had forgotten their wings when I saw Akor last night, and now I was terribly curious about them, and about the purpose of the gems. I would like to say I forgot to be afraid of the newcomer, but in truth I was proud of myself for simply not running. I had never imagined that something that big could be alive.

"Is this the wonder I saw in your mind, Akhor?" he asked. His speech was hard to understand, but I could tell what he was saying. "She is much smaller, and I do not see the radiance about her that you do." He came very close to me very quickly—if I had not been so frightened or determined not to move, I might have been more impressed by the speed at which he moved. As it was I stood there frozen, using all my strength to hold still.

When his head was only inches from mine he stopped. He seemed to be smelling me, which bothered me a great deal—it made him seem for a moment like a huge misshapen beast, a freak of nature, horrible. I could feel a scream welling up; those huge fangs needed only open and shut once. With that speed, I might never know I was dead.

Akor spoke and saved me. "Well, Shikrar, are you satisfied? You could smell Raksha-trace in her grandmother at that range."

I relaxed a little, began to breathe again. Shikrar drew back (for which I was intensely thankful), but he never took his eyes from me.

"Why do you stare at me?" he asked harshly. "I am not the soft fool you spoke to last night, and I will know the truth when I hear it."

I tried for a second to think of something courteous to say, then realised that my idea of courtesy was unlikely to mean anything. The truth was bald, but I dared say nothing else.

"I was staring because it is much brighter out tonight—there are no clouds—and I can see you both so much better than I could see Akor last night. And because you are even larger than he, and I do not know you, and I am frightened."

Akor hissed with laughter. "Well answered, Lhanen!" he said. "There, my friend, was an answer worthy of any youngling. Are you still convinced that she opens the door for the Rakshasa?"

Shikrar snorted; a great puff of steam. "There is much yet to discover," he said in a gravelly voice. "I do not believe the tale she told you. She is not a youngling, Akhor, no matter what you may think, and even for the Gedri she is no child. What brings you here, Gedri?" he growled at me. "What tale has brought you so far from your Kindred? Are you mad? Do you seek after gold? Or is it the thrill of near approach without violating our law, thus to flout death in its very teeth? I charge you now, tell me the truth of your call, or I shall dare my friend's vengeance and break you where you stand, Boundary or no."

I wasn't afraid anymore, though I couldn't tell you why. I suppose any sane person would have become witless with fear or started to stammer something like I had the night before. Though I say it myself, I did not so waste my time. Inspiration had struck and I knew in that moment it was the only answer.

"May I speak to you in the Language of Truth, that you may trust my words?" I asked.

It worked. He was shocked out of anger into silence.

I could almost feel Akor's smile.

"That was well done, Lanen. If you will be advised, collect yourself and concentrate on what you will say. That may help keep some of your underthought a little quieter."

I did as he said, wondering what in the Seven Hells underthought might be, and waited for Shikrar's reply to my offer.

He spoke instead to Akor. "What is this? Does she offer in truth, Akhor? How does this happen? The Gedri are deaf and mute to true-speech."

Akor only looked at him, as far as I could tell. At any rate, Shikrar turned back to me, managing despite his vast immobile face to express both disbelief and curiosity. "Very well, child of the Gedri. You may bespeak me. I am called Shikrar."

"And I am Lanen," I said aloud. I thought then, as hard as I could, trying to concentrate on the words as Akor had said. *"I tell you in all truth, Shikrar, that I have come here on the wings of my dreams, and for no other reason. I first heard of your people many years ago in a ballad, the Song of the Winged Ones, and I have longed to know you ever since."*

He seemed to hear a lot more than I said.

Akhor

I heard her, of course. Younglings have no discrimination, they cannot choose the target of their thoughts until they have practiced for some time. Even though Lanen seemed to have this ability as a natural gift, and to be developing at an amazing rate, still her thoughts were readily audible to anyone nearby. They were a little more focussed than before—she had managed to whisper her greeting to me without too much difficulty—but I heard her on several levels when she spoke to Shikrar, just as he did.

"I tell you in all truth, Shikrar, I wonder what his real name is Shikrar is too short ugly for Dragon name that I have come here still so new a blessing here at last on the wings of my dreams dear Lady those dreams that kept me alive \vision of waking in a dark chamber, staring at the walls, great sorrow at finding herself there\ *and for no other reason. at least not before now there is HIM I first heard of your people what do they call themselves I'd wager it isn't Dragon I know it isn't many years ago in a ballad,* \vision of many of the Gedri sitting around a fire, one singing, feeling of surprise and wonder\ *the Song of the Winged Ones the song in the silence I heard their wings I know I did dear Lady I may yet live to hear them in truth* \great joy at being so near us, at being so near *me*\ *and I have longed to know you ever since* \no thoughts under, but a wash of longing tempered only slightly by joy, as if that which longed did not yet recognise the fulfillment of its desire\ *on my life I speak truth you must believe me."*

The last deep underthought I heard I furiously suppressed. *She is drawn to me because I answered her call, nothing more,* I told myself.

I concentrated on Hadreshikrar's response.

He had obviously heard her, and heard what I heard in her underthought; but he either took it as I pretended to take it or he could not hear it—could not dare to hear it—any more than I could.

Bless his formal soul, he bowed to her. He always did that, bowed to a youngling who had bespoken him for the first time, no matter how scattered the truespeech had been. It was one of the traits I loved in him, a trait that lives warm in my memory to this day.

"Forgive me, littling. Lhanen. There is great reason for our people to distrust one another, but in all my life I have never heard of a Gedri who could use truespeech. And you are so new to it, unless your artifice is greater even than I could manage, I must admit that you speak truth."

"My thanks, old friend," I whispered in his mind.

"I do not say that all is resolved, Akhor, but I admit I am much impressed by hearing the Language of Truth from her. For now I see

no danger of speech with her, if another is present," he told me.

"Will you be that other?"

"For now. I shall withdraw some way, that you may have some privacy, but I shall hear all that is said. Will that satisfy you?"

"It will."

Shikrar gazed at Lanen. "It is well, then. I greet you, child of the Gedri, in the name of my family and as Keeper of Souls. Welcome, Lhanen, to the home of the Greater Kindred."

She sank on one knee, her empty hands open at her sides, her eyes fixed on him, her face joyful yet solemn. "I thank you, Shikrar, Keeper of Souls. If ever I may be of service to you or your family, you need only call upon me."

Shikrar hissed his amusement. "If ever that day comes, littling, I shall do so indeed. Enjoy your time with young Akhor, and remember that even in the midst of joyous communion there is room for caution." He turned and left quietly, withdrawing as he had said far enough at least for the semblance of privacy.

I smiled down at her. "That was well done, Lanen. You have been shown a great honour."

She rose to her feet, brushing the dirt and leaves from her leggings. "I know it, and I thank you." She gazed after Shikrar and said quietly, "He is a good one, Shikrar. He terrified me at first, but he thinks only of the danger to you and your people. I—" She stopped herself. "Akor, forgive me. There is so much I want to know, so much I want to ask, but I am afraid of overstepping the bounds."

"Do not fear it, Lanen. If what you ask is a matter for deepest secrecy, I will not answer. Will that content you?"

"It will indeed." She smiled broadly. "And now, who shall have the honour of the first question?"

"What is the custom in your country?" I asked, bemused.

She laughed. "That fits. You have asked first, and the honour usually goes to the oldest male. At least in Ilsa."

"Why the male? Surely the eldest is the Eldest?"

She looked up at me and I could not tell what she meant to convey. "I agree with you, and so would most of my sisters, but in any event I suspect you are much older than I. How old are you?"

"How do you reckon age?"

She seemed taken aback by the question, then replied, "By the passing of the seasons, of course. Thirteen moons and the three days of Midwinter makes a year. I was born at the Autumn Balance-day, when light and darkness are equal. I have seen twenty-four years, and with any luck I shall see sixty. What of you?"

"We reckon the days nearly the same, with a few variations—and our years are the same, certainly, since midwinter's shortest day is a festival here as well. I am older than you by many hundreds of years."

"Hundreds?"

"Our two Kindreds live very different lives." I settled myself on the ground, content, the *ferrinshadik* silent at last. This way I was closer to her. I laid my head on my forearms so that I was just this side of the Boundary and said quietly, "I have seen a thousand and twelve Midwinters, Lanen, and if I live as long as my father I shall see at least eight hundred more."

She was silent for a long time. "I can't even imagine it," she said finally. "What do you do with all that time? You have seen so much— dear Lady, when you were born there were still people in Ilsa who lived in grass shacks on the plains and *worshipped* horses! And you still have questions to ask?"

"Indeed," I said. "And if you will allow me, I will pose one now. What does it mean when you bend yourself in half?"

"Bend in—oh, a bow!" She demonstrated. "Like this?" I nodded. "I never thought. It means—it is a way of showing agreement or re- spect."

"I am familiar with the concept. So that is a bow. Fascinating. What did you think Shikrar did after you bespoke him?"

"That was a bow?" she asked, delighted. "You've saved me a question. What a strange thing to do, a bob of the head and the wave passing down the neck after it. But then I can't imagine you bend- ing in the middle!" After a moment's pause she added, "It was very kind of him."

Lanen

Akor seemed to find that funny. I let him hiss his amusement and looked more closely at him. The moon illuminated his hide beauti- fully. It gleamed like polished silver, and in the cool blue light it struck me again that he looked like the moon on the sea turned solid and come to life, shimmering and changing as he moved gleaming through the darkness.

I shook myself back to the moment. I decided that if I ever wanted to find out anything important I might as well try now. "Akor, Shikrar spoke of caution, and I don't think he meant only me. Did he?"

"No, he did not refer only to you. We must both be cautious."

"But why?" I asked again. I felt like a child, asking such questions, but I knew that I would never have another chance. "Is there time now for that tale? I cannot imagine a reason for your law. You are ancient and powerful beyond imagination. What in all the world is there for you to be afraid of?"

He lifted his head from where it had been resting, very companionably, on his forelegs near the Boundary. He tilted it a little, as if he listened to something, but whatever it was seemed to satisfy him. "Have you never heard of the Lesser Kindred? They live in the north, in the Trollingwood."

"No," I replied, feeling like the merest idiot. I felt I should know, of course, *everyone* knows about the Lesser Kindred and why Dragons are afraid of people, why didn't I? It was the first time, I think, that I felt the enchantment that I had heard of in the ballads. Those who speak too long with Dragons come to believe everything they are told. . . .

"This may be difficult for you to hear, little one. It is a tale full of darkness."

"I still want to know."

"Very well. I have then a request to make. May I bespeak you? It grows tiresome winding my tongue around the sounds of your language, and I fear I do not have all the words for this that I shall need."

I nodded. "You are most welcome to bespeak me, Akor."

This is the tale he told.

Akhor

The Tale of the Lost Souls, or
The Demonlord of the Gedrishakrim

"When the world was younger and the last of the Trelli but lately departed, our two peoples lived in harmony. The wooden huts of the Gedri circled the caves of the Kantri teachers without fear, and the Kantri taught the Gedri children with great patience and much joy.

"This is the true way of life for both peoples, as I understand it. The Kantri need the quick-living Gedri to remind them that all life passes, that there is a need to live life in the moment rather than ignoring the present as it rolls over them. The Gedri need the ancient Kantri to remind them that their concerns, though pressing, are but a part of life in its vast patterns. In that time, both peoples found in each other a constant source of delight in other minds and other ways of thought.

"So they lived and so they worked, and through many lives they throve together. The huts became houses, farms, smithies. Soon beyond the circle of structures there blossomed fields of grain, and pastureland to feed the cattle that fed both peoples. Beyond that, orchards, groves and gardens. It was not the first time the two had lived in peace, but it was the best. There was plenty, and harmony, and peace.

"At this time the Healers first arose among the Gedrishakrim. It happened that some, those who spent much time with the Kantri and learned about truespeech, began to discover their own gifts in the realms of the will and the mind. In time they found they could heal small wounds; then there came those who could knit badly torn flesh quickly; and once in a generation there would arise one who could join broken bones in minutes. They were deeply honoured, and their services were a blessing to the Gedrishakrim and a wonder to the Kantri, for my people have never had the gift of healing. It was a new gift altogether, and a very great one.

"At the time when Lishakisaan of the Kantri passed to the Winds, the greatest Healer of that time came to see the remains before they were consumed (for our inner fire, released from our control at death, destroys our bodies from within in a very short time). Some years later a youngling of the Kantri was wounded near to death in a fight, and this Healer drew in her will and sent it forth in a blue glow to surround the wounded littling. The youngling was healed in a moment, but in that instant all the Healer's strength left her and her gift never returned. However, she passed her knowledge on to her daughter, who was also a Healer, and from that time some few of the Gedri were able to assist the Kantri when they were in pain, without losing their power in the process.

"It is perhaps not surprising that from this great good came great evil. The balance of all things will not be denied. It was a Healer who turned to the Rakshasa and so to the sundering of the peoples.

"He was a son of that line, the kin of the first Healer of the Kantri. He lived in the south of the Trollingwood at the edge of a settlement. As a child he was content enough, willing to work, listening to the Kantri teachers with a single-mindedness unusual in one so young. When he reached the first stirrings of manhood he demanded to be tested, for Healers were discovered in youth that their training might begin at once.

"His power was shown to be that of the lowest of Healers, able to cure small wounds, help in a small way. Even that little was more than most were given, but for him it was never enough. From the moment he discovered that only the smallest portion of power was his, he sought to increase it, convinced that he was born to surpass his revered ancestor. He began by wanting to learn more from the Kantri, working hard for many years and asking penetrating questions, but he learned at last that there is no way to gain more power than the Winds have given.

"It was his ending and his dark beginning. He left the settlement and burned his home behind him. The fire spread to several other dwellings and one young girl was killed; thus his first death was accomplished without thought or concern. It became the pattern of his numbered days.

"No one knows how he discovered a way to treat with the Rakshasa. Did his curses simply fall on receptive ears, or did he stand in seven circles and call some dark name, or make some offer that degraded race could not deny? It is a moot point. The Rakshasa have always known the needs and the frailties of the Gedrishakrim, and they nurse ever their hatred of my people. It is enough to know that he summoned them, and the world is worse for it.

"He is called only the Demonlord. His name is not remembered. He traded it, before the end, to one of the Lords of Hell for a great power in this world, and when it went to that Lord it took all memory of itself from those who had known it. He surrounded himself with the lesser race of the Rakshi, the Rikti or minor demons. Thus, with no name to give power to another, and a defense that seemed to him impenetrable, he was free to work his will.

"It is difficult for rational beings to understand what moved the Demonlord. Did he seek the domination of Kolmar? Of the entire world? Or perhaps it was an integral part of that small, mad soul to require all power once he had even a taste of it.

"He went first, disguised, to others of the Gedri, in a place where there were none of my people. He demanded that they worship him as their king, showing them but a portion of his power. When they denied him he grew wrathful and stood before them in his new person. The Rikti that surrounded him became visible to natural sight, and the only survivor of that place described a luminous glow about him, of the hue common to Healers but scored with broken black lines like a mad spider's web. The teller of the tale admitted that he ran terrified from that sight alone. Looking over his shoulder he saw that black-shot blue cover the villagers, and he heard them scream as from a great distance. When he returned with others of the Two Peoples, they found nothing but dark steaming stains on the ground stinking of the Rakshasa.

"The Kantri moved as one, silently, terrifying him with their utter, inexorable response.

"They burned the black stains clean with dragonfire.

"When the first tongue of flame reached the first stain, there was a flash of light and a loud moan. The Kantri grimly went about the settlement, flaming clean every stain, every house, every burnt-out shell of every dwelling. As Kantri-fire met Raksha-trace the air was filled with searing white flame, and with the cries of the damned.

"When at last the work was finished, the Kantri met in a circle where the Demonlord had stood. None knew where he had gone, but he must be found. They began to send out word to all the Kindred.

"The Kantri and Gedri met then in a Great Council. Every one of the Kindred who could fly or walk to the meeting place in a day was there, bar one or two who chose to stay with their settlements and defend them. It was the last Great Council. There were four hundred of the Kindred there, glowing in all shades of bronze and copper and gold, and fifty of the Gedri like small, bright children against the vast size of so many of the Kantri. Its like will never be seen again.

"The Kantri knew the Raksha-stink; the Gedri survivor told of the unholy alliance and described the sickening corruption of the Healer's will. More tales reached them, even as they met, of further atrocities, through the links of truespeech between the Kantri. All the news was of a madman steadily destroying settlements of the Gedri.

"The Great Council lasted only a few hours while Kantri and Gedri debated the best way to deal with the Demonlord, for it had become known that he travelled the demon lines and could disappear in moments. The only hope of the council was that the Demonlord would tire or demand more of his servants than he had paid blood for.

"It is remembered as the Day Without End, though some now call it the Day of the End. Before noon, while the sun shone bright and uncaring at the Great Council, a lady of the Kantri called Tréshak cried out as in great pain. Two of the Gedri Healers rushed to her, summoning their power as they ran. They could not have known.

"Tréshak, a kind soul with two younglings, a teacher of the Gedri her whole life long, turned on the Healers and destroyed them with fire. The only kindness is that they never knew her betrayal. They were dead by the time they fell to earth.

"Tréshak screamed her agony. 'Aidrishaan! His Rakshasa have killed Aidrishaan!' Aidrishaan was her beloved.

"There was no more speech. The Kantri broke from their circle, and in seconds the sky was black with them and the clearing thundered with the sound of their wings. Flames preceded them into the sky as they flew at best speed to the settlement where Aidrishaan had been.

"They found the Demonlord. It is not known to this day why he did not simply leave that place when he saw the Kantri coming for him, but he did not.

"He stood laughing beside the smouldering bones of Aidrishaan.

"Tréshak was first. Her fury, her fire burned hottest, and she had flown on the Wind's wings for vengeance. She drew in breath to flame this abomination, though she should die for it. We waited in respect for her loss, knowing that no child of the Gedrishakrim could stand against the armed fury of our Kindred.

"The Demonlord uttered a single word, and Tréshak *changed.* Before our eyes as she flew she dwindled to the size of a youngling and fell out of the sky, for her wings would no longer bear her up. A gleaming blue flame shot up from her blue soulgem, and no one who lived through that day ever forgot the sound of her last cry. It haunts the dreams even of those who were not there, as though time itself is offended and cries out for pity.

"It was cut off in the midst as her soulgem was ripped from her by the hands of the Rikti and delivered unto the Demonlord.

"Perhaps it would have been better if the Kantri had retreated, taken time to consider.

"We did not.

"Four hundred of the Kantrishakrim flew straight at the Demonlord, setting fire to the very air as they dove. He spoke rapidly, the same word over and over, and fully half of the Kantri fell from the air and had their soulgems ripped away by legions of the Rikti.

"He could not get us all.

"He laughed as he died, as the Rikti around him disappeared in our flame (for they are the weaker of our natural enemies and cannot withstand dragonfire in this world). We do not know if he was so far into madness that he did not fear death or pain, or if there was some darkness in his soul that believed even then that he would triumph in the end.

"Fights broke out among the Kantri as we all tried to add our own touch of destruction to the dead body. A kind of madness gripped us, cooled only when the youngest, Keakhor, cried aloud, 'He is dead, we cannot kill him more. For pity's sake look to the wounded.'

"We turned to those who had been struck by the Demonlord's curse. We tried to speak to them, but in vain. One sifted among the ashes of the Demonlord and found the soulgems; they were already shrinking (as is their nature once separated from the body), and even then they bore the taint of their demonic source. In the course of nature, the soulgems of the dead resemble faceted jewels. When the Kin-Summoning is performed they glow with a steady light, and the Keeper of Souls may speak with the dead, but when the Summoning is over they again fall dark. These gleamed—to this day they gleam—at all times from within with a flickering light.

"We believe the souls of our Kindred are trapped within, neither alive nor dead, and despite endless years of our best efforts they still are bound.

"The bodies of our brothers and sisters had become the bodies of beasts. We could not kill them, for old love, but we could not bear to see them either. Someone first called them the Lesser Kindred on that day, and it has become our name for them. They breed now like beasts and live brief, solitary lives. We try to contact the newly born every year in the autumn, but we have had no evidence through the long, long years that a single one has heard or tried to respond.

"We returned in shock, in sorrow, mourning our loss though we could not yet comprehend it. It was a forefather of Shikrar, little better than a youngling himself, who with great effort kept the Kantri from destroying the innocent Gedri who waited still at the settlement. He took the Gedri aside and explained quickly what had happened, and he stopped them from offering to heal those who had been wounded. It was decided then that those of the Kantri who remained must leave the company of the Gedri, for in each face those who were now the Greater Kindred would see the Demonlord, and the memory of their comrades falling from the Winds in agony.

"Without a word, without a glance at the Gedri (who yet had heeded some inner voice and gathered in homage), the Greater Kindred leapt into the sky and left the land forever.

"This is the cause of the Great Ban. Kantri and Gedri must not meet, lest the Kantri take delayed vengeance, or another Demonlord arise among the Gedri.

"This took place five thousand years ago.

"It is the blink of an eye to the Kantrishakrim."

Lanen

I sat on the cold ground, my arms wrapped around my knees and my cloak around all, as he finished his tale. I felt a little drunk and a little ill. The world of the moonlit glade had grown hazy about me as I watched the tale unfold, as a mind older than I could imagine sent thoughts behind my eyes. I sat calm and peaceful in that time when the Two Kindreds lived in harmony, was devastated by death and betrayal, watched in breathless horror as the Lesser Kindred fell from the sky, rejoiced with a dark joy when the Demonlord was destroyed, flew back exhausted with the Greater Kindred, and quietly wept at their final departure from the lands I knew.

In the back of my mind I heard the warning of the bards. *The eyes of a dragon are perilous deep.* . . . I knew then a little of why that is so, a little of our shared history in the world, and I could only weep. I did not meet Akor's eyes when he had finished, letting instead my tears fall silently onto my cloak.

I knew many of the bardic songs about Dragons—I had sought them out since I was a child—and none had more than hinted at a time when the Two Peoples had lived together in peace.

For a time we were both silent. The cold darkness closed in around us, the small sounds of life stilled in the deep night. The moon had sunk down in the sky, but there still was enough light when I looked up to show the outline of that terrifying, expressionless face, like a blank silver shield. His body that had shone like the moon on the sea was now only a lighter patch in the darkness.

"I too am much moved by the tale, Lanen Kaelar," he said softly in truespeech. *"Your tears honour me."*

"They honour the Lesser Kindred," I replied aloud, surprised at the depth of feeling I had discovered for creatures I had been told were little more than cattle. I cannot explain why I felt as I did, but it seemed to me that all my sorrow, all my long desire to speak with Dragons had led me to this place and distilled into this: that I should bring our two peoples together, and that I should set the Lesser Kindred free. What good I thought I could do, all alone, against thousands of years of mistrust and the power of a Demonlord, I cannot now imagine: but such are the dreams of youth, too gloriously stupid to realise what cannot be done.

And without those dreams, how should we ever accomplish the impossible?

"Akor, is there nothing to be done?" I cried urgently as I rose to my feet. My heart was in my voice, as were the tears that had dampened my cloak. "In all this time, have your people found nothing that can help those poor trapped souls?"

He was silent. I stumbled a bit from sitting long in the cold and began to pace the clearing to warm myself, and because the plight of the Lesser Kindred spoke to my heart and would not let me be still.

Akor moved in the darkness. I waited for his words, ached for them; he was silent yet for some time. From what I could see, he stood in an odd position and seemed distracted, as if he warred within himself and only the victor might speak.

I paced back and forth, stamping and rubbing my arms to try and coax a little warmth back into my hands and feet.

Akhor

"Akhor, you must not! Already she knows more of us than any Gedri since the Peace. Would you tell her all? And what more of her people have we learned? Always it is her questions you answer, never she yours."

"And what should we ask of her, Shikrar? Have you questions to ask the Gedri? I have a few, indeed, but they are mere curiosity. The child has barely begun to live, and will surely die long before she has time to learn aught of much interest to us. I have touched her heart, my friend. She will not harm us, and there is no taint of the Rakshasa in her."

"There is always room in the hearts of the Gedri for the Rakshasa. They are free to choose, Akhor, and they may change at any moment. I tell you, be wary! Her very weakness is her strength. Through it she may learn enough to destroy those of us who remain."

"I shall be on my guard. But I must answer her last question. Her concern deserves that at least."

"Very well. But keep your answer short, and end this meeting as soon as you may."

Lanen had begun pacing back and forth, rubbing her arms. It looked most peculiar. I decided to indulge my curiosity and Shikrar's prejudice.

"What are you doing, little one?"

"Waiting for your answer," she replied. I was amused to hear an edge of anger in her voice. How quickly the Gedri change! Not long since she had been terrified of me. Then she said, "Oh, you mean walking around? I'm cold, this is the only way I know of to get warm without a fire."

I couldn't resist.

"Go fetch some wood and set it ready," I told her.

She furrowed her face at me but did as I asked. *"I must ask about that sometime,"* I reminded myself idly.

"Stand clear," I told her.

As soon as she was out of the way, I summoned my Fire and breathed on the wood.

I've always been proud of my aim.

Lanen

I leapt back as a thin stream of fire shot past me and struck the wood. It instantly burst into roaring flame, fiercer by far than any fire I had known. The warmth was most welcome, though, and once I was sure he wasn't going to do any more than that, I stood near. I shuddered gladly with the heat as it began to thaw my hands and face, and smiled when I heard a gentle hissing laugh from Akor. It was just occurring to me that I had at last seen dragonfire when Akor said, "Do you know, Lanen, this is probably the first time since the Peace that our two Kindreds have cooperated in even so simple a thing as this?"

I thought of the lansip harvest, but realised that was not so much cooperation as simple permission. My, no, *our* little fire suddenly warmed me more deeply. A little light in centuries of darkness, just like the flickering soulgems of the Lost Ones. . . .

"Akor, forgive me, I must ask again. Are you certain there is nothing to be done for the Lesser Kindred?"

He drew in a deep breath and let out as human a sigh as I could imagine.

Akhor

"We have sought to aid them ever since it happened, Lanen. We have tried everything we can think of countless times in the hope that some new voice, some new soul's influence might make the difference. If it lay in the power of the Kindred to do aught, they would have been restored long since. Surely you do not think we neglect our own kin, or forget that they lie trapped? At least that is what most of us believe."

"Is there some question?" she asked.

"There are those who say the gems of the Lost Ones flicker only with demonfire, and that the souls of those who bore them are long since passed to the Winds." I paused. "It could be so, in truth, but my heart rebels at the idea. And they do not smell of the Rakshasa. No, since I came into my own I have dreamt of them, the Lost Ones, calling ceaselessly to us, their blood and bone, to release them. It haunts me as it does Shikrar, in whose charge the soulgems lie. I do not doubt that they are imprisoned and aware. The wonder would be if they were still sane."

She stood silent for a moment, in what looked like the Attitude of Deep Thought. It was obscurely pleasing to me that the Gedri seemed to use Attitudes instinctively, as we did, though theirs were as minimal as those of the eldest of my people. They had developed mobile faces to express their thoughts, which meant they used only a small range of Attitudes. However, I was beginning to intuit some of the meanings of those facial expressions, combined as they were with voice and stance. In all my studies, none had ever mentioned how their faces changed. I was entranced.

I watched her closely as I waited for her words. The firelight was playing on her features, strong and blunt, and turned her long hair to the colour of ripe autumn grain. I had never considered that the Gedri might have a kind of beauty. I caught a glimpse of it then.

"I wish I could help," she said quietly.

"Akhor, have you not yet finished with the little one?"

Lanen

Of all things I least expected what happened. Suddenly through the gathering darkness I saw Akor's great head come towards me like a striking snake. I didn't even have time to move away or cry out when I heard his thoughts rolling over my mind, so quickly I could barely understand him, and so soft I could hardly hear.

"Lanen, I beg you do not reply in truespeech, Shikrar would hear your lightest thought. We must meet to discuss these things when he will be elsewhere and not aware of us. Come here tomorrow just as the last light leaves the sky and we shall find a private place. We must end our speech together for now. I will speak with you then."

It took only an instant; he was back at a distance and speaking normally. "You are kind to offer, littling, but there is nothing to be done."

It took me a moment to recover, but at least I knew now what had been going on. I need only think of a way to leave without sounding as though I were sure of another meeting. In the meantime . . .

I moved closer to the fire, which had begun to die but was still enough to warm me. "I must believe you, but I mourn for the Lesser Kindred as I would for my own folk." And that was true enough.

I could hear the smile in his voice as Akor replied, "Perhaps you are part of our Kindred at that, littling. But will not your own folk begin to fear for you? The moon is down, they will soon be stirring."

"I don't care what they do. Must I go so soon?" And for Shikrar's benefit—"Akor, please, may I not meet with you again? There is so little time, and I will be here only four more nights."

"I must speak with others of my Kindred before we meet again, little one. But do not lose heart, I trust my people will at the least allow us to meet once more, if only to say farewell."

Only the sure knowledge of our secret meeting kept me from weeping. As it was, I think I sounded impressively forlorn. "I will do as you command, Lord Akor." And that reminded me . . . "That is what Shikrar called you, wasn't it? Lord Akor? Why 'lord'? Is that the custom of your people?"

"It is because I am the Lord and King of my people, Lanen Maransdatter. And that is the last question I shall answer this night. Fare you well. I shall bespeak you when I have consulted with my people."

My heart was so full of so many things I could not speak. I bowed to Akor and left, hugging myself, and not against the cold. I was so full of joy, of wonder, of fear and anticipation that I could hardly keep from laughing aloud. *Trust you, Lanen,* I thought. *Not just any Dragon, no, the KING of the Dragons himself is the one you find to talk to. I never thought they would have a king. It sounds like something out of a fairy tale. Dear Lady, will I ever believe that this has truly happened when I leave this place?*

That pulled me up short, for it was then I realised that I did not seriously intend to leave.

Akhor

I watched her walk away. I could almost see the joy in her step. Truly there was a universal nature to the Attitudes. If she had been a youngling of my Kindred I would have expected her to take off into the night sky, singing.

"That was well done, Akhor," said Shikrar from the darkness.

"No, my friend, it was not," I replied. "I wished to speak with her for some time yet. Why did you demand that I cut short our speech?"

"You were losing your perspective, Akhor. She is an engaging creature, surely, and for all I can tell she is as free of Raksha-trace as you or I. But that cannot be said for all her people who are here. Surely you have smelled it?"

"Many of them are tainted, yes, and their leader worst of all. I have never smelt a shipload of these merchants that did not have its share of the Raksha-touched. Yet now that you have heard Lanen's truespeech, can you honestly believe that she would have dealings with them?"

Shikrar sighed. "Akhor, my friend, your innocence in these matters concerns me. Surely you know they use force on one another? What is to stop one of the tainted ones from holding a blade at her heart and demanding that she tell all she has learned?"

I did not answer. Truth to tell, I had forgot for the moment how debased the creatures could be, for in her I knew only good. However, I kept my thought to myself when Shikrar asked his question, for the answer in my heart was simply "I am." It did not require thought on my part, it was as natural a response as breathing. I was certain that if Lanen found herself in danger she would bespeak me, and no boundary existed that I would not break to save her.

And still I did not realise. I think Shikrar did, at least in a vague way. He bade me call a full Council to inform the Kindred of my meetings and ask their permission for one more. I agreed, left him as Guardian and walked slowly back to my chambers.

The long autumn night was nearly over; false dawn lit the sky, the leafless trees casting intricate shadows against the light. Their complexity gave me obscure comfort, as though the existence of something so simple yet wondrous as a naked tree against the sky meant that there was in truth an underlying pattern to all things. I hoped against hope that my people would be able to hear my words, that some others who knew the burden of the *ferrinshadik* would listen to me.

And my heart was large with the thought of being Lanen's protector and advocate. I was still unaware of the depth of what I felt for her, or that what I was truly feeling was love—but I had never known love before.

I have no other excuse.

TWILIGHT

Lanen

I arrived back in the camp, being careful to disguise the direction I had come from, just as false dawn began to lighten the sky. Many were stirring but none seemed to notice me. Even Marik, who appeared to be madly busy, spared me little more than a glance. In passing, though, I heard a few words dropped about "fruit," and suddenly the frantic activity made sense.

We had been told several times on the voyage out that finding a late-fruiting tree was like finding your own private fortune buried beneath a stump. The fruits were large and their weight in silver was considerable, but it was a mere fraction of their worth. Lan fruits can restore lost years, or lost health, to any creature still on live, and when the Harvest ships had been used to return from the Dragon Isle every ten years, any fruits that might be found were purchased long ere the ship left the harbour.

From what I overheard that morning, there were rumours that someone had found a sheltered holt where the fruit hung still on the boughs. All the Harvesters rushed where rumour led as soon as they heard it, and several fights broke out even before they left the camp. I could imagine what would be happening at the grove and decided I was not interested in forcing my way in among the crowds. I had to keep gathering leaves for now, lest Marik take note, but I did not seek vast wealth.

I may not have needed silver, but I did need sleep. I decided to stay at the camp and rest a few hours, though I did take breakfast with those who stopped long enough to eat. By that time I was ravenous, and the warmth of chélan was most welcome. It smelled better than usual as I filled a mug and drained half of it in one draught. I was not prepared for the taste.

You must realise that I have had no experience with what some call the finer things of life. I grew up on a farm. Our lives tended to be strong rather than beautiful, and fairly simple (to the point of boredom, I often felt).

Someone had crumbled a few leaves of lansip into the chélan, which had been transformed from a warm spicy drink that got sluggish blood moving in the morning into a draught straight from the Lady's cup. Surely the gods did not have finer drink than this. I instantly shook off my weariness, felt the warm glow of lansip spread like friendly fire through my body. I felt more alert, more alive; and where my memories of the night just past had begun to blur with the need for sleep, they now sprang sharp before me.

I realised that I would have to find some time to sleep that I might be awake and aware this evening, for it might be the last chance I had to speak with Akor. If his people decided he should not speak with me, I believed that he would obey their wishes in future. This night could well be the last.

I also lost my reluctance to join the crowd, and hurried off to where the fruit had been found, carrying my sacks. It would all be gone by the time I got there, I suspected, but the long walk would give me time to think.

I found, not surprisingly, that I felt physical pain at the thought of never seeing Akor again. For all our differences, I saw behind that silver mask a mind much like my own, thoughts that mirrored mine in a way no other's ever had. Even Jamie had not had my dream of seeing the Two Peoples living in peace—and now that I knew it had once been true, it might be done again. I found myself daydreaming about that time as I walked, wondering, wishing that I could somehow bring its spirit back into the world.

The first step must be to undo the wrong that had separated us—to restore the Lesser Kindred. But how, after so many centuries of failure by their own people? I could see no answer, nor could I stop looking for one. I could all but see the soulgems of the Lost lying in some dark cavern, flickering unheeded through their long night; and imagination filled my heart with the agony of the two hundred souls trapped there, living every moment a weariness, waiting in patience, fear, finally in desperation for their kin to release them once more into life.

And even if that were somehow done, how to unite two peoples with such a history behind them?

It seemed impossible. It must be impossible.

I spent every waking moment that morning, as I gathered leaves (the fruits were indeed all taken before I arrived), filled my sacks, carried them the long walk back to camp, wondering how Akor and I might make it happen.

Time was against me, against us. After our meeting at sunset I would have no way of knowing if I would ever see him again. I would have to speak to him of this, of restoring the Lesser Kindred, that very night, hoping he would listen rather than grow angry. I was not sure I was yet ready to risk a Dragon's anger, but I could not stop thinking of it. Of course I had grave doubts as to the wisdom of what I was considering, but that could not be helped, and in any case was not a new sensation. My head was dancing with what I had learned (and with lansip), my heart was full of Dragons, and I did not want even to think of having to leave them so soon.

No. Truth, Lanen. Say what you really mean.

I did not want to think of leaving Kordeshkistriakor.

Marik

"Berys, we have found lan fruit!"

"Excellent. It shall be as my prophet foretold, we shall be wealthy beyond the reach of imagination. It is good. And what of the girl?"

"She will be taken this evening, and blood drawn. Caderan and I have prepared the rite."

"May we both prosper in all things. Farewell."

Akhor

I had just deceived my oldest friend. I had no intention of telling him or anyone else about meeting with her at dusk. I meant it to be a gift to Lanen, and to myself; a few moments of communion between we who for thousands of years had been apart.

I desired to have only the two of us there, as on the night of our first meeting. There was also some obscure part of me that wanted, no, needed to see her in the light of day, and for her to see me.

I could not understand why I felt so pleased. Deception should have lain heavy on me, should have interfered with my very movements. I walked back to my chambers with great difficulty, it is true, but that was only because I did not dare to take to the air so close to the camp of the Gedri. The Kindred had long ago decided to remain largely a veiled mystery to the Gedri who came to gather dead leaves and in their stead provide live cattle, in case their foolishness ever extended beyond those few suicides who stepped over the Boundary. If they did not know our strength, they could not know what they would need to counter it.

I longed to fly, to sing my joy to the Winds, to take her name above the earth and give it to the sky. As I walked, I indulged my fancy and let my mind take flight. I watched myself fly straight up until my wings grew weary and the air too thin, then dive down with my wings close folded and the wind screaming past, pulling up just before I met the ground, into a great loop, into flight for the sheer joy of it.

And in this vision I looked into the sunrise and saw another, a lady of my Kindred but with Lanen's heart and voice. We flew together in delight, without thought, making patterns as we flew, singing to the dawn, singing to each other a new song that only we two . . .

I opened my eyes with a start. My blood pounded in my veins, with fear and with—other things.

I had recognised the pattern at last.

When two of the Kindred decide to mate, they announce their bond with the Flight of the Devoted. It is long, intricate and unashamedly sensual. They create their own patterns of flight; some are based on their families' pattern, some on their own individual style, and something new is added, something that has not been before. Flying separately they fly as one, and at the end of the flight leave all those who have gathered to watch and wish them well. There are places far away from any chambers where they may join in privacy, with only the sounds of sea or forest to keep them company.

I had never chosen a mate, as Shikrar often reminded me. The Lady Idai had long made it known that she would welcome my interest—and by rights I should have welcomed her, she was wise beyond common knowing and devoted to me—but I had told her on several occasions that I had no desire for any lady of the Kindred yet alive. I had reconciled myself to mating late in life or not at all. I began to tremble, standing there on the path to my chambers, as I realised that I had well begun the Flight of the Devoted in my mind, ready to consecrate myself to one lady and to join with her for life.

And the lady was Lanen Kaelar of the Gedrishakrim.

Somehow I made my way back to my chambers. I was horrified and elated at the same time. I had sometimes feared I had no capacity for the love of a mate, yet here it was in all its wonder—but oh, my soul to the Winds, for a child of the Gedri!

Or had I allowed myself that licence in fantasy because there was no possibility of such a joining ever taking place? *Of all the unattainable females, Akhorishaan,* I said to myself, laughing aloud. Yet the vision of her as one of my Kindred would not leave me, and gave me a pleasure and a lifting of the soul I had never known. I felt like a youngling myself, despite my many years of life, and decided there and then to simply enjoy the sensation. It *was* wonderful. And since there was no possibility of such a thing ever coming to pass, I might as well enjoy the feeling while it lasted. Soon she would be gone, my life would return to its quiet ways and I would have but the memory of these times to hold close all my days.

I drew a deep breath. I had to call the Council, as Shikrar had requested. I must summon my people to meet on the morrow at the Great Hall, not far from the Boundary.

I stood in Receiving and began the Discipline of Calm, but soon gave up the effort. How could I call the Council to decide on whether to allow my meetings with Lanen when her very name still sang in all my thoughts?

It would have to wait for a few hours. In the meantime, I allowed my fancy to run free; let her words and her thoughts find their homes in my heart. I knew that after a short while—we had spoken for only a few hours—they would all be settled, and I could trust myself to speak to my people.

Eventually.

Lanen

When the lansip wore off I barely had the strength to drag myself back to the camp with my sacks and go to bed. I slept like a dead thing some hours past noon. The sun, white and insistent at that hour despite the lateness of the year, roused me at last. I woke from a dream of a great light in a forest and with a memory of a song I had not heard before. The sunlight warmed me, I was well rested, and my first and only thoughts were of the meeting to come.

I could not sit still while my thoughts chased themselves in circles, and found myself deeply grateful for the unpredictable hours we Harvesters kept. There were a few souls stirring, some around the cookpot, some heading for sleep after a night and morning of gathering, some groggily arising to drink chélan. None paid heed to me or my movements, and Marik I had not seen at all.

I wrapped my cloak close about me and headed towards the sea. The cold of the night was gone and the day blessedly mild, nearly warm in the sun even as a breeze blew in over the water. I threw back my cloak and reveled in it, for if it stayed clear I feared I was in for a bitter cold night.

I tried, truly, to look around and enjoy simply being on the island that had drawn me for so many years. The sea was like a living thing dancing with the sunlight on it, there were gulls laughing in the air, the wind tasted of salt freshness; but the living face of Akor rose before me, seen only in moonlight yet sharp and present wherever I looked. I could not think why I was reacting so. Yes, he was the first Dragon I had seen—surely reason enough to be impressed— but should I not be remembering his words rather than his eyes? Not that I could well ignore his appearance, but there was another edge to what I was feeling. I couldn't place it, but it was definitely familiar.

Artur.

I stopped short. Artur from Bearsstead, in the Méar Hills above my old home? Why in the name of the Lady had I thought of him? He had been my childhood sweetheart. True, I had longed for him, wept when he wed another—but that was years ago, and what did it have to do with Akor?

You loved him.

Yes, as a child loves. Yes, I loved him.

And for days after his wedding, you saw his face on every farmhand at Hadronsstead.

Yes, but—oh. Oh! No, no, it couldn't—I—oh dear Lady, no, I can't be!

Really?

Give me this much, at least I laughed. In love with a Dragon? Surely not even I could be so stupid! I was no child to be infatuated with a creature so vastly different. I could never—

"We are not so very different, you and I," he said. If he were a man you would love him, wouldn't you?

The thought was immensely appealing. I tried to picture him as a man, and almost without effort he rose before my mind's eye like a portrait already completed. There he stood, lithe, handsome, with silver hair and green eyes full as deep as the sea, beautiful face incredibly smiling and long-fingered hands that took mine and drew me towards him—

Then the huge form I had seen in the night appeared again, soulgem glinting in hammered, horned silver face, voice like a song and thought like love itself speaking its name.

Kordeshkistriakor.

Very well. *(Oh sweet Mother Shia, help!)* Very well, I love him. There, I've said it, I love him whatever his form, all the heavens help me. And what in the Lady's name should I do about it?

The voice from within had no answer to that.

I stood there thinking—even laughing to myself, I am glad to say. I could not take myself seriously. I quite enjoyed the idea of him as a man, but I was still entranced by his true Dragon form for its own sake.

The Lady only knows what I would have thought about had I let my mind wander on, but I soon had more to think about than my love for a creature a thousand years old and the size of Hadron's farmhouse.

I had stopped just past a bend on the path some time back, in the midst of my mad thoughts; now as I stood I heard voices. I did not wish to see anyone in my present mood, so I stepped into the shelter of a thick, low-growing stand of fir trees. They were just the colour of my cloak. In the shadows, with my dark leggings and my hood over my face and hair, I was nearly invisible.

Just as well. The voices had come closer, and one of them was Marik's.

I hoped they would simply pass by and let me return to the camp, but instead they stopped just the other side of the bend in the path. I could hear them clearly.

"It goes well, Master, does it not?" said the other voice. It was high and nasal and extremely unpleasant, and I recognised it at once. It was Caderan, the weaselly creature that danced attendance on

Marik. I had no idea why he had come on the voyage, and as long as I could avoid him I didn't care. "Fruiting trees on your first voyage. It will be a triumph! And you will soon be uncomfortably wealthy."

"I look forward to such discomfort," said Marik lightly. The beauty of his voice was even more marked in contrast to Caderan's. "May I be thus burdened as long as I live! I trust you have worked well this day."

"Indeed, my lord. I have prepared the salve you requested as protection, and the rite is prepared for sunset this very day. But I must tell you, my lord, that what you plan with the articles Magister Berys prepared for you is not possible."

"What do you mean, not possible?" Marik snapped.

"My lord, I am doing what I can—but you ask much, and all takes time." He lowered his voice, but I could still make out his words. "The summoning of demons is a delicate art, my lord. It cannot be rushed, and what you demand is far beyond the ordinary. I am no Magister of the Sixth Circle."

"Damn Berys anyway. Why could he not simply grant my request in full and save both you and me this concern? Only now do I learn that the articles he sent will do but half of what I need!" I could hear Marik glaring at this Caderan. "I must have them, Caderan, and they must serve me as I have said. There is a great deal of ground to cover, and I will need more time. When all is finished tonight, let you consider what you may do to enhance their virtue. I must be able to walk at least ten miles undetected."

"Ten miles? My lord, you know not what you ask! Magister Berys sent me to serve you, but his own puissance could never do such a thing. How should I better his work? The boots he provided will serve you so far, in truth, but the others will not last more than half that time. Such puny assistance as I may render will take you only half again as far, and at that I will be near my limit."

"Then I would recommend that you extend your limit if you intend to leave this place whole as you came," growled Marik. The change in his voice was shocking. The music had gone sour, and in the discord was a heavy strain of menace. "I tell you I must have more time."

Caderan's own voice went hard in response. "My lord, I pray you, leave off this pretence. You hold my life in your hands—but the reverse is also true. Do not try to threaten a demon master. I am still alive because I refuse to listen to threats. It is the essence of my profession." He checked himself and spoke again in a more appeasing tone. "Lord Marik, let us not quarrel. It is neither seemly nor profitable. I will strive for the measure of eight miles, my lord, and nothing you can say will force me to more. Can we not agree on that?"

"Agreed, then," said Marik, his voice recovered. "At that I should have at least some idea of what I can bring out in safety. After the ritual I would ask you to complete the preparation of the other articles, and of the summoning for tomorrow, should it be required. Make certain all is your best work, for my life—indeed, all our lives—will depend upon it."

"So it shall be, my lord," said Caderan. "Do you still intend to speak to the winged ones first?"

"If I can. Why should I put myself in danger if I can win all by negotiation? I have my guards searching for the horse breeder, she can't have gone far. I had hoped we might find her ourselves."

"I told you she would be here, my lord, and there is but one path. We have not met her, therefore she is ahead of us and must return this way."

"So you said. But I have seen no trace of her."

"Only let us wait, my lord. She will come."

Damn. No way out. But what did I have to do with his negotiations?

"You are certain she has spoken with them?"

Ah.

"Yes, my lord. So I have been informed."

"Your informants are never wrong?"

I felt Caderan's laugh shiver down my back. "You are pleased to jest, my lord. No, they are never wrong. I pay them well; they would not dare to be wrong. Even demons can die."

I was barely breathing, keeping as still as I could, praying they would not come any farther. My fir trees suddenly seemed no protection at all. I did not fear Marik physically—I carried a dagger still, and felt certain I could at least hold him off. But I feared that demon master with all my soul. Oh, to be a Dragon—*idiot!* Tell them! Call them with truespeech and warn them!

If I had stopped to think I wouldn't have done it—but I have never been accused of too much thought. I closed my eyes and concentrated.

"*Akor? Akor, my brother? Eldest Shikrar, do you hear me? It is Lanen who calls.*" I waited a moment in silence, repeated myself, still no answer. I didn't know how to do what I needed to do, so I simply opened my mind as best I could and more or less yelled. "*I send warning to the Greater Kindred. There is on this island a demon master, by name Caderan, who is in league with the Merchant Marik. They seek to negotiate with you. They plot some mischief, but I cannot tell what. If I should die, warn Lord Akor, I pray you. Be 'ware!*"

There was no reply. I had no way of knowing if I had been heard or not, and once I took a moment to think about it I blushed there in the trees and groaned silently. If Caderan could detect such things I was dead where I stood. And how many thousands of years had the Kindred been looking after themselves with no help from my worthy self? I realised I had called them simply out of my fear, my helplessness and my anger at Marik. I hoped Akor, if he heard me, would not be too angry. Perhaps no one had heard a thing, perhaps I had to be closer. . . .

Then a voice came in my mind. "*You have been heard, Lanen Maransdatter. Shikrar speaks. We thank you for your warning. Are you in present danger?*" His voice was dispassionate but kind. At least he didn't sound angry.

I pondered the question, and found that the contact had relieved my fears. I concentrated and replied, "*I'm not certain, but I don't think so.*"

"*You have our gratitude. If danger threatens, do not fear to call upon us for such assistance as we may give. Farewell.*"

I breathed a small, noiseless sigh of relief. I hated to ask for help, but once offered I would not refuse it. I smiled to myself. Shikrar had a kinder heart than he admitted to.

Now all I had to worry about was outwaiting Marik here on this lonely path. He and Caderan were speaking quietly about the size of the Harvest and other small matters, and seemed prepared from their voices to wait until midnight if need be, when of a sudden Marik groaned.

"My lord?" said Caderan, his voice touched with just the right amount of concern.

"Unh. The lansip has worn off. Damn it to all the Hells, why now!" His silken voice was rough with pain, though I couldn't imagine what from.

They say all knowledge comes to those who wait.

"Such conditions have no cure and few releases from suffering, my lord," said Caderan, with what almost sounded like a trace of smugness. "When you win back the Farseer, and not before, the ceaseless pain that plagues you will end forever. So much Magister Berys told me. That which you made was invested with much of your own essence, and long parting must needs be painful."

"You can stop preaching at me, sorcerer. I have lived with this for twenty-four years. There is nothing you can tell me about this pain that I have not long known." A low moan escaped him. "I have sworn it, I will find that thief and recover what is mine or die trying. But not here."

"My lord?"

"She may be coming but I won't stand here in the cold waiting for her. She must return to the camp eventually. Help me back along the path. I'll send out my guards for her when I get back to my chambers."

"As you wish, my lord," smarmed Caderan, and I heard their voices dwindle in the distance. I waited the best part of half an hour before I emerged from the trees.

I tried to think straight, to consider what I might say to Marik when he caught up with me—for he would, no doubt, I had nowhere to run—but my mind would not stay still. I was far too frightened, and my mind would not keep on my own danger no matter how I tried to force it. Instead, I considered what I had heard. I assumed that "undetected" meant he was to cross the Boundary, but what did he seek? Dragon gold? Perhaps—but that was only a rumour, and surely with this harvest of lansip leaves, and now fruit, there was no need to face such extreme danger for such a mundane metal, rare and valuable as it was.

I thought about this, for I could not bear to think about what he might want with me, or how powerless I was to stop him.

Akhor

It was well done, I had to admit. If I had thought for a year I could not have come up with a more dramatic way to introduce her to the Kindred.

I had settled my thoughts and let the Discipline of Calm soothe my emotions. It was early afternoon when I began the summoning.

Calling the Kindred to Council is neither swift nor simple. The full Council meets once every five years at midsummer; summoning all of us together in the meantime is difficult and tends to meet with resistance. Some are busy raising younglings (though not in these latter days); some have studies or travels of exploration that take their time; some of the Elders meditate for years on end and find the regular Council trouble enough.

I had convinced perhaps half of my people when Lanen's call rang out like a youngling in distress. *"**Akor? Akor, my brother?** dear friend dear one hear me **Eldest Shikrar, do you hear me?** anyone listen hear me **It is Lanen who calls** fear fear danger."*

That alone would have convinced any who doubted she had true-speech, let alone what followed.

*"**I send warning to the Greater Kindred.** I hope someone can hear me, hear me hear me me danger! **There is on this island a demon master, by name Caderan,** \voice of a Gedri boasting of his ties to the Rakshasa\ horrible man looks like a weasel he's proud of his corruption how sickening **who is in league with the Merchant Marik.** Damn him, fear danger sorrow loss fear \vision of the tall fair-haired hawk-nosed Merchant who had appeared at the place of Summoning\ **They seek to negotiate with you.** He spoke of preparations and walking undetected eight miles that's all Caderan could give him **They plot some mischief, but I cannot tell what.** Marik spoke of 'what he could bring out in safety' what does he seek I don't know **If I should die, warn Lord Akor, I pray you.** \great longing for Akor\ Danger to me now to you soon damn Marik **Be 'ware!** danger beware beware!"*

There was no mistaking the truth of that call, nor the fact that most of the Kindred heard it. It was not unknown—anyone could bespeak us all if they didn't care who heard. I instantly addressed my people in much the same manner, telling them that it was a special case, the subject of the Council meeting at the morrow's dawn, and that most of the danger was in the mind of the youngling. Shikrar told me he had answered her from the guardpost and that she was well. I had to leave it at that, for I had too many others to attend to. She was frightened, certainly, but his response seemed to relieve her fears. She did not bespeak us again.

It took some time to sort out all the replies, but in the end it seemed that most of my people would be there. Even Kédra welcomed the call as a distraction from the coming of his youngling.

I would have to tell Lanen how successful her call had been.

At sunset.

Lanen

I was stopped by Marik's guards about half a mile from the camp. They escorted me—kindly enough, for the most part—into the clearing where the cabins stood. Marik waited at the door to the largest. I walked up the few steps to the door with the guards right behind me.

Damn him, for all I knew about him he was still beautiful. His fair hair seemed to glow in the late-afternoon sun, his eyes grass-green and flecked with gold, his figure slim yet strong, making him appear far younger than he was. He spoke politely as he asked me to come in and sup with him. His voice showed no trace now of the pain I had heard earlier, and even though I knew he used his voice as a weapon I had to fight hard to stay angry.

No, Lanen, truth—I had to fight to keep from agreeing with everything he said.

I was thinking of so many things, I had forgotten the amulet he wore in Ilsa. They are, after all, designed to conceal their existence from those they affect.

"Good Lanen, come inside and be comfortable." I went in and took off my cloak. The guards closed the door as they left. "I thank you for answering my summons," said Marik. "I hope those great boors were reasonably polite."

"They stopped me on my walk and told me I was commanded to appear before you. One threatened to bind my hands if I did not come quietly," I replied, trying to sound more annoyed than frightened.

"Fools!" he cried. "I would never have ordered such a thing. Which was it, that I may punish him as he deserves?"

"It is of no matter, Marik." I swallowed, trying to keep my voice steady. "Why did you want to see me?"

He smiled at me, as though we were privy to a shared secret.

"Why, lady, I have just completed a morning's work that will make the House of Marik one of the wealthiest of the Merchant Houses. I thought I might invite you to celebrate that good fortune. And perhaps after we sup, we might speak more of your mother." He moved closer to me and dropped his voice to a register that melted my fear. "And perhaps speak more of ourselves. I would know you better, Lanen," he said, and he took my hand and carried it to his lips, kissing the back of it as I had been told some men did. Then he turned it over and kissed my palm, gently, tenderly, passionately.

I shivered, sick and thrilled at once. The thought of this man, who might well be my father, kissing me passionately made my stomach heave—but another part of my being had other ideas. My mind had its own firm opinion of Marik as my possible father, as one with a dark soul who dealt with demons, but my traitor body ached with sudden longing. I had never known a man, nor ever truly loved; and I had certainly never been romanced before, twisted as this was. It was the last thing I would have expected from him and I was completely unprepared.

I swayed slightly on my feet, and suddenly I was in his arms and his face was inches from mine. He even *smelled* wonderful, and infinitely desirable. His lips were on mine almost before I noticed. His kiss shuddered through me, jangling every nerve with desire flavoured with a taste of evil, of the deeply forbidden. It was irresistible. It was nauseating.

There was no more than a shred of my mind that held fast to reality. That small part cried out that it was nearly sunset, that one worthy of a genuine love waited for me, but my body had taken over and I didn't care. I am afraid that I let go my better side and kissed him back with all my strength.

He seemed a little shaken. He drew back after a minute and stared at me, his eyes glinting with something unreadable. "So there is a fire within, my lady of the horses. You have built your walls high and well, Lanen, but I shall overcome them." We kissed again. I felt stirrings I had not felt in years. I knew perfectly well that I should leave, but I could no more do that than fly.

Thank the Lady, the idiot moved too soon.

In the midst of a breathless pause (at least *I* was out of breath) while we clasped each other close, he murmured in my ear, "Lanen, lady, I know your secret, I know you have spoken with the Dragons, as I have. I pray you, sweet lady, tell me what you have learned, that we may be together in this as well."

Nothing else could have shocked me out of his spell. I drew away a little. "What?" I asked, my mind fogged with passion. "What did you say?"

"The Dragons, dear one," said Marik, with a glorious smile. He bent and kissed my throat, held me tighter against him, his hands strong and sensual against my back, murmuring, "I know you have been to them, you brave soul. Tell me, what did you speak of?"

My mind was clearing rapidly. I nearly drew away from him, but I managed to realise that I stood to gain more if I kept him believing that I was still helpless. It was not much of a pretence; I was still on the edge.

"Not a great deal, they wouldn't listen to me." I kissed him again, lightly, teasing. "What a thing to ask! Why do you want to know now, of all times!"

"Ah, sweeting, believe me, soon you won't want to speak!" he said laughingly, caressing me.

"Then tell me, you wicked soul, what is it you seek from them?" I asked, trying to sound playful. The words were out of my mouth before I realised they were the wrong ones. This time it was Marik who drew back. He stared at me, his false passion turned in an instant to a cold-eyed suspicion. I tried to feign innocence and went to kiss him again to cover my confusion, but he broke from me. I met his gaze with as open an expression as I could, but he was well versed in lies as I was not.

His eyes narrowed in anger. "And who has told you that I seek anything from the Dragons?" I did not answer. He stepped close again, grabbing my right arm roughly in a grip stronger than I would have expected from him. "Answer me, fool child, or I'll kill you despite all."

Obviously he knew only two ways to use women, seduction or bullying. I can't bear that kind of cowardice, and as I've said, I have a terrible temper. Always have. And all the nausea, the loathing I felt for him (and which now included myself), poured through me and was transmuted into pure anger as I realised I was being threatened by the man who had just enticed me into releasing my passions.

Did I mention that I'm left-handed?

Just like my mother.

My first blow was not from my fist, since my knee was in a much better position, but the second one was. I had never struck with all my force as an adult—even with Walther I had pulled back a little. I have to admit it felt wonderful to see him drop. He hardly even groaned.

I decided it was time to leave. Fast.

I snatched up my cloak and looked frantically round for something, anything that could help me escape the guards outside. I peered through a crack in the door and saw them both waiting outside, so far unaware that anything had happened.

I grabbed up what looked like Marik's sea chest and took firm hold, then called out. "Guards! Guards, help, your master is ill, come quickly!"

Well-trained idiots, at least. They burst into the room just as I had assumed they would. I timed my run and, I must say, it worked rather well. I barrelled into the one in front at full tilt, the sea chest held before me. He, of course, obligingly fell back onto his comrade with a grunt. I threw the sea chest at the head of the one on top just for good measure and he fell back, satisfyingly motionless and still on top of his comrade. I leapt over the tangle of bodies and ran for the trees and the Boundary as fast as I could go.

I got in among the trees in moments, heading northwest to avoid the camp and any awkward questions. I assumed that the guards would sort themselves out far too soon for my comfort. I ran with all my might.

I realised that the sun was just setting as I ran. I laughed aloud, once, for sheer relief that I had escaped alive, but I soon sobered (besides, laughing took too much breath). What did it matter that I was in time for my meeting? Blessed Lady, how could I face Akor after this? And what in all the world should I do afterwards?

I was furious at Marik, angry at myself, angry that I was angry at this moment when at last I would see Akor in the light of day. I tried as I ran to clear my mind of Marik and his lies, and of the sick passion I had felt; I was amazed at the strength of it. Then my mind whispered, *Amulet, Lanen. He was wearing the amulet he wore in Illara, or a better one. It pressed hard against your right breast as you embraced, remember?*

As before, once I realised I had been influenced by a spell much of its force dissipated; but I could not so easily make my body forget the feelings it had been roused to. Still, fear and running helped—as did a certain wild exultation I could not explain, as though by defeating Marik physically I had struck a blow for my freedom. I expected at any moment to hear the outcry, or worse to hear Marik's guards pelting along behind me, but so far there was nothing—and already the Boundary fence loomed before me in the gathering dusk. I ran across the wide pathway before it and stood close against the fence, seeking the lengthening shadow of the trees in case they found me. I caught my breath and listened for Akor. I was not in the place we had agreed on, and I did not dare call to him in truespeech in case another heard. I could only wait, trembling and talking to myself, hoping he would find me by smell or some other sense I might not know of. Fortunately, I had plenty to say to me.

Right, my girl. So you have awakened at last. Is that so terrible? More a reason to rejoice, I would have thought. You are not so immune as you had thought, there is a woman in you after all. And twenty-four years is long enough a maid!

But such a man! He sickens me, he might be my father, I am so ashamed.

He had an amulet. You were responding to the demons, not to him. There is no cause for shame in this. Anger, yes, but the shame is his. It is no crime for you to have such feelings. As for Marik, it is all one; he will not take you in again.

I would kill him first, I thought, listening still for signs of pursuit.

You would not be so foolish. Remember what Jamie said. "Never kill unless you are forced to it, Lanen. The souls so ripped from life do not sleep quietly, and neither does the one who severed them from the world." But come, Lanen, have done! Turn to other things while you can. This is the moment you have awaited all these years. Akor will be with you, just the two of you in concord. There will be no barriers between you for this once. This may be your last speech with any of the Kindred, Lanen, and it may be your one best chance to speak with the one you truly—with Akor.

There were still no signs that the hunt was up and following me. I couldn't understand it, though I blessed the chance. I didn't think

I had done Marik any serious damage, though I certainly knocked him out for a while, as well perhaps as the guard on top. But where was the other?

And where was Akor? Could he not find me? *Oh, blessed Lady, let him find me swiftly.* I took in a deep breath to steady myself, and as I breathed out, I let myself whisper just below hearing, "Kordeshkistriakor."

The very mention of his name seemed a talisman against the false feelings Marik's amulet had engendered. It was as if a bright light had risen in my heart, and by that light the candle flame I had been watching so closely disappeared altogether. I was still terrified, still listening for the hue and cry I knew must come, but of Marik as a man I thought no more.

I could not stand still. I wrapped my cloak close about me and started moving quickly and quietly away west along the Boundary, away from the camp. Akor's true name rang in me like a bell on a winter's morning, crisp and clear and full of promise, giving me hope through my fear, but I had to keep moving. Perhaps I imagined it—I was some long way from the camp, after all—but I thought I began to hear voices crying out in the distance. As I walked in the shadows and prayed for Akor to find me, the last light of the sun lay bright on the lands about me, a gentle end to the day as the world knew it, and I could barely understand how it could be so unconcerned. The light turned the very air golden, granting a last warming glow to the ill-dressed trees and lending even the fading grass a memory of summer splendour. I wanted storms, or a mist to hide me, something as violent as the fear and loathing that had gripped me, but the day ended in calm beauty, ignoring me entirely. I could hardly bear it.

Akhor

The startling thing was that I could feel her approach. The thoughts of her heart were often easy for me to read, but I had not known that kind of bond since I was a youngling first learning to screen out the hearts and minds of others. I heard her say my true name somehow (not in the Language of Truth, but something akin). From that moment I felt her every step, I could very nearly see out of her eyes, and most certainly I felt her fear. I even saw briefly the image of the one she had warned us against.

I called to her, close focussed, in truespeech. She was startled but pleased. **"Yes my friend?** more than friend dear one \oh dear Lady what am I to do?\ "

"Say nothing more, keep silent Lanen for our friendship's sake!" Shikrar at least had surely heard. Where to go?

"I know not where you are, but can you find the place of Summoning the Merchants use? It is some way west and north of where we have been meeting. You will know it easily, there is a narrow way with a gate. Pass into the small space that extends a little into the trees; I shall await you.

"And now, little sister, I must ask you to do something very difficult. You must see a small opening, no larger than your hand can make, and send through it to me only those thoughts we may allow Shikrar to hear. You must give me your thanks for telling you of tomorrow's Council meeting, and that you will wait our decision. Clear your mind first of any other thoughts, concentrate, and send those words to me through that small opening. No larger than it must be, little one."

I was obscurely disturbed by my capacity for deception, but I could not allow this one chance to pass by. I feared the Council would find against me—how could they not?—and I must obey their commands. What I planned to do this night would frighten most of them, but I intended to break no more laws. We would speak as we had before. I would not place my Kindred in danger, and though I would not be so secretive as Shikrar would have me, I would keep such barriers of Discipline about me as I must for the safety of my people.

I felt her make a deep effort to concentrate and try to rid her mind of everything save what Shikrar needed to hear. It was not a bad attempt, and certainly a vast improvement on what had gone before. She learned quickly.

"I thank you, my friend oh dear friend. **I fear what your Council might say** oh please let them understand **but I shall abide by your wishes in all things. I shall wait to hear from you tomorrow night."**

It was very convincing. The last portion was quite clear of underthought. I was pleased; she had a natural talent for truespeech and needed only a little instruction and some practice. *"That was well done,"* I told her.

"And now, little sister," I sent to her, controlled, calm, keeping my heart closed to her as best I could. *"Come to me."*

Lanen

I had come by chance near the place he meant, and as I walked and listened to him I found the little square space with its gate. Somehow, once I was inside, hidden by the trees, separated by only an ancient fence from safety and love, I lost much of my fear. Let them search! How should they find me? And who would dare attack me, with Akor no distance away? I wept then, for relief, then very deliberately loosed my hair from its braid. Let him see me as few others had. It was only fair.

I tried to think of how to tell him about what had happened, or of any of the thousand questions I had always wanted to ask, but I could barely think at all. I felt him near, all my being was moving me, moment by moment, away from fear and towards Akor.

Akor.

The very name hung between us like a silken cord, pulling me towards where he waited; I could feel it tugging at me.

Akor, Akor.

Akhor

I waited in hiding, that she should see me only when she herself requested it. I held tightly to Calm, breathed as that Discipline demanded, tried to keep my mind clear of my foolish thoughts.

I had thought I was prepared, but I could not have known. None of the Disciplines, none of my training, nothing in all my centuries had prepared me for that bond, unspoken, unexpected, unrealised in its fullness until that hour. Nothing could have prepared me for the sound of her voice so full of what I was feeling, for the sight of her in the daylight seen clearly at last.

When she whispered up to me through the trees, trembling, her heart full of love, I nearly stopped breathing. It was as though her words were tied to the strings of my heart, and each note plucked at my pulse like wild, distant music. I forgot my strong resolve, forgot my determination to remain cautious and wary, forgot everything but the sound of her voice and that she seemed to me in all ways more wondrous than any creature I had ever known.

"Akor?" I whispered. "Akor, are you there?"

"I am here, dear one," I replied.

And with those words I released all fears. I would not think of Shikrar, or of the Kindred, or of what might happen. For once in my long life I would live as if there would be no tomorrow.

I felt the Fire stir within me. No more boundaries. There were only the two of us now, and whatever truth we might find together. I moved forward slowly into a small gap in the trees, trying to still this mad riot in myself. I remembered at least to speak quietly for her.

She gasped as I came into her sight. I did not have to ask why. Were we differently made, I would have done so as well.

Her hair like a living waterfall waved gently in the breeze, gleaming the same colour as the sunset, and her eyes were grey as winter storms. She was altogether beautiful, tall for her kind and lithe as I had seen her that first day, and her mind and heart were open to me. There was the true beauty of her.

I found myself wondering what colour her soulgem would be.

Lanen

I will never forget seeing him in the light of the setting sun.

He was more glorious in the day than he had been by the light of the moon. Even in that golden light he shone silver. The sun caught his soulgem as he leaned down to me and it sent out a flash of emerald fire. His eyes were green as well, of the same hue, as though the same fire burned behind all. He seemed for a moment to be the work of some unimaginable jeweller. I could see his scales now, how smoothly they slid over one another. And I had been wrong about his face, it was not truly a mask. There was a wide ridge of bone on top, of a piece with the horns that curved back and up—but below that was what looked like soft skin with small scales on it. I longed to reach out and touch, see what it felt like.

And he said, "My dear one, you are welcome." I didn't even bother to ask how he knew my thoughts. He came close, close, his head near my hand, as he had been the first night when he told me his name. And his voice was soft and more full of song than ever man's could be.

"I permit, Lanen. Touch me. Know that I am here, that I am real."

"That I feel as you do."

I began to reach out and found my hands would not obey. I stared, lost in wonder at this wonder before me. Slowly, slowly, I reached out one hand and touched his face on the long ridge below his eyes.

It was warm, even that smooth silver bone was warm.

I moved my hand slowly, slowly, in awe at what I did, to the soft skin below. My hand trembled as I was trembling, I could bear only the lightest touch of him. The scales were no larger than my fingernail, the skin was soft as a snake's.

I snatched my hand away as though I had been stung, clenched both my fists at my waist as I tried to hold in the emotions that swept through me.

"No," I said, and began to weep.

"And still when we meet you make seawater. But these are not tears of joy, my Lanen."

"Don't call me that!"

He drew away from me. "Forgive me! I thought . . . no, I am certain. I can hear your heart as though it were my own, and in this great folly I know we are one." He came back close, but stayed on his side of the Boundary. "I have not known such a love before, Lanen, but I cannot deny it now. My heart beats with yours, I hear your lightest thought. Do you tell me you do not feel as I know you do?"

I couldn't look at him any longer. "I meant never to tell you! I thought this was no more than my own insanity. I would come to you and you would bring me to my senses with your calmness, calling me little one, littling, so I would realise how impossible this all is. And there you stand talking of love, as though we were one Kindred."

He bowed his head and closed his eyes. It was as he had said, in some way beyond knowing we were one. I could feel his sorrow.

I could not think. My heart was both confused and sure, my head whirling with what was and could not be. But truth calls out truth, and I could not help but tell him my own.

"I will not, I cannot lie to you, Akor. Akor, my dear one." The great gleaming eyes were fastened on me. "I love you, Akor, beyond sense and beyond reason. Not because you are a Dragon, not because you are the first of your people to speak with me. I love *you*." I bowed my head. "Our laws, our forms, even this wall of wood stand between us. But I love you, now and always, may the Lady help me. May she help us both."

Silence fell between us as full as my heart. The sun sank behind the trees and twilight was upon us.

"Please, Akor, say something," I said. "Speak to me."

Akhor

I did not trust myself to speak. I did not know what would come out.

I did not care.

At first I could say nothing but her name.

"Lanen. Lanen. Lanen."

She covered her face with her hands. I knew she wept, but she seemed almost to be laughing at the same time.

I reached out to her, putting my foreleg close to her. "Will you allow?" I asked softly.

She looked up, saw my clawed hand, looked back at me and nodded.

It must have been frightening but she never flinched. I spread my claws back and wide and touched her face with the inside of my palm, where we are most sensitive.

Even water was not so soft as her skin.

I trembled. I, Khordeshkhistriakhor, Silver King of the Kantrishakrim, trembled in wonder at the feel of a woman's skin. I moved my hand away that I might not harm her by accident. Surely the lightest touch of my claws would rend that fragile hide.

"My soul to the Winds, Lanen Kaelar, I am lost as you are lost," I said softly. "And though we know this love cannot be as love for our own kind, at the least we may stand together as friends."

"At the least. But still the Boundary lies between us. Your people will know if I cross it."

"That is so. But they will not know if I cross it, not instantly, and it is in my heart to take you to a place where we may talk for a few hours in peace. We need only wait for true dark, and so late in the year it will not be long coming."

Indeed, it was nearly dark already.

"What will happen if they find us?" she asked quietly.

"I do not know, dear one, but they will have to reckon with me to get to you."

Lanen

I was distracted by the sound of people, not too near but not very far away either. I drew a deep breath, knowing that I risked all by telling him, knowing that I must speak. "I thank you for that, dear friend, but I must tell you, much has happened to me this day. I am hunted now by my own people, for Marik tried to kill me and I escaped him."

"Ah," he said sadly. "So that is the fear in your voice—and something else, I think. Why did he seek your death?"

The noise of pursuit grew louder. "Akor, there is no time. They will find me soon. Dear friend, forgive me, I never meant to bring you into this coil, but if we are to go somewhere, we must leave now."

"Very well, little sister," he replied, the sadness still soft in his voice.

"Is it far to walk?" I asked, hoping it wouldn't be. My legs still trembled.

"Dear one, it would take days to walk there. No, we must fly."

To say I was taken by surprise is like saying the Kai is a river—it's true, but it misses the scale of the thing. All I could think of was one of the dragon ballads, in which the villain of the piece "fell from the earth to the sky in the clutch of the vast-winged beast." It had always struck me as a particularly terrible thing, but time was short and I wasn't going to ask questions.

"Lanen, will you come with me?" he asked, and in his voice lay all my future.

"Yes, Akor. With all my heart," I said. "But how shall we . . . ?"

He looked up. The first stars were out, twilight but a brighter memory in the west. "Wait there but a moment," he said, and was gone in a muted clap of thunder.

Flying. In my wildest dreams I had imagined such a thing, but I never really thought—

"Come, Lanen," said Akor from behind me.

There he stood, gleaming silver even in near-darkness. And there was no Boundary.

"Swiftly now, your pursuers approach. Climb up on my shoulders, there is a place above my wings where I believe you might sit."

I saw the place he meant. It was half again the girth of the roundest-bellied horse ever made. *Bareback and with no reins,* I thought. *And a damn sight farther to fall.* Still, I climbed up—or rather, he lay down as flat as he could on the ground and I clambered up the last few feet.

I fell off as soon as he stood up.

"This isn't going to work," I told him, rubbing my backside and brushing off the leaves. "I haven't fallen off anything with four feet since I was a child." I grinned up at him. "Shame you don't have a mane to hang on to."

"Lanen, we must hurry," whispered Akor urgently. "Will you try again?"

"Believe me, it won't work, your neck is too wide there for me to get my legs around." Again the words of the ballad flashed through my mind. Couldn't hurt to mention it. "Could you carry me in your . . . your hands?"

Suddenly, for a moment, he was again a stranger, a creature out of my ken, a *Dragon.* Did he call them hands? Claws? Forelegs? He had been gentle enough, certainly, but while he was flying? The slightest mistake could crush me, rend me, before he even noticed.

"I shall try." And the moment was gone, as I heard in his voice the tenderness that was almost more than I could bear. His very words were song, they poured over me in a wash of melody that stirred my blood and caressed me all at once, soothed away all my fears. "Come, dear one. Come with me, let me carry you to the star-home, the Wind-home, the Place of All Songs."

I walked to him as in a trance. I would have walked off a cliff, I think, knowing he would fly swift as thought and be there to catch me.

He picked me up, made a seat for me with his hands, so I sat in one and the other held me gently and gave me something to hang on to. His warm, armour-plated chest was at my back.

I felt him crouch, heard as he lifted his great wings. I braced myself as best I could.

There was a sudden jerk as he sprang into the sky, a sound like a far-off storm as his wings beat down again and again, working to get us above the trees.

And we were flying.

xi

THE WIND OF CHANGE

Lanen

How shall I describe flying to you, who will never know it?

I was terrified at first. The wind rushed past me with the speed of a summer storm and a loud roar filled my ears. Akor was carrying me close against his chest—perhaps he was trying to keep me out of the wind—at any rate, it meant that I was being carried facedown and I could see how fast we were going. And with every downbeat of his wings we rose a little, and as they rose we fell. It was quite sickening at first.

When at last I dared to open my eyes, it was like looking down at the trees from the highest cliff in the world *after* you have jumped off. There was nothing between me and the longest drop you can imagine save the clawed hands of a Dragon and the strong, rhythmic beat of his wings. The twilight lingered longer up here, and I could see what passed below brushed and blurred with shadow and with speed.

I was terrified.

I gripped his hands with all my strength. They felt solid as stone, which reassured me a little. Also they were warm with a Dragon's inner fire, and I began to remember that it was *Akor* who held me. That helped a little more. I began to loosen my grip slightly, my muscles aching from being so tightly clenched. His hands held me safe and strong, and ever above and behind me I heard the beat of those great wings. After a time, even the rising and falling gave me comfort.

I would not have believed it possible, but eventually wonder overcame fear and I began to look about me. Just then, Akor's voice sang in my mind, *"These are the lands of my people, dear one. You are greatly honoured. No member of your race has ever seen these hills and valleys, these deep forests, that are home and safety to us. Look well, Lanen Kaelar,"* and I could hear the smile in his true-speech. *"This is the abode of Dragons."*

I looked as well as I could and desperately wished it were day-light. But even in the last light of the sun (which as I say lingered a little on high) I could see the hills and forests over which we passed. There were open fields here and there, some scattered with dark dots that might have been cattle. It was too dark to see anything much beyond the general lay of the land, but I saw what I could only have guessed from the ground—that the island was cut in half by a range of mountains that ran from east to west. I could see no details, but they loomed ahead of us as Akor flew north.

I was growing distinctly cold, despite Akor's warm chest plates behind my back, and it was getting harder to breathe. I think I would have been near frozen were it not for being held close to that living source of fire.

After what seemed like forever (though later I realised was lit-tle more than the half of an hour) I felt something change, a shift in his body. By now it was full dark and not worth keeping my eyes open against the wind. I was cold and miserable and fighting for air, but I wanted to know what was happening. I tried to ask him, but my voice disappeared even as I spoke.

It was then that I understood with a shock why all the race of the Kindred had the Language of Truth, while to my people it was the rarest of gifts. How else could they speak to one another, here where the air was thinner than on the tallest mountain, the wind roaring past them and they separated by at least two wings' distance? Surely the Lady—no, they called on the Winds, of course—surely the Winds had gifted them so they might speak with each other in this world they shared only with the birds. And the Dragons sang, too, I could hear it in their speaking. The music they would make must surpass belief.

I wanted to bespeak Akor, ask how long we had yet to go, but I remembered he had said that I could easily be heard by others. I kept my peace and concentrated on breathing. I longed for moonlight.

From my position, in those moments when I managed to open my eyes, I could only see the stars nearest the horizon.

Akor's thoughts rose soft in mine. *"Forgive me, little one, I had forgot you did not know. Our journey is nearly done. In a moment I shall glide down the Wind. Do not be afraid when the ground comes up to meet us."* I could hear the gentle merriment in his thoughts. *"I know all is new to you, but I have been flying for a very, very long time. You need have no fear."*

When we started to spiral down everything changed. It was the best part of the flight for me. Akor's great wings were outstretched and still as he glided down; the wind still rushed past, but it was not so cold nor so turbulent as when he was beating the air. My eyes seemed to recover a little as my breathing eased; I saw dimly below us, in the center of the spiral, a large wooded hill with a clearing at its foot, and as we came closer I saw a darkness that might have been a pool at the edge of the clearing.

We were very close to the ground now but still moving quickly. I am afraid I yelped a bit when he started beating the air backwards. I don't know what I expected, I had seen birds land before, but this was a bit different.

He landed on his back legs, those vast wings flapping as he fought to stay upright. It seemed very awkward to me, but he neither dropped me nor fell over, so I supposed it was good enough.

He put me down gently. "Are you well, little sister?" he asked. He seemed out of breath, which cheered me. It was the first sign of physical effort I had seen in him, and it made him seem a little more human, or at least a little less distant in kind.

Before my mind's eye flashed the image of that slim silver-haired man with Akor's eyes. I must not think of that.

"I'm frozen solid, but aside from that, yes, I'm fine. Was it very difficult to fly carrying me?"

His laughter made steam clouds in the cold, clear night. "You are lighter by far than cattle. Were it not for having to land upright, I would hardly have noticed I bore you."

"How do you usually land?" I asked. I did not wonder whether I might ask or not. All fear of Marik, all fear of the others of his Kindred had left me, and deep in my soul I knew that now we were here, there need be no long thought before a question was either asked or answered. We were a little like two children finding themselves together without a guardian, delighting in the privacy and whispering secrets together in the dark.

"We are made to land on four feet. It is fortunate that it was I who carried you. I know of no other of my people who has practiced such a landing."

"You've *practiced* this?"

It was amazing to see a creature so noble and so naturally frightening actually manage to look sheepish. "I have. Ah, Lanen, you have found me out! But come, you are cold. My chambers are at hand— if you will bring wood I shall make a fire for you and tell you how I came to do such a thing." He looked around and spied a huge log. "That will do to start," he muttered, and effortlessly picked it up in his mouth. It wasn't until he tried to say something around it that I started laughing. He gave me an unreadable look and moved towards a darker opening in the dark side of the hill.

I gathered a few smaller logs, still laughing. Not that the young tree trunk he carried wouldn't burn all night, but I needed to feel useful. Besides, I was trying to make sense of my feelings. I watched the creature I had such love for walking on four feet, lifting and stretching wide silver wings stiff from the flight, long tail trailing after.

For an instant I saw a giant lizard with wings and was disgusted.

Then he spoke to my thoughts with that voice that chimed in my heart. *"The entrance is here beneath the trees; I shall await you."*

I breathed a sigh of relief. For he was again Kordeshkistriakor, a creature ancient and wondrous, and I did not care what shape he had, for I loved most the soul inside the form.

I followed him towards the hillside, away from the clearing in which we had landed. There was only starlight to see by, but the night was so clear it was enough. The pool I had seen from above lay open to the sky, and showed the vain stars their glorious reflections.

Akor had gone towards two of the tallest trees. They grew side by side and seemed in the starlight to be guardians, old friends who had watched together over this place for many years. He stopped before them, lowered his head and slipped between. I was amazed, there had not seemed that much of a gap. When I came close enough to see, I found there was easily fifteen feet between the two, though their ancient roots effectively blocked the passage between. It would surely be difficult for one of the Kindred to enter who did not know those roots well. It was bad enough for me, clambering over them in the starlit darkness.

Just past the trees there was a low passageway in the rock no wider than the gap between the trees, but tall enough for me to walk upright with headroom to spare. I am astounded to this day that Akor could get in and out of that passageway, but he did so with no trouble.

I took a deep breath before entering. I have never liked caves—in fact, I am afraid of them—and here I was, facing a walk in complete darkness down a passageway to I did not know where. Did the passage narrow ahead? Perhaps it came to a sudden end and Akor had forgotten that I couldn't fly. I gripped the wood, rough in my arms, and forced myself to ignore such idiocy.

I managed to get perhaps five or six steps inside before I stopped.

I am ashamed to admit it, but the cave, the thought of a mountain of stone above me, would not be ignored, and with that senseless fear came the memory of every stupid childish tale I had ever heard about Dragons. In my terror I imagined the floor of the passage littered with human bones and worse things and I stopped moving altogether.

"Akor?" I called out weakly. I tried to force my voice to a semblance of courage but I failed completely. "Akor, where are you? I can't see. Are you there?"

I heard something moving not far away. I jumped, my heart began to race, I dropped the wood I was carrying and put my back against the wall. I was groping for my dagger when his voice came back, loud in the darkness. "Lanen, I am here. Wait only a moment while I set Fire to this wood."

That was the longest moment in the history of the world. I could not go back, I could not go on, I held back a scream by the merest thread. I, Lanen Kaelar, who only moments ago had been high in the air above the world and had managed to look about and forget fear, whimpered in the stony darkness.

Suddenly I heard a loud crack and a swift breath, and light blossomed like the first dawn of the world, golden, warm and comforting.

I looked about me. On the ground was only the earthen floor of the passage. The walls were smooth, the passage short before and behind me. I began to breathe again, to feel much less afraid. How powerful mere darkness was! When I stopped shaking I gathered up the wood I had dropped and walked forward into the light.

At first all I could see was Akor, the fire, and the fact that he was in a large space. I breathed easier. A large space would not be so hard to bear. I laid my wood in a pile by the entrance, for he had broken that whole huge log in two pieces and set it alight.

Then I began to look about me.

Whatever you have heard about a dragon's hoard is both less and more than the truth. I saw no artifacts, no crowns of fallen kings, nor cups, nor stores of coin.

But there was more gold in that place than I had ever imagined existed in the world. The walls of the cave were covered with it to the depth of some inches (I could tell from the deep engraving that covered much of it), and the gold was set all over with precious gems and with nacre. Even a good quarter of the floor in one corner seemed made of solid gold, and extending towards the passage opening was a path of the same stuff, as though it were alive and growing towards the daylight.

I must have stood in the entryway for a full minute, my jaw hanging open.

Akor bowed. "Welcome, Lanen, to my chambers. Come in and warm yourself. I hope your fright is past? I did not know you feared close spaces. It is not unknown even among my people, though it is unusual. Does it help to know that in this corner of the cavern there is an opening above? It runs straight up through the hill and opens on clear air, on starlight and night breezes. When the moon rises you will be able to see it from here."

I shook myself. The news was welcome, but I had to ask. "Akor, what is this place? And why is it—why is there so much—where did it—why do you—oh!" I gave up. I was so astounded I could not make sense of my words or my thoughts.

"Lanen? Come, bring your wood close here where the fire is laid."

Akhor

I was disconcerted and a little sad. I had hoped for a different reaction from the first Gedri ever to see the chambers of the Kantri. She seemed shocked. I had hoped that the firelight reflecting from the *khaadish* would make her feel welcome.

She could not take her eyes away from it.

I was growing impatient with her. To be distracted by such a thing, when even a youngling knew—

Akhor, Akhor, I chided myself. *She is not a youngling. Perhaps she has never seen* khaadish *before.*

"Lanen, is your fear still upon you? It is nothing to be concerned with, it is only *khaadish,* it is a metal like any other. More beautiful, perhaps, and certainly softer." I gouged a trench with my foreclaw as she watched.

She finally heard the disapproval in my voice. "Akor, my friend, forgive me. I did not mean to greet you so in your home." She bowed, her eyes on me now, as I had come to know her. My impatience melted like spring snow. "But you did not warn me. I defy any human to step in here and retain the power of speech! Akor, this is more gold than I have ever heard of. Where does it come from?"

"Gold?" I replied, surprised. It was her turn to amaze me. "*Khaadish* is gold? Oh, Lanen, you make me wise beyond all bearing!"

"What have I said? Akor?"

Lanen

He had turned his head away from me in the most human gesture I had seen him make. I didn't need to ask its meaning.

"My friend, forgive me, I never meant to hurt you. What have I said?"

He answered me with his face still turned away. "In the days when our peoples lived together, there was much concern among the Gedri for 'gold.' It is said they killed one another for it." His voice grew even heavier. "In those days, one of the Gedri held hostage a youngling, and would have killed it for the sake of 'gold.' I never knew what it was when I heard the tale, and none could tell me. I could not imagine what precious, life-giving thing it could be, which they so desired and the Kantri possessed. At one time I wondered if that was their word for our soulgems. I understand now why one of the laws between our peoples in those days was that we must meet in the open, never in the chambers of the Kantri. Ah, Lanen, your knowledge wounds me. For so base a thing!"

I kept my voice as calm as I could. I had never imagined so sen-

sitive a soul behind all that armour. I had hurt him, for all his strength
and my weakness.

"Come, Akor. Speak with me yet, of your kindness. Why do you
call this 'kadish' base? In my lands it is of great value. I have never
seen such wealth in my life. A tiny portion of this is the worth of my
father's farm and every soul on it. Why do you call it base?"

"Because it is!" Akor spoke now with more vehemence than I had
yet heard from him. "Why do you give it worth? Creatures have
worth, their deeds, their words, their thoughts or the work of their
hands have worth, but metal? It is senseless." He turned back to me,
his eyes blazing, his soulgem shining so bright it scattered a faint
emerald light. "Child of the Gedri, I shall tell you a truth that no one
of your race has ever known. This metal, this *khaadish*, is part of my
being, it is part of my race, but we know it is of no value save for its
beauty. *It is natural to us, Lanen. Where we sleep we change the
ground to this stuff.*"

I was silent, trying to understand. Akor kept looking at me, waiting for a reply.

"You change the ground?" I said at last. "But why?"

"There is no why, it simply happens. Where the Kantri sleep, the
ground will change to *khaadish*. That is the way of things." Some
of the intensity had left him, thank the Lady. He even managed a
small hiss of laughter when he added, "We find it most comfortable
to lie upon, which is just as well. Some believe that the earth would
suffer too greatly from our heat without *khaadish* to protect it, others believe that there is something in our armour that works with
the ground to produce it. No matter. It happens." He shifted until
he sat on his haunches in what looked like a formal position and
asked me, "Why do your people put so great a value on this worthless metal that they will kill for it?"

I wished I had a sensible answer to give him, but there was only
the truth. "I have no idea," I told him honestly. "It is beautiful,
certainly—you yourself have used it to give beauty to this cave—but
beyond that I cannot see its value. My fa—Hadron raised horses, and
they were of worth to other men. We bartered for goods or accepted
silver for them—and on rare occasions, gold—and with those metals could buy food for our horses and goods for ourselves, because
others were willing to exchange them. But with all his faults, Hadron
never coveted gold. He only cared about his horses."

Still Akor was silent. I could almost hear him trying to come to terms with this new knowledge that brought sorrow. After a little, I added, "I have not killed for this, Akor, nor set its worth above other things. I am sorry that it has been a source of ill will between our peoples—has anything not?—but I beg you, do not see in me the act of another."

He changed his position then and came down to me, all contrition. "Forgive me, littling. You are quite right. It is hard to remember, sometimes, how swiftly your lives hurry past. It has been many lifetimes for your race—almost as if you blamed me for the decision of the Firstborn. I beg your pardon, Lanen. You must keep reminding me."

The firelight had begun to dim. Dragonfire, it seems, burned hotter than normal fire, for that great log was nearly burned out. It had served its purpose, though, for my chill was gone. I felt warm and welcome. "Does not your fire need more wood, littling?" he asked.

That was when I did one of the bravest and (had I known it) wisest things of my life.

"No," I said. "Let it die out. Then I can't be dazzled by the look of this place, nor by the look of you." I grinned up at him. "The best talks I ever had were at night when the lights were all out. I don't have a blanket, but my cloak will serve, and if you will let me sit near you I'm not likely to get cold." I looked around. "I still don't like caves, but then again I don't think you'll let anything get me."

I was rewarded by a blast of steam. I was surprised, but the warmth was wonderful even though I had thought I was warm enough. I discovered that it was the Akorian version of a guffaw. "Bravely spoken, Lanen, well said! Let no creature small or great enter here, where Akor the Silver King guards Lanen of the Gedrishakrim!"

And just like that the air was cleared of old anger, of the foolishness of others, of anything that was not of the two of us. Laughter is more powerful than many arguments.

As the fire died we arranged ourselves. I was astounded to hear myself ordering him in jest to shift his tail, move his wing this way or that to accommodate me. I think he was a little surprised, too, but he was also amused, and it seemed that among them it was also true that friendship has such licence. We found ourselves curled up together in the corner on the floor of gold (which by the bye was *not* comfortable for me at all), under the opening that led to the sky. I sat leaning against his warm side wrapped in my cloak. His head rested on his forelegs, his wings folded back so they were out of my way. We watched the dying fire flicker on the wall, enjoying simply being together as we believed no two of our races had ever been.

"It is quite beautiful here, Akor," I said, quietly. "I meant to tell you that. And the firelight on the go—on the kadish is warm and comforting."

"I am glad, littling." He looked at me with unfathomable eyes. "And I am glad also that the fear you carried has left you. Will you speak with me of this?"

"Not now, please—soon, in a moment, but this is so lovely I don't want to spoil it."

"Very well. Then what shall we speak of, here in this loveliness, across the long aeons of separation?"

I grinned. "To begin with, what in the world made you practice landing like that?"

He laughed, as I had hoped he would. Nice and warm. "It was foolishness, as I suspect you know," he replied. "I had dreamt—I was recovering after my last Weh sleep and the *ferrinshadik* was heavy upon me, and I had to do something about it or burst, so I imagined that I had somehow a friend among the Gedri who wished to fly."

He had to tell me what *ferrinshadik* was; it was a familiar feeling, and I was pleased to learn that someone had made a word for it. As for his upright landing, he sounded proud of himself even as he made light of it. "Awkward it is still, but it worked." I heard the grin in his voice. "I am glad you did not see me practicing. You would never have consented to leave the ground."

The fire was dying.

"Probably not." I shook my head. "I still can't believe I was flying. It was wonderful."

"Would that you had wings, my Lanen. I think flying would delight you."

And I sighed with longing for wings, and scales, and the Winds to bear me up.

Akhor

She took in a deep breath and blew it all out at once. Very peculiar. I had to know. "What does that signify?"

She was silent a moment. "It's called a sigh," she said, with a kind of melancholy in her voice. "I'm not sure I can tell you just what it means, though I thought I heard one from you not so long ago. I was sitting here longing to have wings and fly, to be a—one of your Kindred, and knowing how impossible it is. It made me a little sad, in a way I can't do anything about. Nothing too awful."

The fire was glowing embers, bright red still and warm, but even in such a minor thing I heard the true sadness in her heart. "Forgive me, dearling, I must ask you again. You know there can be no more secrets between us. I pray you, speak to me of your sadness, and of the fear that darkened our meeting this night."

"You're right, it's time." She told me the story of Maran and Marik as Jamie had told it to her, then all that had happened since she had landed, and finished with Marik's attempted seduction and her battle for freedom. "They were almost on us before we left, weren't they?" she asked, her voice full of weary dread.

"If they did not see us leave I would be surprised."

"When I go back they will take me. I'm still not sure what Marik wants, but I suspect I'll either be killed or given up whole and alive to the Rakshasa." She lifted her hands to cover her face. "Oh my friend, forgive me. I never meant to draw you into this struggle. It is none of yours, and now we have both broken the laws of your people."

"Your life was in danger, was it not?"

"Yes," she replied, certainty in her voice. "I give you my word, Akor, if Marik's men had caught me I would have been killed, or worse. When I go back I still will be."

"Then it is simple enough. You will not go back."

Lanen

I looked at him, my eyes wide, my mouth a startled O. "But—but—won't your people—Shikrar, won't he—"

He lifted his head off his forelegs and looked me in the eye.

"Dearling, I have given you my word. There is nothing will harm you while I live and may prevent."

I covered my mouth with my hand. "Dear Lady," I murmured. "Akor, you must know that I was going to go down on my knees and beg you and Shikrar to let me stay here on this island. I had it all planned, I would stay on the Gedri side of the Boundary in one of those cabins—oh, but I never meant you to break the laws of your people!"

I jumped a little as his near wing came close and wrapped softly around me. It was a gentle touch. "Dear one, I had already decided that that particular law is based on old prejudice and ancient grievance. Were it my province I would revoke the Great Ban and establish the Peace once more. But that can only be done in Council."

"Council?"

"Yes. I know not how your people are governed, but we have a Council that meets every five years. Any of our people who wish to may attend. And sometimes, as now, they are called for special occasions. I have summoned one for tomorrow." His voice sounded, I swear, like Jamie at his most cynical. "It should be interesting."

"Ha!" I snorted. "Interesting! They'll have us both for breakfast."

"It will at least be a novel experience."

And I threw back my head and laughed. Don't ask me why. Somehow the threat of Marik dwindled in the face of a whole Council of Dragons approaching with evil intent and a shaker of salt. When I told Akor why I was laughing, the steam clouded up the cave for some time.

Marik

I woke to find one of my guards hovering over me. "Where is she?" I muttered, cupping my jaw. It hurt to speak.

"I have the Harvesters looking everywhere, lord, but so far we haven't found her. Sul ran after her, but she had a headstart by way of he had to get me off him first." The idiot hung his head sheepishly and explained how Lanen had got past them, the lump on his forehead silent witness to truth. "Fetch my Healer," I commanded as I rose, "and then fetch me Caderan."

Maikel, my Healer, was working on me when Sul returned. The

expression on his face was quite beyond words. "Well," I demanded, "where is she?"

"Please not to speak just now, lord, it is not good for the work," Maikel admonished me gently. I grunted.

"She is gone, master," said Sul, and I heard wonder in his voice. "I was a long way behind her and lost the trail in the woods, so I ran back to camp and started up search parties of whoever was around. I took two likely lads and started off along the Boundary, just in case she'd run that way and been trapped. We must have gone two miles along when I heard noises and saw something up ahead, by where you met the Dragons." His voice dropped to a respectful whisper. "It was one of them, on our side the fence, and while I watched it picked her up in its hands and flew away."

I groaned. Damn it to all the Hells, not only talked with them but befriended, not only befriended but rescued! I had been so close. How had she resisted that amulet? It had been made by Berys himself; she should have thrown herself at my feet. Unless—

Unless she had some innate resistance.

Caderan appeared in the doorway, the darkness kind to his lank hair and sharp face. His eyes were bright with excitement. "The creature was on this side of the Boundary, you are certain?" he asked Sul.

"Yes, lord. I saw it lean down and pick her up," said Sul.

"You are dismissed," he told the two, and they left to take up their stations outside. Maikel still worked on my jaw so I could not speak, but Caderan's face spoke even before he did. "We have them, my lord. Did you not say that the treaty included them staying on their side of the fence?"

I grunted assent.

An oily grin spread over his face. "The Dragons are creatures of Order, my lord, they are bound by it straitly. This is your bargaining point, one they cannot ignore. You may not need to make your excursion at all."

My Healer finally finished and I shooed him away. "I will live now, Maikel, I thank you for your pains. Master Caderan and I would be alone."

He bowed without a word and left.

"Explain."

"My—sources have informed me that if you can find a point of

their law that they have broken, they are bound to make restitution."
He rubbed his hands together gleefully. "She has done it for you,
lord. By escaping to them, she has made them break their own laws.
Think of it! Dragon gold for the asking!" He broke into a high-
pitched laugh that sent shivers down my spine.

"Enough," I snapped. "You will accompany me to the place of
Summoning at noon tomorrow. In the meantime, I will need you to
explain to me how the girl resisted my amulet."

"What?"

"Yes, master sorcerer. She was well in my power, I could feel it,
but the moment I spoke to her of what I needed to know she drew
away from me, and a moment later she struck me."

Caderan did not entirely manage to hide his smile. "Yes, very
amusing I'm sure," I said sourly. "May she smite you one day. Fool!
I care not for the blow. How was she able to resist the amulet?"

"I cannot imagine, my lord. No woman should have been proof
against it. Of course it means nothing to men when a man wears it,
and since it was made very specifically for you, should it be stolen
and used by a woman you would be immune, but—"

"Could it be that simple?" I wondered aloud. "It was made for
me, I am proof against it—how would it affect one who was my own
flesh and blood?"

Caderan's eyes went wide, then narrowed as a sickening smile
crossed his face. "Yes, my lord. You have it, no doubt. I think we do
not need her blood now, though when she is in your power again I
would recommend the procedure for form's sake. Unless she is in
fact a man—"

"Trust me, she's a woman."

"—or a Dragon, then the only explanation must be that she is
your daughter. Your firstborn child, my lord Marik, and the price of
your pain."

His words swept through me like healing fire. I threw back my
head and laughed, despite the aches from the blow, despite the pain
I carried always with me. The price of my pain. Once paid it would
be gone forever. It was worth anything.

Now all I needed now was the girl.

She couldn't stay with them forever. If she was not back in my
hands by morning I would demand her return from the creatures,
along with the gold as recompense for their breaking of the treaty.

If they would not agree, somehow I would use Caderan's servants to fetch her back.

And in the meantime, once Caderan left, I meant to don those articles prepared for me and go walking in the dragonlands. It is, after all, always best to learn what you may, and I suspected this law-breaking by one of their own would not go unnoticed by the creatures themselves.

The Lords of Hell were smiling on me at last.

Akhor

The fire was but a few glowing embers now. We see in the dark a little better than the Gedri, but not much. As the darkness closed about us I began to ask Lanen about herself. She spoke haltingly at first, but I prompted her when she fell silent and she had much to say in the end. She told me of her old life at Hadronsstead, of her friends and her travels since she left.

"I would like to meet your Jamie. He has known you all your life, perhaps he would know whence your dreams of knowing my people sprang."

She laughed a small laugh. "It's a good thought, but he has no idea. He always said I must have been dropped on my head sometime when he wasn't looking. I don't think he even believes you exist." Then she made a marvelous sound, very short notes rising then falling in pitch.

"What was that?" I asked, surprised. I had not thought to wonder if she could sing.

"What was what? Oh—I laughed, that's all."

"Forgive me, littling, but that was not a laugh. Is there no separate word for it?"

"Mmm—well, yes, I suppose it was a giggle."

I tried to say it. The sound of the word was very like the thing itself and made her laugh again. "Usually only children giggle; it's the kind of noise little girls make when they are together," she told me.

"Our younglings sing, though not very well at first. The sounds are similar," I replied. "Do your people sing?"

"Yes. At least, we all sing but we don't all do it well. Jamie always told me I had a voice like a frog with a cold."

I smiled in the darkness. "I have never heard a frog with a cold sing. Would you sing something for me?"

"What, now?" She was surprised, and seemed pleased.

"Yes. I will join you, if I may."

"What if you don't know the song?"

"Littling," I said gently, "I learn very quickly."

She sat up straight and cleared her throat. "Just remember, you asked for this," she said. "This is a lullaby, such as mothers sing to their little ones to help them sleep."

She sang a sweet song, soft and low. Her voice was perfectly fine, though it was very young. I decided Jamie did not necessarily know everything about her. When she began the tune again I joined her in the second voice, keeping the harmony as simple as the melody. She did not stop as I had feared, she even sang it through once more. I was pleased with the way our voices blended.

She let the last notes die away and said quietly, "If the bards could hear you they would fall at your feet and die happy. I have never heard anything so beautiful, if you take my voice out of it. Akor, please, would you sing for me?" she asked. Her voice was very soft, as if she feared to ask such a thing.

There is nothing she could have asked of me that would have touched me more deeply, nor that I would more readily give. Perhaps it was chance.

Perhaps chance had nothing to do with what Lanen and I did together.

I was full of her now, of small things and large, I could hold nothing else. "Lanen, dear one, I am honoured. I shall sing you a new song that my heart taught me this night past."

I closed my eyes. I had not meant to sing that to her; but no matter. I believe that whatever I had set out to sing would have come to that song in the end. I thought I was still safe, for it is only a true bonding if both create the song, if their voices can find a meeting place in the singing.

I drew in breath, lifted my head and sang the song I had heard the night before as I dreamed of a Kantri-Lanen flying the Flight of the Devoted with me.

Lanen

He began softly and sweetly to sing, a lilting melody like a child's voice that made me want to dance or laugh or both together. Then the song changed, became more melancholy; it reminded me of the dark days in Hadronsstead. I understood then a little of what he was doing. I heard my journey through Ilsa, the music of the rivers and the stronger theme of the sea.

Then he let his voice deepen, taking on the beauty of the skies and of the winter's night we had just flown through. I could hear his rejoicing as he bore in hands made for destruction the fragile body of the one he loved.

Me.

And then he made me grow.

He turned me in his song into a Dragon, with wings of air and breath of fire, free and strong and brave. Together we flew on the night winds, made music, became in truth all things to one another as we would have done were the Winds or the Lady kinder. I wept, for joy, for wonder, as I felt my song-self ride the wind, become one with this fellow creature who held my name in his heart.

And I joined him.

I let go my fears; whatever it was that kept me earthbound I left behind. I let my voice join his, let it go where he went, then apart, then he would bring us back together. I had never imagined such music, it thrilled in my blood and pulsed along my every vein. Any part of my heart he did not have I gave him then. I felt my soul melt out of me and join with his as we flew. I could feel the very air on my wings, smell the approach of dawn and the nearness of my beloved; and we were one.

He sang us down. I sang no more, content to hear him, to revel in the glory of his voice and of what we had made between us.

And then there was silence.

Akhor

I was loath to speak. When I came to myself again Lanen was standing beside me, her hand on my side. I leaned down a little farther and she reached up and put an arm around my neck as far as it would go and leaned her head against mine.

It was the closest we could come to one another.

I would not have moved for worlds.

The night poured in upon us from high above, the light of the stars shining in on two lost souls.

She broke the silence at last.

"Kordeshkistriakor," she whispered.

None had ever spoken my true name aloud. The power of it sparked through me, thrilling, terrifying, yet warm with the love of her who spoke it.

"Lanen Kaelar," I whispered back, and felt her tremble.

"Akor, what have we done?" she asked softly. "What was that?"

"Dearling, I wish I were certain," I said. "The closest I can come is the Flight of the Devoted." She shivered against me.

"And what is that?"

"It is the way of my people when—Lanen, dear one, this may be as hard for you to hear as it is for me to say. It is the way of my people when we choose a mate. The two Devoted ones take to the sky and—"

"And sing together and make patterns with their flight and their song, I know, we just did that. I don't know how, but we just did that." I could hear the smile in her voice. "It was wonderful to have wings, and to fly with you like that."

I found myself ashamed, as though in my need I had taken a youngling for mate before it was full grown. "Lanen, please believe me, I did not mean for that to happen. I could not stop myself. I meant only to sing you the song that came to me in the night, but when you joined me I . . ."

"Akor, dear one, enough," she said, stopping me. "Do you think I am a fool or a child? No one could mistake the meaning of that song we gave one another. I asked only because I wanted to hear you say what my heart knew already." She paused. "I think your people take a mate only once, is that so?"

"Yes."

"My people mate quite cheerfully without pledging themselves to one another, though that is done, too. I have never mated, though some have offered; and I have never loved, or been loved, before."

Lanen

I could hardly believe that it was my voice that spoke. I meant every word, but I had not known that I would say them until they were spoken.

"Tell me, do you take this as seriously as if it had happened in truth, with a lady of your Kindred?"

"Lanen," that wondrous voice said to me, "it *has* happened in truth. Simply because we do not choose to leave the ground, it does not make the rest of our song untrue."

"Bless you for that, dear heart!" I sang. "I could not bear it if only I felt that way. For good or ill, Akor, for all the insanity of it, we are pledged to one another soul to soul."

"For good or ill, Lanen my heart. And we may be fools—I would not be surprised—but what extravagant fools we are!"

I laughed for heart's ease, with my one beloved, who would remain always apart from me yet closer than any.

"Come, let us go outside, the night is fine," he said.

I wrapped my cloak about me and followed him out, he on four legs folding his wings close about him, I walking upright. The passageway didn't bother me at all.

I missed my wings of song.

Akhor

It was a fine clear night, frosty and crisp. The moon was finally rising, a blessing on the night. Lanen blew out a sharp breath as we came out of the passageway.

"What was that?" I asked.

"That was me starting to freeze to death. It's *cold* out here!"

I laughed at her. "Dearling, I am fire incarnate. Gather wood and I shall . . ."

"Hold that thought!" she cried and hurried off to collect branches. In moments there was a small fire blazing, Lanen leaning as near to it as she could without catching alight herself. Carefully I wrapped myself round her to keep her warm, to keep her near me. Every moment seemed precious now. I stared with her into the fire, my head beside her as near as I could come. We seemed almost shy with one another.

She spoke first, rubbing her hands together, staring into the fire, thoughtful.

"Akor, what is happening, and why? Do you know?"

"What mean you, dearling?"

"I'm not sure. But I can't believe that our meeting, our—our love for each other, is just part of the normal way of things." She looked into my eyes. "Akor, we first spoke to each other only two nights ago. This night was the first time we had to speak freely of our Kindred to each other, and almost the first thing we said was 'I love you.' Doesn't that strike you as strange?"

I smiled. "No. 'Strange' was when I first saw you step foot on this island. I was serving as Guardian then, did you know? From that moment I was drawn to you, to your laughter and to your feeling of coming home. Since then, I fear, 'strange' has given way to unbelievable."

She laughed and reached out to stroke my face, light as a breath on my armour. "That's what I mean. But here we are, pledged to one another no less!" We both laughed, but I was relieved to hear her add, "Not that I would have it any other way, dear heart. Still, it passes belief. Human and Dragon. Kantri and Gedri. Surely this has never happened in the history of the world." She furrowed her face and stared into the fire. "I don't know about you, my dear, but I feel decidedly peculiar."

Perhaps it was cowardly, but I decided to take refuge for a moment in simpler things. "Then you won't mind my asking you about the way you furrow your face and turn your mouth down. It seems to reflect thought, but has it a name?"

She laughed. "Trust you. It's called a frown. The opposite of a smile, more or less. I frown when I'm thinking, or when I'm angry or upset. Usually angry." She laughed again, wryly. "I have a terrible temper."

"Temper?"

"I get angry easily."

"Perhaps we are related after all. The Kantri are creatures of fire, and I fear it occasionally shows in ways other than flame."

"Like when you are amused, for instance," she said. "I'm getting used to your grins, complete with steam, but I'd hate to see a belly laugh."

"A what?"

"When you find something *really* funny. Just warn me before-
hand, will you?"

"Assuredly I shall."

"And before I forget, I've been meaning to ask you something.
I am quite happy to call you the Kantri or the Kindred, but is there
something wrong with 'Dragon'?"

I was slightly taken aback. "I thought you knew, dearling, since
you have never used that word to me."

"No. I was going on instinct. I was right though, wasn't I?"

"Absolutely. It is—I am afraid it is considered an insult among
us. It is the word your people use for the Lesser Kindred; to use that
word for one of us is as much as to say that we are no more than soulless beasts."

She grinned up at me. "Thank goodness for instinct."

We both fell silent, and I let the night come in on us. It was a relief to speak of such trivia, to take refuge in minor concerns for a moment. However, her question echoed in my mind: *What is
happening, and why?* If another had told me of so strange a thing,
I would have said Meditation of the Winds would—of course!

"Lanen, dearling, I have just realised—if I am to have any hope
of learning what is afoot, I must set my soul in Meditation of the
Winds. To you it will appear that I am doing nothing, but it requires
great concentration, and I must have quiet."

"May I watch?" she asked.

"Certainly, but there is little to see. If you will need more wood
for the fire, please gather it now before I am well into the Discipline."
I was surprised to feel a tinge of hurt from her, though she said nothing. Then I understood. "Ah, Lanen," I said, moving swiftly to where
she was collecting branches. She looked up at me. "Dearling, forgive me," I said, bowing, then in the Language of Truth told her, *"I
could never send you away, dearling, not even so far—I am trying
desperately to be practical. You must know that you are distraction
enough, my heart, without moving about."*

She laughed then, and all was right again. So delicate these emotions at such a time—so similar our peoples, that I knew without
words how my words had stung.

Lanen

He was right, there wasn't much to see. By the time I got back with more firewood he was sitting bolt upright, his wings close-furled and his tail wrapped around his feet (*like a cat,* I thought, stifling a laugh). His eyes were closed, his forelegs resting on his knees.

I sat by the fire and, just for a moment, let the wonder of it all wash over me. I had loved stories of Dragons since I was a child, but what Akor and I had done was not for children. It was real as wind and water, as earth and fire. I had wondered since the night before what was happening, and had no more idea now than when I first asked myself the question.

There was one more thing I could try, at least until Akor was finished.

I am not much given to calling on the Lady, but I have always felt close to Her. I even wear a Ladystar of silver around my neck, though the set rituals that many take part in mean little to me. So, as Akor and I sat in the frosty night before that little fire, I simply opened my heart to Lady Shia, the Goddess, the Mother of Us All, who ruled in the heavens and in the earth. She was the Mother in the ground beneath me, the Old One in the moon that rode overhead, the Laughing Girl in the rains that fell and nourished the land. I called on all three and asked the question that was in my heart.

Perhaps it was my imagination, fired from my "flight" with Akor; perhaps it was being out in the night sitting on the Mother and seeing the Old One high above, with the Girl laughing in her little stream-fed pool off in the trees. Perhaps the night was simply full of magic, and I had touched part of it.

I felt lines of light go through me: the first a white staff straight up my back from the earth; the second a wide, wavery beam of moonlight down from on high; the third a scattering like drops of rain from the direction of the pool. And caught in this web, this net of light, I heard Her speak.

Daughter, have no fear. All is well. Let not its strangeness concern you. All will be well. All will be well. Follow your heart and all will be well.

Akhor

The words of the Discipline were old friends to me. I had always prided myself on clear thought. But then, I had never known emotions like those of the past few days.

In the words of the invocation I called on the Winds to blow clear the cobwebs of emotion, let clear thought remain. I breathed in the sequence I had practiced for a thousand years, felt the whirling passions in me subside.

"I am Khordeshkhistriakhor, Silver King of the Greater Kindred of the Kantri, living on the Dragon Isle in the Great Sea of Kolmar."

That was truth.

"I have spoken with a child of the Gedri, broken the Great Ban set on our two Kindreds."

That was truth.

"I have flown the Flight of the Devoted with Lanen Kaelar, child of the Gedrishakrim, with whom there can be no joining beyond mind, heart and soul."

That was truth.

For all my Discipline, my heart ached at those words. Our people are few, they always have been. I had longed for younglings of my own, I envied that bond in others. Idai had offered herself many times, as mate and mother, but I had refused, for I judged our souls too far apart to meet in the making of younglings.

That was truth.

"I must present Lanen to the Council of the Kindred. We must determine what is to be done. Shall she be allowed to remain here, or must I go with her to some distant shore?"

You will go with her.

"What? Who speaks?"

You will go with her.

"Whither shall we go?"

All will be made clear to you.

"What is happening?"

Your people are dying, Khordeshkhistriakhor. So few younglings, so many elders. You and your dear one may save them, if you will.

My heart leapt. "How?"

You will know in good time. It will be hard. There will be
great pain. But you will live to know joy again.
"Who speaks? In the name of all my fathers, *who speaks?*"
There was no answer, only the wind through the trees freshening upon my face.
Only the Wind.

Lanen

He opened his eyes with a jolt. I knew how he felt.
"Akor? Are you well?"
"I am not certain," he said, coming back down on all fours. "I am—surprised, to say the least. It is a night of new beginnings, Lanen, in all truth. Never in all my long life has that happened."
Don't tell me, I thought, your gods spoke to you, too. Please don't tell me that.
"I heard the voice of another in my thoughts. It was not true-speech, I am certain. I do not know who it could have been."
I stood up, threw more wood on the fire. "Akor, this night I have flown with you above the earth, then under the earth. I have with you defied the rest of your Kindred and all of mine, I have pledged my troth to you on wings I never had and now miss, and I am tired of being surprised. The only thing that amazes me any more is that I am still alive and more or less sane." I found that I was growing angry. "As you sat in your Discipline I called out to the Lady, the goddess of my people, for comfort, or perhaps for inspiration. And do you know what, my impossible beloved? *She answered me!* Not with a vague sense of comfort, but with *words.*"
He did not say anything, only stared. I went on. "What would you be willing to wager on that voice you heard being the voice of the Winds you call on?
"Akor, what are they doing? What do they want of us?"

Akhor

I tried to keep my voice calm, for her sake. I must tell her.
"Hlanen, therre iss much I sstill musst tell hyu," I began. *Damn!*
"It is too important for Gedri speech, will you hear me thus?"

"Yes, if you wish. I'll try not to answer the same way. I'm so tired I suspect they would hear me at the Boundary."

"Littling, that I heard a voice while deep in the Discipline was no trifle. I have never heard of such a thing among all my Kindred. But at least as surprising was what it said to me. I was told that I must go through great pain for my people, but that if I was willing I might save them. No—that we might save them."

"Save them? From what?"

How to tell her that which I had taken so many years to understand, and still bore so ill? *"The son of Shikrar, who is called Kédra, has gone with his lady Mirazhe to the Birthing cove. Many of the females of my race are there, the Elders who remember what must be done, and Idai who stands birthing sister to Mirazhe, and Kerijan. She is the only other female who has borne a youngling in the last three hundred years."*

"Three hundred years?" said Lanen, shocked. "Dear Lady, that must be a long time even as you measure it."

"It is as you say. My people are dying, Lanen Kaelar, and I have wondered these three hundred years and more what to do about it. Now I have heard the voice of the night Wind tell me that I will suffer great pain, that I will come to know joy again, and that you and I may save my people. And that I shall go with you, wherever you fare."

"What?!"

"I tell you only what I was told."

"Akor, I told you, I spent most of yesterday wondering how to ask you if I could stay here on the island with you if I kept on the far side of the Boundary. I was afraid you'd be angry with me or have to refuse outright, but I couldn't think of any other way to stay close to you." She smiled, albeit grimly. "Things have changed now, of course, but still—how could you possibly go with *me?* How could you live in any part of Kolmar where there are people, without your own Kindred?"

"I do not know. I cannot imagine it, unless we were to find a cave far away from the rest of the Gedri. I shall have to think about this. May I ask what your Lady said to you?"

Lanen

"Only that what we are doing is right, and that all will be well if I follow my heart."

He hissed gently. *"Your Lady is kinder than the Winds. Perhaps we could speak with each other's gods? At this moment I much prefer yours."*

I laughed. I was surprised I could still do it, but I laughed. Akor joined me. Suddenly it all seemed so absurd, everything from our first conversation to switching gods, and we both let go our fears. I laughed till I cried, not least because the whole clearing was filling with steam from Akor's hissing.

"Be hwarned, Hlanen," he managed to gasp out, throwing his head back. A wide swath of flame split the night and left me blinded for a moment.

It was, it had to be. A dragon belly laugh. What a mad, wondrous world it was.

Then he began to speak. His speech seemed to have recovered. "Ah, Lanen, what a life I am learning to lead! I stand here in the night and cannot yet believe the truth of all we do." His voice, so warm and alive, grew deeper yet and richer. "For the first time in years beyond living memory, Kantri and Gedri exchange lives and hearts and laughter, and we both are the stronger for it. The Four Winds guide all our destinies, Lanen," he said quietly. "The first teaching rhyme for younglings is our oldest knowledge.

"First is the Wind of Change
Second is Shaping
Third is the Unknown
and Last is the Word.

"It is not elegant, but it is true. All of life is a great cycle. I believe that you are the wind of change, Lanen Kaelar, blowing cold across the Kindred for good or ill, and for good or ill you have come to me. You must know, none of the Kindred have ever had silver armour before. I am the first and only, as best we know, since time began. My birth was seen as an omen by my people, but what it portends none can say. I believe this change is fated, as are you and I."

At another time his words might have surprised me, but I was

beyond it by then. I do not know how or why, but I felt I could almost have repeated that rhyme along with him. I was in a most re-
markable state, as if part of my mind listened to words spoken long
before and only repeated now. Akor was only stating the obvious.

"Does that mean that you are to shape me?" I asked.

"I suspect we have already begun to shape one another, dearling,"
he answered. "I have expected you, or someone, for some time now,
but I did not know you would come so soon. I believe that between
us we will do our share of shaping others as well."

So soon?

Not for the first time I wished to all the gods that I could read
that immobile mask of a face more easily. It was terribly distracting.
The tone of his voice often made his meaning clear, and he shifted
his stance so often it must have some significance, but without thinking I kept looking at his face. Which never changed.

"What do you mean, so soon?" I demanded. I was getting tired
of learning things after the fact. "What do you know that I don't?"

"Ah, dearling, forgive me. We have had so little time together and
there is so much you do not yet know. I have had Weh dreams, and
in one of them I had seen you before ever your foot stepped on this
shore."

He had mentioned this before. "What is a Weh dream?" I asked.
He had said the words with reverence. He answered in truespeech.

*"It is a dream during the Weh sleep. And the Weh sleep is one of
the most closely guarded secrets of the Kindred, my Lanen. I will tell
you of it—I cannot keep anything from you—but you must give me
your word, on your life, never to reveal it to another of your people."*

If I had not been so tired I would have been angry that he could
doubt me even now. As it was I simply said, "You have my word, as
Lanen Kaelar Maransdatter. I will never tell another soul."

And so I have not, and would not here did I not know that the
Kindred are safeguarded now against any danger during the Weh
sleep.

He spoke quietly but aloud.

"The Weh sleep is our one great weakness as a race. If word of
it reached the Gedri, we surely would be slaughtered one by one as
we slept.

"We do not require food as often as you. One meal in a week, if
it is large enough, will sustain us. We also do not require sleep as

often as you do—an hour or so in every day is enough, though some
take more.

"I understand that your people reach a certain size early in life
and never grow from that time on. I have long thought that a con-
venient way of living, but it is not our way. The longer we live, the
larger we become. You have seen the size of Shikrar; he is more than
six hundred years older than I.

"Knowing this, do you not wonder how it is that we can grow surrounded by armour?

"The answer is that we cannot. Every fifty years or so (the time
is different for each individual) the Weh sleep comes upon us. We
may have an hour's warning or a day's, but no more than that. We
have learned that the only thing to do is to find a protected place and
let it happen.

"When it begins, it is little more than a great weariness. That is
the warning. We let our mates or our closest friends know that it is
upon us and leave immediately for our chambers.

"This cave is not where I spend most of my life. This is my Weh
chamber, my safe place for the Weh sleep. That is why it is so far
from my Kindred, so hidden, so difficult to get into.

"Next comes a terrible itching, as though our hide were too tight
(which indeed it is). In the privacy of our chambers we scratch, and
find that we can easily tear off the scales that normally protect us
from all assaults. It is a strange and frightening time. We try to remove as many scales as possible for our own comfort, but usually the
sleep takes us before much can be done.

"The Weh sleep. During it we cannot move, even if we can be
partially awakened for a short while. Our old armour falls from us as
the new dries and hardens underneath, and for that time we are vulnerable to any creature that wishes us harm. And the sleep lasts until
the new armour is hardened, or until any wound we have has been
healed—for it will also come upon us if we are badly injured—or
until the Winds wake us. It can last anywhere from a fortnight to full
six moons, or vastly longer if we are badly wounded. We heal but
slowly.

"In the beginning, and on many occasions since, some have tried
to guard their loved ones during the Weh sleep. The reason we take
the sleep so far away from our Kindred is the same reason that the
idea never worked. The Weh sleep is catching—at least the sleep is.

A mated couple tried it once when I was young. He was fully into the Weh for but a single day when one of us tried to bespeak her and received no answer. She was found fast asleep in the middle of the day, outside the cave. She was awakened easily enough, but she refused to leave. She was awakened anew by friends every few hours for the next two weeks before she at last admitted that it was impossible.

"You see now, dearling, why you must never speak of it. We are asleep, unprotected by Kindred or armour, unable even to call for help or defend ourselves. It is our greatest weakness and our greatest secret."

Lanen

"I understand. But why should dreams then be more important than dreams at any other time?"

"Dreams during the Weh sleep are very rare. They are generally taken to be the word of the Winds, and we are told by the Elders to pay close attention to them."

"And you had one about me?" I asked, very pleased though I was beginning to drowse. All this talk of sleep had made me realise just how tired I was. It had been an unbelievable day.

"I have had three Weh dreams, one each of the last three times I have slept. In the first I met you. It was the first day of the Harvest and I saw you come ashore, as I did in truth. In the second half of that dream I heard someone call to me." His voice went soft and loving. "It was the voice of a child of the Gedri, pleading in the dark, and it called me brother."

I smiled. "I'm glad I got it right. What about your other two dreams?"

"In the second you and I stood on a clifftop, and I helped a pair of younglings on their first flight. There were others there, but I did not recognise them.

"And in the third—ah, it was even more mysterious than the other two. A female of your race, whom I had never seen, approached me and called me by my full, true name, but I was not frightened. It was as if we were old friends meeting after centuries apart."

I liked the sound of them all—very reassuring, somehow. I tried to say something sensible but couldn't think of anything; I was too busy yawning. Looking around, I saw that the sky was beginning to lighten.

"Akor, forgive me, but I think even talk of the Weh sleep must be catching. I don't know about you, but I'm cold and hungry and I need sleep in the worst way. Would you mind if I slept in a corner of your chambers?"

He was amused. "Come, rouse yourself to gather firewood enough for a little time. I shall light that which you took in before."

I dragged myself round the edge of the forest twice collecting wood. Much of it had frost on it. I knew how it felt. Tired as I was, I was thankful for the exercise if only to warm my cold bones. When I brought the second armful in, Akor had already started a cheerful blaze. I found him curled onto the floor of *khaadish*. I purposely ignored the gleam of gold that surrounded me, not that I had to work very hard. I was exhausted.

I stood before the fire for a while, getting as warm as I could.

"Lanen, dear heart, forgive me. I forget that you feel the cold so. Come close by me, take my warmth; it is greater far than the fire."

I grinned to myself. *Too tired, Lanen. You never thought of that.*

There was a space on the ground, in the midst of the curl as it were. I leaned back against him and instantly relaxed against the warmth that poured from his armour. It felt wonderful. I just managed to mumble, "Goodnight, dear heart," before I fell asleep.

Akhor

I lay there for many hours watching her. She was both beautiful and strange. How peculiar not to have wings! I found myself idly imagining a world in which the Gedri had once had wings, but had lost them and been forced to walk on two feet. It still seemed an unnatural way to travel, though it did free the forelegs to carry. That was one thing I had long envied the Gedri.

She sighed in her sleep and stirred. I found myself thinking of her as a youngling again, simply because of her size. Without thinking I lay my near wing over her to keep her warm. She did not wake, only pushed herself closer to me. It was a wondrous feeling.

I knew that I must leave her by midday to join the Council. What I would tell them now, I had no idea. I must give it thought. But I would not give up a moment with Lanen that I did not have to.

They live such quick, fiery lives, the Gedrishakrim. I had known more changes, more surprises, more emotions in the last three days than I had felt in as many centuries. My sense of time was becoming distorted also; I had begun to think in terms of hours instead of days, or moons. Or years. I had, in effect, known a little time of living like the Gedri, and it was a new and wondrous thing. I hoped I could convince the Council of that.

In the meantime I lay beside my beloved in my own chambers, something I would have sworn mere days ago would never happen. *Idai will be furious,* I thought, smiling sadly to myself. Dear Idai, she had wanted me for so long. I simply never felt for her as I must feel towards a mate. I hoped she would understand when at last I had to tell her. I did not think it likely.

My heart was at peace, despite all that I knew must come. The word of the Winds, the Council, having to explain about Lanen and me: none of it would be simple. But for now there were only the two of us, and I let my heart fill with the kind of joy I had despaired of ever knowing.

Lanen, my heart. Lanen, my dear one. Lanen, my betrothed. Lanen Kaelar.

My life had changed forever.

Marik

In the end I waited some hours after Caderan left. It was all very well for him to assure me that the beasts were bound by law—but in my experience, if you fine a butcher, you are more likely to get brains or tripe than the finest cut joints. If I were in their place I would do the same. No, I would go among their dwellings and discover what I could for myself.

I left my cabin normally clad, carrying the boots of silent movement and the cloak of unseeing. The amulet, which would mask my smell, would last but a very short time indeed, and I had decided to save it until the night we were to leave, when I would collect whatever I had found.

I put on boots and cloak and crossed the Boundary some miles east of our camp, near the sea, that their Guardian might have the longer trip to find me. At first, I might just as well have been walking the halls of Castle Gundar, for there was not one of the creatures in sight. The moon was bright enough to guide me easily.

I walked warily but unhindered, seeking their lairs and the storied riches therein, but at first found little. Past the Boundary I went a mile north, keeping the shoreline in sight, then turned inland. I should have known, I suppose. Do not all the ballads describe the lairs of such beasts as being in caves? Half a mile in from the sea I came across a low line of hills, and the first of their dwellings.

From the outside it was plain rock. I approached cautiously, even though the boots masked the sound of my footsteps. I heard no movement, and my dim sight saw nothing, but I did not trust it. I stood and listened a good ten minutes, then crept slowly in keeping well against the wall, but there was no need, it was deserted. I lit a small taper I had brought, lifted it high and gazed about me dumbfounded.

The tales were true and more than true. I did not know there was so much gold in the world. The wall, the very floors were covered with it. I looked all round, noting all but touching nothing, then moved on.

I saw three more caves; the first two were occupied and I went near enough only to hear the inhabitants and leave, but the third was the charm indeed. Its tenant was absent, so I brought out my tinderbox again and lit the taper. When finally it caught I lost my breath, for I had surely found the lair of their treasure-keeper.

The walls were covered with gold to the depth of my second finger joint, deeply graven with strange symbols and set with many-hued crystals from the earth and vast pearls from the sea. But at the back was an opening into a second chamber. I went swiftly towards it, meaning only to glance inside, but I defy anyone to look on such wonders and not linger.

The inner chamber was forty feet on a side and, though it was lined floor to ceiling with gold, you barely noticed the gold for the stones. Faceted all, the largest I saw as big as a duck's egg, and every colour known to man. Emeralds, rubies, wondrous sapphires, topaz the colour of smoke and of sunlight, and huge beryls green as the sea. But even these paled by comparison to the centrepiece of all the splendour.

It was all I could do not to laugh out loud for the sheer joy of it. Before me lay riches even I could not conceive of, a treasure trove beyond price, beyond imagining. There in the center of the room, in a cask of gold on a golden pedestal, lay casually heaped one on another the most wondrous gems in the world. What would not kings or the greatest of the merchants pay for these wonders I had found? There must be two hundred of them, each the size of my fist. Why, I would demand payment for a glimpse of them in their cask before ever I needed to sell off the gems themselves. And when I did sell, I would charge the world for them, sell but one in a year, or two perhaps if times were hard and all my other ventures doing poorly.

Who had seen their like?

Who could resist them, having seen?

Perfectly cut, flawless gems, with the very flicker of life in their depths.

I was reaching out to touch one when I heard a soft clatter outside the cave mouth. I blew out the taper, but not before I caught sight of what awaited me. A vast shape of dark bronze was sliding into the cave and coming straight towards me. I could not see in that sudden darkness, but had the sense to move to the wall next to the entrance to the chamber. I heard the creature sniff, then start to hiss. Sudden as a snake I felt rather than heard it flow past me to the back of the inner chamber. I took my chance and slipped out the entrance, through the outer chamber and on, not pausing for breath until I had run the full two miles to the Boundary and beyond. I dared not look behind me, but I had heard nothing and would not spare the time to stop and see if I was followed.

For all their usefulness, for all their ruinous cost, the precious articles that Berys made were so flawed they were barely worth using. The boots raised such bloody welts on my feet that I could barely walk when I returned, and it took much out of Maikel to ease them. The cloak appeared to work well enough, but the shadow it created affected me as well. I could barely see and found I stumbled like a blind man until my eyes grew accustomed to the lessened vision. My vision was blurred, and my old pain stabbed at me dreadfully.

I spoke with Caderan, and he admitted that the spells could protect me only, not that which I might be carrying. Thus the cloak might hide me from sight, and the spells hid Raksha-scent, but only my footfalls would be silenced. Should I cough I would be heard, should

I strike a light the scent of burning would be evident, as would any light illuming anything beyond the circle of my cloak.

I began to wonder if the Rakshasa were so puissant as I thought. The limitations of these articles, which Berys claimed were the best in the world, made them barely usable.

But these were trifles. Maikel salved some of my wounds and Healed the others, and I knew that I truly had power over the Dragons, for I had myself been in their most guarded places and found their dearest treasure.

xii

THE WIND OF SHAPING

Lanen

I woke in midafternoon to find the cave filled with a grey light from the opening far above my head. Akor was not long gone, for the heat of him lingered in the golden floor. I wandered outside and into the wood a ways, to perform the necessary and to drink from the pool. As I had guessed from the sound of it the night before, it was not a still pool, more a wide spot in a small stream. The water was fresh and clear but icy cold.

It was a good match for the day. Clouds had moved in and covered the sun in winter grey, and there was a deceptively gentle breeze that blew straight through me.

As I stood at the edge of the wood, braiding my hair and looking up at the clouds, I found myself tracking a dark speck in the distance. It was either a very large bird or Akor returning. I watched the flight with some pleasure as it drew nearer and became clearly a Dragon's shape.

It was still a *dark* shape.

I ran for the cave. What would become of me here, without his protection? And who would know this place, he had said it was secret. Did his parents still live? Was this a soulfast friend?

Oh dear Goddess. Shikrar.

The dragon landed just as I bolted into the semidarkness. Ah, well. No peace for the wicked, they say.

Shikrar

//"Akhorishaan, are you here? I have sought you since dawn, I need you, my friend."//

There was no reply, though I would have sworn the cave was not empty. I put my head just inside the passageway. // "Akor, for the love of our friendship, come out to me if you are here."//

Then I smelled her.

I hit my head on the low roof of the passage in my anger, then cried out, furious, // "Akor, what in the name of the Winds are you doing!"//

Lanen

"Lord Shikrar," I said, terrified, "I don't know what you just said, but if you're looking for Akor, he's not here. It's me, Lanen. We spoke the other night." I stepped into the center of the room so he could see me, calmer than I had ever dreamed I could be. "Akor brought me here last night to talk, and I fell asleep. He was gone when I woke."

He rumbled deep in his throat. It was a terrifying noise, like the growl of some unimaginable bear. His truespeech lanced into my mind. *"Gedri, speak to me of this in the Language of Truth or I shall flame you where you stand. Where is Akor, and how came you here?"*

Those were better odds than I had hoped for.

I concentrated as hard as I could. Like a small hole, Akor had said, send your thoughts through it, no larger than it must be, concentrate on what you are saying.

"My lord, I tell you but truth. Akor and I came here last night to speak with each other. A great deal happened that we did not expect and we were talking until dawn. I slept and when I woke he was gone. I swear on my soul that I speak truth. I do not and have never wished harm to any of the Kindred."

I don't know how much of my underthought got through. Shikrar at any rate did not appear to be shocked or to grow more angry than he was, which I would have expected had he gathered more of the truth than I had meant to tell him.

"This must be brought before the Council. Where is Akor?" he asked, in my own language.

"I don't know, truly, my lord."

"I must find him! He will not answer me, his mind is closed." I heard his voice go grim with the thought. "Child of the Gedri, will it be open to you?"

I tried not to shake, with the result that I stood firm enough but my voice quavered like an old woman's. "I believe so, my lord. I will—I will try."

"Come out of there. It will be easier outside," he said. He backed out of the opening. Only then did I realise that he was too large to enter the passageway easily.

I gathered my courage as best I could and wrapped it round me like my cloak. *If he means to kill you outside at least Akor will not have to move your bones from his Weh chamber,* I thought to myself. I stepped out into the middle of the clearing. *Deep breath now, Lanen my girl. See him in your mind, call him.*

"*Akor? Where are you? It is Lanen.*"

He answered me instantly. I could hear the smile in his voice. "*Good day, dearling. I am on my way back to you. I have been hunting that we both might eat. And I thank you for your name, my heart, but I would know your mindvoice among a thousand. I shall be with you very soon.*"

Keep it concentrated, lass; Shikrar can hear your speech but not Akor's. "*Lord Akor, your friend Shikrar is here and would have speech with you. He is greatly concerned about something.*" I tried to keep my fear out of that last sentence, but I don't think I managed it very well.

Akhor

"**Lord Akor** *very formal keep it very formal* **your friend Shikrar is here** *growling at me* **and would have speech with you.** *been trying all day resents that I can bespeak you he cannot* **He is greatly concerned about something** *horribly upset hasn't killed me yet but I fear for my life.*"

I instantly opened my mind to Shikrar. He hardly had to speak; I saw the source of his concern even as he formed his words. "*Akhor soulfriend at last you answer me. No, not me, the Gedri—not now. Akhor, I beg you, it is Mirazhe, her time has come, something is terribly wrong. Help me! I know not where to turn.*"

It happens sometimes that births are difficult for our people. Such things used to be rare, but even in those days they were feared.

I instantly dropped the beast I carried. *"I fly now to the Birthing Cove, Shikrar, but you must swear to do something for me."*

"Anything!"

"Bring Lanen with you."

"NO!"

"Hadreshikrar, soulfriend, you must. You know I do not ask this lightly, I have an idea, you must bring her for Mirazhe's sake. Promise me! For the sake of your son and his."

I cringed at the anguish in his voice as he agreed.

I flew on the Wind's wings to the Birthing Cove and called to Lanen to tell her what I had requested.

Lanen

I wasn't any more pleased to be Shikrar's passenger than he was to have me. He held me away from his body so only his hands would have to touch me. I could appreciate the sentiment, but I got cold very quickly. If his hands themselves were not so warm I'd have frozen.

It was a long flight, but at least this time I could see what we flew over. The Birthing Cove, it seemed, was on the northwestern side of the island, so that I saw a great deal of the island pass below me. We went across the center, a longer way than straight so that Shikrar could fly through a gap in the mountain range that split the north of the Dragon Isle from the south. It was the only gap in that fearsome ridge that I could see.

The northern half of the island was very different from the south. Here the forests were much thinner; in some places bare black rock was all that lay below us for many leagues. A spur of the mountains shot away northward, and at its end another large mountain arose, smoking sullenly in a hundred places. One whole side of the mountain was dark with what looked like rock that had melted away. I could not imagine the kind of force that could make stone run like mud.

It was at the edge of this desolation that we came to ground, after what seemed hours. The sun was nearly down, but in the afternoon's grey gloom I saw a cliff of stone and a wide beach below, rock-strewn and dark, with a large pool a little way inland.

There were four dragons waiting for us. The largest, only a little smaller than Shikrar, was like dark copper. The one sitting in the pool shone like polished brass even on that cloudy day, the one at the pool's edge was close in colour to Shikrar's dark bronze, and the last gleamed purest silver (I breathed again), strange among them, the Silver King come to help his people.

Shikrar dropped me just before he landed. To be fair he was as delicate about it as he could manage, but I was so cold my cramped limbs would not hold me up. I fell to the rocky ground with a cry.

Akor was at my side in an instant. *"What ails thee, dearling?"* he asked, his voice in my mind warm and loving.

"I'm near frozen," I told him through chattering teeth.

Without a word he breathed on me. Gently, steadily, a warm wind in a warmer fog. It was like taking a steam bath.

At first the warmth hurt as much as the cold had, but after a little I began to melt. My face, my hands and feet still ached with cold, but now I could at least move about enough to keep my blood from freezing.

"Littling, the lady nearest you is the Lady Idai," said Akor in true-speech, as he kept breathing warmth into my bones. *"The younger one who gleams so bright is Mirazhe, she who is having difficulty with the birth. The one beside her is her mate Kédra, the son of Shikrar. I am glad you are here. I may need your help if all else fails."*

"Anything I can do I will," I replied aloud. I thought of his words the night before. Kédra's child was the first youngling to be born in three hundred years, and it was in danger. I could all but smell their distress—I think, despite their impassive faces, I would have known something was wrong just looking at them.

Akhor

Shikrar and I went to Idai, who appeared to be the calmest among them, but when she bespoke me her concern rang nearly as loud as her anger. *"Lord Akhor, I have sent all the others back to their own chambers. There were none who remembered more than I, not*

*even Kerijan, or could do anything more here than surround Mirazhe
with their concern, which is the last thing she needs. Akhor, I fear
for her. She has been straining since early last night. Even the more
difficult births took perhaps the half of a day. Those that took longer
we lost."*

"Mother or child, Idai?"

"Both, my lord. Both." She glared at me, standing obviously in
Anger now. *"And you would bring your pet Gedri here to witness it!
How could you so betray your people? Do you care so little for
Shikrar's feelings, for Mirazhe and Kédra, that you would bring the
enemy of our people here, of all places? Shikrar has told me of your
meeting, and of your obsession. It is not right, Akhor. It must leave,
or I shall destroy it where it stands. Never in the history of the world
has a Gedri come to so sacred a place. It should not be!"*

I found I was moving into Anger myself. For Mirazhe's sake I
fought to keep my head, keep some measure of calm as Idai threatened the life of my beloved. *"Lady Idai, how great a fool do you think
me?"* I said sternly in the Language of Truth. *"Or do you believe me
mad, or evil, or so heartless I would throw Shikrar's dislike of the
Gedri in his teeth? This child of the Gedri—Lanen—is here to witness not death but birth, and she may be of service to us. She stays."*

*"No! Akhor, are you bespelled? This is ill done, it is not the way
of things, I will not permit!"*

*"I do not ask your permission, Idai. You will not harm her, and
she will stay."*

"NO!" cried Idai in a great voice, and ran towards Lanen.

Lanen

I had wandered over to the pool. I don't know why, but it seemed
impolite just to stare. I bowed to the one in the pool and to the other
who waited on the far side. "I am called Lanen," I said. Mirazhe
stared at me with unreadable eyes, but did not move or speak. Her
mate leaned down his head and looked at me closely. He said something out loud that I didn't understand, but in a moment what I
guessed was his voice said in truespeech, *"Lanen, may I bespeak
you? I am called Kédra."*

"You are welcome to. You are Shikrar's son?"

"Astounding! So Akhor spoke no more than truth. A Gedri with truespeech! You are the friend of Akhor?"

"Yes," I replied. *"I am sorry for your lady's trouble. Is there anything to be done?"*

He might have answered, but I was distracted by a loud hiss, and suddenly there before me was the large one Akor had called Idai. Then everything moved in a blur—the creatures moved so swiftly I could not tell what was happening until it stopped. Mirazhe, the one in the pool, had thrust her head between me and Idai and hissed back. Apparently Idai was so shocked she backed down, and around the edge of Mirazhe's jaw I just caught sight of Idai lowering her vast claw with its five swords. I'd have been deader than Perrin and twice as surprised.

Akhor

Thank the Winds for Mirazhe; I was too slow to read Idai's intent. When the moment had passed I walked slowly over to the pool. *"Idai."*

She stood frozen in amazement, and Mirazhe kept her head between Idai and Lanen, who never moved.

"Idai! Come thou before thy King and answer!" I commanded in the formal speech of kingship. As I had hoped, it shook her out of herself. She came to me, where I stood near the sea, and bowed as fealty demanded.

"Idai, thou art birth sister to Mirazhe, and in the stead of attending her wishes thou hast driven her, mute as she is, to the edge of challenge. What sayest thou in defence?"

"I say it is thine own actions have brought me to it, Lord King, and thou shalt answer to the Council!"

"Very well. Then we both shall. But you will swear to leave the Gedri in peace while we are here, or I shall banish you, birth sister or no, from this place."

"Very well," she said aloud, albeit through clenched teeth. "It shall live for all of me. But there are more pressing concerns."

"Agreed. First let us bring Mirazhe to delivery of her youngling. You say you know this trouble. What is the difficulty?"

She bowed her head, and I began to see that her anger was half grown from frustration and helplessness. "Akhor, the youngling is turned the wrong way. It cannot make its way into the world."

It was the worst news possible. "Is there nothing to be done?"

"On a few occasions in the past, a smaller female could assist in the birth, reach into the birth passage and pull the youngling out." She lowered her voice. "Sometimes the newborn survived, but our hands are not created for such things. These hands, these claws the Winds gave us for defence, to kill our food and our foes, are not gentle. Even in those few cases where the youngling survived, the mother died."

"Always?"

She stood in Sorrow, her head turned away from me. "Always."

I saw Shikrar and Kédra standing in Fear mixed with Concern, both striving for Calm so as not to overly alarm Mirazhe. The lady herself lay back now in the warm birthing pool with her eyes closed. Her body, so lovely with the shape of new life, was straining to no use. Her soulgem was dull. And to my surprise, there at the side of the pool knelt my dearling, her face furrowed with sorrow. She could not understand the speech between me and Idai, we spoke in our own tongue, but somehow she knew that all was very ill.

Idai's Sorrow was washed with Pain now, and my fear and anguish answered hers. *My lord, I can think of no other way. I must try to save the littling lest both die.*

"Wait," I said aloud. My vague thoughts had finally crystallised.

How I had envied the Gedrishakrim their hands, those tiny, delicate hands.

The two peoples were meant to live in peace. Together.

"Lanen, will you join us?" I said in her own tongue. And to her alone, *"Come, dearling. I need you."*

"Anything I can do, Akor my heart. How can I help this valiant lady?"

Lanen

I realised in a passing thought that I had answered him in truespeech without trying to focus, and the others must surely have heard. I forgot it in the next breath.

"Lanen, have you any knowledge of giving birth?"

I smiled, even then. What a way to put it! "Not of my own, but I have assisted many times, both with my own Kindred and with horses."

"Our history tells us of Healers among your people who could do great things with only the power of their hands and minds. Have you this skill?"

I hoped this was not his only idea. "No. I was tested when I was a child, there wasn't even a glimmer of the Healer's aura in me."

Akor finally let his voice match his mood. It became grim as Shikrar's had been at the cave. "*Come, my friends,*" he said in wide-scattered truespeech, and led us all over to the birthing pool where Mirazhe lay in her pain and fear.

"*Dear ones all,*" said Akor in the same fashion, "*I will not sit by and watch one of my people in pain without doing all I may to help. Mirazhe, littling, can you look at me?*"

She opened her eyes—they were bright blue, beautiful—and gazed up at him as best she could.

"*You have saved this lady from an unprovoked attack, for which I owe you a great debt. I propose now that we ask Lanen to assist you. Her hands have no claws like ours, she might be able gently to coax the youngling out.*"

"*Akhor, no!*"

"*Idai, you will be silent in this. I ask Mirazhe, her mate and his father. What say you, Shikrar? Kédra? Will you allow her to attempt this?*"

I think he expected a chorus of dismay when he finally came to it, but obviously the others—bar Idai, who seemed to hate me on sight—were willing to try anything, even this. I, on the other hand, was not ready for this idea.

"Akor, no!"

"What is wrong, dearling?"

"I—she's—Akor, I have never . . ." Then I realised that none of them had ever, either. "*Very well. If the lady will allow it.*" I bowed to the kind eyes that had saved me. "*Lady, what say you?*"

"She cannot speak, Lanen," said Akor. "During birth our Kindred become silent, and in any case Mirazhe does not speak your language."

"Does she still have truespeech?"

"A little, though it is difficult."

I looked at the lady and even I could tell she was in pain. *"May I bespeak you?"*

She nodded, and Kédra said for her, "She is called Mirazhe."

I concentrated. *"I am Lanen. Lady Mirazhe, do you permit me to assist you?"*

Even truespeech seemed an effort, but she managed it. *"I have not been told all the truth about you Gedri,"* she said, and her mind-voice was gentle despite her pain. *"If you have the Language of Truth, who knows what might be possible. Yes, try what you can. Ahhh!"*

I cringed at her pain in my mind. She was in a bad way indeed. And she was obviously not moving from where she was. I barely stopped to think. I took off boots and cloak, heavy tunic and shirt, and stepped into the water in leggings and my shift—and found it warm, almost hot. It felt wonderful.

At first.

I do not recall much about the rest of what happened. The sun was setting. It grew darker and darker and I had to rely more on feel. Mirazhe spoke with me when she could in truespeech, and I got her to nod or shake her head to let me know what helped or hurt. It kept her from having to speak, which seemed incredibly hard for her.

The worst moment was when I first tried to put my hand in the birth canal. I thought I would faint from the pain. I drew it out instantly and let the water of the pool wash it. It still burned, though not as badly, but what could I do?

I got Akor to tear my cloak, my beautiful green cloak, in half; and so concerned was I by then for Mirazhe and her child that I hardly cringed at its passing. I wrapped each arm, shoulder to fingertips, in one half of the wool. That was much better; its thick double weave was like so much soft armour. I could manage for a long while. When I had finally got the kitling turned, though, I had to use my unprotected hands to pull. I think I screamed as loud as Mirazhe when the littling came out.

But I will never forget the moment when I lifted the small, soft head above the level of the water for its first breath. All pain left me as there in the pool I held, for a second, a newborn Dragon in my arms. It was not much larger than a colt fresh from its mother. Its eyes were open and it *looked* at me, almost as if to speak its thanks. I laughed aloud in delight, then turned it towards its mother. It started to make sounds not unlike a human child just born. Mirazhe nuzzled it.

My hands were terribly burned, and once free of the spell of that greeting I climbed out of the freshwater pool and hurried to the open sea to quench the fire, shaking off the rags of wool that had been my protection. The shock of very cold water on the rest of my body was a great relief, though I could feel nothing on my arms at first. That coldness was all I had sought. Then I looked down and saw great lumps of skin in the water. Then I realised they had come off my arms.

I screamed once and fainted.

Akhor

We all gasped when the youngling came out, whole and hearty. I saw it look at Lanen and smiled to myself. This was likely to be quite an interesting addition to the Kindred.

Mirazhe would not be able to speak for some time, but the way she bent to the youngling and greeted it I had no fears for her. Her soulgem, brilliant now, shone a glorious sapphire even in that light.

Shikrar and Kédra were wholly taken with mother and child. I followed Lanen as she went to the sea. "Littling, the Winds bless you, you have saved them."

She did not answer and I could not see her face, but I did not have to. She screamed then, once from her gut, and fell over.

"Lanen!"

When I lifted her from the water she was limp, she could not hear me, and her arms—her arms were horrible. I could not hear her thoughts. I was terrified. My little knowledge of the Gedri disappeared like the wind, I could not help her and I knew she needed help desperately.

I could think of no other course. I must take her back to her people. They would surely know what to do for her pain. My heart turned cold, but there was no other way.

I gathered her in my arms and leapt into the sky, crying out in truespeech even as I flew. *"Shikrar, Kédra, someone, quickly! Fly before me to the place of the Gedri. Call out to them however you must, bring the Merchant, or better a Healer. Have them meet us at the place of Summoning. Fly on the Wind's wings!"*

Shikrar was beside me before I had finished.

"Shikrar, I fear for her, she barely lives. I take her to her own people to find healing, I will go from thence to the Great Hall when she is in their hands. The Council must wait upon me so much longer."

His greater wingspan took him ahead of me, but I sped after as fast as ever I had flown. I bespoke my dear one constantly, on the chance that she might wake and be fearful. I would not have her feel alone. I held her gently, keeping her close to me for warmth, but she did not stop shaking. I had to hold more tightly than before, since she could not grip with her poor burned hands.

In my passion I overtook even Shikrar, cried aloud to him to follow and flew fast as fear to the Gedri camp. I did not take the time to seek out the pass; instead I clasped my dearling to me and flew up, up into the thin cold air, crossing the mountains in a straight line to my destination.

Lanen never moved.

It was deep night when we reached the place of Summoning. If I had the time, I might have noticed that I still held the mood that Lanen had brought to me the night before, where hours were as years and all of life seemed to take place in a day.

I cared not who heard me. I shouted as loudly as I could.

Lanen

I had the whole story from Rella later.

"Those of us who were here and still awake were just settling to a bite of food when a voice the size of all outdoors rang through the night. We could tell from the first word something was terribly wrong.

" 'Marik! Merchant Marik! Bring a Healer, come here to the Boundary. It is the Guardian who calls!' No one twitched a muscle, we were that shocked. We couldn't believe it, but in seconds it came again. 'Come swiftly, Gedri, or I shall come to you!' it cried. For something that big it sounded amazingly desperate. And angry.

"About then we saw a long streak of light, Marik it was, running hotfoot through the clearing towards the Boundary. His men ran beside and behind—mostly behind—with torches. And we all got up and followed.

"When I got there I saw Marik at the Boundary, standing in front

of this huge silver head leaning over the fence, speaking as quickly
as it could. 'Merchant Marik, I require your consent. I have need of
assistance only your people can provide. May I cross the Boundary?'

"Marik stood there speechless with wonder. The Dragon leaned
closer and spoke again, fangs glinting in the torchlight. 'Quickly,
Merchant, your consent!'

"Give the man credit, he's the cockiest beggar I've ever heard tell
of. Not only did he find his tongue, he found something to do with
it. 'And what do you offer in return, O great one?' he says, bold as
brass. Ah, but he got his comeuppance. There was another voice
from the shadows behind that hissed, 'He offers you life, small-
souled one. I suggest you take it, lest I take it for you.'

" 'I consent,' squeaks Marik, stepping back. He needn't have
bothered. As soon as he spoke there was a sudden wind, loud in the
ears, and behind us all settled the Dragon. He was huge and terrifying, silver all over, and he was carrying something limp in his claws.

" 'This is Lanen, called Maransdatter. She is in great pain, and
there is some thing else that ails her as well. She shakes like a tree
in a high wind and cannot stop.' He set you down and leaned towards
you for a minute, I don't know why. Maybe to see if you were still
alive."

I stopped her. "You know, I think I remember that." Perhaps I
roused a little when we landed, for I remember seeing him in a kind
of haze when he leaned down and bespoke me.

*"Lanen, dearling, I must leave you in the care of your Kindred.
Forgive me, dear heart, I cannot help you in this. I will watch with
you as I may, I will hear your lightest thought. Call if you have need
of me and I will be with you."*

"Mirazhe and the child?" I managed to ask.

*"Both alive and very well. You have the gratitude of all the
Greater Kindred."* His thought became almost a whisper. *"And the
love of their King."*

Rella went on. "When the Dragon looked up, there was Marik
standing to one side. He drops his head down to Marik's level and
says in a kind of low rumble, 'Know, Merchant, that I value this life
more than any other. Restore her to health, tend to her well and I
shall be grateful. Treat her ill and I shall know of it and seek you out,
treaty or no, wherever in the world you fare.' Then he flew away. That
silver hide of his shone like white fire in the torchlight.

"Then we heard the voice of the second Dragon again. It was deeper, and seemed to come from even farther up than the other one. 'We give you thanks for your permission, and for your assistance with the lady; but as of this moment, the Boundary is restored. I am Guardian now. We shall stay on this side, and who of your people crosses the Boundary must die, as our treaty declares.'

"We hurried away from there. Marik's men were carrying you, and he was shouting for his Healer. I think you fainted again."

I remembered nothing for a long time.

Marik

"Berys, we have her! The Lords of the Hells have blessed my petitions with a swift answer, and more. The treaty has been broken by the Dragons, the Boundary crossed, and all to bring to me the dying body of the one I sought!

"I know not what has brought her to such a state, nor why the Dragons care about her, but they do. She was very near to death, her hands and arms horribly burned and her whole body shaking with an ague. Maikel has saved her life, though it took all his strength to do it. When he was done, he shook his head and said it was not enough, and he forced me to cut open a lan fruit, one of my precious lan fruits, and feed a quarter to her tonight and another quarter in the morning. (The second half I shall still have—it seemed to work wonders for her, I will try it myself in the morning if she survives.) Maikel will need to rest for days to regain his strength."

"And the girl?"

"He says she should be fully recovered before we leave the island, assuming the lan fruit is as effective as legend makes it."

"Hmph. All very interesting, Marik, but why do you wake me again so early in the morning to tell me this?"

"There is better news yet, Magister. It happened that there was plenty of chance to draw blood from her, though Caderan and I were near certain before.

"Caderan has performed the rite, Berys. This Lanen is my daughter, my blood and bone, that I promised for the Farseer ere she was born. She is the price of my pain, as you said. And very soon now, once she is fully healed, that price will be paid."

The demon messenger seemed almost to purr. "Excellent, Marik, excellent. Since she is not tractable, let her be dedicated to the Lords of the Hells as soon as may be. That should ease your pain and make her bend to your will; once she is mine I will take stronger precautions. When you return, my share of the profit from this voyage will be rich indeed. Well done, Master Merchant."

I released the creature, hardly noticing now the stench of its leaving, when of a sudden there was a knock at the door.

"Master Marik?"

It was the old woman called Rella, who had taken up with Lanen. "What do you want, mother?" I asked. It never hurts to be polite.

"In fact, master, I was wondering if you'd like some help. I know Lanen's terrible sick, and I've done some nursing in my time. There's some things easier for women to do."

She had a point, but I am a Merchant. I know perfectly well that nothing is free. "And what do you desire in recompense?"

"Well, that depends, don't it? How long am I like to be needed?"

"No more than half a day."

"Well, I've been bringing in ten bags a day, you ask your purser. Half a day, that's five bags lost." When I laughed, she snorted with disgust. "Very well, make it three. The girl has been kind to me."

"Done. Let you begin your service now for your three bags' credit, I haven't slept in as many days. Keep watch over her," I said. "If she wakes in pain, or needs anything, the guards outside will serve you." I stumbled out the door, going to my own cabin. Until that moment I had not realised how weary I was.

The pain was not so bad that night—lansip tea helped—and I limped the few yards across the dark ground serene in the knowledge that on the morrow I would be free of it forever.

xiii

COUNCILS

Akhor

When Lanen's people took her up, I left Shikrar as Guardian and her in his care. I had called a Council and even for heart's anguish could delay it no longer. But before I went, I had to know where he stood.

I faced Shikrar squarely. "Well, my friend? I go now before our people. I have broken the treaty with the Gedri, though my reasons for doing so were good. I have broken the ban, most certainly. And yet good has come of it." He stood silent. "Hadreshikrar, my old friend, how do you judge what I have done?"

He looked me steadily in the eye and replied, "Akhorishaan, your Lhanen has gifted me with life where I saw only the death of all I loved. I know not why, yet, but I know well she is more dear to you than life itself, or you would not have done what you have done. How may I serve you and your dear one?"

I bowed. "Bless you, old friend. For now, I beg you, remain here as Guardian. Watch well, and listen for Lanen's mindvoice should she be too weak to call out."

"Gladly. And do not fear to call on me at Council. I shall be listening."

I had no words. I could only bow my thanks again and go from him.

I feared, oh how I feared leaving Lanen in the hands of Marik. She had told me of the pact that had been made with the Rakshasa, and of her danger should she be his daughter. But there was no help for it. I listened for her every moment, even as I walked among my people.

The meeting place of the Greater Kindred is a vast natural cavern in the southern hills not far from the Gedri camp. We had changed it somewhat, added our shaping to the place, but in large part it was as we had found it when first we came to this island home.

That night I saw it as new. A fire burned in the center of the hall, below that place where centuries ago an escape for the smoke had been created in the roof of the cavern. The walls gleamed with years of carvings, some engraved on a background of *khaadish*, some rough-hewn out of the native rock. It held the smell and feel of my people for five thousand years.

On that night it was warm and alive with the Kindred. I looked around the room carefully to see who was not there, and realised that the only souls who were missing were Idai, Kédra and Mirazhe at the Birthing Cove and three of the eldest of us, who were too feeble to fly so far (they would listen through the ears and minds of their clan members, as Shikrar at the Boundary listened through me). All my people had responded to my summons, and to the tale that had spread fast as the wind about the Gedri who had called out like a youngling.

To my sorrow I noted that the hall held us all easily. I had in my earliest youth heard the Eldest of that day speak of a time when the hall was crowded. My mother later told me that he spoke in his age, that he was remembering tales his father told of other Councils in our former home. Since the Lesser Kindred were cut down in their pain and we came to this place, the hall has never been full.

I did not need that reminder of our last encounter with the Gedri.

I had meant to give much thought to what I must say and not say at this meeting, but since I had begun to live at the speed of the Gedrishakrim I had discovered that time can on occasion move so quickly there is not enough of it for much thought.

I had reached the raised dais at the far end of the hall. There was room there, and place appointed, for the five eldest among us and for the King. Shikrar and Idai would have been there; the other three had not come, and none so far had chosen to claim the right as eldest present.

The five-yearly Council was a place for grievances to be aired, a place to seek wisdom, to speak of those things that affected the Kindred as a whole. In unusual circumstances, any one of us might call the Council for a specific reason.

There had not been a special Council in my time. That was appropriate, surely, for my reason was unique.

There was no help for it now. I must speak and be judged as I stood.

I learned then the sickening sensation that accompanies an act beyond the laws of a society. There must come a time when society will demand an explanation or some form of retribution (especially if the society is founded on Order, as is the society of the Kindred). I found a deep fear then, one I had never suspected lurked within me—the terror of the exile. The fear that I stood for the last time with my own people literally made me reel; I had to stand on all fours lest I fall. Now that it came to the point, how could I live without them, without the friendly voices in my mind and the companionship of my own kind?

And why should I? whispered some coward part of my being.

Surrounded by the souls I knew and had lived with for centuries, my link with Lanen seemed a pale, weak thing, destined to be broken. When I told them what had happened, I need only leave out my Flight with Lanen. They would accept the rest, she would be honoured here for assisting Shikrar's clan, and I could stay. All I need do would be to renounce our bond, treat her as a favoured youngling, no more. After all, what more could we ever be to one another?

I thought with guilt of her plight, left alone in the hands of Marik, and the fate that might hang over her. I touched her mind lightly, and to my surprise there was a faint answer; she must be only just conscious. She knew a Healer was with her, but the pain and the sickness in her washed over me.

"How is it with you, littling?" I asked, in part to take her mind from her pain, in part to ease my guilt. I could not call her by name. It seems I meant to deny her in public soon: I found a need to deny her to myself first, to see how it felt.

Her answer was a whisper, but I noted with a twinge that even then she tried to keep her thoughts focussed that only I might hear. *"There is a Healer (oh hurry it hurts it hurts aaah!), he is helping the burns heal (oh Lady help me oh help oh help) he says I am fevered he has herbs (aaah!) he will give me when he has soothed the burns, I just want to sleep/get away from the pain. You sound strange, what's wrong?"*

"The Council waits upon me. Is there aught I may do for you?"

"Just say my name, so I know my memories are not a fever dream. Please, dear one, dear Kor—"

"Lanen, be silent!" I called sharply. Her sending stopped, thank the Winds. *"Littling, forgive me, but you are weak and your thoughts scatter wide. You must not say my true name, not now."*

Her sending at first was barely audible, a rush and jumble of contrition. *"I'm sorry I'm sorry I never meant to oh I'm sorry please forgive me Akor please I'm sorry, don't be angry with me I could not bear it oh! No noo don't touch my hands nonononono* **aaah!"**

Her thought stopped as though cut by a claw. I learned later that she had fainted again. I hoped her silence was no more than the easing of her pain. But I did know that scream—and indeed most of what she said to me—had been heard by everyone at the Council.

Rishkaan, the eldest there and an old adversary of mine, spoke for everyone. "Akhor, what was that? Or who?"

That was my Lady, said my heart, *rebuking my cowardice with her bravery.* How could I have let such unworthy thoughts live past the moment of their birth? Habit, and old ways, are deeply ingrained in us all; but old patterns can be broken.

We cannot control our thoughts. We can only decide what to do with them.

I called to her, though I knew not if she would hear me. *"Be brave, my Lanen. Thou art truly Lanen Kaelar, dear one, Lanen the Wanderer who has followed her heart to a new country and found it beating in the breast of another. As I am Khordeshkhistriakhor of the Greater Kindred, we are pledged to one another. It is no dream. Be well. I shall be with you as soon as I may."*

I could hardly imagine such courage as hers. Even as she lay in her pain, a thousand leagues from home and Kindred, sick and wounded nigh unto death in the service of those who would judge her here, I had heard only the wounded body crying out. It was not until I rebuked her that her soul weakened. All else she could bear.

Like a distant memory, I heard a whisper of the song we had made. Its beauty melted my heart. If I denied her now, I denied myself for all time.

I drew in a breath of Fire. Let them know the solemnity of this occasion.

"Let the Council begin!" I cried, and loosed Fire with my words towards the distant cavern roof. The breath of Fire is sacred to my people, used outside of battle only at those times when we commune with the Winds or consecrate some deed. Let them know that this was consecrate.

"I am Akhor, called the Silver King. I greet ye all, in the name of my ancestors. Ye are well come, my people!"

"All hail, King of the Greater Kindred," they answered as with one voice. It echoed in that place and sounded like the voices of a thousand. My heart wept at the sound, with pride at their strength and sorrow at the knowledge that I might never hear those words again.

"Answer me, Akhor," said Rishkaan impatiently, breaking the formality. "Who was that? Was it the same Gedri who spoke two days past?"

"My people, I have called you here that you might know what I have done, and what has been done by that child of the Gedri whose voice you have just heard cry out in pain, and who called out a warning two nights gone." I stood in Authority. "Know that our lives all are changed henceforth, my people, because of my actions and hers. The Winds blow cold across our times, but truly is it said that back of the winter is the Wind of spring."

There was a great deal of murmuring.

I ignored it.

"My first news is of the clan of Shikrar. Mirazhe has brought forth her youngling, a fine son. Both are at the Birthing Cove and both are well. The Lady Idai stands birth sister to Mirazhe, and Kédra is with them now to dote on his family."

This was news indeed, most unexpected good news. Some laughed as they remembered Shikrar's ostentatious pride in Kédra. Most had known of Mirazhe's distress, one way or another, and many stood in delighted Surprise.

"Is Shikrar not with them?" someone called.

"He stands Guardian at the Boundary," I replied. "I know his feelings on at least part of the matter I wish to put before you, and I cannot say that of another of our Kindred beside myself and two of those at the Birthing Cove. But I begin at the end of my story."

And in a style I have used a thousand times since, I lifted my head and spoke to the Greater Kindred. I did not know it at the time, but I have been told that my voice changed as I spoke. It grew deeper and clearer, no louder than before but ringing so as to fill the Great Hall itself.

"Harken well, O my Kindred. I have a tale to tell you of dreams and waking life beyond all imagining, of danger and sacrifice and love beyond all reason.

"Harken, O my people. This is the tale of Lanen and Akhor."

✿   ✿   ✿

I told them everything.

Everything. From my Weh dreams to our first meeting, her words with Shikrar at our second meeting and his warning. (Much was made of this, that she had truespeech. It was undeniable and still seemed little less than miraculous.) I told of our third meeting, that I had arranged it without the knowledge of any other but that it had saved her life.

With a deep breath and a prayer to the Winds, I spoke then of our reactions to one another, how we had been drawn to each other beyond all reason and beyond all denying. I told of our flight to my Weh chamber, of much that was said, and was about to begin the story of our souls' Flight when some kind Wind blew my thoughts ahead to what their reaction would be at this stage of the tale. Better to save that particular blast of fire for the end, when they knew her better.

All I gave them of that time was the knowledge that there was more to hear.

Next I told of the Discipline of Clear Thought, and the answer both of the Winds we revere and the Lady of the Gedrishakrim. There was a louder murmuring at that. The Winds had spoken before to our people, but not for many lifetimes. I heard the word "omen" muttered around the room. I knew some still saw me as a living omen, with my silver hide.

The events that took me to the Birthing Cove were already known to many. Shikrar had indeed sought me everywhere, and of course Idai had sent the elder females away when she realised they knew no more than she (Idai was eldest after Shikrar and could so command the others). I was grateful that Idai's voice was not there at that moment, but the duties of birth sister may not be neglected and are most needed just after the birth. She would have her say about me later.

When I told the Council what my Lanen had done for Mirazhe, for Kédra, for the youngling, all murmuring stopped. At first they could not believe that such devotion by one of another race could exist. I felt the first stirrings of doubt, even of disbelief. I had thought of that.

"My people, I call upon Shikrar, Eldest and Keeper of Souls, as

witness to this thing beyond belief. Will you take his word as truth?"
They would. All knew that Shikrar was beyond reproach.

He was waiting.

He spoke with us all from the Boundary, using wide-scattered speech that all might hear. He spoke simply and with great reverence for Lanen and took them to the end of the tale, that she lay now so terribly burned and sick and in the hands of her people, hence her cry of pain. He gave then an account of our arrival at the place of Summoning, and seemed almost proud of his part in the proceedings.

I was wondering how to fill in the final verse, the tale's heart that I feared would turn my people from me, when Rishkaan saved me the trouble.

"And what is the last refrain, Akhor?" he asked sourly. "Your song is not complete, you have left out a verse in the center. Why should this Gedri child do such a thing? She is no Healer by her own admission. Did you threaten her? Or beg? I cannot believe either. All she had to say was no, and no shame to her." His voice grew harder. "And why did she speak so to you, before the Council was begun. 'Dear one' she called you. Why, Akhor? What have you not yet told us?"

Trust Rishkaan, I thought. He knows me well, and his disdain of the Gedri verges on hatred.

It was time.

"Because, Rishkaan, my people: she loves me. She would do anything for me, and I for her." *My soul to all the Winds, preserve my dearling and me, bring us home to that joy you spoke of, for at this moment it seems a thousand leagues and ten thousand years away.*

"There is one last thing I have to tell you, my people, and try though I might there is no way to ease the telling.

"I flew the Flight of the Devoted with this child of the Gedri as we sat in my Weh chamber two nights past. We flew on the wings of our souls and made a new song together.

"We know it is foolish, it is impossible, we know there can be no joining save mind to mind; but I swear to you she is my heart's beloved, and my mate for now and ever. As I am hers."

There was a brief moment as a hundred and fifty of the Greater

Kindred were stunned into silence, some for the first time in centuries, some for the first time in their lives.

Then the Great Hall was awash with sound as they found their voices and, as one, protested.

My own reaction was not what I had expected. I knew a chastened pride in myself for speaking openly about Lanen, but apart from that I was excited, and in the main I rejoiced. For the first time since I could remember not only were the Kindred united—albeit against me—they were *awake*.

My people have slept too long, this is snow on their faces. It is good for them, however it may turn for Lanen and me.

Indeed, I began almost to be amused as the most outraged stormed up to face me on the dais. They stood in Admonition or Disgust or Anger, as it took them, and I could not possibly hear more than a few words from each.

"You cannot, it is unholy. . . ."

"What spell has this Gedri witch . . . ?"

"It has always been death for the Gedri to pass . . ."

"Akhor, how could . . ."

"You fool, you were our hope for the future, touched by the Winds. . . ."

"What omen now, Akhor? Will the Silver King lead us into the arms of the *Gedrishakrim?*"

This last was Rishkaan. He stood where I could see him, his body twisted in the extreme of Fury, his wings half-raised and rattling, and spat the word "Gedrishakrim" at me like a curse.

I stood in Sorrow. I could think of no words for him, nothing to say to ease his pain and anger, and I would not dignify this fury with a direct response.

Turning to the others, I stood and called in the loudest voice I possessed, pitching it again to make the cavern ring. "Silence! Silence, O my people! Is this the Council of the Kindred? Silence I say!"

The habit of obedience is strong, as is our pride. Those on the dais stepped off, save Rishkaan, who had the right of age and claimed it now. He had controlled his anger and now took the place of the Eldest, which was due him as the eldest of those present. All kept

silence (out of curiosity as much as anything else, I strongly suspected: there had not been this much excitement at a Council meeting for centuries).

"Who has laid a spell on you to draw you from your true nature?"
cried Erianss. She was about the age of Mirazhe, mated to a good
soul, but she had never quickened from their flights. "Our people
diminish and you, the King, give your heart to one who is but a flicker
in our lives! Even should she live past this sickness, she will be dead
in half a hundred years. Is such a creature worthy of the love of our
King?"

There was a general murmur of agreement.

"Erianss, you know that no spell could be hidden from you all.
How could the Rakshasa be involved and leave no trace for our
kind? We know such a thing cannot be done. And as for my—as for
Lanen's life being short, you are right, and my mind knows that you
are right. But I cannot deny love, no matter what form it takes. Was
Yrais less worthy of Hadreshikrar because she lived but thirty years
after their joining? I have not taken a mate from our Kindred because there has never been a lady who could understand the *ferrinshadik* that has haunted my heart all my life. One lady even told me
the kingship had made me too solemn, that I should try to think less."
I had to smile; it had, of course, been Erianss. "I suspect that lady is
now less than happy with the outcome of her advice.

"My people, I am your King by your own gift. When that office
was bestowed upon me I changed, as a king must. In many ways I
have lived not the life I wanted, but the life I was required to lead.
I have not shunned that duty. I have held what I believed to be best
for us all in the front of my heart for nearly eight hundred years. In
that time, I have come to know that I must think of you at all times,
and of our Kindred as a whole, our future and our past.

"It is no secret but a great tragedy that we are fewer than ever
before in our history. In the last eight hundred years there have been
but three births, including Kédra's youngling. We are declining, my
people, even from the few we were before, and I have wondered
what was to be done for many long, long years. Now I believe that
it is time to attempt a reconciliation with the Gedri. They were great
Healers of our people at one time. Perhaps if we can communicate
with them they might be able to discover what it is that has so
changed us of late."

"It has always been death for the Gedrishakrim to pass the Boundary," said a voice behind me. Rishkaan had mastered his fury and stood now in Anger and Rebuke. "I do not recall there being anything in the treaty or in our laws which allowed for any other fate, no matter how they happened to come there. Why should there be any other consideration? She deserves death."

My heart fell when I heard a murmur of assent; at least, that was my first reaction. Then I began to grow angry.

"Is your respect so lightly given, my people?" I demanded, fighting my instincts to take on Anger myself. *Calm, Akhor, calm, that alone will sway them.* "Not a breath ago I heard your praise for this child of the Gedri who put herself in peril of her own life that two of us—strangers to her—might live; this child of the Silent People who has the truespeech, as none of her Kindred had even in those times when our two peoples lived in harmony and the Peace was in flower. And I charge you to remember, it was I who crossed over to her, and that to save her life."

My words met only silence. Still mistrust, still anger, still vengeance. When would it end? I felt my words falling as on stone. I was suddenly weary. I gave them my last words.

"Consider well, O my people. I did not invite this, and neither did my dearling. When Lanen and I met, it was with the simple hope that our peoples might speak with one another, not that we two would join in a hopeless union. For we both have doomed ourselves to barrenness, to loneliness, to a life apart from all those we hold dear.

"When our several gods spoke to us at the same time outside my Weh chamber, we realised there was more to this than we can know. I hope you also will realise that there is more to this than madness, and will see in this joining the will of the Winds and of the Lady.

"Let any other speak who will; I have done," I said. "I am heartsick with my beloved's pain, and weary with this day. I shall be in my chambers hard by if any should require speech of me. I will rejoin you at midday."

I stepped off the platform and found a way made for me.

I could not tell if it was an honour or if they simply did not want to touch me, nor did I care. I was hungry and thirsty and I needed to know how Lanen fared, and to talk with Shikrar.

Lanen

I woke in a bed, warm and comfortable. The last thing I remembered was searing pain as the Healer took my hands in his. I
could feel my hands and arms now only as swollen lumps lying outside the bedclothes, and blessed the Healer for it. I opened my eyes
slowly and saw that I was alone save for Rella, who snored in a chair
against the wall near the fireplace. There was a bright blaze, and I
was warmer than I had been for days.

Fireplace?

Wall? In the camp?

"Rella? Where am I?" I creaked.

Rella opened a red-rimmed eye and said, "In Marik's second
cabin, where his guards slept until now. Thanks to you I got to spend
the night in a chair and my back is killing me. How are you feeling?"

"Terrible," I murmured. "But better than I was. My arms and my
hands don't hurt at all." I could see them now, wrapped carefully in
bandages. I lifted my left arm and tried moving a finger. It didn't go
very far, but it didn't hurt either. From the shoulder down I was, for
the most part, blessedly numb. "What hour of the day or night is it?"

"It lacks but a scant hour of dawn, and you'll oblige me by putting
your hands back down and keeping still," said Rella. "The Healer said
leave them be for the rest of the day, you're not to move 'em or touch
anything. They still glowed bright blue when he bandaged 'em, my
girl, I'd do as he says."

I gingerly tried to bend my right arm a little at the elbow. There
was no pain. "That must be some Healer Marik's got," I said in awe.
Our village Healer had been nothing special, able to speed healing
a little, cure small aches and pains. This man had healed my arms
and hands almost completely—I shuddered again at the memory of
great lumps of skin in seawater—and I knew that, beyond even the
burns, he had saved my life.

I had little memory of the night before until Rella told me of our
arrival in camp, but I vaguely remembered when the Healer was just
beginning to work (when Akor bespoke me), and the fact that even
when he had taken the pain from my burns, I could not stop shaking. I was roasting and freezing by turns, I could barely breathe, and
I had started coughing horribly.

Now, only a few hours later, I felt as though I had the remains of a cold, and that on the mend.

"Aye, 'twas his own personal Healer. Third rank he is, and aiming for fourth already, but there's no airs about him. He's a good lad, gentle-spoken as you could wish, though he's so powerful so young."

I summoned the strength to smile at her. "How do you know he was third rank?"

"Asked him, didn't I? For now, though, my girl, Marik's left me in charge of you. He said I was to call him when you woke, but first—" She went to the table and brought over a small bowl. "—you've to eat this."

Even in my weakened state, I had enough strength to doubt. It was too strange seeing Rella here in what must be my prison. "You first," I muttered, trying to make it seem a jest.

Rella grinned. "Well, better late than never," she said. "Dear Lady knows I could use this after last night." She speared a piece of the orange flesh with her knife and ate it with obvious relish. "And so I become the first of my family ever to dine on lan fruit," she said, and shivered. "Blessed Shia, that's wonderful! But I reckon you could use it more than me."

I have never tasted anything in my life so glorious. Imagine the sweetest peach, the tartest pear, the lushest berry you have ever tasted, and combine with them a rush of strength to a wounded body. I could feel the virtue of the fruit as it rushed down my arms, healing, renewing. She fed me a quarter of the fruit—she told me I had had the first quarter the night before, I mourned not tasting it— then, looking at the rest as it lay in the bowl, said quite calmly, "Hmm. Seems to be going brown at the edges. You'd better finish it before it spoils. I'll help you if it's too much."

She barely had two more tiny pieces for herself. And where a quarter, for all its vigor, had restored some of my lost strength and started the blood moving around my slowly healing injuries, the added half Rella stole for me rushed wildly through my arms to my very fingers' ends. I could feel the knitting of skin and muscle beneath the bandages even as I ate.

For all that, it did not really satisfy hunger. I found, as health and strength flowed back into my body, that I was ravenous. I counted back and discovered I hadn't eaten in two days. Rella had prepared a stew with roots and dried meat, assuming I'd need food, bless her, but even she was surprised by the amount I put away. She would not let me feed myself, but insisted that I leave on the bandages and let her feed me.

Between the first and second bowls of stew I took the chance to ask her something that had been nagging at me.

"Rella, why are you being so kind to me? You're the only soul I've seen here who cares whether another human being lives or dies. Please don't think me ungrateful, but why?"

She stared at me for a minute, and somehow I was made more aware than usual of her crooked stance. "Child, I told you, I have come to this place to make my fortune, and with what I have gathered already my old age will be spent in ease. I have had a hard enough life thus far, and I have seen every kind of rogue there is over the years, and there are more than a few of them on this voyage. You were like a breath of clear air on that ship. I remember you asked my name, you brought me soup one night when I was tired so I needn't stir. You probably don't even remember, kindness is natural to you as breathing, but I do." She stared into the bowl she carried and her voice dropped. "Besides, I had a daughter once. She'd have been about your age." When she looked back at me her eyes were alight with a dancing admiration. "And I hope she might have been something like you, too, brave as brass and tell 'em all where to go." She grinned. "There's even rumours Marik tried it on with you and you knocked him silly! He spent a while closeted away with his Healer, but not afore some'd seen his bruises. That was well done."

She started feeding me again, but for some reason simply looking at me seemed to catch her just so and she started laughing. "Ah, girl, never mind me—but dear Goddess, will I ever forget the sight of you, half dead and carried here by a Dragon! Or the look on Marik's face, or the squeak he made when that Dragon told him to do well by you or he'd know of it! Marik would've killed the two of you for a pin if he could have, but he had to put a bold face on it. Ah, dear girl, you've made this a voyage to remember!" I had never heard her laugh before. It sounded a bit rusty, but it was a good laugh.

"Besides," she added, calming down, "you'll find there's another interested in your well-being now, even if his life didn't depend on it. It's not your kind soul has got you inside the only real walls on this forsaken island and a night in a real bed treated by his own Healer!

Nay, there's a price owing to Marik; and make no mistake, Merchants collect on their debts."

I was instantly sober. In my pain I had forgotten just what Marik thought he was owed. And now here I was, in his power again, even in his debt. Why had he healed me, when surely he and his pet Caderan could have simply offered me to the demons? My heart sank. Of course. I was to be handed over to the Rakshasa whole. In any practice, sacrifices are better received if they are perfect before they are killed.

"Rella," I said, keeping my voice low as she bustled about, "I need your help. I don't know if I can get out of here on my own."

"Not for a good few hours anyway, until those hands of yours are healed," she said lightly. "Marik's orders."

"No, I mean I have to get away. Now, if possible." I reached out clumsily with my bandaged arm and blocked her path, looking her in the eyes. "He's going to kill me, Rella, or hand me over living to the Rakshasa. Probably tonight. Please, for pity's sake, will you help me?"

"So—you know about that, do you?" she said very quietly, and in a voice I had never heard from her. I drew back in horror. Was she privy to Marik's counsels, was she in league with him? But she smiled and put her hand oh so gently on my arm. "Come now, my girl, do I look like one of them?"

"I wouldn't know."

She grinned. "Like I said before, better late than never." She pulled the chair next to the bed and sat, her face on a level with mine, and her whole demeanour was changed. Gone were the rough edges of a practical countrywoman. Her eyes were sharp with intelligence, her carriage even of that twisted body spoke of hidden strength, and her voice, low and intense, bore only a trace of a northern accent. "You are not the only one with secrets. I am a Master of the Silent Service in Sorún. I was sent to learn what I could of Marik and his doings, for he has gained power in too many quiet corners of Kolmar far too swiftly to suit us, even before he determined to come here. That he should set out on such a chancy venture drew our attention, for he is in all things a cautious man. We suspected he had foreknowledge of his success from—other sources. Caderan and his demons, for example."

I lay back and tried to grasp the change in her, tried to understand what she was so carefully not saying. "Rella, what are you talking about? I thought he sought only wealth."

"Child, child, since when has anyone ever sought wealth alone? Wealth is a means to an end, and that end is power. There are more branches of the House of Gundar in the Four Kingdoms than of any other Merchant House, despite its relative youth." Her voice was thick with disgust as she added, "And each one is well supplied with men and arms, and each one has its own sorcerer." She spat.

My head reeled. "Sorcerer? Blessed Shia, do you mean there is a demon master in each of the local merchant enclaves, even in the towns?"

"At least one."

"Mother of us all," I breathed, a curse and an invocation. "Rella, do you tell me he is using demons to gain power throughout all of Kolmar?"

"As fast as he can. And you are the key, Lanen Kaelar."

My heart leapt with fear at that name, but her gentle manner stopped me from trying to get out of bed. She smiled, a smile full of knowing that somehow suited her far too well. "Never wonder, child. I told you I am of the Silent Service. We have ears everywhere. I risk my master's wrath for speaking openly to you, but you are too vital a piece in this game to act in ignorance."

"How did you find me?" I asked softly.

"Pure chance. My partner and I found ourselves trapped one night in a nameless village in central Ilsa, driven to the inn there by torrential rains. We rose late the next morning and sat in a corner in the tavern. The only others there when we sat down were an older man and a tall young woman with hair like ripe wheat. The older man did a great deal of talking."

Blessed Shia. The couple in the corner, sat there all the time, hearing every word. I had never looked close enough to have seen her crooked back. Dear Lady, how could I have been so stupid?

"It was a fine tale, Lanen. Are you Marik's daughter?"

"I don't know," I said miserably. "I think I must be. If I were not and he knew it, he would surely have let me die."

"Mmm. You didn't hear your Dragon friend speak to him last night. I think Marik would have tried to keep you alive for that one's good will, at least for the moment. But probably best to assume for now that he is your father. In any case your time is short. The ritual is set for this very night, as soon as true darkness falls. We have only until then to get you out."

"Truth, then," I said, my eyes locked on hers. "Why are you helping me?"

One corner of her mouth lifted. "Marik's as nasty and vicious a son of the Hells as ever drew breath, or hadn't you heard? And I've no wish to live under the rule of demons. Besides," she added, touching my cheek softly, "I spoke true about your kindness, and my daughter. Now, quickly, tell me what you can about the Dragons."

"Rella, I can't, I promised—"

"Idiot. I don't want to know their secrets or yours. Just tell me how to get in touch with them if I need to. Just in case."

I was taken aback. "Very well. There are three who might help you—us. Akor first, if he is there—that's the Guardian, the silver one who brought me back. Or Kédra, or Shikrar. Go to the place of Summoning, or anywhere on the Boundary, and call out. Someone will come, and if it isn't one of those three"—I grinned—"just don't get them angry."

Behind her the door opened and the guard I'd hit with the sea chest came in. He had a horrible bruise on his forehead and he didn't look any too pleased to see me.

"Well, mother," he said. "Is she fit to speak with my lord?"

"Aye, soon enough, soon enough," said Rella calmly, her accent thick with the north. "Just you tell M'lord Marik to wait a bit. There's things unattended to yet. Tell him half an hour."

"Now, mother."

She whirled on him in obvious anger. "If he fancies watching my lady make water, let him come now. She's never even been to the necessary, and it'll not be swift or simple with her arms as they are and all she's been through. Half an hour!"

The guard, looking daggers, nodded. "Half an hour then. Be certain she is ready."

"Yes, yes," she replied absently, fussing with me as he left. Once he was gone, she caught my gaze. "Very well, my girl. We have only so long to make all ready."

We held a swift council of two.

Akhor

I bespoke Lanen quietly when I left the Great Hall some hours before dawn—she did not answer. I assumed she slept still. Shikrar had heard nothing from her.

As soon as I reached my chambers I bespoke Shikrar once more. He stood guard still at the Boundary, waiting to hear my side of all that had happened. He had heard what I had said in Council and I filled in the few gaps in his knowledge, asked his pardon for keeping our twilight meeting secret, and told him all that a friend would want to know about my perilous love for Lanen, and of our Flight.

"And because of this, this Flight taken in your fancy, you consider yourself bound to the child? She is a singular creature, to be sure, but—Akhor, you must know such a thing is not binding."

"I know that, my friend. But I do not seek to escape this bond, mad though it seems, impossible though it is. She is my soul's other half, Shikrar. I never knew it, but I have sought her all my life. It is the wisdom or the folly of the Winds that she has taken the form of the Gedri, not of the Kindred." I did not tell him that I had seen her in our flight as one of us. I suspected even Shikrar would have had trouble with that.

But I could not forget. I found that I now understood what Kédra had told me once, about the new song of the Devoted. The music was always there. I had only to think of her and I heard our voices joined as on that night, and saw her in her Kantri form. Her soulgem was clear as water; it had no colour, only light. And her armour was the dark gold of her hair. . . .

"How fares Mirazhe? And the newborn?"

His tone shifted dramatically, I could hear his swelling pride. *"Both well, both beautiful. Idai is trying to get rid of Kédra, but he cannot tear himself away yet. My son's youngling! The thought is wondrous."*

I reveled for a moment in his rejoicing. It gave me new strength, and a measure of hope. Surely he would not take my request in the wrong spirit.

"Shikrar, I rejoice with you. In our decline, how bright shines such a birth. Yet I fear I have a request to make of you, even at this time. Believe me, were there anyone else I could call upon—but I have little choice. The Council debates now my fate and hers. There

are no Elders there save Rishkaan, and he is shocked to his bones by everything I have said and done. He cannot separate my actions from Lanen's." I could not keep even my mind's voice steady; it wavered like the rawest youngling's. "*Please, my friend, I beg you, let Kédra do as Idai asks that he may relieve you at the Boundary, and let you come to the Council. Rishkaan is the Eldest present, though he is so much younger than you, and that gives his words more weight than they deserve. He has already called for Lanen's death—you know he can never forgive the Demonlord for destroying his ancestor Aidrishaan, and the making of Tréshak into the first of the Lesser Kindred. To him the Gedri are makers of death and agony, Shikrar, nothing more, never capable of more, and he wills to return that evil to my dearling. Shikrar, soulfriend, I cannot bear it. I would never ask this at so sacred a time, but I have spoken already and they can hear no more from me; perhaps they will be able to hear you.*"

There was a long silence. When he spoke again his tone was somber and more kind than I had heard it since this all began. "*Ah, Akhorishaan. I know now it is true, she is your mate no matter what anyone says. I know that voice. I heard it last when my dear one, my love Yrais, was dying, and it came from my soul. I will summon Kédra, Khordeshkhistriakhor. I will be there by morning.*"

"*Hadretikantishikrar, I thank you with all my heart.*"

Then he was gone. I reached out to Lanen again, but she was still asleep.

There was nothing else I could do. I closed my eyes in meditation, took myself through the Discipline of Calm and waited.

Towards morning I slept for a brief while, and in that time I dreamed. At first it seemed a dream of our Flight, for I saw Lanen in her Kantri-form, but it soon became something other. She had become more real, more fully herself in that form; I watched as we lived our lives together as one Kindred, brought younglings forth, raised them, taught them all our joint history and all we knew of the Two Peoples. It was full of joy, that dream, until the end. We both became Elders, well respected by the Kindred, and died so, but it was not our deaths that disturbed me. As I rose slowly to consciousness I saw the soulgems of the Lost flickering through our ashes, almost in accusation. We had made no difference to them, our lives though rich and well lived had made no difference.

I woke some hours after dawn feeling disturbed, and obscurely

angry at the Winds for such a vision of personal happiness that left
me so deeply unfulfilled.

I discovered on waking that Shikrar had been better than his
word. Kédra had already arrived and taken up his station at the
Boundary, and Shikrar stood outside my chamber, requesting entry.
I welcomed him, trying to dispel the cloud of the dream that hung
over me. "I thank you from my heart, my soul's friend. You honour
me."

Shikrar's eyes smiled. "Yes, I do, and so does my son. I am glad
you recognise it. Now, how may I help you and your dear one?"

My heart was warmed, enlarged by him. Of all my Kindred, only
Shikrar had yet referred to Lanen with anything but a curse; his
words were balm on a raw wound. "Bless you for that, my friend. As
for helping us, I beg you, go into the Great Hall and find how the
Winds blow in the Council. I must know what they say now about
me—about us."

"Bespeak me in a few moments, you shall hear with my ears." He
turned to go.

"Shikrar, I—"

"Be at peace, Akhor," he said gently, turning his head towards me,
answering my thought. "Our friendship is old and tried. You and
Kédra alone in this world know my true name, and for you as for my
son I would do whatever lay in my power. Now your Lanen has
given me the free gift of my son's dear one and their child when death
seemed inescapable. How shall I not do my utmost?"

I bowed to him. I had no words. He smiled back at me and left.

Lanen

As Rella and I were making our plan of escape, I rose and tried
to dress. I had forgotten that much of my clothing, of course, was
still at the Birthing Cove—I had arrived in leggings and my shift,
both of which were now a pile of rags against the wall. I sighed, only
once, for my ruined cloak. Rella had to send one of the guards to
fetch the contents of my sea chest from our tent (he refused to bring
the chest itself).

It may seem a small thing now, but I remember clearly my intense relief—almost delight—at discovering not only a spare shirt,
clean leggings and an old patched tunic, but the extra pair of boots

I had bought in Corlí (with my boot knife tucked away inside, little use though it might be) and my old black cloak. I felt a thousand times better when I was dressed.

The lan fruit had worked wonders. There was no pain when I tried using my hands, and when I dared unwrap the bandages a little, from the shoulder end, I found pale skin underneath, delicate but whole. And it was not even the pale pink of a normal healing burn—it looked like ordinary skin. I did not dare hope that I would avoid the scars of such a burn, but perhaps they would not be so bad as I feared. And still no pain. I understood then why lan fruit was so valuable. The Healer's efforts had drawn me back from the edge of death, but without the lan fruit, I would still have needed weeks to heal fully. With it, I was nearly healed within *hours*. It almost passed belief.

I left the bandages on for the moment, to give the illusion that I was still injured enough to need them.

The guard, unfortunately, was true to his word. The first fingers of sunlight were just reaching into the clearing when he returned with his master. Despite my efforts I shivered when I saw Marik. Dear Lady, that this vile creature might be my father—it was all I could do not to retch.

I watched him from my sickbed, for after the effort of dressing I had found I needed to lie down again. I was desperately weary, despite the lan fruit and the healing. Healers use their own power, but the body of the one being healed must supply the materials and bear the changes enforced on it by another's will. I felt I could sleep for a week.

"Go," Marik told the guard. When he saw that Rella lingered, he snapped, "You, too."

She sneered behind his back. "You're welcome. I'll expect those three bags' credit."

"Go!" She closed the door behind her.

Marik turned to me and bowed, his lovely voice warm and his eyes unreadable. "Lady Lanen." He seated himself in the chair by the bed.

"Marik."

"How are you feeling?"

"My hands don't hurt anymore," I said, truthfully.

"I am delighted to hear it, lady. I do not wish to shock you, but have you any idea how close to death you were last night?"

"No. I remember I couldn't stop shaking." I hoped he wouldn't notice that I still hadn't.

"Maikel drained himself saving you, lady. He will be no good for anything for two full days, and without the lan fruit you might have died anyway. That is his calling, of course, and he is well paid for it— but we feared you would not see the morning. Aside from the fever, your hands"—he let that glorious voice falter—"your hands and your arms had but shreds of skin left on them." He moved closer to me, concern writ large on his face. "What happened, Lanen?" he asked in husky tones. "What did those creatures do to you?"

"It was—my choice," I said at last. "There was a way I could help them. They didn't know it would burn me." I think I managed to sound pitiful enough, and wished that more of my weakness were an act.

"What happened? You must tell me, lady." He smiled gently, his whole demeanour intent on kindliness, the amulet around his neck brilliant in the bright dawn light. "Come, Lanen, I have saved your life, surely you owe me so much."

I could feel the glamour through my weariness, but never again could I be fooled in that way. "Forgive me, Marik. It is true I have learned much about them: but they have enjoined me to silence, and surely you see that I will not, I cannot betray that trust. I hope for a day when our two peoples will be able to speak freely one with another, but until that time I—"

"Spare me your fool's dreams!" he spat angrily. Despite all I knew of him, I was shocked. That voice, so musical it reminded me of the Kindred, turned to cracked bells in an instant when he was angry. He rose and flung himself around the room, pacing, half wild with impatience. "I want to know why the Dragons, who have instantly killed everyone else who has ever crossed their border, did not kill you. Not only do they not destroy you, the Guardian himself crosses the border to take you away, and a day later brings you half-dead into the camp and demands that I break their precious treaty and weary my own Healer near to death—for what? For *you*. I want to know why, girl. *Why? What are you to them?*"

I was becoming befuddled with fright and weariness, and his intensity cowed me in my weakened state. *Swiftly, Rella,* I begged her silently. I looked up at Marik. "I don't know what to tell you," I answered. "I did not cross the Boundary like poor Perrin. He was after gold or some other gain, no matter who he had to kill for it. I was not. Please, I cannot tell you more. So far as I know I am nothing to them. Let me sleep." I bowed my head.

He was back beside the bed in an instant; he snatched a handful of my hair right next to the scalp and yanked it back as hard as he could. I screamed, of course. (Jamie always said I should never cheat anyone in earshot of the chance to help.) "You have slept enough at my expense, witch," he snarled into my face. "Talk, or I will make you. What pact have you made with the creatures? Tell me, damn you!"

In the brief silence I thought I heard voices outside, and in through the window came just the slightest hint of the smell of smoke.

"I have made no pact!" I cried out.

"Have you not?" he said grimly, and a dagger appeared from nowhere in his hand as he gripped me by the hair. My bandaged arms were worse than useless. He held the blade against my throat, I could feel the cold steel press against my flesh. "Yet I know a way to find out the truth of the matter. Why will you not speak of the Dragons to me? What do you owe them, against the life you owe me? You were willing to tell them about me fast enough," he growled between clenched teeth. "What kind of creature are you, with Farspeech that you use against your own kind?"

I was almost too shocked to be frightened. "What? How did you . . . ?"

"I know," he spat. "Leave it at that. Repay your debt, daughter. Use this Farspeech to tell them I am a man of honour, that you were wrong about me."

"I cannot!" I cried. Even if it were possible to lie in truespeech, the vision of Marik at large among the Kindred, hidden by who knew what agency, bearing the Lady only knew what sort of weapons to use against them—never.

And below thought, down deep where I thrust it until I could bear to think of it, I heard him call me daughter, and knew it was the truth.

"So. You cannot." His face was mere inches from mine, his eyes blazing with hatred and a kind of triumph. "Then I shall take what I want without your assistance. For I have ways and ways, Lanen.

You are not the only one to have set foot across the Boundary and lived!"

I gasped, which made him laugh. The smell of smoke was stronger now, and the voices outside louder. I could not make out what they said.

"Yes, I thought that would catch you. And I did not crawl to the beasts that live there, as you did." He smiled at me, a mad smile, but the most chilling thing about his whole demeanour was that it seemed so little different from his usual manner. Aside from an indefinable something in his eyes, his smile was still the charming smile I had first seen in Illara. I was terrified. "And now that you are healed, there is no more cause for delay. You are no more use to me, daughter," he said, making the word a curse. "I shall turn you over to my demon master as payment."

"The Guardian—" *Hurry, Rella, damn it, it can't be that hard....*

"If you had called him, he would be here already." The knife blade pressed hard against my throat.

I could make out what the voices were shouting now. Fire. I heard the running footsteps of what I desperately hoped were the two guards. Marik ignored it, possibly did not even hear it.

"I have not called upon them," I managed to say past the blade. "I have no wish to destroy you, Marik." I managed to choke out the word. "Father."

At that instant, thank the Lady, the door burst open and Rella rushed in. "What are you doing to her?" she screamed. Marik was caught off guard, she ran straight to him and dragged him away from me.

Now it was my turn. I rose swiftly and snatched up the chair that stood near the bedside, raised it high and brought it crashing down with all my strength. Marik dropped with a groan.

Rella stood and faced me. "Come on, in the eye like we agreed," she said impatiently. "Quickly!"

"Come with me!" I whispered urgently.

"I told you, if this doesn't work you'll need me here to help. Hit me, damn it!"

There was no time to argue. I drew back, muttered "Sorry about this" and hit her.

She fell back. I had held back my strength, but she had said it should be realistic. I ran to the window farthest from the door and threw open the shutters.

In just a few moments, Rella sat up and screamed. "Help, guards! Help!"

I ran.

Both Marik's grunts came rushing back in, the idiots—if I'd done the same as last time they'd go down again the same way. Stupid.

"She's gone!" yelled Rella, pointing at the open shutters. One went straight through the opening, the other ran round the cabin on the outside.

I rose from behind the bed, winked at Rella and flew out the door. The woods beckoned in the dawn light, and, all my weariness forgotten, I took off like a deer for their shelter.

I had gone no more than a few steps when I was seized by a sudden horrible weariness in every limb. My movements were drugged and stretched out as in a nightmare, when every step takes all your strength and no matter how you struggle, you never get anywhere. I used the last of my will to look up at the strange noise before me, and managed to catch sight of Caderan gesturing in the air and grinning wildly before darkness took me once again.

Akhor

When I next bespoke Shikrar, as noon approached, it was to find the Council still divided on my fate and Lanen's. Our union they all (save Shikrar) discounted as madness and agreed it would have to be severed. As for our fates—there was still much debate on whether Lanen should be allowed to live. If so, it seemed most felt she should be kept here and not allowed ever to rejoin her people. A few, led by Shikrar, kept her deeds before the others' eyes and argued for her freedom, combined with her sworn word that she would not return on pain of death. As for me, some argued that I be forced to give up the kingship and another appointed; some felt I had been gripped by a passing fancy or subtle spell and that I would be fine once Lanen had gone, one way or another; still others that I must simply be kept away from the Gedri for the rest of my life, never again to be the Harvest Guardian, and that in all other ways I was still fit for the kingship.

Shikrar's arrival had caused quite a stir, it seemed. Rishkaan, disgruntled, had no choice but to give way to him as Eldest. At the beginning of the latest debate on Lanen's fate one of the younger males, a distant cousin of Idai's, called out, "Let us ask the Eldest. He is Keeper of Souls, it is his family that is most deeply involved. Let us hear the words of Hadreshikrar!"

Shikrar waited for complete silence before speaking (and got it—our people revere the wisdom that comes with age). He raised up to address the Council and stood in Righteous Anger, taking quite a few by surprise.

"My friends and my Kindred, what is this that I have heard? Much discussion of whether we should do to death the beloved of our King, or let her live alone in exile in a foreign land? I cannot believe I hear such things from the children of the Winds. Is it our place, is it our law, to deny love? Akhor has been faithful to the kingship, faithful to us all, his life long. Are we now to turn on that faithfulness, tell him he is bespelled, deny him the love he has found at last?"

"But it is the love of a base creature. A Gedri!" one voice called out.

"You, Rinshir, should know better than to flaunt your ignorance," Shikrar shot back. "The Gedrishakrim are intelligent creatures, they can speak and reason. They are by nature no more base than we. They can become so, surely, by their own actions. If they choose to deal with the Rakshasa, then truly they are debased; but in and of themselves they are not an evil people."

"This is a new song, Hadreshikrar," said Rishkaan bluntly. "The debate on the nature of the Gedrishakrim is as old as our people, as old as the Choice. Always before you have spoken against the Gedri. Why are you now so changed?"

Shikrar let the appreciative murmur die down before he replied. His Attitude had not changed, but it was overlaid with Teaching, the most natural in the world to him. "Tell me, Rishkaan, was there not a time in your earliest youth when someone described flight to you before your wings were strong enough to bear you?"

"Yes, of course. What of it?"

"And was their description a good one?"

"It was good enough," replied Rishkaan. He stood now in Defence, not liking this nor able to guess where it was going.

"And do you remember your first flight?"

"Who does not? It was the beginning of true life for me, as it is for us all."

"Yet tell me, Rishkaan, had that good description captured the essence of flight?"

"Not for me," he replied instantly. "There was no way the teller could describe the joys of flying to one who was earthbound. It would be like telling a fish about singing." There was some scattered laughter. I laughed myself, in the brightness of my chambers. Shikrar had made his point well.

"Then, my old friend, how should I not change my view of the Gedri once I had met and spoken with one of them, especially this one?" He turned to the others, and his voice began to deepen. He stood in Anger and Teaching still, but with Authority now behind all. "All of you, my Kindred, have spoken of the impossibility of this joining between Akhor and the Gedri female Lanen, that they must dissolve a bond of love, a Flight of the Devoted even if only flown in the mind. But of you, who has ever spoken to a child of the Gedri? Speak now, let me know your names."

The silence spoke loudly indeed.

"Yet you are so quick to condemn. *Why?* What harm does their love do to you? They have no illusions of joining, they have both condemned themselves to a life of barrenness, for the sake of this bond they did not ask for but cannot deny."

"How can they have flown the Flight of the Devoted in mind only!" cried Erianss. "It is impossible. Flight is part of our being, we are made for it, it is life and rejoicing to us. Can Akhor deny it? The Gedri is earthbound, the two of them can never meet in the skies. Why then should such an imaginary 'Flight' be honoured?"

Shikrar altered his Attitude, and Rebuke was clearly reflected in his stance. "Erianss, hear now the words of the Eldest. We respect age for many reasons, among them the fact that age has seen much that youth has not, and does not have to rediscover fire. Youngling, in my own youth I knew both a lady with a misshapen wing and an Elder who had found his mate late in life. Neither could fly when they took their mates, yet both flew the Flight of the Devoted and lived out their lives together with their chosen ones, none the worse for it. I spoke to the lady once about it and she told me they had flown together in a vision, just as Akhor described his Flight to me."

"With respect, Eldest," said Rishkaan with a hiss, "you are not impartial in this. I believe you would defend a Raksha who had saved the lives of your loved ones. You do not see the Gedri with clear eyes."

Shikrar did not respond immediately, but drew in his breath and began the Discipline of Calm. When it was completed, he answered.

"I have a question for you, Rishkaan. If a Raksha had saved your life, would you not question its very existence as a Raksha, a creature of chaos and darkness? For in saving your life it would have gone against its very nature. Thus it would be an unnatural demon, which might be a very good thing indeed for it as a soul, but very bad for it as a demon.

"My Kindred, Akhor did not exaggerate when he said this little one might well die from her efforts on behalf of Mirazhe. We all heard her cry of pain; I saw with my own eyes the wounds she had from too close contact with Mirazhe's inner fire. Before you condemn my impartiality, before you deny my wisdom in your own outrage and ignorance, think well on this and speak who dares; who among you would undergo such torture for an unknown child of the Gedrishakrim?"

There was silence in the Great Hall, but my heart rejoiced at his words. *"Bless you Shikrar, the Winds bless you, you have saved us. I have never heard you speak so. I thank you from my soul in the name of the Winds of our Kindred and the Lady of the Gedrishakrim."*

"Thank me when all is over, Akhorishaan. There is much yet to do."

Marik

This time the Messenger appeared from Berys. Just as well; Maikel would not be able to heal my arm again for some time yet.

"Yes, Magister? What would you?"

"How go your preparations for the dedication?" he asked.

"Well enough. Caderan seems in no difficulty," I replied.

"I would speak with him. Is he nearby?"

"Near enough." I sent for Caderan to attend me. "The girl is fully healed."

"How?" Berys sounded faintly surprised. "From what you told me of her injuries I thought it would be days at least."

"So did I. The idiot old woman I have attending the girl fed her the whole lan fruit instead of half. It means I have had none, but I know now that legend, if anything, is less than the truth. Even with all the effort of my Healer, he was not certain that she would live through the night." I rubbed my head absently, cursing when my fingers found the lump at the back. "The bitch is well enough to have knocked me out with a chair when she tried to escape. Caderan has her in a sorcerous sleep; she will not be allowed to wake again until the ritual is prepared."

"Good." The demon Messenger had a slimy smile on its grotesque face, and I got the impression that Berys was laughing at me.

"Magister?" said Caderan's voice from the door. "What do you want of me?"

"I would go over the ritual with you," he said. "Marik, do you leave us. This is not for you to hear."

I left cheerfully. The minutiae of demon summoning has always bored me. It is best left in the hands of those who find interest in such details. I went out to supervise the salvage of what was left of the storage shed. Luckily very few bags of leaves were actually destroyed, as I have them conveyed to the ship on a regular basis, but it was a nuisance and had distracted my guards long enough to allow the woman Rella to disturb me.

I had her brought to me for a fitting rebuke for that disturbance and for giving the girl the whole of the lan fruit, though I moderated it as she was the one who had discovered the fire in time to save most of the contents of the shed. Still, she looked unbalanced with one eye swollen and black. The second, which I gave her, was a great improvement.

Lanen

The day passed in a confused welter of dream-tossed sleep and worse waking. In dreams I wandered lost, trying to run in stretched-out time from the darkness that followed behind me, calling aloud to Akor for help, seeking him in the forest and not finding him. As I ran I cried out that I wanted true speech with him, only true speech.

But worse, far worse, was the nightmare that alternated with this one. In it I would seem to wake, but that waking found me in my old bed in Hadronsstead, alone as ever and a world away from what must have been no more than a vivid dream of the True Dragons. I screamed, unable to make a sound, and longed for death, so much kinder than that false waking.

Then I would wake in truth, fuddled in mind from the nightmares of loss, only to find before my open eyes a demon of the lesser kind, one of the Rikti. In futile panic I fought my bonds, struggled, but the padded chains that bound me were strong and solid. The demon would cry out in a high-pitched shriek, and Caderan would come. I do not remember how many times it happened, but I seem to recall that he was surprised the last few. Each time he spoke a few words and poured some liquid onto coals, and I would sleep again. And each time as I fell back into the darkness, my last thought was that I should have used truespeech and called out to Akor.

Once as I dreamed, it seemed that Akor's mindvoice called to me, asking if I were well, if I were yet awake. I tried to reply, to call out for help, but the dream that gripped me left my mind so befuddled I could barely remember my own name, much less recall how to use the Language of Truth.

I only stayed awake long enough each time to begin to be terrified before the Rikti cried out again, Caderan performed his rite and blackness claimed me once more.

xiv

RAKSHASA

Akhor

At times through the day I listened for her, but there was no response. At first I was not overly worried. Could I not hear her lightest whisper? I knew she would call out if she needed me, and I had no idea how long she might sleep after all the healing was done.

The Council was going badly, but Shikrar and I had done what we might—now it was up to them. My people had much to discuss, and they were not accustomed to acting swiftly in such matters. I had no choice but to leave my fate and Lanen's to the Council.

As I awaited their summons, for further debate or to hear their decision, I set myself in Meditation of the Winds. I heard no voices this time, for which I was deeply thankful. I let my soul fly on the Winds, let calmness and order take my thoughts that I might see my way clear.

Do not mistake me, I had no intention of simply accepting the word of the Council if they demanded her life—but I had little time in which to think of a more reasonable alternative. It was harder than I had imagined, since every answer seemed to include exile from our people, indeed from both peoples, for both Lanen and me. Still, perhaps time would heal these wounds.

My heart grew heavy then, for it was the first time I truly gave thought to how short my dearling's span of years would be. I could easily live fifty years alone, in contemplation. Many of the Kindred spent that much time in seclusion simply by preference.

In fifty years, at best, Lanen would be in her old age. It was more likely that she would be dead. Coward that I was, I could not sit alone with that thought. I left my chambers and went to the Boundary to speak with Kédra.

He, of course, was full of a joy no other doings could displace. I played willing audience to his need as he spoke of his pride in Mirazhe and his newfound delight in their youngling. If that had been all the tenor of his speech I might have tired of it sooner, but he could not say enough in praise of Lanen, and he in his turn listened when I spoke of her as I had not dared do with any other, even Shikrar.

As time went on, however, and the sun sank into the west, I found I was calling out to her more often and becoming more and more disturbed at the lack of answer. Surely she should have awakened by now? The wind had turned with sunset and blew from the south, and in the darkening twilight suddenly I caught a whiff of Gedri nearby. Kédra had smelt it as well, and we both knew it was not Lanen.

In moments a figure appeared in the twilight at the edge of the trees, looking all ways, then speeding to the place of Summoning. It was a female, smaller and darker than my dear one, but swift and sure in her movements despite an odd twist to her body. There was no trace of the Rakshasa in her, though her eyes looked strange.

She could not have been more than a tree's length away when she called out in a loud whisper.

"Akor? Akor? Guardian, are you there? Lanen told me to seek you here."

I waited. She spoke very quickly, and fear surrounded her.

"Akor, I need to talk to you. Akor?" Then, as if to herself she muttered, "Damn, what were the other two—Shikrer, something like that, Kaydra—the Hells—Akor?" she called again, louder. "Akor, damn it, Lanen told me to come here. She's in trouble!"

My heart fell like a stone. I moved swiftly to her and leaned down all in an instant so that my face was barely a length away from hers. "What kind of trouble?"

She let out a yelp and leapt back. I had not desired to frighten her, but it occurred to me once it was done that I might more swiftly learn her tidings if she had some fear of me to spur her on.

I drew back a little, but stayed down on the same level. "I will not harm you, child of the Gedri. You are friend to Lanen?"

"Yes. Are you?"

I admired her courage. "I am Akor, the King of the Greater Kindred," I said solemnly, "and I would give my life to protect her from harm."

"Then now would be a good time to start. Marik's got her—"

"I took her to him to be healed."

"Yes, yes, she's healed right enough, but he's got other plans for her. His demon master, that Caderan, has her drugged or ensorcelled or something like. I saw her, she's chained to a wall in his cabin and there's a demon not a foot from her face. As best I can tell it just sits there and sings out when she wakes. I've heard their talk, though, and sure as life they have worse in store for her when true night falls." I shivered, as though the winds of deep winter blew through my soul. True night was all but upon us.

Kédra spoke quietly from behind me, the anger in his voice barely held in check. "How can you know this? Is it in some public place, where all may approve?"

"Sweet Lady, do you think we're all depraved?" she replied sharply. How swiftly the Gedri move from fear to anger. "He's got her behind locked doors and bolted shutters. If the rest of the Harvesters knew about this they'd either go for his hide or bolt in terror. I went looking for her and I saw her through a break in the shutters."

"I think you have put yourself in danger by coming to us," he said, chastened.

Her voice was also more gentle as she replied, "I like the child, and despite what happened to her, she trusts you. If anyone can help her against demons, surely you can. The legends say you dragons are life-enemies of the Rakshasa."

I had not spoken, for fear I would scorch the ground. Fire swelled within me at the thought of the Rakshasa near my dear one. Even as I crouched I spoke to the messenger through clenched teeth.

"What is your name?" I demanded.

"Lanen calls me Rella."

"Then for your tidings, Rella, I thank you. Where is the place where she is held captive?"

Her directions meant little to me, but the place was not far, thank the Winds. "Do you stay here with Kédra," I said. "I believe it is not safe for you to be in that place." I bespoke Kédra even as I sprang into the night sky. *"Tell Shikrar where I am gone and why, and protect this Rella from her people and ours. And in my name, summon Idai from the Birthing Cove if Mirazhe is well. In the face of this madness I fear I shall need her. I will return with my dearling as soon as I may."*

My words to the Winds, I prayed as I flew, *let my speaking be true.*

Marik

The guards' cabin was changed beyond all recognition. More than anything else it reminded me of that hidden room in my first Merchant House in Illara, when Berys and I made the Farseer that was the cause of all my pain.

I had trebled the guard, and all six had strict instructions to let none nearer than thirty paces, including themselves. My own cabin was more than fifty paces distant, and I could only hope it would remain free of the taint of our activities. Such things make it hard to sleep.

As for ourselves—Caderan had spent all the hours since dawn placing wards and other things in readiness, in and about the cabin and the grounds. Since the girl had Farspeech, we would be in danger as long as she was awake, until the dedication was complete. His preparations were exhaustive. The girl herself sat slumped in a chair and chained to the wall, as she had been all day. The Rikti who guarded her perched on her knee, alert, and whenever she struggled to consciousness Caderan spelled her asleep again.

On his advice I wore the Ring of Seven Circles.

He had provided a small wooden altar—no more than a table, really, but in the last few days he had carved things deep into the wood. I recognised the seven circles of the Hells, but outside the largest circle there were sigils I had never seen before. When I looked at them, they seemed almost to move—but that might have been the candlelight. On the floor around the altar were scriven in chalk seven more circles, to keep the demon bound.

On the altar were seven candles, all short, stubby things, placed evenly outside the carvings. A cup I recognised from earlier in the day, when he had drawn my blood into it, lay in one corner, along with a wand and a large bowl full of choicest lansip leaves. In the center a round brazier sat piled high with coals. I was surprised that they were yet black and cold, but at a word and a gesture from Caderan they lit themselves. In moments they glowed deep red, like so many malevolent eyes gazing out at us. "The sun is well gone, night approaches," he said. "Let us begin."

He reached into a pouch at his waist and threw something on the coals. I was amazed to smell lansip burning. For just an instant the place was filled with rare perfume, the very touch of bliss—but at a word from Caderan the smell went instantly rancid. He laughed. "So eager they are for lansip," he said, and his voice shocked me. From its usual high nasal register it had sunk, now far deeper, into a rough and powerful range. It seemed almost to echo in that small room.

Now he began to chant, low and soft, his voice steady. All the while he sang he gestured in air with his hands, drawing out symbols (I recognised one or two of the strange carvings from the altar), making passes over the candles each one in turn. At first I thought it my imagination, but it soon became obvious that the room was in truth filling with a foglike haze. The very air was thicker, crowded almost. It was hard to breathe.

It was also, obviously, hard to concentrate. Caderan's voice went more slowly now, the syllables (which I had heard him rehearsing by the hour for days) taking more and more effort to pronounce. His tongue stumbled now and then, and each stumble was greeted by a flare of flame from the brazier as if some intelligence waited there for him to falter. The last words were preceded by long pauses, but when they left his lips they were whole, and when the last was pronounced he drew a deep breath of satisfaction. From the altar he took up the wand and touched it to each of the sigils in turn.

"Come, Dark One, thou art summoned. Lord of the Third Hell of the Rakshasa, I call upon thee—by circle, by sigil, by offering, thou art compelled. I charge thee by my power, I charge thee by these sigils, I charge thee by this offering of blood—" Here he poured the dark liquid from the small cup into the coals, setting off a hissing and a stench. "—and of lansip—" Here he emptied the large bowl into the brazier. "—come to this place. By my own power I summon thee, by the power of Malior, Magister of the Sixth Circle, I summon thee, and to bring and to bind thee I call thee by name."

The name sounded to me like a string of grunts and clicks and curses, but there was no mistaking it for anything but a demon name. Caderan had warned me and I had fasted now for a full day, so that when the sound of it made me heave naught escaped me but a little bile, that I caught in a cloth. Even I know it is unwise to leave such personal essences in the presence of demons.

When I looked up I saw that the thick air had begun to congeal above the altar. It outlined limbs surprisingly fair and well made, though the shape of the head made me reach again for my cloth. As it grew more solid it appeared to be the torso and upper limbs of a comely man, though the skin was deep red streaked with black, but above sat the head of a nightmare. It had far too many eyes and mouths, scattered it seemed at random about the many disparate lumps that made up what sat on its thick neck. When it spoke its breath was the stench of rotting meat, and its voice was flat as death.

"Behold, fools, I am come," it said. "None may summon the Lord of the Third Hell and live. Die in agony." And with those words the mouth nearest Caderan grew ten times its size, ringed with teeth like daggers, and reached for him.

Without a word Caderan leaned back, and the Raksha (to my shock) found itself unable to pass the carven circles that surrounded the brazier. Its attack was arrested as though it had hit a wall, though naught but air blocked its way. It screamed, a gut-wrenching scream, and pounded at the barrier, to no avail.

"You waste my time," said Caderan calmly. "Behold, dread lord, you are bound and summoned. You have no choice."

Its yells cut off instantly, as if they had never been. "And what is so worth your life that you summon me thus, puny mortal?" it asked in the same flat tones it had used before.

"Behold, lord," said Caderan, gesturing at me. I went to the wall and unlocked the chains that bound the girl. I put one of her arms about my neck and lifted her, carrying her like a bride to stand before the demon. "This is Marik of Gundar's blood and bone, a pact made and an offering sealed when this one was in the womb. We come to make payment for the Farseer, that Marik's pain may cease."

"Let her speak her dedication," the thing said.

"The offering resists. I would have you dedicate her."

"Wake her then, fool. She must have a will for that will to be taken."

I let her down, let her feet touch the floor and whispered her name softly.

"Lanen. Lanen, wake up."

I shame to admit such weakness, but in that moment I hesitated. She was so near, so young and strong—my daughter, my only child, my blood and bone . . .

And then the pain the demons had cursed me with, the pain that has followed me since her birth, stabbed through me in a great spasm, and I was myself again.

I felt her take her own weight and stand on her own feet. She put her hands to her face and rubbed her eyes. "Where am I?" she said groggily. Then she looked up, and in that instant knew all.

"NO!" she screamed with all her might, and strove to throw me off.

Lanen

I might as well have wrestled with a Dragon. Marik was proof now against my strength, and I felt in his wiry frame strength the equal of my own. I could do no more—

true speech, I desire nothing but true speech

"AKOR! SAVE ME!" I screamed, in truespeech, aloud, with every fibre of my being. My voice was pitched so high it frightened me.

There was an instant of silence, in which Caderan laughed and the creature before me reached out, but in the next moment all sound was swallowed up in a vast roar.

It came from just outside the cabin.

Akhor

I was frantic. I could not find her. My people can smell the Rakshasa if they are anywhere near, and in truth the stench from the camp had been heavy of late, but now it was gone. I could not find the place Rella had spoken of, I could not find my dearling, though the Fire within me knew well that she was in deadly peril. I flew in circles around and about the camp, lost, maddened—

And her scream tore the night, rent my heart, brought me arrowing down to a structure I had passed fifty times. I roared once, Fire preceding me as I came to land, for I found myself surrounded by Rikti. I would have laughed, were my Lanen's terror not ringing still in my brain. My Fire swept them effortlessly from the air, from the ground, cleansed the sigils I could now see dimly scratched into the very earth. But they were many, and all took time.

I had no time.

"Lanen, I am here, I come!" I cried, as I swept the Rikti from my path.

Her answer was the merest whisper in my mind. *"Now, Akor, or it is too late."*

Lanen

Despite his arrival I was still before the altar, and though I struggled with all my might, Marik thrust me forward towards the demon with a grip of iron. "Take her, dread lord, take the offering swiftly. A Lord of the Kantri rages nearby and would keep her from you."

"That shall not be," said that dead voice. "Come, offering," it said, stretching out its red-black arms for me. Marik released me, and as I tried to run it grasped me by my shoulder.

I tried to scream. I tried to run. I had no will, no voice, barely a flicker of my own self remained. "You are given as sacrifice," the thing said. "Now you—"

"Lanen, I am here, I come!"

I summoned the last of my strength and shouted in truespeech, *"Now, Akor, or it is too late."* It was barely a whisper.

"—belong to me," it finished, and a red veil fell before my eyes—

The splintering of wood behind me shook me even from that cold, dead place. I still had no volition, but I could tell from the sound and the feel of air at my back that the wall behind me was gone.

Caderan and Marik had turned to look.

Marik screamed and ran. Caderan was cooler—he turned where he stood and spoke to the demon, even as Akor was making the hold large enough for him to enter.

"The offering will be made later. For the price that was paid, I charge you now, destroy the Kantri lord." And before my eyes, Caderan vanished.

The thing said something I could not hear, but in that instant I was restored to myself. I ran from the circle, past Akor and away as he hunched into that cramped space, breathing fire and swiping a clawful of daggers at the demon. I knew that the only thing I could do in this fight was to get out of the way.

I learned then what Akor meant when he called the Rakshasa "life-enemies."

The demon grew in stature until it rose high above where the roof of the cabin had been. It was now nearly of a size with Akor, though it was still bound within the circles Caderan had drawn. Akor did not even pause in his attack. He flamed it, dragonfire searing the face and body of the creature, and raked at it with both front claws leaving great gashes behind. The thing spat at him, its essence scoring his silver armour, and, reaching out with its mangled and flame-scorched arms, took him by base of the throat and squeezed.

Akhor

Those hands were near to stopping my breath, but even in that moment I blessed the Winds for its stupidity. If it had grasped my throat near the jaw, things might have gone ill, but our long necks are very flexible and I kept my head well out of range of its arms. As it was, I drew my head back, pulled in what air I could and spat a great gout of Fire at its face. It burst into flame, and while it was thus distracted I turned my own head sideways and snapped at its neck once, twice. Again. Again. Its blood burned my tongue, and the taste nearly made me stop. Nearly.

It took several bites, but these jaws the Winds gave us are made for such battles as these. The burning head dropped from the shoulders; the thing gave a drawn-out scream and vanished. The only traces of its presence were dark stains on the ground where the head had rolled, and in the cabin where it had been bound.

I flamed them clean with Fire, and burned what was left of that building to ashes. I stood watching the fire scorch all clean, when I heard a soft voice behind me.

"Akor. You're hurt."

It was Lanen.

Lanen

I was afraid to speak to him. I was in awe. When I finally got up the courage to say something, I could only think of his wounds.

"They do not pain me, dearling. A moment, though," he said, and proceeded to cleanse each of his gashes with Fire. "There. All is done."

I had begun to shake with reaction, but somehow I managed to look around me. I shouldn't have been surprised. They weren't coming any too close, but the noise and the flames had drawn a crowd. One finally got up the courage to speak—it sounded like one of Marik's guards.

"What happened?" He was addressing me. I nearly laughed. Here was this wonder, this figure of legend standing before them, and this man was talking to me. Best they know the truth, I thought. If Marik is still alive, at the very least he isn't going to have many friends.

"Marik and Caderan summoned a major demon, a Lord of the Rakshasa, and he was going to give me to it. The Dragons"—*"Forgive me, Akor, it is the word they know"*—"do not tolerate demons on their island. The Guardian has destroyed it."

"Come," he said to me, and turning to the people said calmly, "There is no need to fear. I have delivered both you and my own people from a great evil. I will not harm you." *"Let us leave them, dearling,"* he said in the Language of Truth. *"It seems your people are no more prepared for our friendship than are mine. Will you come with me?"*

"With all my heart," I answered. *"Is there somewhere we can go to rest?"*

"We shall go to my chambers near the Great Hall. Come."

He gathered me in his hands and leapt into the night. I held tight for the very few moments of flight until we came to land outside his chambers. He brought wood and lit a fire, then curled around it and let me sit against him.

I thought I was doing well until I sat down against his warmth. It was as though someone had suddenly cut the strings that had held me up, for I began to shake and to babble about nothing, and finally to weep in earnest. I sat huddled against his neck with his head beside me and his wings soft about me, and I told him as I sobbed of the haunted dreams and tortured wakings, of the demon and the dread sinking in my soul when it touched me, of the horror of helplessness in the face of so great an evil. He had the wisdom to say nothing, but when I had finished talking and had only tears left, he kept repeating, "It is gone, Lanen, back to its dwelling place. It is destroyed in this world, it cannot return until it has recovered so far as to enflesh itself again, and that will not be in your lifetime."

My lifetime. So short a time we had together. As long as a Weh sleep, no more— "Dear Goddess, no!" I cried.

Akhor

She seemed so fragile in that moment. I had not been prepared for her storm of tears, though when it came I understood. In times of great stress my own people take to the air, and flame and sing to the sun or the stars until the madness has left them.

"What is it, dearling?" I asked gently in truespeech. *"I am here, I will let no harm come nigh you."*

"Not me, you," she said, and I felt her fear. "Akor, your wounds—" She dropped her voice. "Blessed Shia—will the Weh sleep come on you?"

I closed my eyes in relief and pulled her close with my wing. "No, dearling, they are not so bad as all that. They will heal of their own in time."

She let out her breath in a great sigh, and her fear was gone as swiftly as it had come. I thought for a moment and was surprised at the conclusion I came to.

"*Lanen Kaelar!*"

"Still here," she said aloud, smiling gently now, wiping the tears from her face, reaching out to touch me.

"*You feared that the Weh sleep would take me from you.*"

"Yes."

I had no words, no response, but unbidden my mind rang with the first notes of the song we had made between us, and I opened my mind to my beloved. She joined me, just for a little while, and in the Language of Truth we sang again our joy.

Soon, though, Shikrar bespoke me. He had gone to tell the Council of the killing of the Rakshasa, as I had asked, but it had not helped matters. They wished to ask me particulars of the battle, and if I knew which of the creatures I had fought. I left Lanen safe in my chambers.

Kédra

I was greatly relieved when Akhor bespoke me and said all was well with them. He asked that I keep Rella company until the Council could come to some decision. My father was in the Great Hall now, telling them news they would not wish to hear. For my part I was intrigued by the Gedri who sat before the fire I had made, and I understood Akhor's wishing to speak with them. The Boundary was safe between us—I stood a little back in hiding and listened on all levels for any trespass by others of her race—but I longed to hold converse with her. Yet I was bound even as Akhor was bound; I could not speak first. She had gathered the wood in silence, and when I had lit it for her she only looked at me. She would have to—

"Dragon? Are you still here?"

"I am, Lady Rella. I stand Guardian, and Lord Akhor has given you into my keeping."

She moved so that she could at least partially face me. "How kind. Am I your prisoner?"

"Forgive me, lady, I am not so fluent in your language as Akhor. I do not know that word. What does it mean?"

"Will you hold me here against my will?"

I was shocked. "Lady, what do you think of us? My Lord Akhor thought you would be in danger if you returned to your own people, so he has asked me to watch over you here. We await only the word of the Council to bring you where the Lady Lanen waits now."

"So I am free to go."

"Wherever you wish, though we cannot cross the Boundary to protect you."

"Why not? Akhor did. Three times."

"All three were to save the life of—of Lady Lanen."

"I see," said the Gedri. "And I am not as worthy of protection as she is."

"It is a different case, Lady Rella. Lady Lanen is—"

"Oh, spare me the 'Lady'! Just use our names, Dragon. And I don't see why her case should be different." She put her hand to her face. "I have two black eyes thanks to that girl—though I did ask for one." She made a noise which I guessed was a kind of laugh.

"And thanks to Lady Lanen, I have a living mate and a son, where all was death before," I answered a little sternly.

"What?" She stood and came up to the Boundary. "Do you tell me that she saved your wife and child?"

In as few words as possible, I told her our half of the tale. She told me the rest, then fell silent for some time. "Wretched child," she said, shaking her head. "Idiot. Burn your arms off for—oh, dear Lady." She put her hands before her mouth for a moment, then looked up at me. "Dragon, did you see her before Akhor brought her here? Did you see her wounds?"

I bowed my head. "I did not. I never thought she might be in such pain, she made never a sound, all her heart was in the saving of my child—"

"I am—my work has taken me many places, and I have seen death in forms more terrible than most have to know, but in all my life I was never so sickened by anything as by the sight of her burns. Her arms were naught but shreds of muscle stretched over—oh, I can't." She turned away for an instant, then looked straight at me. "If your Akor had taken a single moment longer to get her to the Healer, she would have died in agony. You owe her two lives, Dragon, you know that."

I bowed to her. "I know it full well. And my name is Kédra, Lady Rella."

"I told you, it's just Rella."

"No, lady," I replied. "By your actions this night you have pre-served the life of the Lady Lanen, and that for no hope of gain that I can see, simply of your kindness. 'Lady' is among my people a term of respect, and for that kindness I am afraid that you shall always be Lady Rella to me."

She smiled at me then, a crooked grin that suited her well. "Oh, well. I suppose I'll just have to put up with it."

Marik

I finally stopped running about a quarter mile from the place. I was heading south from some instinct of finding safety on the ship, but my true fear was that there was no safety anywhere. Call me cow-ard, but what is the point of bravery in the face of certain death? Per-haps Berys could stand up to an angry Dragon, but I couldn't. When I realised it did not pursue me, I began to walk cautiously back along the dark, rough path to the cabins.

I met Caderan running in my direction. He slowed when he saw me. He was badly out of breath. "The Raksha—held off the Dragon—long enough for me to get away. But the cabin is gone—and so is the girl."

My hands were around his throat without my thinking of it. "And what good are you to me now, sorcerer?" I asked, finding satisfac-tion in the feel of his throat beneath my fingers as I tightened my grip. "Now I must live with this pain forever, and in the matter of the Dragons all dissembling is useless. I never thought to live this long when that beast came through the *wall*. Now that the Dragons will kill me on sight, what good are you to me?"

I shook him once more and pushed him away. He fell to the ground.

"I am your only hope, Marik," he said, coughing as he lay in the dust. "How else will you survive if it comes to an attack? Remem-ber, Merchant, only I can provide a shield against dragonfire."

The worst of it was that he was right. I would have to suffer him a little longer, at least until tomorrow, the last night of the Harvest. Then I could—no.

Tonight.

It would be the last thing they'd expect, to do so bold a thing after so great a defeat. And who in his right mind would leave a Harvest early?

Only one who intended to be long gone by the time the Dragons noticed anything was amiss. I hauled Caderan to his feet and drew him swiftly after me. We slowed when we drew near the smoking remains of the guards' cabin, but as the beast was nowhere in evidence, we slipped into my own cabin unobserved.

I closed tight the door and threw wood on the fire. "Now, demon caller, you will learn for me if this night is a good time to go into the dragonlands."

He looked surprised, but only for a moment. "I have ascertained it already, my lord. You asked me to consult them when first you purposed to go there. I learned at that time that tonight and tomorrow night are equally auspicious."

"You never said anything about tonight before," I growled at him.

"It did not seem important. I knew you planned to wait until the last night." He must have seen my displeasure and doubt, for he went on, "My lord, the creatures hold some kind of assembly among themselves for these two nights. They are well distracted. There is still a Guardian, but its thoughts will be far from you."

It was then that my vague thoughts became a plan of action. I mastered my anger and spoke softly. "Very well. Good master Caderan, I pray you send for my guards. Let word be spread that the Harvest is over, for fear the Dragons will attack again. Send out to the farthest reaches where the Harvesters have gone and tell them they must return, for we leave at dawn. Let the Master of the ship be notified that as soon as may be, we shall decamp and take all on board." I turned to him, my anger turned to determination. "I shall keep to the timing we arranged, that I may come straight from that place and onto the ship by morning. Go now. I would be alone."

He left, and I heard him shouting for my guards. Good.

A vision of the gems rose before my eyes, bright and enticing. By night's end the creatures would pay for robbing me of my only hope of pain's ending. I shuddered again as the vision of that silver beast pulling down the wall rose in my memory. By the powers, I would have mastery over it yet.

I ran my fingers over the ring on my hand, its circles warm now with my heat, and I felt a slow smile spread over my face.

Let it come.

Lanen

As I sat recovering in Akor's chambers I heard a curious voice. *"May I bespeak you, Lady Lanen? Kédra speaks."*

"Of course," I replied, bemused. For an instant I feared for Mirazhe, but his mindvoice was calm, even pleased.

"I stand Guardian and so may not come to you, but I have not yet given you my own thanks for saving my dear one and our youngling."

"Is Mirazhe well?" I asked.

I could hear the smile in his voice, even in truespeech. *"She and the babe are wondrous well. They send you their greetings."*

I grinned. *"Surely the little—uh, the littling is a bit young to speak yet!"*

"I see now why Akor is so drawn to your people," said Kédra in a curious tone. *"There is great pleasure in teaching. When we are first born, Lady, we have little control over our bodies, but our minds are well awake. My littling cannot send thoughts, not in words, but his mother can see the pictures he makes and get a sense of his feelings. She sent him a picture of you this morning, and he remembered with pleasure."*

He remembered.

Newborn, and he remembered me.

I would never have forgotten that face, those eyes gazing into mine, but I never dreamed that *he* would remember.

"Oh, Kédra, what a gift you have given me," I whispered. *"I had no idea. We don't start remembering until we're three or four years old, and then only in patches."* I hugged the thought to me. It was a kind of immortality, to be remembered by a creature who would live so far into the future I could not imagine it. *"Has he a name yet?"*

"His use name is Hjerrók," said Kédra proudly.

I almost laughed aloud. Why couldn't they come up with something a human could actually pronounce for a change? I tried it a few times out loud and replied in truespeech, *"Well, the best I can do with that is Sherók. Bless Sherók and his mother, and you Kédra, for all you have given me. Your friendship and your kind regard are gifts beyond measure."*

"They are yours and your family's for all time, Lanen Maran's daughter. You have saved the two lives I value most in the world, and though I can never repay such a gift I will do what I may."

"Akor has told me that Rella is with you. Your greatest gift to me now is to guard her well," I replied. "Akor has been speaking with your father, and he comes now to tell me how the Council is drifting. I must go."

"Then fare you well, Lady Lanen. I am at your service as long as I live."

"Farewell, Kédra. The blessing of the Lady on you and your family."

Akor entered his chambers slowly, his soulgem dull even in the bright firelight. I wished yet again that he had an expression I could read—but no, he had told me, with them it was the stance and the way they held their wings, what had Akor called it—oh, yes. Try to read his Attitude. "What news then, dear heart? Has the Council come to a decision?"

"Not yet, but they approach it." I heard the weary note in his voice, like a sigh. "It does not bode well for us, dear one. That was the last word Shikrar gave me. He has been most eloquent in our defence, but the tide of the debate goes badly against him."

I was almost afraid to ask, but my choices were rapidly disappearing. "And what exactly can the Council do to us?"

His voice was right at the edge, I could hear his control slipping. The glorious rescuer, the tender beloved who had left not an hour since was gone, and in his place stood a defeated soul. That frightened me as much as his words. "They might find against us both, or against either one of us. They might demand that we part, that we be exiled, that I give up the kingship, that you be kept here forever apart from your own Kindred, or—"

He did not finish, but I did not need to hear him speak the words. If the Council was against us, I must of necessity ask Akor to decide between me and his people, the one thing I had sworn to myself not to do. I felt my heart plummet into my boots. This last defeat, from so unexpected a quarter, was the one too many. My legs gave way and I fell to my knees. "Are we lost, then, after all we have done?" I asked, my voice deep with despair and barely above a whisper. "Will they call for our deaths, Akor?"

"I do not know, dear one. It is possible. Shikrar thinks not."

"Have you no voice at this Council? Can't you argue with them?"

"I have. I did so last night, while you lay wounded."

The events of the past days swept over me, tumbling images of death and life and love. Was it only last night that I lay dying, burned beyond belief, for doing a good turn? I lived only because of Akor's lawbreaking. *Akor, beloved.* I bowed my head. Why should I expect good from those who saw only the broken laws, not the healing, not the charity to another soul? What good could we hope for, who had so disregarded all in the name of love?

My fists were clenched, my teeth ground against themselves, and I discovered to my amazement that in the last extreme my despair had turned swiftly to something else.

Anger.

"Well, I haven't had my chance," I said in a normal speaking voice. It sounded like shouting. "I am still trying to understand that not an hour since you saved me from my father, who gave me to demons before I was born and was trying to make good his vow with my life. I was in his power because I had nearly died saving the lives of Kédra's wife and son, and *these* people are debating about what to do with me." I faced Akor. "I would address the Council."

"You cannot, Lanen, they would—"

I did my best to yell in the Language of Truth. I didn't want anyone to miss it. *"I have a request to make of the Kindred, the Kantrishakrim, the People who chose Order, that justice may be served. It is Lanen Maransdatter of the Gedrishakrim who speaks."*

There was no answer.

"In the name of the Winds and the Lady, I demand that I be allowed to attend the Council and speak in my own defence. It is only just."

Silence.

"ANSWER ME, DAMN IT!"

Silence.

Akhor

"Akor, you have saved my life once this night. Will you try your arm again?"

I was still shocked at the intensity of her truespeech, and more amazed yet that there had been no answer. "Yes, of course," I replied without thinking.

"Then come on, you may have some defending to do."

And with that, Lanen strode out of my chambers. When I hurried to join her, she only looked up at me and asked, "Which way is the Great Hall?"

I gestured towards it with my chin. "It is near for me, dearling, but some distance for you."

She started walking as quickly as she could. *"Kédra, it's Lanen,"* she called out as she strode through the night. *"Akor will not stop me, but as Guardian you should know that I'm on my way to the Council. I mean and will do no harm to any, I swear on my soul to the Lady. But if your duty lies in stopping me, I will understand, and I forgive you. But you will have to kill me to do it."*

Kédra replied in the same kind of speech Lanen was using, scattered and heard by all, and his truespeech was bright with a strange joy. *"Success and long life to you, Maran's daughter and Akhor's Lady!"*

I had followed her perforce, walking slowly at her side. I was dazed still by this madness that gripped her, but I found my blood answering hers, felt the Fire building within me. "Come, dear one, it is a long way. Will you not allow me to bear you?"

"How?" she asked, still striding as fast as she could. She managed to be in Anger even as she walked; there are some advantages to having such mobile faces.

"Here," I answered, putting my head nearly on the ground in front of her. "I have been considering this. Sit just behind my face plate, where my neck is thinnest. I do not know if they will be within your reach, but you might try to take hold of my horns to steady yourself."

She stopped then and grinned. Her anger abated a little, tinged now with delight. She leapt up the little distance. I could feel her pull herself onto my neck, where she seemed to fit nicely. "Your horns are well within reach, my dear, they might have been put here just for that purpose," she said.

And she laughed.

Lanen

I was still angry, but as he lifted his head to its normal position I felt like a child on the shoulders of its parents. It was wonderful. There was none of the terror of flying, and he was so big I could see over the trees. He was right, he did move a lot faster than I could; and I felt much safer as well. I had decided that if I was going to be hanged, as the saying goes, it might as well be for horse stealing as for chicken feed. At least this way I might make it into the Council chamber and live long enough to get in a word or two.

I was counting on shock to do a lot for me. I had begun to realise that, aside from my dear Akor, these creatures who lived so impossibly long found it hard to adjust to change. With any luck the sheer surprise would buy me some time.

Besides, I had stopped waiting for someone else to make my life's choices when I left Hadronsstead. I had been faced with far worse than death already, and if I was condemned to die for doing nothing truly wrong, and in despite of all we had done that was right, I was damn well going to let someone know about it before I went.

Of course I was crazy. I do not deny it. But it was a glorious madness, marching with Akor to beard the Council of the Kindred in their hall! Like the heros in all the ballads, fighting against impossible odds. And I realised then that I would rather die fighting for myself and for one I loved than live to old age in the quiet safety of a lie.

I remember.

xv

WIND OF THE UNKNOWN

Akhor

I did not even slow down. There was none but Kédra to stop me in any case, and his voice sang with ours as I strode to the Great Hall. I even heard a snatch of the song of his clan, Shikrar's own melody with elements of Kédra and a lilting theme that could only be Lanen. That more than anything lifted my heart high, that the son of my namefast friend sang us to victory. Lanen also was singing, a martial air without words.

At the entrance to the Great Hall we were met by Shikrar standing solemn in the entryway.

"As Eldest I beg you, Akhor, do not do this."

Lanen's voice came from behind my head. "Your pardon, Eldest, but he is not the one to talk to. I am." Her voice rang with excitement.

Shikrar stood in Concern. "My friend, hear me in this. You must not let her in. She has no voice here, Akhor, you know that. She is of the Gedrishakrim!"

"You mean I'm human. That's what we call ourselves, Shikrar, human. If I can call you the Kindred, instead of Dragons, you might at least return the favor."

Lanen

"Be silent!" he yelled at me. I was glad to finally get a direct response, but a yelling dragon is impressive. And *loud*. "You put yourselves in peril even by standing here."

"Then let's not stand here. Can we get in, Akor? Is it physically possible?"

"A moment, Lanen. Shikrar, why such fear? Has the Council reached a decision?"

He bowed his head in a very human gesture. "They have. I dissented, and I am glad to say mine was not the only voice. I reminded them at every turn of what you both have done—but Rishkaan's faction was strong. There is much hatred yet for her people among us." Still gazing at the ground, he said quietly, "You are to be exiled, Akor. Relieved of the kingship and sent to live out your life away from your people on some rock in the ocean."

"And Lanen?"

"She may go with you, to survive as best she can. Or . . ."

My voice was calm, even reasonable. "Or they'll kill me and save me the trouble of having to survive."

He bowed to me, a sinuous, graceful Dragon bow, then did me the courtesy of looking me in the eye. "Yes, lady. That is correct."

I laughed. What more did I have to lose? "To the Hells with that. Come, Akor, let's go in. Or let me down and I'll go in myself."

He lowered his head to the ground and I slid off. *"Go before, dearling,"* he said, turning to me with a smile in his voice and his soul-gem gleaming like emerald fire. *"I shall come behind and keep all harm from you. Let us tell the Council ourselves what others have not managed to say."*

I paused and gingerly took out my boot knife. It was the only weapon I had about me. "Shikrar, you who have so gallantly fought for us, will you do me another kindness? Will you take this? I would not enter the Council chamber armed."

He held out his great clawed hand and I put my tiny knife in it. Again he bowed. "I shall keep it with the treasures of my people," he said, strangely moved. "So valiant a lady and so courteous, I do not wonder Akor feels kinship with you. And despite my anger just now, I do not forget that I owe to you the lives of my dear ones. In the teeth of the Council I stand with you."

Despite the reminder of teeth I grinned at him. "Well, that's two," I said gaily, and started down the corridor. Nothing could stay me, not the weakness of my so-recent brush with death (which yet affected me), not my new-healed hands that still smarted though the bandages had been removed, not the Council's sentence of death, not even walking down a dimly lit underground corridor towards the hostile unknown. A kind of wild exultation had gripped me. I trusted in Akor and in Shikrar's goodwill, and in whatever force had brought me to this place at this time. The Winds and the Lady were behind me and fear, I thought, was far away.

The corridor seemed endless, twisting and doubling on itself, but there was always at least a little light ahead, and after some time I heard the low hum of deep voices in a large chamber.

The entrance came suddenly, a blazing opening in the darkness, filled with firelight and Dragons. I stood at gaze, staring at an assembly I had seen so many times in my dreams but never hoped to see in real life. For a moment I wondered at the firelight and the torches that lined the walls, for Akor had told me that his people saw well enough in darkness not to need much light; then I realised that in this formal setting they must be able to see the Attitudes assumed by all who spoke, and that fire was sacred.

Akor had said their numbers were dwindling, but it was hard to believe that in the face of a sea of Dragons. The fear I had hoped to avoid rose up in me then, when I saw them all assembled. How dared I hope to stand and defy them? The lightest breath from the least of them and I would be a memory. Throughout that vast hall they stood and sat and lay, conversing, arguing, a great patchwork of all sizes and all colours of metal, from steel blue and leaden gray through bronze and brass, copper and dull gold. But none like Akor, none silver.

I remembered his words. *My birth was seen as an omen, though what it portends none can say.*

This seemed as likely as any. Akor's voice whispered in my head, "Courage, dear heart. Now we are here, let us do what we have come to do."

It was kind of him not to speak of my fear.

At the far end of the chamber there was a half-round dais, as it were in the bottom of half of a large bowl, and on it sat a Dragon with a skin of copper bright as a new-minted coin. I gritted my teeth and aimed straight for the front of the dais, but I was overtaken by Shikrar, who hurried ahead of me and started to speak.

I had only ever heard a few words of the Old Speech. It was the first tongue of all the peoples, the language of Dragons, and though it was in aeons past the basis of my own language there were few words left of it in common speech. The ancient name I took as my own, Kaelar, the Wanderer, was from a ballad. Songs and places alone kept even the memory of the Old Speech among men, but for all the time and distance the sounds were somehow familiar, and hearing Shikrar speak I felt I had stepped back in time. The words hovered just on the edge of understanding. I caught one or two, and felt that I was near as a breath to understanding all he said.

When the world was younger and the last of the Trelli but lately departed, our two Kindreds lived in harmony.

Akor stood behind me, his massive bulk shielding me from the view of most of the others. Few, it seems, had seen me come in, for which small mercy I was deeply thankful.

"What is he saying, Akor?" I whispered.

"He is calling for attention, saying that another has come with words for the Council. It is brave of him, dearling; by our laws you have no voice here. And we are a people of law."

Even in his mouth it sounded sour. "Are you indeed?" I asked, a ghost of my mad bravery lingering. "Well, now I'm here I must do what I can. I've dealt with legal-minded Merchants before."

"*Lanen, my people are not Merchants!*" he said, sounding shocked.

I would have answered him, but Shikrar stepped back and bowed to us. "Let you speak now for your lives, my friends, and may the Winds guide your words and your thoughts," he said in Common Speech. He moved then to the back of the dais to sit beside the copper-coloured one.

"It's time, dear heart," I said quietly.

"*Yes. They are expecting me alone to stand and speak. Shall we go?*"

"Age before beauty." He stared at me. "You first," I said, smiling. "I'd hate to be fried on sight by accident."

"*I see. You would rather it be done intentionally,*" he said as he stepped gracefully up. It wasn't fair, really, I didn't mean to be laughing when I clambered up the tall step to stand beside him on such a solemn occasion. But it did make for a hell of an entrance.

I gathered later from Shikrar that they had expected to find a demure, silent soul, obedient and willing, waiting for their verdict and generally thick as a plank. Lady knows why. Just because I had been an idiot in love didn't mean I was stupid altogether.

"My lords and ladies!" I called out, in my best horse-fair voice.

That got their attention. The sound nearly deafened me. The Great Hall was wonderful, it magnified my voice so well I could speak almost in normal tones. That yell had been something, for a human.

"I greet you all, in the name of my ancestors and my people. I am called Lanen Maransdatter of the Gedrishakrim, and I greet you as my brothers and sisters in the name of the Winds and of the Lady."

Dead silence.

Well, even in my dreams it hadn't been easy.

"*Lanen, few of my people understand your tongue. Shall I translate for you?*"

"Yes, Akor, please, but only if you promise to say exactly what I do. Some of this is not going to be pleasant, and you must not soften it. We know the tones of voice are roughly the same, I'm sure they'll get the general idea."

"*I'm sure they will,*" he replied dryly. "*You would not care to re-*

consider, would you, dearling? Thus far we have merited only a swift death."

"Perish the thought," I said, responding in truespeech. The fey mood was still upon me. "*I'd hate to disappoint them. They won't have had this much fun in years. Now stop distracting me and start translating.*"

The response was gratifying, but I must admit it was my turn to be surprised. I had forgotten that they could all hear my truespeech, it now seemed so natural to use it with Akor.

"*Why have you waited so long to speak in the Language of Truth? Or had you nothing true to say?*" sneered a smaller, bronze-hued Dragon.

"*So now you can hear me. Why didn't any of you answer when I called you from the Boundary?*" I shot back. Somehow rudeness from the Kantri snapped me back into that anger and exultation that had brought me storming in. "*Could you not admit that I have the gift you value so highly? That I am not Silent, not Gedri in that sense, but a creature of standing equal to your own? Or did you think I could lie even in this language?*"

"*You have no voice here . . .*" began one lady feebly, but I could not bear to hear that again. Instinctively I spoke aloud.

"I should have a voice here! I am not a beast, I am an ensouled creature as you are, and I never heard that the Winds gave you the power of the high justice over me and mine!"

"*Would it not be best to continue in the Language of Truth?*" asked Shikrar quietly. "*It is thus that we may best hear you.*"

I thought about that for a moment. "*I believe you are right, Shikrar, and I thank you. I spoke in my own tongue in my anger, but were you to come among us we would wish you to speak our language. I shall continue as long as I may, though I cannot use the silent speech for long without some discomfort. It is natural to your people—and to me, it seems—but I am newly come to it. Still, I shall try.*"

Akhor

Obviously there were many who had not believed, even after hearing her distant calls on several occasions, that she, a Gedri, could be the source of truespeech. There could be no doubt now. When she lapsed into her own speech again, I translated for her.

I had meant to establish her right to speak. The right was mine, and would have been hers if she had been of the Kindred. I at least was due an appeal. But I did not dare interrupt. She was inspired, and I was glad enough to wait and watch. Our people are prone at times to sudden ill-conceived actions—it is the hazard of being creatures of Fire. I would make certain she was protected from any who threatened.

Otherwise, I merely sat and marvelled at her. She was a wonder.

Lanen

"People of the Greater Kindred, I stand before you as your sister in this world. True, we are made differently, but we are far closer in spirit than you are to the Rakshasa, or either of us to the vanished Trelli. In the first days of our meeting, Akor and I quickly came to understand each other's Attitudes and expressions. And even when words failed us, we learned that tone of voice was a near-infallible guide. As I understand Attitudes, I stand somewhere between Defiance and Respect."

One voice rang out. *"We read you well enough, Gedri. You are sentenced already."*

"No, *Dragon,* I am not," I cried, lapsing into my own tongue and putting as much venom in my voice as I could. They all stirred at that; some who had been in what looked like it might be Listening or some such now stood in Anger. As soon as I saw it I understood, I knew what I must do.

"Yes, Akor has told me how that name offends you. Very well! You are the Greater Kindred, I will pay you that respect; but I have told you my own name. I am Lanen Maransdatter. To call me Gedri, a Silent One, is in any case not correct—but among my people if you deny the name, you deny the person, and I think you have done quite enough of that already."

"Who are you to judge us?" called a voice from behind me, dripping with hostility but speaking in my language. I turned back to face the bright copper Dragon I had merely glanced at before. *"Rishkaan,"* whispered Akor in my mind.

"I have told you. I am Lanen Maransdatter, beloved of Akor the Silver King, and whatever you do you cannot unmake that which already is. You could crush me with a fraction of a thought, with the

lightest breath of fire, but you cannot destroy the change that I bring."

I turned back to the assembly. "*Don't you understand? Have you not heard? How can you censure your King when he is caught in the web of the gods? Yours and mine! How absurd, for us to be so devoted after so short a time. Can you imagine we do not know it? We are not fools. When we came to ourselves after the joining of our souls, we stood apart and called on our gods for understanding, each to each. And the Winds and the Lady spoke to us.*

"*I did not come here to fall in love with one of the Kindred! Blessed Lady, what a pointless thing to do! I suffer from the same* ferrinshadik *that is so deep a part of my beloved; I longed only to speak with another soul that felt as I did, once in my life to hear the thoughts of the only other race in this world that can speak and reason. Why should I not? I had no idea. I knew nothing of the ban until Akor told me of the Lost Ones. That tale itself is long forgotten by my people.*

"*I speak with you now as I have a thousand times before in my heart. I left my home gladly to follow the merest rumour of you, for I knew in my soul you were no legend. I gave up my home to find you, to learn of the Greater Dragons who lived apart from my people. You were the old ones, the wise ones, and I desired to learn from you.*"

I spoke now aloud and let my voice rise, partly from some memory of the tricks of the bards, partly because I was now hard put to it to keep stray thoughts out of my truespeech and I wanted this clear.

"And thanks to your King, I have indeed learned. I ask you now, do you not remember your own history? Kantri and Gedri are meant to be together, to live in harmony. Yes, you had reason to be angry at the death of Aidrishaan—*but he was only one.* By that time the Demonlord had destroyed several villages full of my people. You are creatures of Fire, I can understand that you would be driven to too great an anger, to too-hasty action—*but that is what it was.* And is.

"I believe you never accepted my people as your equals, even in the days of the Peace. Always we have been the Gedri, the Silent Ones, our very name in your language a dismissal, a cause for contempt. We are smaller, weaker, we live a fraction of your lives, we cannot fly—but you have never admitted that we have a greatness that you do not possess."

There was much muttering at that. More stood in Anger. I had no plan, no idea of what to say, but the words came for all that. I still did not understand why I sought to anger the Kindred. I trusted in whatever was leading me and followed as best I could. But the hall had begun to hum, low and deep, with murmuring, and the beginning of the most unsettling melody I had ever heard.

"What of the Gedri is worthy the name of greatness, Maran's daughter?" growled Rishkaan from behind me. *"They have brought only darkness and blight on the world. My mother's granddam was changed by the Demonlord in the flower of her youth, she was riven from her daughter when she could barely fly, along with all the rest of my family that ever was. I shall bear the Gedri ill will always."*

"That is your choice, Rishkaan of the Kantrishakrim, but you do not speak for all the Kindred." Akor's truespeech rang clear and firm. *"Now silence all, by our own laws, and let her continue."*

I took a deep breath. "I have never heard of a Healer among your people," I said calmly. "Has there ever been one?"

All was silent.

"No, Lady," said Shikrar, trying to keep a quiet delight out of his voice, *"you are correct. None of us has ever had that gift."*

"Many of my people are Healers now. They are better than you remember, if the last you knew was what Akor told me in the Tale of the Demonlord. Not a full day past he carried me to the camp nearly dead, my hands and arms so badly burned I thought I should never use them again. A Healer came to me and, I am told, spent his whole strength on me—but this very morning I was recovered and nearly managed to escape from captivity. A captivity in which I was being held for dark reasons I had nothing to do with. I could have made my life easier by betraying you to the Merchant Marik, but I did not, and some time before I warned you to beware of him."

"Your people have Healers and you are not traitors," came a voice (translated by Akor). "The first is a gift of the Winds, the second but the lack of a weakness, and neither of them true achievements of your Kindred. What else have you to recommend your kind?"

"Generosity and courage!" I shouted back. "I know you have heard how near I came to death. I saved the lives of Mirazhe and her son, I drew the child—the youngling—out of her body with my hands when I already knew that pain would be my only reward."

I stopped a moment. "Why do you think I did that?" I asked calmly. I turned to Akor. "Even you, Akor my heart. Why do you think I did what I did?"

He drew breath to answer, changed his mind, stood in what I guessed was Curiosity and said, "I do not know, littling. Why did you?"

Akhor

"She is besotted with you, Akhor, she would throw herself into the fire if you asked her," growled Rishkaan from behind me in the speech of the Gedri.

"No, I would not!" she cried. Her eyes were blazing, were she one of us she would stand in Defiance and Instruction. "I am no child. I am a woman grown, no young fool to kill myself for love. Not even for one so dear to me as Akor." She glanced at me briefly as I translated, almost an apology, but her warrior's blood was afire and she had no time for delicacy.

"I helped Mirazhe because I wanted to, not because Akor asked me. I have learned the midwife's skills with the females of my race, I have helped bring forth newborns before. *I would do the same for any soul who suffered in childbirth.* It was because I saw Mirazhe as a fellow creature in need that I risked burned hands and sickness to save her and her littling."

She lifted her voice, all her frustration and anger ringing in the Council chamber. "Who among you would do as much for one of my own? And how? You could not, you cannot assist so, your hands are made for rending and killing. Those claws, so formidable as weapons, can barely touch one of my people without wounding. That is a thing you must learn, O people of my beloved. How to touch without destroying!"

The murmur of discontent grew swiftly louder, the unsettling melody now easily heard. My people began to stir, fluttering their wings in anger. *"How dare you speak so, we are the Eldest of the Four Peoples and have you in our charge!"* cried Rishkaan in true-speech, ignoring Shikrar's commands to be silent. *"All know it. Why else are you made so much smaller and weaker, with only your short lives to live and no remembrance of others to guide you? You should hold us in reverence!"*

"Reverence must be earned!" she yelled back. "Let you learn of my people before you condemn. You would have sentenced me to death or exile without ever hearing my voice. How dare you take such judgement upon yourselves! Who made you the keepers of life and death over us? Are we so terrifying, so evil, that we must be killed on sight? Dear Goddess! What courage!

"A few nights past, one of my people was killed for daring to cross the Boundary. Akor tells me the idiot had had dealings with the Rakshasa; I am sure he did, in some way at least—an amulet for luck, perhaps. Perhaps more. But is death the only answer? His name was Perrin, and though I did not know him we had travelled together. He was a youth and foolish in the way of youth. Youth makes mistakes.

"Maybe Perrin deserved death, O Kantri, but maybe he did not. You are so bound by your laws, you creatures of order, they dictate so much of your lives. They are killing you! As you forget how to value time, as you lose sight of the joy of each single day as it comes and passes, I believe you forget how to value life itself. Even—especially—your own."

Her eyes blazed as she stood tall and faced the Kindred, her courage bright around her, her heart high as and fierce as any of the Kindred that ever lived. "Every time the Harvesters have come, I would guess that there is at least one who crosses the Boundary against the treaty. Is that not so?"

"It is," I answered her.

"And what is the fate of that one, or two, or however many?"

"By the terms of the treaty they have written their own death in the crossing," growled Rishkaan in truespeech.

"Death! Always death! Yet consider, O ye of the Greater Kindred. In all these centuries, what retribution have the Gedri demanded? What restitution for all those deaths?"

"They are due none," Rishkaan replied coldly.

"And if my people claimed that Akor broke the treaty in crossing the Boundary to come to my aid, that he interfered with Marik, destroyed property, and that restitution was required? As I understand it, there is no provision in the treaty for such a thing, though he did what he did in full view of all my people. What if we in our foolishness were to demand his death, as we have paid with death so many times? Do you tell me you would sit calmly and accept it, treaty or no?"

The murmur died down, as many stopped to consider her words. However, from one corner a mindvoice rang out.

"You cannot kill us, Gedri. You are not strong enough."

She paused a moment for effect, then said one word, her voice very low and calm.

"Demonlord."

Every soul in the assembly drew back and hissed, but she raised her voice and called above the noise, "All it would take is one demonlord, from among the many thousands of my people. One demonlord, to exact revenge for all the deaths over all the centuries. Yet there have been none!"

"Do you call for Akor's death?" hissed Erianss.

"Sweet Goddess, no! *No!* Not death! Don't you understand, do you still not understand me? I call for life. Life!"

I smelt the seawater as it ran down her cheeks. "Life for both races, dear people of my beloved, life truly shared between Kantri and Gedri—as when the world was younger, and our two peoples dwelt together in peace." She bowed her head. "Oh, my brothers and sisters," she said brokenly, suddenly spent and weary, "I call for life."

She had no more words. The final echoes of her voice rang round the walls and met only silence.

Lanen

I had them. One more word and Akor and I would walk free. Ah, well.

I heard Kédra's voice clearly. *"Lanen? Lord Akhor? The Lady Rella whom you left in my charge bears news of the Gedri that you must hear. She says it is urgent."*

"How could she have news if she has been in your keeping?" I asked him.

"One came from the camp seeking all of the Gedri, and spoke with her as I kept out of sight listening. She followed after him and was gone for some while, but she has returned."

I stood motionless on the dais, filled with the fear that I had not reached the Kantri, and aware of a rising dread. What news could possibly have sought her out so far from the camp? Dear Lady, what had happened *now?*

Kédra's voice was grim when he spoke again. *"Lady, it is the Merchant Marik. His order has gone out among your people that you are to leave on the morrow. They are beginning even now. And the Lady Rella says that there is no sign of Marik, and that you will understand when she says that she saw him with the demon master not half an hour gone. She says you will know what this means."*

I did. I knew as if I had heard it from his own lips. I whirled on Akor.

"He got away, didn't he? He got out of the cabin before your battle."

"He did."

I nearly choked on my own words. "Akor, don't you understand? He has already been across the Boundary and returned. He boasted of it to me!" I ground my teeth. "I meant to tell you earlier, but in the face of that demon I forgot. Akor, he and that slug Caderan must have found a way to hide all trace of his passing from you and yours, even the smell of the Rakshasa!" My fists clenched, my gut tightened, I felt the whole fabric of my impassioned plea to the Kantri crumbling from under my fingers, but there was no help for it. "Akor, I tell you he is here in your lands even as we speak. I know in my bones that he has found kadish or something he desires even more. As sure as I live he will take it with him tonight and be gone in the morning. He must be stopped!"

Akor stared at me. "It would explain much. I could not find you in your imprisonment until you bespoke me, though once past the wards the Raksha-sign was obvious and the very air was thick with it." He looked away, a very human gesture. "Name of the Winds, is such a thing possible?"

"It must be. He told me, Akor. He meant to kill me, he taunted me with it. Oh, dear Lady. Now we are lost." I bowed my head, despair rising in me like a flood until I could hardly bear it. Here I had stood before the Greater Kindred, forced them into silence with my version of the truth, forced them to see their failings as a people, and now I must tell them their fears were true and my words the ramblings of a dreamer. I felt as though I had held out a new beginning for Kantri and Gedri shining in my hands, and Marik had snatched it away before ever it knew life.

There was nothing else for it. I mustered my thoughts, how to tell them, how to—

"*My people, hear me!*" called Akor. His voice caught me unawares, stirred my blood. Even those few words had my heart hurrying to answer. His truespeech sang like a call to battle.

"*Truly it is said the great balance will not be denied. While we work here to find justice, another has brought a great evil upon us. The Merchant Marik, he who would have sacrificed Lanen to the Rakshasa, has made some new league with them.*

"*He has been in our lands already, though no Guardian sensed him sight or smell, and none felt the Raksha-trace even so near. We must disperse now and find him. He seeks plunder or worse. Go carefully, find him if you can. If not, find what has been taken. Look even unto the* khaadish *in your chambers. Go, my people.*"

There was some movement among the gathered Dragons, but suddenly a voice rang loud in my mind. Someone else was shouting in the Language of Truth.

"*She is here as distraction, Akhor, it is a plot between them!*" cried Rishkaan before any other could speak. His voice flew high, cracking with emotion. I shrank back. Suddenly Rishkaan reminded me of Marik, Marik with his knife at my throat. "*She must be kept under guard lest she escape the Council's decree!*" He moved towards me with the grace and speed of a striking snake, he was upon me in an instant. I cowered and raised my arms, turning my head away, for I knew that my death was come upon me.

And it would have been so, but Shikrar was faster. He all but flew to stand between, taking across his chest plates the swipe that was meant to appear accidental. It barely scratched him. It would have cut me in half.

I fell to my knees.

None of the Kindred had moved.

They watched.

Akhor

Shikrar stood, wings spread wide to protect my Lanen, all his being fixed on the furious figure before him.

"Why, Rishkaan?" I asked quietly. "This is not for some ancestor you never knew. This burns in your heart."

"Burns! Burns! Yes, yes, you speak truth at last, Silver King. She must die, she is a Lord of the Hells in Gedri guise. You have not seen what I have seen!" he raved. His voice echoed in the shocked stillness of the chamber, throbbing with a truth that spoke only to him. "I have seen, I know what is to come. I too have had Weh dreams, Lord Akhor, but mine have been of death and ending. My people, she would mingle the blood of Kantri and Gedri! Her children will be monsters, the world will fill with Raksha-fire and none to stand between because of *her!*"

Shocked silence swept the low murmurs out of the air. Where could such thoughts, such words come from? I had heard tales of madness among our people but never thought to see it myself. I did not for a moment believe that he had had such a dream in Weh sleep.

Kédra called out to all of us, his voice urgent in our minds. *"Akhor, what is happening? Are you there yet? Time is precious. The Lady Rella says that this Marik will not wait, and I believe her. Find him, I beg you, lest he do more harm. Quickly, Akhor my friend!"*

I needed time to think, but there was no time. I could make only a few swift plans. "Shikrar, take Rishkaan with you to my chambers. They are nearest, there you will find water and a place to rest until this is over."

"Akhor, no!" cried Shikrar. "The Chamber of Souls! I must go, I am Keeper of Souls, I cannot—"

"Then call Kédra to watch over Rishkaan for you, but guarded he will be. I know Kédra is Guardian tonight, but I think we need not fear other Boundary crossings for this while. Wait for Kédra to arrive before you go to the Chamber of Souls." When Shikrar and Rishkaan had gone I turned to the others, my people, tumbling as was I in a wind we had never known. "The rest of you, go now out into your chambers, into all our lands. Find if there is *khaadish* missing or aught else. And if you can, find the hidden thief."

For one last time they obeyed me. Still in silence, the Greater Kindred left the Council chamber quickly. I had seen vengeance in some eyes, fear in others, wonder and excitement in the very youngest, but below and beyond all of these something new. I did not know what it might be, and I had no time to think.

Lanen

I knelt still, unable to move. So close to my dream, so near the joining of the Two Peoples, and the shadow side of both rose up to blight my bright, shining vision of peace. Rishkaan's words had pierced my armour of courage with the shaft of a dark vision at least the equal of my own.

She would mingle the blood of Kantri and Gedri! Her children will be monsters, the world will fill with Raksha-fire and none to stand between because of her!

The black pull of despair closed like dark water over me. If I was truly destined to bring such evil to the world, better far that I should die at the hands of the Kantri. Shikrar at least would be merciful.

"Rise, Lanen. You must hurry, there is no time."

It was Akor, speaking in tones that dragged me to my feet. Whatever I might need must wait now upon a larger purpose. I stood ready and asked, "What would you have me do?"

"Wait outside this chamber for Kédra to arrive. Then you must go with Shikrar to safety."

"Akor, please, let me do something! Anything! I have to help you, I must, there must be something I can do to help stop that damned son of a bitch—"

Akor waited, a very little time, until I ran down of my own accord. "Littling, I will not allow it. What should you do that I and my people cannot?"

The worst of it was that he was right. I've thought since that if I had any decent sense of the dramatic I would have begged, nay, insisted on going with Akor, as so often happens with the women in the bard's tales. I never did have time for those idiots. Why stand by unarmed and helpless in a fight, waiting to be taken hostage or distract your loved one's mind during a battle? Despite my anger, my despair, my frustration, I did no more than bow my assent and say, "The Winds and the Lady keep you, dearling. I will await you here." And in truespeech, focussed as tight as I could, I added the blessing that Jamie had given me when we parted. *"Akor, beloved, go you safe and keep you safe, and come safe home to me."*

His own farewell was a swift touch of the mind like a caress, and then he was gone. I took a small brand from the great fire that lit the chamber and followed the passage out. I had little hope now for my-

self, but in the face of Marik and his demon master I cared little for
that. In my heart I begged the Winds and the Lady to keep Akor from
the evil of the Rakshasa, and protect him from Marik.

It was deep night when I emerged, some hours past midnight. I
had not realised we had been so long in the Council chamber. A brisk
wind blew past, carrying the glorious scent of lansip on the night air,
sharp and crisp.

I sat, leaning back against the rocky entrance to the Great Hall.
Weariness wrapped round me like my old cloak as I waited for Kédra
under the clear cold stars. Pain and terror, exultation, delight and despair may sound the very fabric of adventure from a distance, but
even singly they are exhausting. Together I was no match for them,
and sleep took me.

xvi

IN THE DEEP NIGHT

Marik

Ow! This damned spike hurts, I've scratched my chest with it
already. Thirsty for blood the damned thing is. Now take it in the
right hand, run the middle finger of the left onto it—*damn!*
Shouldn't have hurt that much. Never mind. It looks rusty as well,
I must have Maikel salve the wound once I am on board the ship.
Now, what did Berys say—yes, that was it, fill each of the four little wells at the corners with blood. It's damned hard to see the
things in the dark. This cloak that hides me from other sight leaches
colour from the world. Still, on balance I come out on the profit side
of the ledger—I pass unseen, and can see well enough to get where
I am going. And anything that gives off light shines like a beacon.
Ah, the moon! Such pain in my eyes. It is overbright but at least I
can see what I'm doing.

There! The flash Berys said would signal the beginning, then it
goes dark again. Two hours only have I now, in which to make my
fortune and that of my House forever, but for these two hours I shall
leave behind no spoor of either world; no natural human smell, no
Raksha-trace to lead the Dragons to me.

I move in a mist of blurred outlines and shadows, drawn by

vengeance and desire, glide like a ghost across the Boundary and speed towards their treasure chamber.

Shikrar

As we left the Great Hall, Rishkaan (much subdued) asked if we might survey his own chambers, which were close at hand, before we examined Akhor's. I itched to be gone to the Chamber of Souls myself, but I understood the concern behind his request. When I bespoke Kédra, he agreed to meet us at Akhor's dwelling as soon as he might, but said he was searching along the Boundary for sight or smell of the Gedri Marik and would be some little time, and that we might as well make certain of both our chambers first. He would come as escort to Rishkaan as soon as he could, that I might guard the Chamber of Souls. In passing I bespoke Idai, who flew at best speed from the Birthing Cove. She had just set out, leaving Mirazhe and the youngling in a protected cave. She said little beyond that she came as swiftly as she might.

When we reached Rishkaan's chambers I was hard put to it to mask my dismay, for the disrepair and neglect could not be ignored. I had begun, over the last few decades, to suspect that he was one of those for whom long life was no blessing. It sometimes happens that one among us will grow old in mind before his time, and so it appeared to be with Rishkaan. The only relief is that those so afflicted often pass into the last Weh sleep well before their full years are accomplished. In sorrow I began to hope for such an ending for Rishkaan. In any case, it was swiftly apparent to him that nothing had been disturbed.

My own dwelling and the Chamber of Souls stood nearby and we were there in a moment. Stopping outside the door I lit a branch and offered in truespeech a prayer of Remembrance to the Winds as I entered, the flaming brand in my mouth. The ancient soulgems of my people, ranged against the back wall in symbolic patterns and set in *khaadish*, blinked reassuringly back at the fire I held now in my hand, and the soulgems of the Lost lay still in their rough cask, flickering as they had through the ages. I bowed in the old sorrow of their presence, and as always renewed my vow to release them if it lay in my power. It occurred to me to speak to Lanen and Akhor about them, if (as I hoped) the Council changed their minds after hearing her words. Perhaps in this new blending of the peoples there might be new hope for the Lost Ones. I breathed a thought to the Winds to guide the Greater Kindred to wisdom, bowed to the Ancestors, and we left.

As we returned to Akhor's chambers, close by the Great Hall, we found that many of the Kindred had assembled nearby after ensuring that no intruder had been near their chambers. The talk was all of the Council, and of the Gedri, and of seeing one of the Silent Ones close to at last. This they had a good chance to do, for Lanen slumped fast asleep against the outer wall of the Council chamber. All spoke softly so as not to disturb her—I wondered what she would dream, for all the speech was in our ancient tongue and beyond her ken even were she wakeful.

Most, I noted with pleasure, remembered to speak of her by name, and as I listened I realised that Akhor was right—she was truly the Wind of Change. For many, the anger that Lanen had stirred up in them had been transmuted all in a moment to shame at her words, at their realisation that perhaps the Kindred had been unfair to the Gedri through the ages. She had touched a deep truth and most of our people were responding, despite the threat of a demon-aided thief from among her people, for which she could hardly be held responsible. Few save the eldest spoke now of death or exile; I even heard in passing a suggestion that she be honoured as a teacher. I allowed myself a secret smile as I escorted Rishkaan into Akhor's torchlit chambers. Akhor would have so much joy at least.

No sooner were we inside, however, than Rishkaan spoke his frustration. "Hadreshikrar, I obey our King, but in truth I do not know why I must be held here. I have seen what I have seen, and spoken truth in Council. Are my Weh dreams worth less than those of Akhor?"

"No, Rishkaan, of course not," I said sadly, "but you have attacked Lanen, the Gedri child, while still she addressed the Council, and that action has yet to be considered. She is not a Raksha to be killed on sight."

"I tell you she is the end of our world! I have seen it!" he cried.

"Calm yourself, old friend," I said gently. "I heard you both in Council. But I do not understand how both could be true. Akhor saw our people's salvation arising from his joining with Lanen, he told us the Winds spoke with him and said as much. How should I believe such communion false?"

"Perhaps he did not tell the whole truth," growled Rishkaan. "You well know that our Kindred are not above stretching the truth if it suits their need."

I bowed. "True enough. Akhor concealed his twilight meeting with Lanen from me, he has admitted it. But Rishkaan, did his words in Council not strike you as those of one who has done with conceal? And why should he invent so clumsy a lie? If he sought to justify his actions, surely the voice of the Winds would be more use to him ere ever he and Lanen were joined. What good does that good word do him afterwards? No, to me it has the ring of truth. And—forgive me if I am blunt—how could there possibly be a mingling of the blood of Kantri and Gedri? I agree, it is a thought to sicken the mind, but surely it is beyond possibility. It is as if you asked us to beware the offspring of a bull and a butterfly."

"Fool!" cried Rishkaan. "I tell you I have seen it! She had our form, Shikrar, she was one of us! And her children I saw in terrible guise, half-Gedri, half-Kantri, caught between in a black hour, changing from one to the other. The sky was filled with hideous forms, the world was aflame with Raksha-fire, and because of her there was no Akhor to stand between the Lords of Hell and the last defenders of Kolmar." He bowed his head and did not speak for some time. "Ah, Hadreshikrar, I grow old before my time," he said sadly.

"Rishkaan, my friend, I hear you," I replied, "and well I know the years bring sorrow with wisdom. But I cannot believe the world is doomed, not by love, though I hear the truth in your voice and know that you at least believe it. I beg you consider though, for the sake of Akhor, that perhaps he and Lanen might also be right. It may be that you have seen most but not all of what is to come. Might there not be a last verse, a final turn on the wing or beat of the heart that has not been revealed to you? Or," I said, quietly voicing a thought that had been growing in my mind, "perhaps you have each seen only one side of a balance that might go either way. Perhaps the Council's decision to exile them will bring about its destruction, while allowing them to stay together would be the saving of our Kindred, as Akhor has foretold."

Rishkaan was mustering a reply when we both heard the sound of someone arriving outside the cavern entrance, and the sudden silence that came with it.

We did not wonder long. Kédra entered the cavern. "I could find no trace of him, Father," he said, his voice in some strange place between defeat and merriment.

"Are you certain the Gedri who spoke with you told the truth?"

"And who might you be, to call me liar to my face?" asked a high voice I had not heard before. And in behind Kédra walked the second child of the Gedri I had ever seen close to. She stood bent over, and I saw that she could not straighten. She was smaller and darker than Lanen, but full of the same fire. I was too surprised to be angry.

"I am the Keeper of Souls, lady," I answered sternly. "Who are you, and know you a reason why I should not slay you for crossing the Boundary?"

She did not flinch, but Kédra answered me. "I stand her advocate, my father. Lanen commended her to me though this lady knew it not. She sought protection where she might, for Marik has learned that she aided Lanen in her escape, and seeks her life. She told me—"

"I told him, Master Keeper of Souls, that I'd rather die clean and fast than go the way Marik would send me," said the crooked one. "I am called Rella. And I would still rather be sent to my rest by you than by his fools of guards." She bowed to me. "Do as you wish, Master. I am old enough, and now I've set her free I've done my duty and shall sleep peacefully."

I looked Kédra in the eye and saw there the curious merriment I had heard in his voice. It was clear he had come to like this creature and her boldness. To my amazement, I found that I agreed.

"If you stand friend to Lanen, how should I do other than welcome you?" I said.

She bowed again. "Then I thank you for my life." She gazed straight at me. "Seems you are true friends to her, after all, though I must say sometimes you've an odd way of showing it. Where is she?"

"I heard Akhor ask her to wait outside the Council chamber. My son, if you will keep the watch with Rishkaan I will swiftly escort this lady to Lanen, then go to the Chamber of Souls as guard."

"As you wish, father. Go well."

I leant close to the crooked one's face. "Come, mistress, let us walk together to the Council chamber. I would speak with you."

She bared her teeth in what appeared, by her voice, to be pleasure. "It will be an honour, Master."

Strange that so short a time could change so old a feeling.

I looked forward to speaking with her.
The Wind of Change, indeed.

Marik

I walk through dry leaves and feel small twigs snap under my feet,
but no sound escapes to my ears or any other's. I am like a small boy
that has outwitted his parents; I suspect I am grinning like a death's-
head. My breath comes faster now as I approach the cave where I
saw the gems in their golden cask. The time limit on my amulet beats
in my mind as my heart beats in my chest. I know well that it has
taken me little more than the half of an hour to get to this place from
the Boundary. There is plenty of time in hand.

And there, just before me, darker in the general blackness, lies
the entrance to the cave I seek. Steel your nerves, Marik, stir up your
courage to enter and seize the treasure—

Hell's teeth! What was that? Freeze, don't breathe, turn slowly—
aah! What's that brilliance that burns my eyes?

Fire. Hell's teeth, it's a blossom of fire from nothing, searing my
eyes, near but not yet upon me. Back away, remember there's no
sound, duck so as not to move the branches, hide beneath the shadow
of the bare trees, better than nothing. My mind knows they cannot
see me, but if they turn suddenly or run into me by chance all is over
with me. By damn, those things are huge, and two of them draw near
to the cave mouth.

The largest—dark bronze, with a gem in his forehead that winks
deepest ruby in the firelight—enters with the flaming branch, while
the other, bright copper with lackluster eyes, sits without not twenty
paces from me. Breathe, Marik, breathe, if this one waits the other
surely will not be long.

At last! I have waited an eternity here, and at last it comes out
again. The painful fire is quenched in the leaf mould, the bronze one
joins its companion and they move away northward. Breathe, Marik.
It is astounding. For all their size they move swiftly and silently as
cats, leaving only the least trembling of the grass, the lightest whisper of rustling leaves to mark their going.

Wait but a moment longer, beat steady my heart, breathe deep
and lose the fear that caught me. The peril now is past. Before me
the cave mouth beckons with the promise of riches untold, lying

there now unguarded. I see in my mind's eye the open cask full of flickering gems and enter the Dragons' treasure chamber.

The outer room is huge and lined with gold to a depth of some inches. Its call would be difficult to resist were it not for the gems.

Even in this cave the dark is not absolute. My eyes, now recovered, catch the glint of the many vast gems thickset in great slabs of gold on the back wall. Still I am not tempted, it would take far longer than I have to dig them out of their settings. I step closer—

And there, on its golden pedestal, sits the object of all my cost, all my travail. A rough golden cask, like a great bowl, filled nearly to overflowing with the gems that flicker and change with the patterns of their inner fire. It is all I can do not to laugh aloud. Here at last, and so simple withal. I put my hand out to touch, and pause.

They are so very beautiful. I, with my good head for business and sharp eye to the value of a thing rather than its artistry, stand entranced by the wonder of what lies before me. Time seems to pause, hovers in my hand, in the eternal moment between thought and action.

How long have I stood here spellbound? Listen for the beat of the amulet—still strong and steady, I have not tarried too long. These gems have blinded me, deafened me, immobilized me, until at last some deep instinct has warned me that I am bounded by time and must do what I have come to do or leave.

Or?

No, not or.

And.

The cask is heavier than I thought it would be, surely this much gold alone is worth many lives of men. In seconds it lies with its contents in the pack I have brought, a dead weight, a precious burden on my shoulder beneath my cloak of borrowed darkness.

Now to leave swiftly, back into the night, back towards the Boundary. I gather my strength and start to run. Lords of Hell, this thing is heavy! But the worst is that I have lost track of time and cannot tell how much longer my amulet will last.

What is that noise? A high keening sound that grates on my nerves, speeds my heart even faster, sets my teeth on edge.

Hell's teeth. *It's coming from the gems.*

Lanen

"Lanen, child, wake up. You'll catch your death out here."

I swam reluctantly up from a deep well of sleep to Rella's touch on my shoulder and her voice in my ear. I blinked in the moonlight, slowly realising that many of the Kindred were standing in the clearing talking in very low voices. It took me a moment to work out exactly where I was—leaning against rock, cold and stiff—a cave, no, the Council chamber—then I was wide awake.

"Rella, how did you get here?" I asked, stumbling gracelessly to my feet.

When I heard the hiss of amusement, I turned to find Shikrar on the other side of me. I nodded to him, trying to hide my disappointment at seeing bronze instead of silver.

"Is there any word from Akor?" I asked. "Has anyone found Marik?"

"Lord Akhor bespoke me not long since, Lady," replied Shikrar. "He has overflown the Gedri camp, and says that Mistress Rella speaks truly—all is being removed and taken in darkness to the southern shore. Of Marik there is nor sight nor smell."

"Well, there wouldn't be, would there?" said Rella. "He's been in once and out again and you none the wiser. Have you something he would want, some treasure perhaps? He's here to make his fortune, sure and certain, and if the camp is all broke down he'll take what he's after and straight to the ship with it."

"By the treaty he must meet with us at dawn to tell us he is leaving," said Shikrar, obviously distressed at this reminder of Marik's ability to come and go unnoticed. "If he does not, we are within our rights to attack him."

I could swear Shikrar looked pleased at the idea. I couldn't blame him. So was I.

"Yes, well, he's sure to stick to the treaty, isn't he?" said Rella wryly.

"Why not have all the Kindred go to their own chambers and stay there?" I asked. "If there is something he seeks in one of these caves, I'd guess that finding it occupied would slow him down, at the very least."

"It is well spoken," replied Shikrar. He called out aloud to those of the Kindred who were still nearby. "Let us return to our homes, my people, and each keep safe his own dwelling. When the intruder is found, the Council will resume. This is the counsel of the Eldest and the Keeper of Souls."

And the Dragons melted away like ice in sunshine, swift and silent, until only Shikrar stood with Rella and me. "I too must go, the Chamber of Souls must be guarded," he said, and suddenly the idea of waiting helplessly so far away and so alone terrified me.

"Let us come with you," I said, ashamed of my fear but sure of what I asked. Shikrar looked surprised, so I added, "We can't go into Akor's chambers. I suspect Rishkaan would take his chances with the Council and kill me if he had half a chance, despite Kédra. And if Marik comes here, hidden from sight and sound—well, it wouldn't be as clean as Rishkaan, but the end would be the same. Please, Shikrar," I begged, despising myself. Just like the idiots in the ballads. Damn.

I did not recognise the Attitude Shikrar took on, but his voice sounded an odd mixture of annoyance and approval. "Very well. Come, we must hurry. Both of you sit upon my neck, as Akhor bore you, Lanen. It will be the swiftest." And he put his head on the ground.

I was just reaching out to clamber onto his neck when with a hiss and a deep rumbling growl he sat bolt upright, knocking me to the ground, his head whipping round to the southeast as though his gaze would pierce darkness, distance and all. My heart dropped into my stomach, for I knew the instant he did. I cannot imagine how, but I knew, even before Akor's cry echoed in my mind.

The soulgems of the Lost.

Marik had them.

Akhor

I was stabbed with the theft as with a lance of ice, as I rode the night wind to the north and west seeking I knew not what. My back arched, my neck snapped skyward and I split the night with a plume of Fire to hallow my vengeance, for I was seized in that instant with a purpose beside which all else was nought. I would save the Lost ones from this final desecration or die in the attempt.

I cried out to Lanen, a wordless cry of loss and desolation, as in my soul I knew this must be the death of all our words in Council. I turned on the wind and flew fast as thought, calling to Shikrar as I went. *"Shikrar, Keeper of Souls, command me!"*

"Akhor, soulfriend, meet me at the Chamber of Souls," cried Shikrar, his mindvoice faint in despair. *"Lost, lost, twice cursed and twice bereft, all my ancestors bear me witness I will have them back!"*

We are brothers in the soul, after all.

Lanen

Shikrar crouched to fly but I cried out, aloud and in truespeech, *"Eldest, leave me not here! I know what has befallen, I heard the Lost cry out as did you, bear me hence I beg you!"*

I might as well have kept silence. *"There is no time!"* he cried, and sprang into the night with a clap of his vast wings. It blew us over.

"Damn," I said aloud, as Rella and I stood and brushed ourselves off as Shikrar disappeared. "What in all the Hells is going on?" she asked. "I'll tell you as we run," I replied and was starting to follow after Shikrar when behind and above me I heard a roar like nothing on earth. I threw myself to the ground from sheer instinct and felt the wind batter me, heard the clap of Dragon wings, and watched as another took to the skies. It was hard to tell in the moonlight, but it was too large and too bright for Kédra and I only knew of one other nearby—one whose bright copper hide would reflect moonlight well.

Rishkaan.

Damn, damn, *damn!*

"Kédra! Swiftly, to me!" I cried, dragging Rella behind me, and met him coming out of Akor's chambers.

Marik

My legs are weak, my old pain has come back even as I run with this burden of wealth. I stumble as fast as I may.

Curse it, the sign Berys warned me of! A tingling at my throat, the amulet drags at my neck and sends sharp stabs into my heart with every step. The wound on my chest where I scratched myself with the spike burns with the nearness of Raksha-fire, and I cannot get rid of the high voices of the gems. How should gems speak? They are cursed, perhaps they are demons themselves, Lords of Hell what have I *got?*

My two hours are all but sped.

I cannot find the Boundary! How can this be, I returned only last night with no trouble—but the gems, they sing, I hear them try to speak, their sounds confuse me, I cannot see despite the bright moon. The gems and their golden cask drag at me. Hells and damnation, I have to get out of here!

I can only run and hope I will blunder into the Boundary by chance. Lords of Hell, guide my steps who seek to serve you. The first of these gems will I give in free offering to you, if you will get me past the Boundary.

Hells and damnation. I hear in every breath their step behind me, feel every moment the hot wind that precedes my death. I saw the fury of the one who destroyed the demon, I know my life is forfeit if my amulet fades while still I walk in the forbidden lands. I remember the corpse of the youth who crossed over, I could not eat for days after—what will they do to me if they catch me with their greatest treasure?

Faster, man, faster! Hell's teeth, the gems are keening high and shrill, terror creeps up my spine bone by bone, freezing my legs and my heart, threatening to leave me here forever, the frozen statue of a running man. Your life, Marik, stay alive! Run, run with what strength you have left, for the amulet beats now its pulse to match my heart, faster, faster—there!

Dark in the moonlight the Boundary rises before me, safety in wooden rails. Fast as thought, Marik, run, run—through! Through and beyond, tear off the damned amulet that burns now where it touches chest and hand, throw it from me. I slow, out of breath, I watch as it glows brightly once more, bright as it flashed at first, but the glow now is a rich red, like light through blood. It lies on the ground, gleaming brighter and brighter. I cannot look away, it fills my sight like a red star fallen to earth.

I tear my eyes away at last and run, now south, where the ship lies waiting that will carry me safe from this place of horror.

Shikrar

Every bone in my body cried out when the soulgems of the Lost were stolen, every instinct told me to fly to the Chamber of Souls, and so I did, swift as wings would carry me. I had only just landed when Rishkaan arrived, a fury in his eyes that frightened me. Akhor came as swiftly as he could, but he had been far to the west.

I tried to reason with Rishkaan, but I might as well have spoken with a stone. He rushed past me into the Chamber, sniffing for all he was worth. "No scent, no scent, how can that be, there must be some trace, there has to be—"

"Rishkaan, remember what the Gedri Rella said, that he had come and gone without our knowledge before. We will never find him this way."

He snapped his head to face me. "You are right," he said in a voice of iron. "He must have gone—" He did not not stay even to complete his thought, but sped away past me into darkness.

I could not follow, and did not want to. If Rishkaan needed vengeance, if in his fury he slew this Marik, I would not stand in his way. I would await Akhor here, in my ravished Chamber, where the soulgems of my ancestors looked down in contempt on the failure of the Keeper of Souls.

These are the true words of Rishkaan, from the Kin-Summoning requested by Akhor, Silver King of the Kantri.

The soulgems of the Lost sang loudly of their theft; I could not ignore it. I took Kédra by surprise and pushed him aside—he is much younger and smaller than I, after all—and leapt into the sky as soon as I was out of Akhor's cave, flying towards the Chamber of Souls.

It was not only the theft that compelled me. I could not rid myself of that vision, it lingered before my mind's eye like an image of the sun. Akhor, dead, his body turned to ash—that was bad, but death comes to all in their time. Far worse, worst of all, the horrible clarity of the Gedri Lanen with her younglings. They were a monstrous union of the two Kindreds, able to change from one to another at will. It was the sight of that perversion that struck bright flame within me. Such abomination I would spend my life to prevent.

The Silver King, Akhor the Wise, I had hoped for so much from him. Still, he would get over this Gedri child. It was merely a passing madness. He had many years yet in which to accomplish the purpose for which he had been born.

As long as my dream remained unfulfilled.

I saw Shikrar land before me, but the time for subtlety and obedience was past. I ran before him into the Chamber, where stray glints of moon and starlight filtered down from the airhole above and struck brief gleams from the soulgems of the Ancestors on the back wall. *Someday I shall have my place there,* I thought briefly, *a good end for a long life, rest and peace and the voices of your descendants to call you forth from time to time—* but as I knew it must be, when I turned to look at the flickering depths of the Lost Ones, I could but stare, for all my knowledge silent and openmouthed, at the pedestal where they had rested near five thousand years, empty now of anything but memory.

Shikrar reminded me I could not trace him by smell, so I must outwit the creature. Where should he go but the fastest way back to the Gedri camp?

I hurried out of the Chamber of Souls and made the straightest way to the Boundary, searching still as I went for the smell of the Gedri or for Raksha-trace. I found none, but still I followed the way the evil one must have gone.

xvii

THE LOST

Shikrar

It was but a moment after Rishkaan had gone that Akhor bespoke me. *"What news, Shikrar?"* he asked urgently.

"Rishkaan is gone after the thief," I replied, and in the Language of Truth I could not keep my underthought from adding, *"and I did nothing to stop him."*

"You are not to blame," he said instantly. *"Where has he gone?"*

"Towards the camp of the Gedri," I replied. *"He is in a fury, Akhor. What must I do?"*

"Keep you in the Chamber of Souls, Eldest, lest against all reason Marik should return. Reason seems to have little sway this

night. I will await Rishkaan and Marik in the camp of the Gedri."
And he was gone.

Lanen

"Kédra, please, I must be with Akor. All is changed now, I beg you, take me to him!"

"Lady, ask me anything but this," he replied, deeply troubled. "I have already lost my charge Rishkaan, I dare not so disobey my King as to do this for you. Lord Akhor would not thank me for taking you into such danger."

"I don't care!" I shrieked. I was dancing with frustration and the need to be gone. "Damn it, Kédra, I can't leave him alone in this. I tell you I heard the Lost cry out before Akor spoke word, I am called, I cannot stay here!"

He stared at me in silence for a long moment, then leaned swiftly down. "Come then, lady, the Winds and Lord Akhor forgive me."

"Bless you, true friend," I cried as I scrambled onto his neck.

"If you think I'm staying here without either of you, you're both crazy," said Rella's voice from behind me, and there she stood, arms on her hips. "Kédra, of your kindness, either take us both or give me directions so I can walk."

"Get on, then. Quickly!"

She scrambled up nimbly enough behind me. Kédra was not as strong as Akor, and had twice the burden. "I do not dare fly thus," he said, "but I can run. Hold tight."

He sped off in the direction of the camp. I called in truespeech, *"Kédra, may I bespeak you?"*

"Of course."

"I'm sorry I have had to ask this of you, my friend, but I must be with him. How should I bear it if—" I could not say it aloud, but there rose in my mind the image of the wounds Akor had from the demon. No, no, I would not think of it. . . .

"Lady, fear not. Rishkaan is with him, and though he bears you no love he is loyal to the King. There is no demon spawned that could stand against the two of them."

"I'm not very good at hiding underthought yet, am I?" I said ruefully. *"I vowed I'd stay well clear of this, but I can't. I can't. Damn.*

Damnation. Hell, blast and damnation." And I can't tell you why, but that opened the floodgates. Poor Kédra. I started cursing, aloud and in truespeech, beginning with the wide-ranging matter I had learned from the seamen on the voyage out, through the many choice oaths of the stablehands at Hadronsstead, and ending with a good long string of simple old-fashioned swear words. I must say, it helped, and I heard Rella behind me laughing quietly.

When I had done, Kédra bespoke me. Even in the Language of Truth, they hissed their laughter. *"Lady, I am impressed. I thought I knew your language, but through all of that I caught little sense. Extraordinary. I could feel the shape of the words in my mind, but I had no sense of their meaning."*

"They don't have much, really," I said, deeply pleased that he hadn't understood. *"I was swearing. I don't know if the Kindred do it, but for humans it's a necessity."*

"I shall remember."

Rella tapped me on the shoulder. I half-turned to hear her.

"You talk to them, don't you? Without words. Farspeech."

"Yes," I said. It seemed so trivial now.

"Dear Lady Shia, is there no end to what I am to learn on this voyage?" She laughed. "I must remember that little skill of yours."

In the darkness I had no idea of how fast we were moving, but now as false dawn began to lighten the sky, I could see the trees flashing past. It was frightening, a little, but at that point it was mostly satisfying. And there before us was the Boundary.

Akhor

I had flown first to the southern shore, where the last of the Gedri were taking their goods onto the ship that lay out in the harbour. The soulgems of the Lost were nowhere near, so I flew north along the trail that we kept clear.

Even as I approached the settlement I could smell the Rakshastink. The camp reeked of it, growing ranker as I passed through the cleared spaces. There was the blackened site of my fight with the Raksha, smouldering yet—there the second of the wooden dwellings that had been here for centuries, there at the north end the doused ashes of the great campfire that had burned night and day. I landed in the clearing where the tents had been—it was the largest—and faced north and east. As I stood, I heard again faintly the soulgems' wail.

The sky to the east began to lighten, an end at last to this end-less night. I listened and waited, and wondered what I would do when the creature arrived.

I did not have long to wait. I smelled them long before I saw them, Raksha-stink and Gedri-smell, two of the creatures hurrying towards the clearing.

When they saw me they stopped abruptly.

Rella

Kédra leant down and let us off at the Boundary. Lanen took off at speed as though she knew exactly where she was going, but I'd not had even the little sleep she had and I was tired. I also did not wish to be any too close to whatever was going to happen. I dragged myself along, drifting some ways east along the Boundary.

Sudden as lightning a Dragon landed a good ways ahead of me (ignoring me entirely, thank the Lady) and started sniffing along the ground. I could hear him from where I stood (some distance down-wind of him), so I decided to stop and watch. Didn't take him long to find what he sought; he turned his head and shot a blazing stream of fire at the ground. Content with that, it seems, he ran straight on—and those things can run, let me tell you. He seemed to move even faster than Kédra, low to the ground and fast as a snake. He was out of sight in a heartbeat.

My way lay in the same direction, so after a few minutes I fol-lowed him, and came upon the empty campsite just as true dawn was beginning to break. I moved forward cautiously, past trampled grass and ashes of dead fires—

And there before me sat a young battle ready to begin. On one side stood the silver dragon, Akor it was, who had saved Lanen's life; I had lost track of the copper-coloured beast I had just seen. On the other was Caderan, looking fresh and strong, and Marik looking like a man at the end of his tether and ready for desperate measures. At the north end of the clearing, Kédra and Lanen had found one an-other again. He crouched like a great cat about to spring, but Lanen held desperately to the trunk of an old ash tree, as though that was the only thing keeping her from leaping into the fight.

I stayed well back and well hidden.

The true words of Rishkaan, from the Kin-Summoning

I stood in the trees to the northeast, silent and hidden, waiting behind the two Gedri that had just arrived, waiting for Akhor to destroy them. To my disgust he did not, but spoke to them instead.

"Give them back, Merchant. Put down your burden and give them back to us, and we will let you live."

"And so again you break the treaty, with not even the show of ceremony this time," drawled the shorter one, the one who reeked of the Rakshasa. "I had heard it said that the Kantri were creatures of Order. I must have been mistaken."

"Chaos breaks order, *rakshadakh*, when it oversteps its lawful bounds," hissed Akhor in deep anger. "Do not speak to me of treaties, you who have brought the Rakshasa to this place. Be glad I do not slay you where you stand, holding my kinsmen against their will."

"What do you say? Kinsmen?" said the tall one. "How should we constrain your kinsmen? We are mere men, we cannot command Dragons."

It was an unfortunate word for the Gedri to use. Dragons. The Lesser Kindred. Whose helpless soulgems he bore.

I could bear it no longer. I ran out, flaming, meaning to destroy these vermin as they deserved and recover the soulgems of the Lost.

My flame did not affect them in the slightest.

Akhor

I moved as one in a dark dream, slowly, as time sped on and left me behind to fight limbs like stone. Rishkaan's flame did not touch them. He stopped, wide-eyed, and sent again a blast of purifying fire against the *rakshadakh*, the demon slave that stood beside Marik and spoke with the tongue of falsehood and darkness.

The *rakshadakh* laughed, untouched, and lifted his hand. An answering flame shot from his fingers, black and red, not like true flame at all, and I heard Rishkaan cry out in pain.

And time snapped back into its place, my limbs were mine again, and I leapt into the air. If flame did no good, I might at least injure them when I landed. I was not thinking clearly, of course, for the Lost called to me endlessly. I flew so that I would fall on the Gedri with extended claws and that was my saving, for no sooner had the large claw of my foot come nigh the *rakshadakh* than it was sheared off. If I had practiced I could not have managed to do what I did, but somehow I swerved and tumbled gracelessly to the ground beyond them, unharmed as yet. I felt that dark flame pass over me as I fell, and unlikely though it seems I finally began to think.

How could we fight them? Our flame was useless, and now it seemed we could not reach them physically—what was left? Then Lanen's voice rang in my mind.

Lanen

I couldn't help myself, I called out to him without thinking. *"Akor! What's wrong, what in the Hells is happening? I saw Caderan shoot flame from his fingers, he's Marik's demon master, why don't you fry the bastard where he stands?"*

Akor's answer came swift but wearily. *"Tried—flame no effect— can't touch him either, the* rakshadakh *has some protection against us. Where are you?"*

"Kédra and I are on the north side of the clearing, in the trees. Are you hurt?"

His answer chilled me.

"Not yet."

Fear, loathing, anger—in a lucid moment they transformed into cold, calculating thought, as Jamie's drills on battle came back to me. *If your enemy is unarmed, use your fist, you've a long reach and he won't expect it. If he's wearing light armour, use your dagger to pierce the joints. If his armour turns your dagger, use your sword. If it turns your sword, get under his guard and push him over backwards across your ankle, he won't expect that either.*

I knew Caderan must have several spells going at once. It couldn't be easy to keep all that up. If only I could find something to distract him—

The Lady's servants say that thought is the birth of action. I believe it, for no sooner had the thought come to me than Rishkaan, glowing in the sunrise, leapt into the air and beat his wings, climb-

ing swiftly into the morning. I couldn't believe it, he was running
away, leaving Akor to face the two of them alone.

Marik, who had seemed to be mumbling to himself since
Rishkaan first attacked, raised his hand, and in the dawn light I saw
the sun glinting off something on his finger, a ring of some kind. Then
I realised it wasn't sunlight; the ring was glowing a bright and hideous
red. He said something I couldn't understand and turned the back
of his hand to Akor.

Something small and swift, glowing even in daylight, flew from
his hand and struck Akor in the chest. I watched helpless as red blood
flowed from him, obscenely lovely against his silver armour, while I
hid unmarked in the trees, horrified, helpless, furious.

Akhor

I did not know I was wounded until I heard Lanen cry out. I
looked down and saw a small red stream trickling from a perfectly
circular wound high on my chest, and I knew. Nothing pierces our
hides save Raksha-fire. Marik was in their service, and I would kill
him if I could. If he didn't kill me first.

I began to understand for the first time the actions of my people against the Demonlord. Foolish as it had seemed, at least they
did not stand still and wait to be wounded. I longed to launch myself at the *rakshadakh* again—instead I leapt into the air, seeking
height, calling out to my dearest companions, to Shikrar, to Kédra,
even to Idai as she flew: "*'Ware, my Kindred, the demons are among
us! The Rakshasa have sent their slaves and our doom is upon us. To
me, my friends, to me!*"

I heard the chorus of their replies (along with Idai's curses at
being too distant to aid me as yet), heard Shikrar from the Chamber of Souls and Kédra not five lengths away rising in anger as I
looked down on the *rakshadakh* and saw the last thing of reason I
can recall before I threw myself at Marik.

It was Rishkaan, diving with wings folded from a great height,
straight at the demon master Caderan. From the Gedri's fingers
shot out a blinding gout of black flame, and I am certain that
Rishkaan died even as he fell—but still he fell, all the size of him,
falling like the end of the world down towards the demon master.

Caderan screamed, like a beast that sees its death come upon it, and tried to run. He might as well have tried to outdistance the dawn. He cried out only once as he died, and my heart rejoiced in the sound.

My heart was afire, Fire rippled through me and burst out of my throat with a roar. Rishkaan may have been my adversary in Council but in his dying he was my brother in blood, and I would destroy this other of the Gedri vermin or die trying.

Shikrar

When Kédra bespoke me, telling me that Marik and his servant stood at bay before Akhor and Rishkaan, I told him I would leave that minor matter to them.

When Akhor cried out to me that a demon slave, a *rakshadakh*, was his enemy, I ran from my chamber and was in the air before I could think. So short a way, but once I was in the air a thought did come to me. I bespoke Kédra.

"Khétrikharissdra, I charge you as Keeper of Souls to stay out of this battle."

"Father, no!" he cried, entreating.

"It is not your father who speaks, it is the Eldest of the Greater Kindred and the Keeper of Souls," I replied sternly. *"Should I be killed in this battle you will become the next Keeper, you alone beside myself have the gift of the Kin-Summoning. You will not risk losing that in battle."*

"Father, I beg you!" he cried, his heart in his voice. I knew how he longed for vengeance, but I could not permit.

"Obey me in this, my son," I said, more kindly. *"I do not charge you by your fealty, but by your love. I lost my beloved, I will not see my son die before me. And above all, Kédra my son, you have a youngling newborn. He will need a father."*

And I was there.

Lanen

I couldn't believe what I saw. Marik was laughing, the bastard. He watched Shikrar arrive even as Akor attacked him, and he was laughing.

Dear Goddess. *Akor!*

Even as I watched, Marik sent the deadly circles flying from his hand, one after another, each a little worse, each striking Akor in a new place, wounding him more deeply than the last. Four of them followed the first, striking Akor unerringly even as he flew. He fell from the sky before ever he came within reach, streaming blood, great gouges in that glorious silver hide.

I ran towards Marik even as Shikrar thrust himself between Marik and Akor and attacked. For his pains he received the worst yet of Marik's circles, a terrible hole in his shoulder.

Marik's mind was all on the Dragons.

I ran into him at full tilt, with no thought for my safety until it was too late. I might have saved myself the worry; whatever he had to protect him from Dragons didn't seem to apply to his own kind. I did as Jamie had taught me and it worked a treat, knocked him off his feet, long enough at least to give Shikrar and Akor a breathing space. In seconds I was sat on his chest trying to slit his throat with his own dagger—but it did not bite. I tried again, and again the blade slid harmlessly off his skin.

He laughed and started to gesture at me with the ring he had been using on the others. I tried to knock his hand aside, but he was too quick. He pointed at me and said something in a foul language I had never heard before. We were both surprised when nothing happened.

I recovered just quickly enough to hit him, but I didn't have much leverage and it hardly bothered him. Then I saw an idea strike him harder than my fist had. He raised the hand with the ring on it and pointed towards Shikrar, who despite his pain stood now between Akor and Marik.

"Choose who will die, Maran's daughter," he cried in terrible delight. "For no matter what you do they cannot touch me, and no weapon of yours will bite any more than their useless teeth and claws."

And in that instant it came to me how he must be defeated.

Thank the Lady for truespeech.

"Akor, beloved, thus may he be stopped—"

Akhor

I heard her through my pain, through the fury that still burned white-hot within me. I bespoke Shikrar, who moved away to let me see, and together we turned our thoughts to the figure that struggled now with Lanen on the ground.

Even against such a strange form of attack, never so much as imagined in all the history of the Kantri, Marik must have had some defence, for his mind lasted long enough to work the last evil from his ring. As Shikrar and I together attempted to reach his mind with truespeech, to stop him with the sheer force of our wills, he managed to point the cursed thing at me and send through the air a final circle of dark fire that burned agony into my chest. I looked down in shock to see a gaping wound.

My bones, I noted, were intact. I knew, for I could see some of them.

Then, blessedly, as the pain began to sear through me, my legs would not hold me up and I fell insensible to the ground.

Marik

The gems sing louder, even in victory I cannot stop them, that horrible noise invades my very bones and shakes me. But Maran's daughter fails to save the silver one, and I have defeated—

light white light voices screaming in my head shut up get out get out GET OUT
FIRE
       my head is on fire
                it's inside my head the gems are screaming
the Lost
       Lostlostlost
              Die in agony rakshadakh
               White flame inside my head
    then darkness   all darkness   nolight noair allgone alllost
and all is gone
        all gone
           all lost
               lostlostlostlost
                  nononononooooo
                     . . . .

Kédra

My father called me to come when Akhor fell, for he judged that Marik was no longer a danger.

"Kédra, help me, we must bear him to his Weh chamber," Shikrar my father cried, his own wound ignored, his voice struggling to get past the tightness in his throat. I had to look away. Could it be that Akhor still lived? I had never seen, never imagined such wounds.

"Help me, Kédra, I cannot bear him alone," said my father. I braced myself and moved towards them, wondering how we two could lift him and Shikrar so hurt himself, when I heard an unexpected voice.

"*Kédra, Shikrar, I am come. Where are you?*"

"*In the Gedri camp, Lady Idai,*" I replied with relief. Idai was older than I, large and strong, with her help we surely could lift Akhor.

"*Be warned, Idai, his wounds are grievous,*" said Shikrar as she approached. "*We must carry him to his Weh chamber, and we desperately need your strength. Save grief for later, it is action he needs from us now.*"

Nevertheless, she cried out when she saw him. Lanen was beside him, bowed in what I guessed was grief or despair, unable to do ought to help. "*Who hass done this?*" Idai demanded in truespeech, even her mindvoice hissing with hatred. "*It iss the Gedri witch, it iss her doing,*" she said, and with all the power of her will she shouted at Lanen. "*Stand away frrom him!*"

"*I will not!*" Lanen screamed back at her, using the Language of Truth now as one born to it. She stood with her back to Akhor, looking for all the world like a mother protecting her youngling; her feet were planted in the ground (as well as two feet can be), her knees bent to spring, her forearms raised and her fury plain, and she all but hissed back at Idai. "*Akor is mine as I am his, I will stand with him if you kill me for it, damn you.*" They stood thus braced against one another for mere seconds, when Lanen fell to her knees and I smelt seawater. "*Lady, he bleeds as we stand here. If it would heal him I would die gladly. What can I do? Dear Goddess, what can I do?*"

Idai's wrath abated somewhat, for she knew agony when it stood before her defiant, defeated. "*Let us lift him, child. He must go to his Weh chamber and sleep, there to heal or to die. Move away, littling.*"

Lanen hurried from Akhor's side and spoke briefly with Rella. The three of us turned him to carry him on his back, when I stopped for an instant and knelt. *"Come, lady. I will bear you,"* I said to Lanen. She nodded at Rella and leapt up onto my neck. *"Hold fast, this will be difficult,"* I warned her, and together we three Kindred gathered ourselves and, as one, leapt into the air, beating our wings furiously, carrying our King to his rest.

Lanen

I had just thought enough to spare to bespeak the Council—well, everyone, actually—to let them know that Rella would be bringing the soulgems of the Lost in their cask as far as the Boundary fence at the place of Summoning. Then I forgot about it entirely.

I hope I never live through such a horrible time again. I was terrified for Akor. Goddess, Dear Shia, Mother of Us All, I could not stop looking at him, borne senseless through the morning by his companions. Those great gaping wounds bled terribly. I had never imagined that anything could bring such destruction to so powerful a creature. Dear Goddess. It was past bearing, it was unendurable, but I had no choice. Endure it I must.

I did not weep. I think I was beyond tears, though my cheeks felt wet. I clutched at Kédra's horns when the flight of the three was worst, begging the Winds, the Lady, whoever would listen, to let Akor live. Nothing else mattered.

Finally, beyond hope, I saw the hill and the little pool below us. The three started to spiral down, slowly, carefully. The landing was rough, and I thanked years of hard work for the strength in my arms to hold on. I let go and dropped off as soon as I could, for Kédra had told me that he was the only one small enough to enter Akor's cave and he would have to drag him. I followed behind, as one who is already dead but has forgot to lie down.

Kédra managed to get Akor to his floor of gold, where he lay in a pool of sunlight from the opening above. Akor lay on his back with his wounds uppermost, and—I couldn't believe my eyes—Kédra was scraping gold from the walls, breathing flame onto it until it glowed, shaping it like clay with his great claws into what could only be a bandage.

"Kédra?" I asked quietly.

"It will keep what blood he has left within his body and speed the healing," he said, not even glancing at me. "It is our way, Lanen. Let me finish."

I backed away, both hands covering my mouth lest I distract Kédra again, and watched, tears unheeded washing my hands.

When he had finished, when the red-stained, silver wreck of Akor's body was decently covered with gleaming golden bindings, Kédra bowed his great head, sorrow at last coming into its own. "Lanen," he said quietly, "he will not hear me. I must know if there is aught he desires. When we are wounded our bodies have different needs and only the wounded know what they are. Bespeak him, I pray you, that he may be healed. You are his beloved, he will rouse for you."

I clenched my teeth and made myself stop weeping. I knew instinctively that I must be calm for him lest my distress take his mind from his own needs. Deep breath, Lanen. Now.

"Akor, dearling?"

He did not answer.

"Akor, beloved, it is Lanen who calls, Lanen Kaelar. Dearling, speak with me, I beg you, for one moment only before the Weh sleep takes you. Akor?"

Nothing. *Forgive me, dear one,* I thought to myself, *but Kédra is here and I cannot make him leave. This must be done.* Then I said aloud and in truespeech, in the best tones of command I could muster, "Kordeshkistriakor! Wake to me. It is Lanen Kaelar who calls."

Like one rising from deep waters he raised his head. *"Hwat would you, ssweeting? I musst ssleeep. . . ."*

"Akor, it is Kédra," said he in truespeech, loud enough for me to hear. *"You are wounded, what have you need of?"*

"Ssleeep onlly, Khédthra," replied Akor as loudly. *"You haff sstopped the woundss with khaadishhh?"*

"Yes, lord," replied Kédra. *"Need you meat or water, heat, iron—"*

"Ssleeep onlly, younglinng," he replied. *"But where iss Hlanen who called me?"*

"I am here, dear heart," I answered, clinging to calmness with all my strength. *"How may I help you, my love?"*

"Let me but feel your hand, little one," he said, more clearly than

he had spoken yet. I stepped up and laid my hand on the soft skin under his jaw and saw him relax. *"Ahh, hyu arre perilouss, Hlanen Kaelar. Around you the world changess sso quickly I cannot learnn onne thinng beforre the nexst iss upon me. But you do make life interressting!"* He smiled. *"Ssleep on the Windss, Hlanen Kaelar. I will look fforr hyu hwen I wake. . . ."* His mindvoice floated into nothingness and he slept.

I gazed at him. He had gone beyond his pain, forgotten the Council, Marik, anything that might ever have been a danger to either of us; but he remembered that he loved me. And he remembered my name.

"Sleep on the Winds, beloved," I said quietly, lightly touching the dulled soulgem in his forehead, and unbidden from my mouth came softly the words of parting. "Go you safe, and keep you safe, and come safe home to me."

Then I began to cry in earnest.

xviii

THE WINDS AND THE LADY

Lanen

When Kédra and I left the chamber, Akor was already deep in the Weh sleep. Kédra was pleased that his breathing was regular; it was a good sign, he said, and promised well for the healing. He had brought a large quantity of *khaadish* outside with him, and applied it to the gouge in Shikrar's shoulder. The process appeared to pain Shikrar, but after it was done he seemed better able to bear the wound.

Shikrar and Idai had thoughtfully lit a fire for me in the clearing, for the day though bright was sharp with winter's approach. I thanked them and stood as near the flames as I could, wondering why I was so weary. Dear Goddess, was the Weh sleep affecting me? No, it couldn't, surely. Then why was I so weak? I was even starting to tremble—

And the voice that lives always at the back of my mind spoke up, its tone lightly mocking. *Well, my girl, aside from nearly dying two days ago, having no more than an hour's sleep last night, fighting for*

*your life with the Council and watching as the one you love best is
butchered before your eyes, you haven't eaten since that stew in
Marik's cabin a day and a half ago. Remember?*

I swayed as I stood and said, "Please, is there anything to eat
here? Goddess, I don't even know what you eat. I'm starving."

Shikrar brought his head down to my level and spoke quietly. "We
eat meat and fish, littling. Can you eat of the beasts your people
brought with you?"

"Everything but bones, hide and hair," I answered. "But I don't
think I could catch one now, or butcher it either."

Shikrar hissed softly. "Sit you down and rest, lady. You have the
soul of my people, and I can almost forget that you have not the body.
How often do your people require food?"

"At least once a day—two or three times is best," I said, sinking
down beside the fire, and despite my hunger and fatigue had the satisfaction of seeing a Dragon stand in what was obviously Astonishment.

"Rest now," Shikrar repeated, recovering. "Kédra will keep watch
over Akor, Idai shall watch over you, and I will bring food." He
bowed, that graceful sinuous Dragon bow, and took off at once. I
managed to watch Kédra going into the Weh chamber, and muttered
a kind of thanks to Idai (despite her obvious annoyance at being
made my guardian) before sleep took me.

I had hoped to find rest in sleep, but it was not to be. From the
instant my eyes closed I was assailed by dreams. The first was lovely,
to begin with. I am almost sure that Shikrar's words caused it, but I
saw myself as a Dragon, with a hide of gleaming gold and a soulgem
of adamant. I felt even more truly the wings I had been gifted with
in spirit during the Flight of the Devoted. I flexed them, I learned
to fly, and in great joy lived out my days as one of the Greater Kindred. Akor and I lived a long and wondrous life together, we had four
younglings and flourished with them—but for such a sweet dream
it had a most dreary ending. It showed our deaths as a gentle passing in sleep and the burning of the body from within, as Akor had
described it to me. But here, through the soft ashes where our two
soulgems lay gleaming, I saw that which I had seen only for a few
moments on the battlefield: the endless flicker of the soulgems of
the Lost, unredeemed, unrestored, as though Akor and I had never
lived.

I woke then, crying out, but Idai was there and her real (and grudging) presence consoled me. I slipped again into sleep. I walked again in the same dream, but this time it was the other side of the coin—Akor appeared to me again as the tall, silver-haired, green-eyed man of my imagination. Our lives were hard, full of wandering and adventure, danger and darkness set against our joy in each other and in our children—but when this dream ended and we were laid to rest I saw a great number of the Kindred flying above our graves, more than could possibly be born in so short a time as I would live, and I knew that somehow the Lost had been restored.

I came slowly awake, knowing in the depths of my soul that I was being given a choice—but I forgot about it as soon as I was fully conscious, for Kédra was standing above me speaking my name softly, and there was a glorious smell on the breeze of roasting meat nearby. It was late afternoon. Idai and Shikrar were speaking together in low voices by the pool.

As I ate, Kédra would tell me no more than that Akor was now deep in the Weh sleep, and that he himself was about to leave. There was much to be done now, not least of which was the restoration of the soulgems of the Lost to their rightful place in the Chamber of Souls, and he alone would Shikrar trust with such a task.

"Should not Shikrar be going into the Weh sleep himself? That wound looked terrible," I said as softly as I could.

"It will happen soon enough, but for now he has chosen to remain. Neither he nor Idai seems affected by the Weh as yet."

"Oh, Kédra," I said, longing to reach out to him, wishing for an instant that he were human enough to hug. "I wish you could stay longer, though I would not interfere with your duty."

He bowed. "I would if it were possible. My heart is heavy with this sorrow, lady, and I ache for your own."

I bowed and held out my hands to him, futile and senseless gesture though it was. "Kédra, dear friend, I do not know the words to thank you deeply enough for all you have done. I—without you—"

"I have but begun to return that which you have given me. Farewell, Lady Lanen. Go with the love of me and mine," he said, and slowly, gently, leaned down and brushed the end of his snout against my hands.

I could not speak. I held my hands palms together, hallowed by his touch, and watched as he climbed into the darkening sky.

When he was gone I went to the pool for water, to drink and to wash. Idai and Shikrar, standing at the water's edge, fell silent as I drank.

"Very well," I said, when I had drunk my fill. I looked up at the two of them and sighed. "Now, what exactly is it that you aren't telling me?"

Shikrar sighed and bowed to me. "Truly, there is no good reason for our silence, save that we would not burden you beyond your strength. Lady, I fear—it is most likely that—" and I, who thought myself beyond astonishment, was amazed to hear Shikrar's voice break on his words. I did not know then that Shikrar had lost his beloved soon after Kédra was born, that he knew well the pain that he spoke of.

Idai finished it for him. *"May I bespeak you, Lanen?"* Her mind-voice was harsh but at least for the moment not angry. *"I know we have spoken already in truespeech, but I would begin again. I am called Idai. I have not much of your language."*

"Do and welcome. Please, Lady Idai, what is it that so grieves Shikrar that he cannot speak?" I felt my throat tighten and was glad that we used the Language of Truth, for I was suddenly aware of an endless river of tears waiting to break forth. *"Please, I beg you, lady. I would know the truth."*

"It is Akor. He has told you of the Weh sleep?"

"A little. He said that when you are wounded it comes upon you." Just tell me, Idai, quickly, I thought to myself, forgetting that she would hear.

"Very well, Lanen. Akor may live or he may not. If he does not, death will claim him soon. If he survives"—and for an instant I heard her mindvoice break as mine had—*"child, his wounds will take long and long to heal. Some half century, at the least. I do not know how many years you have nor how long you may expect to live, but I know that at the best you will be in your age when he awakes."*

So—my heart was numb—so either my beloved would die soon, or he would live, but not awaken whole and strong until I was in my seventies, most of my life already spent. *Some half century at the least.* If I even lived that long.

"Forgive us, lady, that we pierce so brutally to the heart of the matter, but you needed to know, and we have little time," said Shikrar sadly. "The Weh has taken Akor, it will take us all if we do not leave swiftly." He paused to lick at the edges of his own wound, which had begun to bleed again around the patch of gold after his exertions in bringing me meat. "It may be that I shall be taken by the Weh in any case, but not here."

I was surprised at my own calmness. Too much reality will do that. There is a strange state beyond mourning in which life is as it is, and we do what we must.

"Can you stay long enough for me to say farewell?" I asked, my voice calm.

"Certes, lady," replied Shikrar, bowing formally. I was briefly surprised at his words, but reminded myself that he was Eldest of a people that lived millennia. The surprise should rather be that, speaking my language at all, he should most often use words known to me instead of those used by my distant ancestors.

Beyond hurt, beyond thought, beyond mourning, I went into Akor's Weh chamber to bid him farewell. Evening was closing in rapidly, so I took with me a brand from the fire for light. I would see him clearly before I left, that when I returned somehow in fifty years I would remember.

Akor slept still, but as I approached I was shocked at the heat. He was hotter than a baker's oven, I could barely come nigh him. He did not lie still, but twisted and turned in his sleep—for he slept still—and as I watched he went rigid. It was terrifying, and all so strange. I went as close to him as I dared, for the heat, and spoke to him gently. I did not use his true name for fear he might rouse to pain, but spoke the soothing words one uses to a child. Eventually he relaxed. I was greatly relieved, but not for long. It soon happened again, and then again.

I had never seen Weh sleep, but Akor had said nothing of this. I had assumed it was like a human sleep. I might have been wrong, but he had seen me sleeping the other night. If sleep itself was so different for our separate Kindreds he would have mentioned it, I was certain.

No. This was *wrong*. For healing it was wrong.

Then he began to moan. It was a terrible sound, deep and rich even in pain but cracked as mud in the sun. For all my love I could not stay. I ran outside, calling I know not what.

Shikrar waited in the firelight and I fled to his side. "Shikrar!" I cried. "Oh, Shikrar, something is wrong. He's so hot, he was sleeping but now he cries out, it can't be right, I've never seen Weh sleep but this can't be right."

Shikrar was moving at a flat run by the time I finished speaking, with Idai on his heels. I followed after and found that even a Dragon of Shikrar's size could manage that small opening at need.

Inside the cave the brand I had brought in (and dropped) gave off light enough to see; but I could not feel its warmth, a tiny drop in the ocean of heat that ran in waves from Akor. He fairly glowed with it.

Idai called to him, aloud and in truespeech. But there was no answer, no response at all. She would not give up, calling again and again in the hope of some reaction. As we all watched, Akor's body was gripped by another spasm. He went rigid for what seemed like forever. Finally, slowly, he relaxed.

Shikrar stood beside me, watching, looking very old indeed. I would know now without being told that he was the Eldest of them. His eyes in that cave were ancient and completely unreadable.

He turned to me and spoke gently. "What has happened here, Lanen? Did you call upon him in truespeech to rouse, or use his true name?"

"No," I said, managing to keep my voice more or less level. "I didn't use truespeech at all, and aloud I only spoke the words humans use to comfort their children in illness." I drew breath with difficulty; my chest was tight and I was so caught in deep sorrow I hardly cared about breathing. "Shikrar, this is wrong, isn't it? Akor never told me what the Weh sleep was like, but this must be wrong." I felt new tears run down to join the ashes of the old on my salt-crusted cheeks.

He bowed his head down to my level and spoke softly. "Yes, child. It is wrong. In the healing of the Weh sleep we grow cold. He should be chill to the touch by now, and still as a stone."

Shikrar

I closed my eyes and bowed to Lanen as I saw the pain in her eyes, the echo of my own sorrow and Idai's despite her youth. Perhaps, I thought, our races are not so very different.

"Hadreshikrar, on your soul, I beg you, tell me the truth. Is he dying?"

I looked long on the sleeping, painracked body of the friend of my heart. I could hardly bear to hear Idai; she still called to Akhor, but quietly now, as though she could not stop herself. Her voice was a mourning lover's.

Without turning back to Lanen I answered her honestly. "I do not know, lady. I have never seen this before."

Idai eventually fell silent. She turned from Akhor with bowed head and left the cave without glancing at either of us. After a time I nodded to Lanen that she, too, should take the chance for air untainted by Akhor's pain. I saw that she had begun to flinch every time Akhor groaned, saw her muscles twitch in sympathy with his, and fresh before my eyes rose a clear vision of my own watch on my beloved Yrais as she had neared death.

Without speaking her eyes commanded me to call out to her if there was any change; without words I swore I would. She tore her glance away from Akhor, put on her cloak against the cold, and went out wrapping her arms around herself to keep out a cold far sharper and a thousand times more bitter.

Lanen

I found I was thirsty again after the heat of the cave. I walked over to the pool at the edge of the forest, my way lit by the bright moonlight. It was only so helpful. I could see no further than my own pain, I sought only a moment's relief from cool water.

Idai was there before me, on the far side of the pool, drinking in the manner of beasts. Her long tongue flickered in and out of her mouth, hissing in the cool water. I knelt and drank double handfuls; I was parched after that long time in such heat. The cool water felt good on the new skin of my poor hands.

When I looked up she was staring at me through the tree-shadowed darkness. I could not tell anything about her thoughts, she was just staring, her eyes gleaming in the filtered moonlight.

"You are so vulnerable when you drink, like all beasts," she said. The tone of her truespeech was flat; like me, she had gone beyond caring. *"Lanen, do you know what is happening to Akor?"*

"No, Lady Idai. I would give my life, I swear, would it help him,

but I don't know what is wrong or what I could do." My own mind-voice shocked me, it was low and as flat as Idai's. *"Why? Do you know?"*

"I am not certain," she said, *"but I have an idea."*

"For love of the Lady, tell me! Is there aught we may do to save him? I beg you, tell me your thoughts, even an idea is more than I have now."

"How well do you love him?" she asked me.

"As I love my life, Idai, I swear it on my soul," I said. *"In that cave lies my dearest dream of love and all my life to come, suffering torments. If I can help him I will, nor ever count the cost."*

"Then renounce him," she said coldly.

"What!"

"Renounce him. Go into the clearing and call upon the gods, ours and yours, and swear on your soul to the Winds that you do not love him. Perhaps then he may live."

I did not move. I was beyond surprise, I had no more capacity for it, but I did not understand.

"How should that help? It would be a lie. I do love him, as much as you do."

"How could you so?" she hissed at me, and her coldness was turned in an instant to raging fire. *"I have known him all his life long, full a thousand winters! He is blood of my blood, soul given wings and fire. How dare you say your love is like to mine! A few paltry days you have known him, hardly a breath of time between you! How dare you!"*

I knelt on one knee to her on the cold ground, partly out of respect, partly out of weariness. *"Lady, I honour you. I see that the very depth of your love is pain to you now—but still I dare to say I love him as you do."* She looked as if she were going to spring at me. To be honest, I didn't much care. *"Lady Idai, a life is a life. I have spent mine longing for your people and dreaming hopeless dreams in the dark to keep myself alive. Akor is those dreams made flesh, the summit of all my life—but more, infinitely more, he is himself. And I love him with all my power. If you want to kill me for it, then do so and welcome."*

My words shocked her. I could see her force herself to relax. *"I do not wish your death, only to prevent Akor's,"* she said.

"Do you truly think it possible?" I asked.

"It may be."

I waited.

"I believe I know what is happening, Lhanen of the Gedri," she said, her mindvoice gentle now. She stared into my eyes, as though seeking truth there, and said, *"This love that you and Akor share, it is wrong, and not only because you are so different. I believe that in the sight of the Winds it is too great a sorrow for both Kindreds to bear for so many years as Akor will live. I fear the balance is being restored by the great leveler of all life."*

Death.

"And if I renounce him?"

"Perhaps the balance will be restored, and Akor's life spared."

It was the only ray of hope I had and I clung to it. I did not, could not stop to think. The vision ever before my eyes was of Akor in agony, in torment even beyond his wounds, and if this would save him I would do it.

If I can help him I will, nor ever count the cost.

I ran into the clearing, found Shikrar waiting there. Above us the moon, just beginning to wane from the full, was riding above the trees and shone down into the glade bright and clear. I planted my feet and raised my arms to the heavens. I did not know what I was doing, but the words came to me as naturally as if I had known them all my life.

"I call upon the Lady of my people, Lady Shia, Goddess thrice holy. Mother of Kolmar beneath our feet, Ancient Lady of the Moon, Laughing Girl of All the Waters, I call upon thee to witness my words." I drew a deep breath, sought the memory, found it. "And to stand beside thee, Blessed Lady, I call upon the Winds of the Greater Kindred of the Kantrishakrim.

> "First is the Wind of Change
> Second is Shaping
> Third is the Unknown
> And last is the Word."

The moon stood directly above, the earth under my feet listened as it held me, the waters of the pool gurgled their attention. And a wind, a light cold breeze, blew into the glade and played about me,

seeming to come from all four directions in turn. My cloak was like
a live thing, swirling and lifting on the hands of the Winds.

"Hear me!" I cried aloud, and there was silence. I opened my
mouth to speak—

—and I could not draw breath. The lie stuck in my throat; all
my soul bowed down before the gods and acknowledged what truly
was. . . .

Perhaps the balance will be restored, and Akhor's life spared.

"I do not love him!" I cried with all my strength. My voice seemed
to come from my gut, not my throat. I was surprised by the power
of it. "Let the balance be restored. I do not love him!"

That was twice. Three times I must say it, three for the Lady was
the charm to make it true. I ignored my heart that screamed its denial, I ignored the winds that grew stronger and seemed to come now
from all directions at once. I drew a final breath, for after this was
done all that I cared for would be lost—

—when in my mind I heard, impossibly, his voice. It was the only
thing in all the world that could have stopped me. His truespeech
whispered softly in my thoughts, echoed in my heart. I heard the
agony of his body, I knew it as he knew it, I could almost feel the
heat and the suffering that surrounded him, yet he spoke as gently
as the first time I had heard from him the voice of love.

"My soul to the Winds, Lanen Kaelar, I am lost as you are lost."

No, it couldn't be. He was in the Weh sleep, I heard but an echo
in my mind of what had gone before, he couldn't be—

*"Lanen Kaelar, dearest one, it is I, Khordeshkhistriakhor. Do not
cast me from you. I love you as my life. Lanen, Lanen, do not deny
me a third time, it is worse pain than the wounds or the fire. Let me
die still in your love."*

And I had no strength to deny him. I had thought never to hear
his voice again this side of death. I fell to my knees and bespoke him
without words, let my love stream upon him in a clear light that surrounded us both, I in the dark clearing, he in this impossible wake-
fulness from the Weh sleep in his cavern. Even for the saving of him,
I could not let the lie be spoken a third time.

Aloud and in truespeech I bespoke him. *"Akor, my heart, you are
in my love beyond life's ending. Before the Winds and the Lady, Kordeshkistriakor, I say that I love you, I love you, I love you."* I rose

on shaking legs, brushed the leaves from my leggings. *"I come, dear heart. I will come to you, I will wait with you. I cannot save you, but I will not leave you to die alone."*

I walked slowly into the cave, leaving Idai and Shikrar standing wordless in the clearing, in the wind and the moonlight. I believed I went to my death, or at best to watch his.

I do not know how he had roused from the darkness of his pain and the Weh sleep to speak to me, but he was no longer awake when I came nigh him. He lay curled up on his floor of gold, quiet now, a silver statue splashed with gold. He seemed to be more at peace than he had been since this Weh sleep began.

But the heat was worse. The whole of that great chamber was as warm as high noon on midsummer's day, and Akor himself was the sun. The very air shimmered.

I went as near to him as I could bear. I wanted to bid him farewell, to touch him one last time, but the heat drove me back. I had no words. In the end I could only speak his name, give it back to him and to the darkness that waited for him.

"Kordeshkistriakor," I whispered. So beautiful, the name, the form of my beloved. I even managed a tiny smile when I said it, knowing that I could never say it as the Kindred pronounced it.

I sat as close to him as I could. I would watch by him, as I would watch by any I loved at their deathbed.

I prayed the Winds and the Lady to deliver him from this terrible fate, but if they answered I never heard it.

I cannot say how long I was there, through that endless night. It felt like forever. The brand I had carried in died out quickly, and I discovered that Akor was indeed glowing, a silver beacon, like the moon come to rest in that small place. Sun's heat and moon's light, my dear one.

My birth was an omen, though none knew what it might portend.

It was near dawn, I guessed, when I gradually realised that something else was happening. The heat was growing rapidly worse, the light brighter. Then suddenly Akor cried out, one final deep cry of pain that tore my heart and brought me to my feet. The heat doubled, driving me back from him with a blast of wind straight from the deepest circle of Hell. He writhed, his eyes still tightly closed, his soulgem blazing green fire, his tail whipping from side to side, his wings vainly trying to fan in that enclosed space.

In the glow I could see it. I felt my heart in my throat, I could not breathe.

Akor had begun to smoke.

All my resolve dragged at me, trying to make myself stay, forcing me to see what I had brought upon my dear one—but I found that the urge to life was stronger than I knew, too strong for my mind to overcome. It would have been death for me to stay one instant longer. I felt my traitor feet turn me away from him and I fled for the entryway.

I emerged just ahead of a great gout of flame. By the grace of the Lady I tripped over one of the tangled tree roots and fell flat. I felt the fireball come searing past me, over my head, and heard it strike a tree on the far side of the clearing.

I lay where I had fallen and wept, my body shaken by racking sobs. I knew I would never see Akor again. Even a Dragon could not have survived that. I could not hear him or feel his presence in my heart.

I had come to the dragonlands so full of dreams. I had finally found the one soul in all the world that was the match of mine, and the body that housed it was now ash in the place where we had joined our hearts and minds.

I longed for oblivion.

It was not granted me.

For a long time I lay as I had fallen. Cold and sharp against my face pressed the dead leaves of autumn, wet with dew and smelling of decay. The sky was lightening, dawn but a thought away, the birth of a terrible morning.

I lay unmoving, my eyes wide and staring at the earth as I tried to understand what had happened.

Akor was dead.

I could not grasp it. It seemed a tale told by a stranger of a distant land. How could it be? Not a day past I sat on that living silver neck and rode high as my spirit and strong with my love into the Council of the Kindred. How could he so quickly be gone?

And I heard a sound like tearing glass, joined by a cry of pain deeper than any sound I had ever heard, it shook me where I lay.

Idai and Hadreshikrar mourned.

Akor was dead.

I sought him despite that truth, called out with all my heart and mind, cried out aloud, met only silence. His voice in my heart was stilled, the last words he gave me lost to the echoes of memory. I would not forget his words, but I would never hear them again.

Dead.

He should have wept over my grave for a thousand years.

I curled against the pain as though around a dagger in my gut. This was no life, I was but half a person. My other half lay in smoking ruin there in the cave, gone forever, beyond all hope.

I rocked as I knelt on the wet leaf-fall, my arms wrapped tightly around me, holding on for dear life. I was holding back screams; they found their way out as whimpers, as a high-pitched moan dreadful even for me to hear. Death echoed in my mind, in my body, and I could not bear its presence.

I had lived my dream and found it perilous beyond imagining. I cursed the day I left Hadronsstead. If I had let my dreams alone at least I would still have them, and he would still have life. Now were we both bereft.

I was alone in a dry place. The pain of this grief was more than I could bear. I longed to die, for my heart to break, for death to cease its wanderings and come for me.

And in the still air, above the sound of my grieving, a wondrous voice rose to greet the dawn. The song was deep and rich, and through the cracks of grief shone the love of the singer. It grew like a tree, putting down roots in the past and rising straight into the morning, true and full of life and laughter, and it named the life it sang.

Kordeshkistriakor.

A high voice like crystal bells joined it, twining round the melody like a vine, soft buds of harmony bursting into flower as it climbed. The two would echo one another, join in a clear harmony, separate into their own ways.

The song lifted me to my feet, when I would have sworn no power on earth could do so. I stood in mute thanksgiving for his life, in honour of his song, but in time it seemed to me that there was something missing. I stood in the bright morning, my face wet and dirty with tears and dew and leaf mould, and joined in the song of passing for my beloved. I was no more than a creaking murmur that came and went added to the glorious voices above and around me, but somehow it was fitting, and three were complete where two were not.

With a strength I had never known, with all my soul grown old in the night with grief, I sang my dearest love into the morning.

Rella

I did as Lanen asked and returned the gems to the Dragons, along with one of a different kind I found in the ashes of the Dragon that died. It seemed the right thing to do; at least, the Dragon that met me at the Boundary accepted it along with the others. It wavered its head at me—I suppose it was a kind of bow—and left.

I returned to the clearing and looked down at Marik's body. It lay without movement, save that his wide staring eyes blinked occasionally. I left him as he lay—I remember hoping that the son of a bitch would die while I was fetching help—but no such luck. I trudged down to the shore and, waving and shouting, called out the boat. It took some time, but I managed to have his body taken aboard. He was not dead, though I thought death might be preferable. His mind was gone. I watched it happen.

He had something from Caderan that protected him against the Dragons, against flame and claw, but *they destroyed his mind.* He lies like an infant now, with as much life and as little thought. Maikel was with him for hours, and he says that it might be possible to recover some of what has been lost, but it will take years. It is frightful.

I find that, despite their leaving Marik alive (it would have been kinder to kill him), I quite like the Dragons. I am surprised. Shikrar, the Keeper of Souls, seems to be a kindred spirit. He reminds me of my grandfather. His son Kédra is a good soul and looked after me well through that cold night—I think I even made him laugh once or twice. Certainly I will never forget his "Lady Rella."

They seem too old and too deep to be casual companions, but in such an adventure as this one—ah, the Silent Service can go whistle. I will think on my report on the voyage back, surely in all that time I will find a way to tell them as little as possible about the creatures.

On a more practical note, I do not know how long I can make

them hold the ship for Lanen. As long as their fear of the Dragons lasts, I suspect. If all else fails I will go back to the island myself to-morrow morning—the Master of the ship was willing to wait that long—but I hope she will somehow come to us. Despite all, I have seen enough of that island for one lifetime, and if I never step again on its shores I will die happy.

Shikrar

I bespoke Kédra, telling him of my soulfriend's death as gently as I could. The calm after the song held me still, my mindvoice was steady enough. He replied soon afterwards, saying that Rella had come to him again, wondering if Lanen was coming to take ship, and that the Master was anxious to be gone.

I decided such a thing could wait until all was done that must be done.

Lanen

The song was finished. I was not at peace—I did not believe that I would ever be at peace again—but at least I could move and act.

I knelt to Idai and Shikrar, in thanks, in friendship. They stood silent until I rose, then bowed to me as one. We stood together un-moving, unspeaking, in shared grief that went beyond tears, beyond words to the silence of souls.

Until, finally, there came a moment when we stirred, when life made its demands heard once again. I looked about me.

"Is there anything yet to be done?" I asked. "What are the customs of your people?"

"We have sung him to rest, there is only his soulgem to bring forth, that it may join his ancestors' in the Chamber of the Souls," said Hadreshikrar. He was beginning to show signs of weariness, and it seemed to me that his wound pained him deeply. "I will do that service for you, if you so desire."

"It is my place as his mate to do so, then?" I asked.

"Yes."

"Then I will. I thank you for your offer, Shikrar, but I think I must do this. I can understand the meaning. I must see his ashes and bid him farewell. I was his mate."

I turned towards the cave. The body that had insisted I live was reluctant now to carry me there.

This time I won.

It was dark in the chamber, dark and very warm. The walls had taken up the heat Akor had given off; it would be warm in there for days.

It was fairly dark, but I could see my way. The sun was no more than an hour risen, but even that much light coming through the smoke-hole above allowed me to see, if not very clearly. I looked slowly towards the place where Akor had lain. Having seen I had to look away, horrified, sickened. That vision haunts my dreams yet. *Fool, fool, he tried to spare you.*

Akor had told me but I had forgotten. At death the fire that sustains the Greater Kindred is let loose and, unchecked, destroys the body from within. All that lay on the floor of *khaadish* were a few charred remains of his ash-covered bones.

I forced myself to look again.

I should find his soulgem close by what was left of the skull.

Taking my courage in both hands I moved slowly, reverently, towards the huge pile of bones.

In the faint light I thought I saw something move.

I ignored my traitor eyes. "Lanen, come, it is only bone," I said aloud, to steady myself. As I finished speaking I heard a small sound, like a sleeper makes at the edge of waking. Surely there was something there?

No, there could be nothing, nothing but ash. And one green gem the size of my hand, that I must steel myself to take out to Hadreshikrar.

I was nearly on top of the skeleton now, and this close I could see that there *was* something, a large pale something lying still within the protective circle of bone.

My first instinct was to run towards it yelling, to chase away whatever pale creature had crept here for warmth, dared so swiftly to desecrate the remains of the one I loved. But even blurred in the darkness, half-seen, it was somehow a familiar shape.

It stirred.

The sun climbed higher, sending more light into the chamber.

No. This could not happen. This was insane. I had lost my mind.

For there before me, surrounded by the charred, ash-covered ribs that crumbled as I watched, was the figure of a man. He lay naked in that warm place, curled on his side in his cradle of bone. One arm pillowed his head, the other hand clutched something near his forehead. Long silver hair spread gently over broad shoulders pale as new snow.

Song whispered wild and distant in my heart, the song that Akor and I had made for each other in this place, but I dared not hear it. I could not speak, I feared to breathe lest this spell should break.

For in that place lay the form of the Akor of my dreams, the silver-haired man that was Akor in human form.

Not dragon.

Man.

My legs failed me and I fell to my knees, my heart scarcely beating as I knelt, shaking, lost in terror and wonder. This could not be. I must be mad. Had my mind in desperation made this phantom for heart's ease?

Was he real?

I forced myself to speak.

"Akor?" I breathed, reaching towards him through the cage of dead ribs. "Akor?"

He did not stir and I could not. I knelt there captive, trembling, lost. What then, if not flesh and blood? Waking dream? Demon-sending? Insanity?

Still he did not move.

With a vast effort of will I got to my feet and turned to go, to call Shikrar and Idai to come and see, when behind me I heard a rustling of movement and a clear voice saying sleepily, "Lanen?"

I turned in a dream, slowly, as against a strong current.

He stood before me, still within the high circle of bone, shaky on his two legs, gloriously alive in a body new-made. I could not speak, only look with all my soul.

"Lanen? What has happened?" he asked, his voice slurring slightly. I reached out to him. He tried to walk towards me, but he was still accustomed to four legs. He stumbled.

I caught him before he fell, held him up, helped him back onto his feet. I moved without thought, lost in wonder at the touch of him, skin against skin. My love alive, healed of his grievous wounds, made whole—made human.

When he stood firm again, I saw he used only one hand to steady himself. I reached for his right hand, to see if it was injured, when he raised his clenched right fist between us. In silence he turned his hand palm up, opening his fingers like the petals of a rose, to reveal a faceted gem that filled his palm, flashing in the torchlight, green as the sea.

His soulgem.

I had to speak. And there was only one word I could say, holding his soft hand in mine, filled with wonder. First and last, a word of love.

"Kordeshkistriakor?"

"Yes, Lanen. I am here." His eyes darted here, there, to me, to himself. "Unless this is a Weh dream. But no, you are real, this is all real. Why can I not speak? So strange a mouth. What has happened? What have I become?" He looked at me with the eyes of Akor beneath long bright hair, emeralds set in a silver sea, opened wide now in wonder, and said, "Lanen?"

I had to say it. The impossible. The truth. "Akor, you—are human. A man, one, one of my people, one of the Gedrishakrim." And the truth of it washed over me like a sudden waterfall, thrilled down my spine like rain on a sleeper's face, and in that place of death I laughed for joy, loud and clear. "Akor, beloved, we thought you dead, but you live. Bless the Winds and the Lady, you live, you live!"

I turned towards the cave entrance and shouted, my voice soaring high with delight. "Shikrar! Idai! Come and see! He lives, Akor lives!"

He had moved carefully out of his bony coffin-cradle, and it struck me that it was not meet for his Kindred to see him thus naked. I took my cloak off quickly and wrapped it about him.

Shikrar and Idai stood at the cave's entrance, their eyes adjusting from bright morning light to near darkness. I stood between them and the new-made man. At first all they could see were the bones of Akor in the light from the high window. Shikrar spoke kindly to me, his voice sad and gentle.

"Lanen, be at peace. I know it is terrible, but death comes to us all. I fear—"

He fell silent as Akor stepped shakily out from the shadows behind me. His new body was flawless, healthy, clean-limbed, and his long silver hair gleamed richly in the growing daylight. He held up his soulgem that they might see it clearly; then he handed it to me. I put it reverently in my scrip.

It seemed to me that he tried to bespeak Shikrar, for he frowned at him at first. Then he spoke, in a voice growing clearer and more fully human with each word, but which bore yet an echo of the deep music of Kordeshkistriakor.

"I greet you, Hadreshikrar, Iderrisai, dear friends," he said. "You are as welcome as the sunrise, for in all truth I never expected to see either again in this world." And suddenly he laughed. It was the most glorious sound in all the world, a laugh of pure joy from a throat that had never known sorrow. "Let us go out from this place," he said gaily. "And you, my Lanen, come bear me up lest I fall." He held out his hand and I took it and put his bare arm around my shoulder.

Shikrar and Idai were struck dumb and motionless, and could only watch as I helped Akor walk out through the entry passage, watch as he discovered he did not have to lower his head to pass. His eyes glowed with the knowledge and he grinned at me as we walked, putting his free hand to his mouth to feel what it was doing as delight took him.

I held him up, held him close, walked as in a dream on two legs beside my two-legged love, and prayed to the Lady that I might never wake.

Akhor

When I stepped out into the morning I was dazzled by the light. My new senses were assailed from all sides, I did not know which way to look. First and strongest, though, was the feeling of air on my skin. Never, even when my new armour was still damp and weak, had I known anything like it. The feel of Lanen's rough cloak on my skin, the ground beneath my feet, the strength of her beneath my arm on

her shoulder, even the touch of her hand on mine to steady me—
small wonder I could hardly walk. The sun was brighter than I had
ever seen it, the very air bore upon it a glorious scent like nothing I
had ever dreamed.

I turned to my dear one, now grown to a giant as tall as I and able
to help me walk. "What is that smell?" I asked. I delighted in the
strange movement of my new mouth, so different, so similar.

She sniffed once and smiled. "Lansip. Can't you tell? Or does it
smell different now?"

That was hlansif? Now I understood. "Dear heart, it was nothing like this to me before. This is the very smell of paradise. I know
now why your people seek it out."

Her smile broadened. "Wait until you taste it."

Her joy had nothing to do with hlansif and all to do with me. I
gazed at her until I could bear the brightness of her face no longer.
I turned instead to face my old friends, come now out of my chamber and blinking in the sunlight.

When I looked at them, really looked for the first time, I knew
fully how much smaller I was grown. They had not changed, they
still had all the stature of our people. I barely came to Shikrar's
elbow.

I tried to bespeak Shikrar again, soulfriend for almost a thousand
years, but even I could not hear my own truespeech. "Forgive me,
Shikrar, Idai. The Language of Truth has deserted me for the moment," I said. They could not answer; they were robbed yet of speech
by wonder.

I had to speak, if only to touch reality thus. Holding fast to
Lanen—for balancing on two legs was proving most difficult—I
faced them and tried to speak in the tongue of the Kantri, but my
new mouth would not make the sounds. No truespeech, no Kantriasarikh? Was I to have nothing left of who I was?

I spoke again in the language of the Gedri. "It is I, Shikrar. Truly,"
I said. "Do you know me for myself, my friend? Lady Idai, do you
know me for Akor?" When they did not reply, I added, "I am glad
you have tended to your own wounds, my friend. I thank you from
my heart for bringing me here after the battle. I would have died
there."

"Akhor did die there!" cried a high voice. We all three turned to
look to Idai. Her eyes were wide and her Attitude spoke violent De-

nial. She was backing away from me, flapping her wings as if to take
to the skies. "This is not Akhor! It cannot be. Akhor is dead!"

I opened my mouth to object, but in that moment I knew she
spoke truth. I waited for the echo of her words to die to silence, then
said gently, softly, trying to make my voice sound as normal as I
could, "Idai, Iderrisai, come, come, my friend, be calm, you are
right. But for all that I am not to be feared. I am no wandering
soul, no creation of the Rakshasa, though my bones—" I shivered.
"—Akhor's bones—lie yonder. You are right. That name is a part of
me, and all my life before I remember in the way of our Kindred,
but I am made new, and I will need a new name."

"Name of the Winds," swore Shikrar softly, as Idai fought to control herself. He gazed full at me, and his Attitude swung bewilder-
ingly between Fear, Denial, Friendship, Wonder and (I was amused
to see) Protection of a Youngling. "I hear you and in your words and
your voice I hear my soulfriend, but I cannot believe my ears or my
eyes. Akhor, Akhorishaan, is it, can it be that you are trapped inside
that body?"

"I am here, Hadreshikrar, but I am not trapped. Though the
world is so huge!" I could bear it no longer, I laughed for heart's ease.
"It is like being a youngling again, looking up at the trees and being
so close to the ground! I am alive, Shikrar, beyond hope, and the *ferrinshadik* is silent at last! Behold these hands, so dextrous, so gentle, and this supple body!" I tried to bow in the fashion of the Gedri,
and only Lanen's strong arm held me up. She laughed as she caught
me, helped me to balance, delighting in me.

I reached out my hand, so soft, so useless in the eyes of the
Kantri, and touched her cheek. The tips of my fingers (though I did
not know the word then) were sensitive beyond belief. I shivered
again with the sensation, not only on my hands but all over this new
vessel of mine. Lanen's smooth skin beneath my hand was like nothing I had ever known.

Now it was my turn to swear. "Name of the Winds, Lanen! I feel
every breath of air on these hands. How could you bear to burn yours
so terribly, no matter whose life you might save?" I wondered at my
new body, for suddenly it was hard to speak past a thickening in my
throat. "Dear one, oh, forgive me, I never knew it was such agony
for you."

She smiled and took my hands in hers. "Akor, dear heart, I grew up on a farm. My hands were covered with calluses—places where the skin had grown hard. It happens naturally, for protection, and it helped a little at first. You'll get them, too, given time." She blinked, surprised at her own words, and laughed. I rejoiced when I recognised it as the laugh of delight I had heard when first she set foot on the island of the Kantri. "Your outer form may have changed," she said, "but I would know you for Akor in ten thousand. Who else is so full of questions?"

"At least now I do not have to contort my tongue to speak them. The sounds make sense with a mouth like this."

Lanen

I am afraid that my first thought was that a lot of other things did, too, but I managed not to say anything. "I notice you can say my name now." I grinned. "I miss that little hiss you added—but what's done is done."

With that I turned to face Idai, who was still standing well away from Akor. "That's a human saying, lady, that you would do well to listen to. This thing has happened whether we like it or not, and denying your old friend will not unmake it." I did not want to be harsh, but why should this all be so much harder for her to believe?

And with the thought itself came the answer. *Lanen, Lanen, she has loved him for a thousand years, and now he is gone from her people forever.* I spoke more gently, ashamed of my show of temper. "Lady Idai, your pardon, but this is the word of the Wind of Change, here as we stand. For good or ill the world will never be the same for any of us. At the least, let we who are at the heart of the change keep friends for the sake of one another."

"Step back, child of the Gedri," she said to me. Akhor seemed steady enough on his feet now, so I stood away.

She leaned down until her head was at his level, her eyes locked on his. "I once told Akhor my name, when I was young and foolish and hoped that he might one day come to love me." Her voice shook me—she was speaking in the same tones she had used the night before, calling to Akhor in his Weh sleep. The voice of one whose beloved has died.

"Do you know my true name, youngling, and where and when I told it to Akhor? For only he and I in all the world know that."

For the first time sadness appeared on that face. "Idai, Idai, of course I know your name. But how should I speak it before Shikrar and Lanen? I would not so betray your trust. In eight hundred years I have never breathed it to any but you, and then only twice. I do not have truespeech, Lady. What would you?"

"Tell me," she said, and I sensed a kind of reckless madness rising in her. "Speak it aloud, Gedri. Shikrar is Keeper of Souls, he will know it in time. And surely you will not hesitate to speak it before your dear one."

I bowed. "He might not, lady, but I will not put you in such peril." I bowed to her. "I was promised by my father to demons ere ever I was born. If they ever catch up with me—I was in the power of one for a brief moment, and I had no strength to resist. If I don't know your true name, I can't tell it."

I turned and walked away, as far on the other side of the clearing as I could get, and stuffed my fingers in my ears like a child.

Akhor

Shikrar, I was glad to see, was also quietly moving away.

"Very well, Iderrikanterrisai," I said, as softly as I might, "you told me your true name at moonrise on Midwinter's night the year I was come to my prime, the year I had seen my full two centuries and a half." I could not keep old sternness out of my voice when I added, "You said you had waited for me to achieve my majority, that you longed for me, and that now you might speak of it without rebuke. When I protested that I did not know you well enough, that I was still young and had given no thought to a mate, you gave me your name. I do not know why, though I have wondered about it often enough. Perhaps you meant to shame me into giving mine."

I bowed my head, thinking (irrelevantly) as I did so that the gesture had not the power it had in my former body. "Several times since then, for your constant friendship, I would have given you my true name in return," I said sorrowfully, "but I never have, for I would not encourage you falsely nor build hope where there could be none."

She stood in Shame and Sorrow, and all the years of goodwill between us rose up clear before me. "I would give it to you now, if you will receive it," I said, reaching out slowly to touch her. "Or would that be injury added to insult?"

She did not speak. I lowered my voice. "Iderrikanterrisai, I am— I was—Khordeshkhistriakhor. I can think of no truer way to speak long friendship's love."

"Khordeshkhistriakhor, you honour me," she said at last, adding with the ghost of a hiss, "though a little late for my taste. But I cannot deny. You are Akhor."

The truth, though, was that I was not. When the true name is spoken, especially by one who has never said it before, there is a reaction in the hearer. I felt nothing.

"Lanen," I called. She strode quickly up to where we stood. "Call me by name."

She looked startled. "Do not fear," I said, "both Shikrar and Idai know now. But I must hear you speak it."

"Very well. Kordeshkistriakor," she said, and without thinking added in truespeech, *"dear one."*

I jumped. "I heard you!" I whirled to face Shikrar, very nearly falling over in the process. (I think Lanen was getting used to catching me.) "Shikrar, bespeak me I pray you!"

"Akhorishaan, what is it? Can you hear me?"

"Yes!" I cried, and felt for the first time the tears of joy I had seen Lanen shed. "Ahhh! My soul to the Winds, Shikrar, I hear you! I had feared it gone forever!"

Shikrar's mindvoice was full of quiet delight. *"As did I, old friend. Perhaps in time you will be able to speak again. After all, Akhorishaan, you have not had much practice being human."* I laughed again. "But why did you have Lanen speak your name just now?" he continued aloud. "True, we here all know it, but surely there is still danger for you if—"

"No, my friend," I replied solemnly. "That was why I asked her to make the trial. It is no longer my name. I must find another."

There was a pause, then Shikrar said, too casually, "Perhaps Deshkantriakor?"

I stared at him. It took me a moment to react, then I started to laugh. He was hissing loudly, and behind him Idai, who obviously thought we were being far too irreverent, finally let go and sent a cloud of steam into the clearing as the laughter burst from her also.

Lanen turned to me. "What in the—?"

"Forgive me, dearling, but it seems my old friend Shikrar has re-covered, and his jests, as always, are terrible. He says I should be named Deshkantriakor, the Strange King of the Kantri."

She glanced at Idai and Shikrar as they recovered their bearing. "Very funny," she said dryly. "I wouldn't recommend it, myself."

"Perhaps you are right," I said, with no little reluctance. "It was worth it for heart's ease, in any case." I had been turning over ele-ments of the Old Speech in my mind, though, even as we laughed, and I knew what my name must be.

"My name is chosen, Hadreshikrar, Iderrisai, Lanen Marans-datter, I pray you attend."

In the silence that followed, in the clear morning, I stood before those I loved best and spoke the words of the Naming.

"I reveal my name unto you, dear love and oldest friends, that you alone may know the truth of me, may with my consent call me by name and speak as friends of my soul. My usename shall be Varien, the Changed One, and so I shall commonly be called. But my true name is Varien Kantriakor rash-Gedri, Kadreshi naLanen: He who is Changed from the Lord of the Kantri to a Man, Beloved of Lanen. It is the truth of who and what I have become. If it seems overlong, I beg your indulgence, for my heart tells me I shall require the safety of such a name. I charge you, my dear ones, guard it well among you."

They all three repeated my name aloud. I had chosen well, for the words rang in my heart with the truth of the naming, tied now to my soul. For years afterwards, though, when anyone asked my name I could hear the laughter of Dragons.

Lanen

In the silence after the Naming (which was not so different from the human ceremony), I was ashamed to notice so minor a thing as the weather, but it could not be ignored much longer.

So far we had been fortunate. Winter had backed down for the moment, leaving behind a clear, cloudless morning; but the air was still cold, and I saw gooseflesh on Akor—on Varien's skin where my cloak did not cover it.

Varien. The Changed One.

"We must go back inside, or find another place where there is warmth," I told Shikrar and Idai. "I think we should return to Akor's cave near the Council chamber. From there Rella might be able to help us, or I could go to the ship myself and get clothing for him." I wondered as I spoke whether the ship would have left already. Suddenly it was important. "We will also need food, both of us," I added, for I was hungry again. "Will you two do us the honour of bearing us thence?"

Without hesitation they agreed. I cut off a great slab of the meat Shikrar had brought for me the night before, knowing I—we—would want it when we arrived at Akor's chambers. As there was nothing else to be done where we were, Shikrar and Idai picked us up gently in their great hands and we left the ground.

I thought it would be the last time I ever flew. I watched the ground pass beneath me in the sunlight, a wondrous and varied green carpet of forests and fields, and tried to enjoy the mere sensation of flying in daylight when I could enjoy it, but my body's demands were too strong. Held close to Idai's warmth, her strong hands safe about me, knowing at least for the moment that all was safe, I closed my exhausted eyes and slept.

Idai woke me as we came near Akor's chambers to tell me that the Council was meeting again as we returned. I could not spare a thought for such matters. My body was importunate in its demands. Warmth, food and sleep were all I could think of. Indeed, my memory of that journey is in great part lost, for on the heels of grief, joy and wonder I had no strength left.

I know Shikrar brought wood and started a roaring fire in Akor's chambers for Varien and me. I cut the meat I had brought with me into smaller pieces and roasted it on a stick over the fire. It seemed to take forever but it tasted like very heaven when it was finally done. It was Varien's first meal; I wondered what he made of it all, but I was too weary to ask and he was no better. As soon as we were finished we lay down as near the flames as we dared and slept, facing each other across the fire.

I remember nothing after that until Shikrar woke us hours later.

THE WORD OF THE WINDS

Lanen

When Shikrar woke us it was late afternoon. Idai had kept watch over us and kept the fire warm and bright, while he and Kédra had taken Rishkaan's soulgem and the soulgems of the Lost to the Chamber of Souls and reverently restored them to their rightful place. He apologised now for disturbing us, but we had been summoned by the Council, and there was news from Rella that he had forgotten to tell us. (I only learned later from Akor how extraordinary it was for one of the Kantri to forget anything, no matter how slight.)

I dragged myself upright and found that I could not turn away from Akor—no, no, he was Varien now—still unable to believe it, still not knowing why we had been granted such a grace. It was long and long before I could look at him without a measure of awe.

I put the rest of the meat on a spit and began to cook it as Idai left to attend the Council and tell them our tale in her words. We ate as quickly as we might. Our drink was spring water, but I had to smile—we drank it from rough, heavy vessels of gold that Idai had fashioned for us, remembering how I had needed to kneel to drink from the pool. Kings would envy such vessels.

Shikrar told us that Rella had spoken with Kédra that very morning. It seems the Master wanted to start as swiftly as possible on the journey back. Kédra had asked her to request a delay of but one more day, and she had promised to try. I found myself wishing that she had truespeech, and began to discover some of the frustration the Kantri must always have felt around my people.

Finally Varien stood. "Very well. It is time. Let us go before the Council that they might see what I have become," he said. "I am yet unsure on these two legs, Lanen. You must be my strength."

"I thought we had already agreed on that," I said, smiling. "But first give me a moment to make you more presentable." Two quick knife slashes for armholes and my belt around all, and Varien stood clad in a makeshift tunic rather than wrapped in a cloak. "Now, my dear one," I said as I put his arm about my shoulder and mine around his waist, "let us beard the Council once more." I turned to him, to that wondrous face mere inches from mine, and grinned. "I can't think of a thing to say to them, dear heart, but perhaps they won't need many words."

"Before you go, I too have a gift for you . . . Varien," said Shikrar shyly. He handed Varien a rough circlet of *khaadish,* with a gap at one end. "I made it while you slept. I thought—your soulgem—perhaps if you are seen thus, it might lessen the shock."

Varien's eyes went wide.

I drew the green gem from my scrip and handed it to Shikrar. He scraped from the floor a quantity of gold and breathed fire onto it until it glowed, then made of it a flattened strip, melding the edges to make a circle the size of the soulgem. Taking the gem in his great claws, he placed it gently within the circle and bent the edge above and below, finally joining the set stone to the circlet with Fire. I longed to help him, lend nimble fingers to those huge unwieldy talons—but even if there had been some way for me to work near-molten gold, I would not have dared. Such a gift can only be the work of one pair of hands, however ill-suited to their task. He quenched it in the stream that ran in one corner of the chamber.

The setting was rough, but it held. Shikrar bowed and gave it to Varien, who pushed himself gently away from me to stand on his own. He received it reverently in both hands. He lifted it to put it on, but with some inborn hieratical sense, stopped short.

He faced Shikrar. "From you, my soul's friend, Hadreshikrar, I accept this gift and bless you for the honour." He bowed stiffly (so as not to fall over, I suspected), then turned to me. "To you, Lanen my heart, I give it freely."

I did not even pause. I took the rough crown from his hands, held it aloft, and said quietly, "In the name of the Winds and the Lady," and placed it on his head.

His soulgem lay again on his forehead, framed by silver hair, beautiful and heart-piercingly familiar.

There were no more words. We all walked together into the golden sunlight of the dying day and down to the Council chamber.

Varien

I have never since done so hard a thing as to walk through the aisle my people made for me to the dais of the Council chamber. Idai had told them the tale and Shikrar came behind to add his word, but what would you? Full of wonder, they stared in disbelief, in silence, for what words had ever been made for such a thing?

I climbed awkwardly onto the platform and stood with Lanen's help. What had been a slight ledge was now become an obstacle, taxing my fragile coordination and balance. I stood shakily before my people and a sea of souls looked back. I could see they all bore the sorrow of Rishkaan's ending, yet still from old habit they reached out to their King, to me, even as I stood in my small, helpless Gedri shape, as to a sheltering cave in deepest winter. Most stood in Wonder; some held to Disbelief, though that could not last. And over all there was the faintest hint, like the green haze of earliest spring, of something very near to hope.

I did not know what to say. I feared I had lost the truespeech altogether with my Dragon-form, but now my soulgem lay in its proper place. I had to gather my thoughts like the veriest youngling to be heard—this body of mine was not accustomed to such effort—but to my soul's deep delight, I found that I still had the Language of Truth.

"*My people, I greet thee with the love of thy King,*" I said. It was the broadest kind of truespeech that all could hear, but it was undeniably the Language of Truth, and my mindvoice though weakened was unchanged. I understood, though, why Lanen so reluctantly bespoke anyone if she could avoid it. It immediately caused an ache behind my eyes that threatened to grow worse. Still, I knew that only thus would they believe.

"*I am the soul you have known as Akhor, the Silver King. My people, I stand before you changed beyond all possibility; and I cannot tell you how or why this has happened, for I do not know. My love and care for you have changed no whit, but I am shaped now by the Winds into the semblance of a man, and must so live. I return to you the kingship you gave me so long ago, and desire you to choose another to serve.*

"*I am no longer Akhor the King; I am become Varien the man.*

My fate is in your hands, whatever may befall; but I ask you for old love to spare my dear one, Lanen Maransdatter."

I leaned against her, my strength spent, the pain of truespeech too great.

It was enough. There was no more to be said.

Lanen

I held him and waited. There was nothing else to do.

The silence seemed to last forever. The tension in the air bore down upon me like a heavy cloud and time slowed to a crawl. I felt an hour pass between each breath, and in that time there sped through my mind any number of wretched ends to this mad act of the gods, each worse than the last; but I began to wonder when the silence stretched on still unbroken, and I yet breathed.

And finally I began to think that perhaps they had all had enough of death and destruction and had no desire to do us injury. I could not be certain, but among the various Attitudes they stood in, I did not seem to see Condemnation. It seemed rather the opposite.

Hope?

And in the moment I knew, as though the Lady had told me herself, that the taking of the soulgems of the Lost and Rishkaan's dying had wrung their hearts as it had wrung ours, and that in the Lost they saw their own future if naught else was changed. Their saving, so dearly won and now so dearly paid for, was become the saving of the Kindred; our hope was become their hope, standing before them now on two legs in a rough black tunic and ill-fitting crown.

And all their longing was like to my longing, to hold communion with the eternal Other and make a place for it in the heart.

And the silence was broken at last by a single voice like the music of heaven, high and gloriously triumphant, and it cried out, "Long live King Varien! Long live the King!"

And hundreds of throats joined to it their music, voices raised in wonder and glory. "Long live King Varien! Long live the King!"

And the King knelt, humbled, before them.

And in the center of that music I found a remembered silence, and in the silence heard music still, wild and deep with wonder beyond all knowing, and bright with rejoicing beyond all hope.   .

Varien

I never dreamt such a thing could happen. I knew even as they called my name that I could not be King in truth, but the blessing of their acclamation overwhelmed me. When once again there was silence I stood, with Lanen's aid, and bowed to them in the manner of the Gedri. I tried once again to speak in the Kantriasarikh, for the return of truespeech had made me hope, but my tongue and jaw made mockery of it. I concentrated, ignoring the pain that true-speech brought.

"Dear my Kindred, I will carry this memory to my death, and ever in my heart I shall hold it dear. We have all grown, my people, and the Word of the Winds is the seal to the learning, but I will not leave you without a King. It grieves me, but I cannot even speak to you in the Kantriasarikh. If you would be guided by me, for old love, I here offer unto you Hadreshikrar to serve in my place."

"He is Keeper of Souls, Lord Varien," said Erianss respectfully. "Surely that is more than one soul should be asked to do."

"It is, Erianss, you speak truly, and I had considered it. I therefore would ask Shikrar to surrender his position as Keeper of Souls to his son Kédra, who has already shown a facility for the Kin-Summoning and a constant and deep respect for all life."

There was a silence, broken at last by Shikrar in the Language of Truth. *"These are deep matters and will require much thought and much time. For the moment, if it is agreeable to the Council, I will remain as I am and guide the discussions as Eldest, which is not open to debate."* There was some scattered laughter. *"In any case, both Lord Varien and the Lady Lanen must soon leave us to go east with the rest of the Gedrishakrim. Has the Council considered the Word of the Winds regarding Lanen Maransdatter?"*

Lanen

Somehow I had never thought of my fate being different from Varien's. Just for a moment my heart dropped to the pit of my stomach.

"The Winds have spoken, Shikrar, and we dare not ignore their words," said a voice in my mind, and I turned in surprise to Idai. *"She*

is the beloved of our King, and for her sake the Winds have given him new life in the shape of the Gedrishakrim. How then should we speak against the Winds? It is my thought that she be honoured as Varien's beloved, and sent back to her people with him."

I held my breath. After some few minutes of silence, Shikrar said, *"Is there a voice to dissent?"*

None spoke. Shikrar turned to me and bowed, that lovely sinuous wave of his long neck. "Be well, Lady Lanen, and go with the blessing of the Kantrishakrim," he said aloud in my own language.

"I thank you all, O people of my beloved," I said, finally breathing again. *"Never has one of my race been so honoured, and never blessing was more precious."* I turned to Idai, my eyes awash with unshed tears. *"And to you, lady, I say that more generous soul never lived."*

"Be thou then as generous in thy love to him who was Akhor, Lanen Maransdatter, for that thou dost love him for us both," she said privately to me, the formality of her words a seal and a benison. *"And remember also that distance is no hindrance to truespeech. Shouldst thou need me, here am I."*

I bowed to her. *"I hear thee, lady, and will remember."*

Varien

I stood on the dais as I had hundreds of times and gazed deep into the eyes of my people. I knew well that I would never stand before them all again.

"Be well, my Kindred," I said, working to keep deep sadness out of my truespeech. *"Prosper and be well, and strive ever to restore the Lost, as shall I. O my people, my Kindred—know that the love of him who was your King is with you ever. In the name of the Winds, my people, I bid you farewell."*

I bowed one last time and stepped carefully down from the dais. Unaided, I walked slowly down the aisle they made for me, gazing at each in turn as I passed—then through the long dark passage and, finally, out under the stars.

LANEN THE WANDERER

Kédra

That Lord Akhor lived, in whatever guise, banished the raw wound of grief I had borne since hearing of his death, and left me rejoicing. When my father told me of the Council's final decision, I was astounded, and found hope in my heart for my people at last. At dusk, when the Lady Rella came once more to the Boundary, I answered her summons swiftly, my heart light with wonder and a reckless delight.

"Kédra, old son," said Rella, "the ship's Master is not going to wait for her forever. He's leaving at dawn and that's flat. I did my best, even suggested that we all come back ashore to get more lansip, but they're all spooked and won't come near for fear of DRAGONS." The way she said the word made me laugh. "Aye, I know, but true enough they'll leave without her sure unless she's at the landing before dawn."

"I thank you, Lady Rella, and I have a boon to ask. The Lady Lanen has asked that she might speak with you—will you come?"

She looked up at me with a curious arrangement of her features. Her Attitude seemed to have something of distrust in it. "You'll return me here in time, will you? Whatever she wants is her own affair, but I mean to be on that ship when it leaves."

"You have my word, lady," I answered, bowing. "Will you walk, or shall I bear you upon the Winds?"

Her eyes widened. "Fly? You'll take me with you while you fly?" As best I could tell she was well pleased with the prospect. "How? Shall I sit where I did before?"

"No, lady. I bore Lanen thus aloft, but only of desperate necessity, and my neck aches yet. If you will permit, I shall carry you." I felt a curious sensation as I took her carefully in my hands. Her weight was barely noticeable, though my balance changed of course. It was the feel of it, though, that took me by surprise.

How should so new, so unheard-of a thing, feel so customary and so right?

Rella

I was terrified by the idea, but how could I refuse such a chance? "Very well," I said as he gathered me into his front claws. Oddly enough, it felt safe. "Now what?"

"Take hold of my hands and hold tight," he said. I'd barely taken hold when he launched himself into the air. It was better and worse than when he had run so swiftly with both Lanen and me on his neck. Scared witless and enjoying every moment, I held on like grim death until he came to ground again. I felt like a child, every dream of flying come true. It had been too short a trip, I didn't want it to end.

We landed in front of a cave (he had to drop me a little way to the ground so he could land). Firelight flickered from within, and when we entered I recognised it as the same one I had gone into before. Shikrar was there, a golden patch on his shoulder gleaming in the firelight, along with the other Dragon I remembered seeing on the battlefield.

Kédra

"They are not here yet, lady, but they should not be long," I said to Rella.

"Who else are we expecting?" she asked. "I wouldn't think many more Dragons would fit in here."

I found my mouth closed with wonder, I could not answer her, for there at the cave mouth entered the Lady Lanen, and on her arm—Name of the Winds, I could see it in his eyes. I had heard the words of the Council, but I had not yet seen.

It was Akhor become human.

Lanen

I was surprised to find Rella waiting for us. She seemed a bit confused, as well she might be.

"Who are you, lord?" she asked, looking at Varien. She spoke in her true voice, with little accent. She seemed to feel instinctively the awe that surrounded Varien, and he still wore the circlet that Shikrar had made.

"Rella, you are welcome here. I am called Varien," he said simply. "Come, stand by the fire and be warmed."

She approached cautiously, looking from me to him. "Kédra told me you wanted to see me," she said at last, forcing herself to look at me. "What do you want? I came to tell you that the ship leaves at dawn tomorrow no matter who is or isn't on it."

"I was afraid something like that would happen," I said. "I was going to ask you to scare up some spare clothing for Varien from the ship's stores. It doesn't look as if we're going to have enough time for that."

I turned to Varien. I hated to say it, but it had to be said. "Dear heart, could you bear to leave so soon? I was hoping to persuade the ship's Master to stay on for a time while you got used to—things, but it doesn't sound like he's going to listen."

Varien

"And what should we tell them, Lanen?" I asked. I found myself growing senselessly angry at whatever powers were forcing us to move so very swiftly, with not time even for me to find my balance on these new legs. "Have you any thoughts as to how we shall explain my presence?"

"I wouldn't explain it at all," said Rella's practical voice. "They don't need to know, and if they ask just tell them you are under the protection of the Dragons. That'll be true enough, I've no doubt," she muttered.

"And do you think that will be enough?" I asked. She paused for a moment, thinking, when Lanen laughed and clapped her hands.

"Yes!" She turned to Idai, Shikrar and Kédra, her eyes shining. "My friends, will you consent to bear us one last time on the Winds? Not now. At dawn." She laughed again. "Oh, Akor, they will not question our protectors if they are the ones that take us to the ship!"

I laughed with her. "True enough, though it may be a long, silent voyage."

"Oh, you don't know them as I do. Give it a few days, they'll need all the hands they can find. We'll hear from them soon enough."

"*Look to the lady,*" said Kédra in truespeech.

Lanen

Varien and I turned as one, to see Rella sat on the ground, her face white as a fine sheet. "Akor. You called him Akor. That was the big silver one, I remember," she mumbled to herself. "But he can't be Akor, Akor's a Dragon, he was near death just yesterday at the battle, I know he . . ."

"Rella, I misspoke. This is Varien," I said, flustered. I hadn't noticed my slip. "How could he be Akor?"

"How could a man I've never seen suddenly appear from the dragonlands?" she asked sharply, then lapsed back into frantic muttering. "Can't happen, they kill the ones who cross, save you and me—oh Blessed Shia. You didn't come on the ship, so either you've arrived from thin air or you've been with the Dragons all these years. There isn't anywhere else."

"We asked you here because we thought you deserved an explanation, after all your assistance," said Varien, his voice gentle. I marvelled at his patience. "Do not worry, Lanen, I know what we agreed, but I think only truth will satisfy the Lady Rella." He knelt down to her and said gently, "It is true, I am he who was Akhor. Do not ask me how this transformation came about, for I do not know, but accept that it has. I shall be coming with you."

Rella nodded, her eyes wide. He turned to me again. "I think you have hit on the way, Lanen. If you are all willing, my friends?" he asked the Kantri, and all three accepted.

There was not much more to be done, though I did insist on one thing. Kédra obliged by scraping a large quantity of *khaadish* from the walls of Akor's chamber. I laid it close by for morning, when I meant to wrap it in my tunic until we were private on the ship. I'd be cold in just my shirt, but it would not be for long. At my request, Varien allowed a quantity the size of my fist to be taken for Rella. By that time she was so overcome that she simply thanked him and put it in her scrip.

It was well into the night, and though Rella seemed fine (despite her shock), Varien and I were still exhausted. Shikrar agreed to wake us at dawn. We stoked the fire and lay close to each other. The last thing I saw was Rella wrapped in her cloak, sitting by the fire and talking in a low voice with Kédra and Shikrar. *As if the Peace had been restored,* I thought, and slept.

✿   ✿   ✿

I woke to Shikrar's soft voice in my mind. *"Lady, the sky lightens. It is time."*

Varien was stirring. I went to Rella and touched her shoulder. She was instantly awake. "Time to go," I said. She grunted and rose to her feet.

I had been dreading this moment. I had warned Varien that he must not wear the circlet with his soulgem openly on the ship. Men have killed for far less. What that really meant, of course, was that he must say farewell here, before we left.

He bespoke them, of course, the green soulgem of Akor bright against his pale hair and skin. I was deeply thankful that I could not hear what was said, for my own heart was full enough, and I had only known these people for a few days. How should I bear hearing my beloved's farewells after a thousand years? Varien's cheeks were wet when at last he took off his circlet and wrapped it in my tunic with the rest of the *khaadish*.

"Seawater?" I whispered to him, drying his face with my sleeve.

"Tears," he replied, and smiled.

As for my own farewells, I found that after a few stumbling words all I could do was to open my heart to them in the Language of Truth. Wordless, my thoughts flew to them all with love and deep gratitude. From them in return came clear images: from Kédra, a vision of Mirazhe and Sherók playing on the beach at the Birthing Cove, and behind all gratitude mixed with love deep and strong. Idai sent an image of Akor in his youth, and the barely heard thought *"Even then he never turned to me. It is the Word of the Winds that you belong to each other."* From Shikrar, images I could barely understand, they were so complex and many-layered—but they spoke of a friend closer than a brother, of years beyond counting spent in one another's company, of wonder and thanksgiving and hope for the future. And the last image I had from Shikrar was of the soulgems of the Lost, combined with his regard. I caught his eye and he whispered in truespeech, *"Do not forget the Lost, lady, for it is in my heart that your destiny and theirs are intertwined. Seek ever their restoration."*

"I will," I replied softly.

There was no more time. We all went out into the breaking dawn.

Rella

At least this time I could see where we were going. I will never forget being borne through the air by a Dragon. It is astounding beyond words, but twice is enough.

Kédra carried me across first. The ship lay still in its place in the harbour, but the decks this morning were black with scurrying forms as they prepared to weigh anchor and be off.

Until they saw us.

I couldn't hear anything, of course, but it took only moments for there to be a clear space on the deck for Kédra to land. He dropped me a little space, then landed and bowed. "Fare you well, Lady Rella, and know that you have the regard of the Kantri," he said loudly. "Should you need our assistance, you have only to call upon us." It was what we had agreed, but he leaned down to me and added a quiet "Though I have no doubt you'll manage well enough. Be well, lady. It has been an honour to know you."

I bowed and bade him farewell. The whole ship rocked when he took off.

Lanen

Idai bore me gently and in silence. She flew low and backwinged, as Akor had done, though not so smoothly. "I can see this will take some practice," she said as she landed, amused. "Shall I then practice? Will you return one day to the Dragon Isle, Lanen Maransdatter? Will you and Varien come here again, where you are most welcome?"

"If it lies in my power, Lady Idai, I shall," I replied.

"Fare you well then, Lanen, and know that you have the regard of all the Kantri. You have only to call upon us," she said aloud. She bowed to me one last time, crouched on the deck, and leapt into the sky. The ship pitched violently from her leaving.

Varien

"Shikrar, my friend, you are wounded. You have done enough. Let another bear me thence," I said as he prepared to take me in his hands.

"*If you think, Varien Kantriakor rash-Gedri, that I am going to let anyone else deliver you to the Gedrishakrim, you are deeply mistaken.*" He gathered me in and took off. "*After all my years of suffering with you through the* ferrinshadik, *should I let another have the honour? My wound will keep. In any case, the others are all aloft already.*"

"What?" I tried to look up, but of course there was only the bulk of Shikrar to see.

And then I heard them.

It happens occasionally on the first warm spring day after a long winter, or when autumn breaks summer's heat, or when there is a reason for rejoicing, that many of my people will take to the skies and sing the Hymn to the Winds. I have done so myself many a time. The pleasure we have in riding the Wind is made manifest in song, both aloud and in the Language of Truth. It is a celebration, and a reverence, and an expression of joy.

And, in this case, of farewell.

Lanen

Never in all my dreams of Dragons had I imagined such a thing. The sky was full of wings and voices, singing to the morning, and their music echoed in my mind as I heard the language of the Kantri in truespeech. It was lovely almost beyond bearing. Voice rang with voice in harmonies that lifted the heart and gave it wings, with new voices ever swelling the chorus and tuning to a new melody, words and serried ranks of souls touching memories older than life. Dragonsong on the dawn wind—if I close my eyes, I stand there yet and marvel.

Most of the others on the ship cowered in the stern, crying out occasionally in fear, but a few I noticed were looking up in awe, and I remember thinking that perhaps we were not all lost.

When Shikrar approached, it was swiftly obvious that he would not fit on the deck. Rella and I rushed forward as he came as low and as close as he dared and let Varien fall from a little height, more or less onto us. "Farewell, Varien," he cried, circling the ship. "We are ever at your service. Call and we shall come." And in truespeech he added as he joined the others high above, "*Be well my brother, my dear ones. Remember the Lost.*"

So it was that the ship *Sailfar* weighed anchor and left the Dragon Isle under the benison of music more lovely than men had known for thousands of years, and (for a time) in the company of the Kantrishakrim.

When the crew had recovered from the sights and sounds, and realised that no more Dragons were going to try to land on the deck, the Master began bellowing orders, fast and furious. Varien chose to go with Rella to watch over Marik (she had told me no other was willing to tend him), and I set to work with the rest of the crew. True, we were all three avoided at first, but once we were under way there was more than enough work for all of us.

Marik's second-in-command had been Caderan, so that now a man named Edril was left in charge who had never dreamed of such prominence. Once we were well under way he sent for the three of us. I believe that, at first, he meant to confine us belowdecks, but a small nugget of purest gold in his hand and the promise of twice as much more on landing ensured our safe passage. (Of course, I might have told him that this was enchanted dragon gold, and that it would turn to base lead if we did not come alive to Corlí. Varien might have gestured to the Dragons, who followed us at a distance for some time, to emphasize a point. It was a long time ago, and I am too old to remember such details.)

Rella was not best pleased to find herself in Marik's company every day, having to tend him like an infant, but she took great delight in providing Varien with more suitable clothes from Marik's overflowing chests. I had to explain a few things about human clothing, but he learned quickly.

I suppose Marik was a pitiful sight—I glanced in on him once, the day we left—but I at least had no pity to spare for him. It was long and long before I could stop seeing the torn and bleeding body of Akor being borne on the wings of his dear ones from the battle with Marik and Caderan. Shame to say it, perhaps, but I hoped fervently that Marik would die on the voyage. We were not so blessed.

I was amazed (as, I think, were the Master and crew) that all the rumours about the Storms were true. I had feared a journey back twice as long as the one that took us to the Dragon Isle, beating against the wind all the way—but the winds blew now from the west, and the sea, while not smooth as glass, was not a third the strength of the raging tempest that had greeted us on the way out. The work was as hard and the hours as long, but not having always to cling to the rail for very life made it seem no hardship at all.

Do not wonder that I say little of my beloved. The men and women were berthed in different parts of the ship, and though I spent as much time with him as I could, I like the rest of the crew had a great deal to do. To my surprise, I learned that he spent much of his time with Maikel and Rella, in Marik's quarters. He was yet too unstable to walk well, and his soft hands still reacted to every breeze. He tried to help setting the sails at first, but after the very first haul away his hands bled. We put it about that he was unwell, and though the story was received in stony silence, he was allowed to perform the more delicate task of assisting the cook, as well as apprenticing to the ship's sailmaker. He was really very good with a knife, though none were ever sharp enough to suit him.

Varien

I would not have chosen such an entrance to my new life, but there were some advantages. My balance, hardly established on land before I went to sea, ended by being superb out of necessity. I worked a little each day—on such a small ship no one could sit idle, nor did I wish to—and by the end of the short voyage I began to have some strength in my hands. I had learned a little about Gedri food as well, its great variety and savour—though most of this was by way of report from the crew, who told me what they would prefer to be eating.

As time went on I learned more and more about my new body. Fortunately I seemed to have the instincts I needed for this new form, but I also had a few very curious conversations with Lanen before I understood some things. Truly the Gedri are astounding creatures, but I could not help thinking that they were put together rather oddly. The Kantri are of a more sensible shape altogether.

On one of the few occasions when Lanen and I had a moment to speak to one another in private, she asked me how I could bear

to spend so much of my time in the same room with Marik. When I
told her that I was looking in the face of my actions, she said she did
not understand. For answer I took her with me to see him.

Lanen

He lay on the small, hard ship's bed, his hands lying motionless
outside the heavy blankets. His eyes, when finally he turned to look
at us, were open and clear as a newborn babe's, and as free of
thought. By the end of the voyage he no longer had to be turned—
he had begun to do at least so much for himself—but that was all
the improvement there was. Strange to say, he looked healthier than
I had ever seen him, but it was hard even for me to grudge him that.
At first, Maikel attended him daily, putting forth all his strength. He
also fed Marik with another of the precious lan fruit.

Maikel told Varien once that he was certain that without it
Marik would have perished on the voyage. On hearing that I wished
the fruit had never been found in the first place—but then I remembered it was that same fruit that had saved my own life. I could
hardly object, as I looked down at my arms. The vision of them in
the sea was with me yet, but they appeared surprisingly unmarked.
There were a few scars and puckers, but for the most part they were
whole. My hands were soft and weak, no better protected than
Varien's, and at first I had to wrap them in cloth to work the lines,
but by the end of the voyage I had begun to regain some of my calluses.

I never did know what the crew or my fellow Harvesters thought
of Varien. Our entrance had done all we could wish for, and no one
asked any questions. I suspect that the seamen, a superstitious lot,
decided among themselves that they did not want to know.

After some eight days at sea, Maikel approached me late one afternoon. We could not have been far out from Corlí. I was hauling
in sail as the Master's orders snapped across the decks.

"Lady, I am concerned," said Maikel quietly to me. "Marik is a
little better in body, but he tosses in his bed like one who dreams
nightmares and cannot wake."

"Why do you tell me this?" I asked harshly, tying off the line. "I
bear no love for Marik."

"I know it, lady, but Master Varien sent to ask that you come to Marik's quarters. He believes you might be able to assist."

I left my place instantly and followed him. He led me to Marik's quarters and left me in the company of my friends.

He had not exaggerated. Marik was tossing and moaning like one haunted. Even Rella looked concerned. Varien took me by the hands when I entered. "Lanen," he said softly, and his voice was balm to my heart. "We believe he is trying to speak."

"So Maikel said. What do you want me for?" I asked, trying to keep the disgust out of my voice. I could not look at Marik without seeing Akor bloodied near to death, or a vision of the Raksha reaching out for me.

"Littling, listen to me," said Varien, putting one hand to my cheek and turning me gently to face him. "What has been done, on both sides, is in the past. For the moment we are responsible for him, and he suffers. Maikel has tended him as best he may, but says that he cannot yet make himself understood aloud."

"You want me to bespeak him, don't you, to see if I can hear what he is trying to say? Despite the fact that he is Gedri and most likely deaf and mute?" I said in truespeech. I was feeling a little dazed.

"Yes," he replied, smiling. "It is good to hear your voice, dearling, would that I could respond in kind. But I cannot, and I believe that you are his only hope. I cannot be certain, but I believe that I have heard a scattered voice, and I believe it to be his."

"So, I must help him, who would give me to demons." Varien only looked at me, waiting, his green eyes old and patient, and behind him sat Rella, saying nothing. I had expected to find myself fighting my own temper, but to my surprise I began to understand a little of pity. Marik's plight, however richly deserved, was making me grow despite myself.

"Very well," I said, with no good grace. I loosed Varien's hands and went to sit beside the bed. "Marik, it is Lanen," I said. "Your daughter. I am going to speak to you without words. Try to hear me, and say what it is that troubles you." Taking a deep breath, I said in truespeech, *"Marik of Gundar, it is Lanen Maransdatter—your daughter—who speaks to you. Can you tell me what troubles you?"*

To my amazement, I heard a kind of response. Scattered it was indeed, but it could only be coming from him.

"*Marik?*
         Lanen?

                                             daughter
demons   *nonono*   *light out of darkness*
            nono
                              lostlostlost
destroyer comes   *Corlí*   *Caderan stop*
        Caderan stopped

                                       dead
dead dead   death comes   light goes   *where*
                where   *lostlostlost*
        the swift destroyer   *stop*   *who where*
demons   *lostlostlost*
                    nononoooo . . . ."

I broke the connection, shuddering. Marik lived now in a vast
darkness, but something in that broken mind sought light and life,
after a fashion. "It's hard to tell, but he seems to be thinking about
something called 'the swift destroyer.' I think he wants it stopped,
but he wants Caderan to do it." Varien frowned. I turned to Rella.
"Have you ever heard of such a thing?"

"Yes," she said grimly, looking daggers at the troubled form of
Marik. "We should have strangled the bastard long since. It's a dis-
ease. The Swift Destroyer. Fever, chills, vomiting, and one of every
two who get it, dies within the day. It's a demon-spawned illness.
Takes a strong demon caller to bring it on, too. Damn Caderan and
all like him."

"But surely if Caderan is gone he cannot bring this down upon
us," I said.

"Don't count on it. The damned stuff is almost always left behind
by a sorcerer as a final piece of viciousness, while they get clean away.
There's some physical component to the spell, some fetish that sets
it off. If we could find that, we might be able to stop it."

I looked at Rella in amazement. "How do you know so much
about this?" I asked, shocked.

"I told you," she said with a grin. "I'm in the Silent Service. All
that we do is learn things and remember them. You can believe me."

"What would this fetish look like?" asked Varien, taking all this in his stride. I was surprised at his calmness, until I remembered that, in a sense, it must be his usual state. You can't live more than a thousand years without gaining a certain composure about most things.

"It should be pretty obvious. I'm trying to remember—there should be a mudball about the size of a fist, a few feathers, and a handful of the incense used for the dead. Probably wrapped up together in a cloth somewhere on the ship."

"Start looking now," I said.

Rella

Well, that was another sleepless night. We looked high and low, all over the ship, for hours and hours, and found nothing. I began to wonder if Marik wasn't just babbling in his delirium, until one of his guards fell ill.

The one who had taken over Caderan's quarters.

We quarantined the man and went back over the room. We thought we had already searched it thoroughly, but I had been taught that the Swift Destroyer always struck first in physical proximity to the fetish that bound it. It must be in that room.

It was Varien who finally found it, in a hidden panel above the small desk that was bolted to the deck. He removed it with gloves on, as I instructed, and dropped it over the side, then followed it with the gloves.

The outbreak was not nearly so bad as might be expected. The guard died, poor sod, but the rest of us who contracted it had little worse than what felt like a bad cold. Varien seemed to escape the infection, which surprised me, as he had come in closest contact with the fetish. I suppose the gloves held it off.

Maikel helped us as he might, letting Marik fend for himself for a few days. By the time we started expecting to sight land, there were a lot of us on board still sniffling and sneezing, but no worse. It would have been terrible had we not found that thing in the desk. I'd never seen the Destroyer, but one look at what was left of the guard's body was enough.

And of a sudden, in the late morning of the twelfth day out from the Dragon Isle, there was a cry from the crow's nest. Corlí had been sighted away off the starboard bow.

We were home.

Lanen

We drew nigh to Corlí as the sun rose to a splendid noon, and some three hours later I tossed the mooring ropes over the side to those who waited on the pier to haul them in and make us fast to the dock.

I sought out Varien as the ship erupted into a mad confusion. We had all been provided with tallies of the lansip we had gathered, and we were to be paid on the landward end of the gangplank. The moment we had docked all the Harvesters ran for their packs, aching to walk again on land and to collect their pay from Marik's people (and, if I had known it, to get away from this Dragon-cursed ship).

Rella and I collected our tallies from the bursar, and I went with Varien to seek out Edril, the merchant we'd bargained with for our passage. We honoured our word and handed over what now seemed to me a tiny amount of gold. Edril's eyes widened and he went so far as to bow his thanks to us. Well, fair enough, gold is exceedingly rare, and Marik never was the sort to inspire personal loyalty.

At the far end of the gangplank there was a milling crowd of Harvesters seeking payment, receiving payment, grinning madly, laughing wildly at family and friends in the crowd that had gathered to cheer and greet the first Harvest ship to return in a hundred and thirty years.

Rella was behind me when I collected my pay for the lansip I'd gathered, but I did not mean to linger. Varien and I, at least, had but one desire—to get away from there as far and as fast as possible.

Varien

I had never imagined such a great crowd of Gedrisha—of people. The quay swarmed with them, shouting, laughing, working, begging, a great seething mass of souls intent on their own business yet moving as in a great dance with their fellow creatures. It was dizzying.

We were past the paymaster and heading into the crowd when Rella called out to us. Lanen was in a hurry but she stopped, waiting for her to catch us up. "Whither now, Rella?" she asked. "Now you've made your fortune proper, where will you go?"

The old woman smiled, her pack resting effortlessly on her bent back, a mysterious something in her eyes. "Home, I think," she said.

She stared at Lanen, her smile growing wider. "It's a long way to go alone, though. I wondered where you might be headed. If our paths lie together, perhaps I might ride with you—some of the way, at least." When Lanen did not answer, Rella delighted me by standing in what could only be an Attitude, the backs of her hands on her hips, her weight all on one leg and that hip higher than the other, with a quirk of the lips and an expression I had not seen before. Now if only I could learn what it meant.

"I'm making for a little village in the North Kingdom, maybe you've heard of it. It's called Beskin."

"What?" exclaimed Lanen. "Beskin?" Her eyes glowed with delight. "Heithrek. Do you—have you ever known a man called Heithrek, a blacksmith? It would be—oh, near thirty years ago, but his family might still be there."

Rella grinned with delight. "Never met him." She paused, and I'd swear she savoured her next words. "I know his daughter, though. Tall woman, looks a lot like you, name of Maran Vena."

Lanen let loose a little cry and her mouth dropped open. Her eyes were shining and she couldn't speak for a moment, lost in wonder at something I could not imagine.

And then from nowhere, out of the seething crowd of humanity, a small dark-haired man came close behind Rella. I saw something flash in his hand and heard Rella cry out in pain. Lanen cried out as well and caught her as she fell, but from where she stood she could not have seen what happened. I left Rella to her care and ran after the man, or tried to. There were simply too many people. I could not keep up with him—it seemed almost as if the crowd parted to let him through, then closed up behind like an impenetrable forest. In seconds he was out of sight.

I went back to Rella, now covered with blood and lying in Lanen's arms on the ground. She was badly wounded, though I could not be certain that the smell of death was on her. I ran to seek Maikel, not knowing if he could do her any service, knowing only that there was no other hope for her.

Lanen

I had seen such a wound before, though Jamie was better at it. Rella still lived.

"Who has done this?" I asked urgently.

"Caderan's master. Berys. Demonlord," she said, breathless. Her face grew paler by the second and I feared death was not far off, but she managed yet to speak. "Beskin. Maran—give her . . . love . . . warning," and then, staring into my eyes and speaking very clearly, she said, "Go to your mother."

Then she fell back. I did not know if she had fainted or died.

Varien

Maikel and I came as swiftly as we might. He found the pulse of life in her yet, weak but present, and taking her body in his arms he bade us follow him to the Healer's residence hard by. His fellow Healers laid her on a clean table and began to put forth their power to save her. We could only watch.

Lanen stood in shock, helpless and angry. She stared into nothingness for only a little space of time, then with a jerk opened her eyes wide and turned sharply to me. "Come on. They'll take care of her. We have to go."

"Where?"

"Away from here." When I still did not respond, she gripped my arm tightly with the strength of her fear. "If they found her they can find us. We have to go *now*."

And so it was that our first days in the land of the Gedri were spent in flight.

Lanen

I still regret there was nothing I could do for Rella, not even wait for her to be healed, but I knew where she was going. And she was alive. That would have to do for now.

On our journey it occurred to me that those who tried to kill her may have expected me to wait for her to recover, to stand useless vigil by her side. To this day I do not understand why so many people think that a kind heart is an indication of a weak mind.

Varien and I bought the first decent horses we found—not as good as Hadron's, of course—and rode out of Corlí barely two hours after we had arrived. We journeyed north overland, keeping to the main highways, staying at crowded inns along the way, travelling as

long as the sun was in the sky and keeping watch turn and turn
about at night in our room. The late-autumn days were closing in,
so we made the best of the shrinking daylight hours, riding until the
last drop of daylight was wrung from the sky, rising well before first
light to break our fast and be on our way.

We passed through the great plains of southern Ilsa. The
ploughed fields were shorn now of their burden of grain and lay
around us in untamed stretches, brown with winter's approach. I
found great beauty in the land, perhaps because I was given to see
it with another's eyes.

Varien

Once I had learned to stop falling off my horse—and I had an
excellent teacher—I began to enjoy the stark beauty of the plains
through which we rode. I missed the mountains and forests of my
home, but the rising sun shone red-gold and kindly on fields where
the Gedri had toiled, and I was content.

With the land, at least.

I found as we journeyed together, learning more of each other
at night and morning in those few moments we had in peace, I could
let sorrow and amazement and fear each have their place and yet
have room for one feeling more. I would not have thought it possible, but my love for my dearling grew with each passing day. Everything I learned about her I cherished, her high heart and brave soul
proved as true in everyday life as it had been on the Dragon Isle in
the midst of high matters and great changes. I have found over the
years that, as with my own people, the true test of character is to deal
with others kindly from one day to the next. It is not so difficult to
rise to the best of one's being when matters of great moment are at
stake. It is very difficult indeed to rise each morning with a kind
heart.

As we travelled north, I found that other things were rising as
well. The incredible sensitivity of my skin was gradually wearing
off—clothing was no longer uncomfortable to wear, I had to think
about it to notice the wind on my hand—but other things were happening that concerned me. The Kantri mate perhaps a dozen times
in a lifetime spanning many centuries. It is a response to the urge to

procreate, and though the joining of souls is a wonder, the act itself is difficult and, I understand, more than a little painful. Certainly there is no great pleasure in it.

When first I noticed something unusual happening to my body—we were some four weeks out of Corlí—I innocently asked Lanen about it. Then I had to ask why her face had turned red. At that time, she mumbled something incoherent and swiftly changed the subject. The next evening, however, she seemed to have come to terms with the idea. She sat me down and explained the technical details of human mating. It sounded dreadfully awkward at best. She laughed at my puzzled expression and put her arms about me—I had learned what "hug" was, and returned it gladly—and said we should discover more about it later.

Lanen

Dear Goddess, it was hard. At first I never mentioned the subject of sex, for we were still learning about each other, and Varien was busily coming to terms with a new life and a new form.

The problem was that his new form was to me the most alluring I had ever known. And I slept near him, and longed for him as a drowning man longs for air, and had not yet allowed myself so much as a lingering kiss.

It was not that I was, as the foolish maidens in Ilsa put it, "saving myself" until we were wed. The thought never crossed my mind to do any such thing. But for all his length of days, Varien was yet but a month or so old as a human, and in honour and simple respect I made myself wait until he had grown into his new body before I did anything about my own desires.

Typical, of course. When he finally asked me about "mating" (as he called it), I was in the blood of my moon-cycle. I tried to keep a straight face about explaining the details, but when he looked so skeptical—and at one point absolutely disbelieving—I laughed and held him tight and said we'd work on it later.

Goddess, it was hard to let him out of my arms. I longed for him more each day, and we had never yet truly kissed. He was still learning how, though his pecks on the cheek were rapidly progressing from the buss of a toddler to something more interesting.

I am not by nature a patient soul. Thank the Lady we were working so hard to put distance between us and Corlí, and were keeping watch over each other through the nights. It meant we were seldom in bed (when we slept in a bed) at the same time.

Damn, damn, damn.

Varien

Lanen said we were making for her old home, Hadronsstead. She had told me about the Gedri custom of "wedding," and when I asked if we might not be wed on the morrow, she laughed kindly and explained that the whole idea was to have friends and family to witness the formal joining, and we would need to wait until we reached her home.

It made perfect sense. There is a formality of roughly the same kind among the Kindred, in which the two who wish to be joined go together to their families and announce their intent. By happy chance I heard a ballad one night as we supped in the common room of that night's inn. It was a tale of two lovers, and though it ended badly—very badly—I suspected that I could do worse than follow the hero's early example.

Accordingly, a week after she had explained things to me, I judged that the time was ripe. When we returned from our supper,

> "I went and took her hand in mine,
>   and down upon one knee
> I begged my true love me to wed,
>   and gave her kisses three."

Of course, I kissed her thrice on the cheek, though my rising blood told me that something else entirely was called for.

Lanen raised me up and took my face in her hands, smoothing back my hair, and said in truespeech, *"Of course I will wed with you, Varien Kantriakor, did you think otherwise?"*

"Never, dearling, since the Flight of the Devoted. We became one that night"—and with great satisfaction I leant down, such a little way, and kissed her on the lips, full and long and deep. It thrilled me, a simple kiss shivering down my spine, and I said in a voice now grown rough with longing—"and now we are of one kind and Kindred, and a true joining is possible. Come, my beloved, Kadreshi na Varien, join with me in love."

"*Varien. Akor. Kadreshi naLanen.*"

Lanen

I have tried to write of that night, the first of our loving, a hundred times, and each time it sounds worse—full of gushing sentiment, the words of a green girl with her first true lover. But despite our lack of experience we were neither of us children, and after the first fumbling starts we laughed, kissed again deeply, and went about it with light hearts and urgent bodies.

It was wonderful. I suspect I did more than my fair share of laughing at Varien's astonishment at finding things so pleasurable, but my love laughed with me, and it was good.

We had seen no sign of pursuit in all this time and dared to hope ourselves safe, at least for the moment. I had asked the hostellers along the way, and we were no more than halfway, if that, when we began our loving. The days sped past as we rode swiftly, still with the thought of escaping a threat, but also trying to outpace the onset of deep winter; and the nights were spent in love and delight as we learned each other's bodies and rejoiced in their blending.

We were blessed in the weather as well—at least, when I remember those times, the sun is always bright with the edged golden light of late autumn, the sky is blue and only spotted with clouds enough to make a goodly show. There again, if we had ridden through another such tempest as had tossed the Harvest ship on the way to the Dragon Isle, I don't think either of us would have noticed.

I do remember, though, that it was on such a day that we came to Hadronsstead at last. It was only two hours after noon and already the sun was sinking, but we saw the stead first in daylight as we came over the rise. I could hardly bear the joy that possessed me—for not only was I come home, I saw in a field not fifty paces distant the face of all my kindred.

"Jamie!" I cried, and in the instant I was off my horse and running.

Varien

If there had been a hundred men in that field, I would have known Jamie among them. His face gleamed like a sunrise when he saw her—and when I touched my hand to my soulgem (I carried the circlet under my coat), I could feel his joy and his deep rejoicing.

He held her tight, the embrace of a father and daughter, and over her shoulder he looked into my eyes. I dismounted and strode over to them, stood waiting while yet they communed in silence.

When at last he could bear to let her go, she stood back and would have spoken (to give us each other's usenames, I learned later—a curious but useful habit when there are so many to know), but Jamie silenced her with a gesture. He gazed deep into my eyes. I smiled, for he stood in what was unmistakably Protection of a Youngling, as I had when first I met Lanen. I met his gaze in quiet rejoicing, for Lanen had told me so much of this man who stood father to her.

Suddenly he grinned, and his first words to me were "Yes, you do love her truly, don't you?"

"More than I have words to say," I told him.

"Come away in, my children," he said, taking an arm each of ours in his own and leading us towards the building. "We have much to do in little time, if there is to be a wedding at midwinter."

Lanen could not speak for joy, and I would not interrupt their communion, so in the silence of kinship we came to Hadronsstead and in at the kitchen door.

It was late that night when at last all tales were told in full. I could not read Jamie's expression as he glanced from Lanen to me and back again, but it was certain he could not be mistaken in our regard for one another.

Lanen retired first, pleading weariness, but we all three knew well enough why she left Jamie and me alone. He gazed at me in silence for some time. I returned his gaze openly, though I found it hard not to laugh.

"I'm glad I amuse you, at least," he said gruffly. "What's so funny?"

"Forgive me, Master Jameth. I wondered if you thought to outwait me in silence, as we do with the younglings of our Kindred when they have some minor disobedience to admit to their elders."

"I am not as gullible as Lanen," he replied. "I don't believe in wonders. Where had you been hiding in that cave, and for how long?"

"Ah, youngling," I sighed without thinking, "and still our Kindreds mistrust each other. What could convince you that I am who I say I am?"

"Nothing that I can think of. Unless you were to use this truespeech on me, and I heard you."

"Most of your people—forgive me—most humans are deaf to the Language of Truth, and in all the history of the Gedri only Lanen has not been mute. Most likely you would hear nothing."

"I'm willing to chance it," he said, challenging me.

I sighed and rose. I fetched my circlet from my pack in the corner, where I had stowed it when I arrived. I placed it on my brow, breathing deep, remembering that when last I had worn it I stood before my own people. *"May I bespeak you, Jameth of Arinoc? It is Varien who speaks."*

I waited. "Well?" he said. "Go ahead and try."

I tried again, using the broadest kind of truespeech. *"Master Jameth, would that I might convince you of that which is simple truth. I am he who once was Lord of the Kantri. I am become human by the will of the Winds and the Lady. And I love your heart's-daughter Lanen with a love that will be remembered in song on the Isle of Dragons when we all are dust and gone."*

Jamie's expression did not change. I removed the circlet. "Forgive me, Jameth. I spoke, but you did not hear."

"Ah, well. You tried," he said, much of the rough concern gone from his voice.

"Yet despite your deafness you are well content. I do not understand."

He half-smiled at me. "You might just be telling the truth. I've seen conjurers at fairs who claim Farsight. They moan and groan and frown, there's a whole act goes with it. You didn't even twitch. Did Lanen hear you?"

"Yes, I did," said a quiet voice from the door. It was Lanen as I had never seen her, with her hair all loose about her, and dressed in a soft green gown that flowed when she walked. I was enchanted.

Lanen

"I thank you for those words, dear heart. It's a shame Jamie couldn't hear them."

"You know, my girl, in the end it doesn't matter," said Jamie, smiling a little sadly at me. "Whether he's just a man or a Dragon become man is all one in the end. I have never seen you so, Lanen. You are positively glowing. Do you love him so very much, then?"

"Beyond reason, beyond death, beyond all understanding I love him, Jamie."

Jamie stood and held out his hand. "Then welcome, Varien, whoever you may be. Come, stand up and face the fire, let me see your eyes."

Varien

"Why?" I asked, as I moved to oblige him.

"They are called the window of the soul, and I would look in yours if I may."

I obeyed, kneeling that he might see better (for he was much smaller than I).

I think perhaps my eyes convinced him.

Lanen has told me since that, despite all other changes, my eyes (though human) have yet the semblance of the eyes of Akhor, who had lived at that time a thousand and twelve winters. I think perhaps Jamie saw in my eyes the years weighing upon years, the memory of time beyond his imagining. Or perhaps he simply saw my love for Lanen, and was content.

"Be welcome, Varien," he said, and took my hands to help me up.

"I rejoice in thy welcome, for thou art dearest kin to my beloved," I said formally. The words came as a surprise to me. They were the words used by the Kantri on such occasions, and though I had taught them to a few younglings (notably Kédra) I had never thought to find them on my own tongue. "I fear I come ill prepared, for I do not know thy customs well, though Lanen hath tried to instruct me. Our wedding is set for three days hence, but what have I to give thee, in thanksgiving for so rare a gift as thy heart's-daughter?"

"What is the custom among the Kantri?" asked Lanen, when Jamie had no answer.

"The usual gift is a song," I replied.

"Then that will content me," said Jamie, his face unreadable. "Let you sing a new song at the wedding, before you take your vows, as Lanen's bride-gift." He took me by the shoulders. "But Varien, know that I am giving into your keeping the only thing of value I have ever had claim on. If you do not treat her well, I will come for you."

Lanen laughed, making light of his words, but I knew well that he meant them with all his heart. I was grateful for his honesty. I was beginning to learn that it was a rare gift among any people.

I spent the next three days and nights working on my gift. I was beginning to discover that, if I needed to, I could do with as little sleep as the Kantri needed. It was just as well, for I had not had time to learn how to use this new voice of mine. It resonated in a completely different way, and it took some time to find the best placement, but I had been singing for a *very* long time and I found it soon enough. The melody was obvious, a variation on the theme of our Flight, but it was very difficult to make meaningful verse in another language. It was not perfect, but as an idea of the finished whole it was a good beginning.

Lanen

I hardly saw Varien those next three days, which I suspect was just as well. Jamie and I went over the year's accounts and finished the business of the stead for the year, which had to be done, but every spare moment I had I spent in making a gown. Had I time enough to have sent to Illara, I'd have been wed in samite, but as it was I had only homespun cotton cloth on hand. Still, with the help of a better seamstress than I and three nights of pricked fingers as I embroidered, I was not so ill a sight on Midwinter's Day.

There were few to come to the ceremony at noon—Walther and Alisonde, brave souls (I think Walther wanted to apologise, but I wouldn't let him), a few women from the village, all of the stable lads and Jamie in the place of honour standing for my family. I thought briefly of Marik, babbling still, with only part of a mind left him, and of Maran, away in Beskin—but they were no more than phantoms, while Jamie stood real and solid beside me.

The priestess of the Lady stood waiting at the end of the hall, which Alisonde and some of the village women had made gay with such flowers as bloom in winter. Around my brow holly and ivy were entwined, vivid green and red against the cold white of winter, and green and gold the embroidery on my white dress. Jamie took me by the hand and walked with me down the hall, to where Varien stood waiting.

He took my breath away. He was all in green, a simple belted tunic over stout leggings, but upon his brow sat the circlet that held his soulgem. His silver hair blazed against the green he wore, and his soulgem seemed to shine with its own inner light, clear and steady.

When we were come nigh, he opened his mouth and sang.

It was the Tale of Lanen and Akor.

I suspect you have heard it often, though it is certain you have never heard it sung so. For he wore his soulgem on his brow, and I heard all his song echoed in truespeech, where he still had the voice of a Lord of the Kantri.

Jamie cried. That strong, toughened soul, farmer, horsemaster, assassin, wept openly at the beauty of Varien's bride-gift to me. I was beyond tears, in a place where joy has wings.

In the name of the Winds and the Lady we were wed, lighting candles at midwinter to drive back the darkness. And in the silence of our minds, we pledged to each other in the Language of Truth, in which lies are impossible.

"Varien Kantriakor rash-Gedri, Kadreshi naLanen, I take you as my husband and my mate for as long as life endures. In the name of the Winds and the Lady, beloved, I am thine."

"Lanen Kaelar, Kadreshi naVarien, I take you as my wife and mate for as long as life endures. In the name of the Winds and the Lady, dearling, I am thine before all the world."

That is the true tale of Lanen and Akor.
There is more to tell, but there always is.
True stories never end.

GLOSSARY

Chélan Name of a plant and the brew made from it. It is drunk as a stimulant. We would say it tasted rather like maté with a hint of cinnamon.

Ferrinshadik The longing felt by (esp.) the Greater Kindred to join in fellowship with the Gedri, though they describe it more generally as the longing to speak with other races.

Gedrishakrim Humans. Usually shortened to **Gedri.** OS: "the silent people."

Kadreshi na Kantriasarikh phrase, meaning "beloved of."

Kantriasarikh The OS word for the language of the Kantrishakrim.

Kantrishakrim The Greater Kindred of Dragons (originally all dragons). In Old Speech (OS) the word means "the wise people." Usually shortened to **Kantri.**

Khaadish Kantri word for gold.

Language of Truth The telepathy natural to the Kantri. It also has elements of empathic awareness. The Gedri call it Farspeech.

Lansip Name of a tree and the brews made from it. It grows only on the dragonlands, all attempts at transplanting having failed. Made into tea, it is a tonic and general remedy for minor ailments from headache to heart's sorrow; taken in quantity, it is an elixir of youth. The precious and rare fruit of the lansip tree, called lan fruit, is a sovereign healer, and when eaten will heal nearly anything outside of death.

Old Speech   The name in the common tongue for the language created by the Kantri and used by all the peoples before the Choice. Since that time it has developed into distinctly separate languages.

Rakshadakh   Literally "demon droppings" (that is the polite translation). It is the ultimate insult as far as the Kantri are concerned, and generally refers to a demon master or one who treats often with the Rakshasa.

Rakshasa   (obs. form: **Rakshi**) Demons. Singular, **Raksha** (greater demon) or **Rikti** (lesser demon). OS: "peoples of chaos." This is plural because, at the time of the Choice, the Rakshasa were already differentiated into two distinct peoples.

Trellishakrim   Trolls. OS meaning is simply "the troll people," as this word came from the **Trelli** themselves, and they never translated it. It is almost the only word of their speech that survives, notably in the name of the great northern forest of Kolmar, the Trollingwood.

PRONUNCIATION GUIDE

As a translator/transcriber, I feel the frustration common to all those faced with similar difficulties. The jaws, throats, teeth and tongues of Dragons are vastly different from those of humans. It is not, therefore, surprising to realise that the written forms of these names are approximations only. The names of Dragons are not commonly known, nor are they often seen in print! I have therefore attempted to spell them as they are pronounced. Often in English there are graphs (letters) that are present for historical purposes; this is not the case with Dragon names in this volume.

Vowels are essentially those of Italian or Hawaiian, each with a consistent value and always pronounced. A rough guide would be:

    a = ah, as in father
    e = ay, as in say
    i = ee, as in see
    o = oh, as in vote
    u = oo, as in true

Consonants are essentially as in English, with a few exceptions:

    K before a vowel is always followed by an aspirant (^{h})

    R, unless initial, is always "soft" and slightly rolled

Labials (m, p, b) are generally unpronounceable by Dragons without a great deal of practice, with one exception. The "m" of Mirazhe's name is so written to indicate the nearest English equivalent of the actual sound, which is very like a nasal liquid. Lanen heard it as "m."

The plosive that occurs between s and r (-khistri-, -issdra-) may be represented by either d or t in English—the pronunciation lies somewhere between.

Hadretikantishikrar (Hah-dray-tee-khan-tee-shee-krahr), primary accent on the last syllable, strong secondary on the first, weak secondary accent on the fourth. Usename **Shikrar,** accent on the second syllable. He also has a formal usename, **Hadreshikrar** (Hah-dray-shee-krahr), accent on the third syllable.

Iderrikanterrisai (Ee-deh-ree-kahn-teh-ree-sah-ee). Primary accent on the last syllable, strong secondary on the first, weak secondary on the fourth. Use name **Idai** (Ee-dah-ee), accent on the second syllable. Formal usename, **Iderrisai** (Ee-deh-ree-sah-ee), accent on the penultimate syllable.

Khétrikharissdra (Khay-tree-khar-eess-drah). Primary accent on the penultimate syllable, secondary on both first and second. Usename **Kédra** (kay-drah), accent on the first syllable.

Khordeshkhistriakhor is pronounced roughly, in English (core-desh-kiss-tree-ah-core), with the primary accent on the penultimate syllable and a secondary accent on the first syllable. His usename, **Akor,** is pronounced [ah-core], accent on the first syllable. The fact that Lanen's pronunciation of his name is written without the aspirant throughout indicates that she could not reproduce the aspirant, or indeed was unaware of its existence. A diminutive of his name, **Akhorishaan** (Ah-core-ee-shaan), is occasionally used.

Lanen There appears to be some confusion as to the proper pronunciation of **Lanen**'s name. It is pronounced (lah-nen ky-lar). The accent is on the first syllable for both names. And since English does not often make use of the "ae" spelling, it should be noted that the first syllable, **Kae,** rhymes with sky.

Mirazheshakramene (Mee-rah-zhay-shah-krah-may-nay). The primary accent, again, is on the next-to-last syllable, with a secondary accent on the second syllable. Her usename, **Mirazhe,** is simply the first three syllables of her name, accent on the second syllable.

Shurishkerrikaan (Shoo-reesh-kher-ree-kahn). Primary accent on the last syllable, secondary on both first and second. Usename **Rishkaan** (Reesh-kahn), accent on the second syllable.

ACKNOWLEDGEMENTS

I count myself fortunate to have been the recipient of so much love and support from so many good friends over the years. I cannot possibly say in this small space the thanks I owe to them all, but let me do what I may.

A deep bow and a thousand thanks to Claire Eddy of Tor Books for taking on the mammoth task of breaking in a new writer, for her encouragement in the face of endless revisions, and for being willing to take a chance on my work. Thanks also to Betty Ballantine for making the time and taking the trouble to read the original manuscript and pass it on, and again to Deborah Turner Harris for a well-timed kick in my direction and a kindly word in Betty's ear.

And, in chronological order—thanks to Sue Davis Claus for putting up with me and this story from the very beginning, and for being the inspiration for "Mead Paul and Brandy," where this all started (and Sue, here is your formal apology for the time I knocked you over in my rush for a pen and paper); to James Quick, my hanai brother, for his constant love and support over the long years; to the late Harry Phelps, for confidence in my work and belief in myself; to Mary and the late Curtis Scott, for their solid friendship and for reading my short story and telling me it was a nice sketch, but when was I going to write the book; to Jan Buckley for reading damn near every version (now *that* is friendship) and telling me she actually enjoyed it; and to Betsy Palmer, soul-sister, patient friend and teacher, for throwing me a rope when I most needed it.

Thanks, guys.

—Elizabeth